SONG OF THE ABYSS

Emma Hamm

ALSO BY EMMA HAMM

Deep Waters
Whispers of the Deep

The Otherworld
Heart of the Fae
Veins of Magic
The Faceless Woman
The Raven's Ballad
Bride of the Sea
Curse of the Troll

Seven Deadly Demons
The Demon Court
The Demon Crown
The Demon Prince

Dragon of Umbra
Fire Heart
Bright Heart
Brave Heart
Torn Heart
Taloned Heart

and many more...

In the first book, I made a forward of telling people to let the science go. Again, I'm going to say that again. There is no science in this monster fucker book, so please just sit and enjoy the nonsense.

Now that that is out of the way.

I want to say a special thank you to the sensitivity readers who were kind enough to paw through this book for me. It was my absolute pleasure to have you see through Anya's eyes, and to make sure that I represented the Hard of Hearing community in a way that was respectful and felt accurate.

This story wouldn't be what it is without all of you. You're absolute Queens, and I adore you all so much.

Chapter 1

The leviathan called to him.

The kraken knew his name.

The depths of the sea were part of him and Daios was part of it. But at some point, recently, he'd lost that connection. He'd felt it snap and sever in a wild moment of freedom where he had thought he was saving others. Now, the sea had left him alone.

And Daios had never been alone like this before.

He floundered. Tossed and rejected by the currents that had once always pushed him through the sea with unnatural speed. He had been the favored son, the largest of his hatchling group, and the one who was supposed to honor them all. Though he would never be a leader— his rage had always run too hot for that—he would be the wave that stood between them and all danger.

That was his purpose. Yet, he had failed them. He had led his people to certain death, and he could not forget that.

"Your mind is with us, brother?" Maketes called out, the yellow flash of his fin spearing through the water to his right. "You know we need you all here for this."

Maketes had been the only brother to stay close to him in the aftermath of... all of it. Even though he probably shouldn't have. Maketes had been the one who still saw something worthwhile in the bleeding, broken form that Daios had been left with. Even when he'd been enraged. Even when he'd promised to destroy the only thing his blood brother had found dear.

These memories threatened to overwhelm him. He'd suffered through them swelling in his mind multiple times before, and now he knew the warning signs before it was going to happen.

His hearts shifted in his body, one moving to his throat and the other dropping beneath his stomach. They both beat so hard that it was difficult to think beyond the thudding that never seemed to end. It was all he could focus on. All he could think about.

And then the memories came.

"We're here to find the girl, remember?" Maketes's voice filtered through the palpitations and ragged breaths. "We're here to find the General's daughter. She told us what the girl looks like, and where in the city she usually is."

He remembered.

How could he forget? It was the only task they had trusted him with since he had... since everything had happened.

Again, his hearts thundered, pushing through his mind and forcing him to think of the achromos again. The humans, as Mira called them. They were creatures that had no place in this ocean and the monsters he had fought against since he was nothing more than a boy. They'd taken apart this ocean, poisoned it, spread and multiplied in their numbers until he wasn't even sure they could be beaten.

They came at his people with weapons so powerful, even the

fathoms below couldn't fight against them. He should know. He'd seen them firsthand.

His head started to spin. His vision skewed to the side and he couldn't quite see where he was anymore. There was... something ahead of him. Something that he probably needed to brace himself for. They were close to the city, weren't they?

Alpha, Mira had called it. And his brother's human mate would know. The golden city of light where only the most important of her kind lived. This was the city that he needed to infiltrate, and he was the only one mad enough to do it.

The only one they could spare.

He reached for a stone in front of him, intending to brace himself against it just for a few moments. The currents were suddenly wild around his body, tossing him around, and all he wanted was a moment of peace for just this one second.

He reached and missed. Because there wasn't an arm there anymore. It had been taken from him just like all the lives of the people he had led.

Everything warped around him. The stone shifted, wobbling as though it wasn't solid anymore. He could hardly feel the cool touch of the ocean on his skin. It was all wrong. And then he heard it. The loud booming noise of shots being fired at him. He tried to twist out of the way, but that only turned his attention to the nightmares that followed him.

He could see pieces of his own people floating in the distance. A limp body, the torso sinking faster than the tail, so graceful it was almost as beautiful as it was heartbreaking.

Then a flash of light, and there were more of them. Blood soaking the water, filling his gills with that metallic taste. And he was ashamed to admit he almost enjoyed the taste. He always had. Daios was a warrior. He had battled his entire life and the taste of blood in the water always made him fight harder, yet this was the blood of his people.

His fault.

All those bodies, floating there, never to swim or breathe again. They were his fault. He had done this.

And suddenly he could feel the pain in his arm again. The sting of saltwater burning through the useless stump that marked him as other for the rest of his life. He was unworthy of being their shield.

He was unworthy of being anything at all.

A weight struck his side, shoving him against the stone and pinning him down. For a moment, Daios thought he had been attacked again. He fought back. His writhing tail coiled around whoever dared to touch him, pulling the other closer and squeezing hard enough that he heard the pained wheeze from whoever was foolish enough to think him weak. Even at this moment, he was not weak.

He was a powerful warrior and he would kill all who stood in his way. Because all he could see were bodies floating in the distance.

And it was his fault. He was the nightmare that had come to his people and promised hope. But all he'd given them was death.

"Daios." The wheeze came from within his grip. "You're losing it again."

Losing it? He wasn't losing anything other than the people who had relied on him to keep them safe. And his arm. By all the gods of the ocean, he could still feel it. It still felt like he could flex his fingers and reach out for something, but he couldn't. It wasn't there.

Squeezing tighter, he froze when whoever was within his tail's grip slapped against his scales. "Daios. We have to get out of the way or the achromos will see us."

Everything snapped back into focus. Suddenly, he could see where they were again. The ocean cleared of flashing lights and screams that came from his mind only. They were not at Beta, where he had lost so many of his loved ones. They were in front of Alpha and he had put them in another compromising situation.

Looking down his heaving chest, he could see that he'd coiled his tail around Maketes. Red lights flashed up and down his scales, all the way from his massive fluke to his chest. Warning lights for nothing to get close to him. His brother was wrapped completely up in his tail, shockingly, but Daios forgot that his yellow finned brother was so much smaller.

Maketes tapped against his side again, his claws scratching harmlessly against Daios's much larger scales. "Let me go."

He did.

Daios didn't know what to say, though. He'd never been good with words, and an apology stuck on his tongue because it didn't seem like it was enough. He'd attacked his closest friend, without reason, because he'd lost the knowledge of where they were. What was he supposed to say in a situation like this?

So instead of talking, he just grunted. A deep sound, but one that he hoped portrayed that he wasn't in his right mind. That he wouldn't have done it if he had realized where they were.

Maketes darted away from him, his tail flashing a few times in agitation. Even his gills had flared around his ribs, likely to get more air into his body after being squeezed so tightly.

"Ridiculous," Maketes muttered. "They put me with him to watch over him, but how am I supposed to fight against that?"

"You aren't," Daios replied.

"Exactly. You lose your head like you've been doing so often, and what am I supposed to do?"

He stared his brother in the eyes, seeing the concern and the fear in those wide orbs, but he knew there wasn't a good answer. "You stay out of my way."

"That's not an option. What if you decide to turn the ocean red with their blood? What if you get yourself killed?" Maketes smoothed his hands down his rib gills, trying to push them flat and failing miserably. "You want to lose your other arm? That's how you lose your other arm. So keep your head on straight, stop thinking about whatever you were thinking, and let's stay together, yeah?"

He wasn't so sure they could do that. Because the moment he turned his attention away from Maketes, the more he was certain this was not going to be easy.

Alpha spread out before them like a giant bubble. Mira had explained to them what they should expect to see, but he had never thought it would be like this. Beta was spires of buildings, jutting and reaching into the ocean. Alpha had a shield of its own.

The golden city. Every spire and building within that shield was gold. It glimmered with interior lights, shimmering like a tiny world held safe with a glass dome set atop it. Even from this distance, he could see the greenery. Trees, Mira said, although she had never seen one herself. There was some kind of fancy light that allowed plants to grow within it. Dots of people moved freely through the streets, all in a massive dome rather than the thin and hidden corridors they had seen in Beta.

And everywhere around the city was flat. Completely and utterly flat. Destroyed by machines a long time ago, razed to the ground, so that there was no way for anything to swim near the glass walls without being seen. He narrowed his gaze, focusing his attention on the small pillars dotted around that flattened landscape. Even as he watched, a school of fish started toward the dome. One of those pillars came to life, a light within it gathering before it lasered toward the swimming creatures.

They evaporated into a plume of blood.

Maketes let out a low whistle. "That will not be easy to get into."

"It'll be easy enough." Daios settled down on the sand, flattening his body and his tail against the very edge before the ground flattened out. Narrowing his eyes, he waited.

And waited.

Long enough that Maketes dramatically rolled onto his back and stared above them. "Easy enough, you say? Sure feels like we've been here forever."

"We've been here for only a few moments."

"We've been here for hours on end and all you're doing is staring. How do you not move for that long?"

Daios took a deep, steadying breath. "Do you remember how you just said traveling with me is hard?"

Rolling his head to peer in Daios's direction, Maketes replied, "Yes."

"You are hard to do this with. Now, if you could focus your attention on finding the pattern between these pillars, then we can get somewhere. Otherwise, go back and report to Arges that I am here."

"I'm not supposed to leave you alone."

Of course not. Because everyone was afraid he would suddenly believe he was more powerful than he was and try to attack Alpha on his own. As if he was that foolish. He was a warrior with too much bravery, that much he would admit, but he wasn't about to do something that would get him killed.

"Just go," he growled.

"Are you sure you aren't going to—"

A low, rumbling growl erupted out of his chest. Gills flattened to his form, he glared at his friend until Maketes held up his webbed hands for peace.

"Right," Maketes said. "I'll leave you alone. Just don't go blasting into that city without anyone knowing where you're going or how you got in there, yeah? I'll let the others know that we're here and that we're figuring it out."

His brother disappeared in a swirl of bright gold, nearly matching the city itself before he swam off into the distance. But then Daios could focus on the task at hand.

For all that they didn't trust him, Daios was a seasoned warrior. He knew how to wait. How to have patience. Such things were impossible for Maketes to even consider, because his brother had ever been the trickster. He found joy in every part of life, and never once thought about how difficult it could be if he was wrong.

Daios laid in the sands, unmoving, for days. It took a while for any other fish to test the pillars, but when they did, he could see how long it took to charge up the weapons. There was a pathway through it. He knew there was. He just had to be patient enough to see it.

No true warrior would count days or even think about worrying about how long he had been there. He grabbed a few of the fish that swam past him for food, even an eel that slithered close enough. Slurping down the electric eel had given him a charge of electricity that played down his sides and ran through the crimson gills at the sides of his neck.

Then he saw it.

It all clicked into place. The pattern that would lead him to the destruction of this city and all who lived within it.

With a sudden burst of movement, he shoved himself out of the sand and blasted toward the pillars. There were only seconds while the pillars charged up, but by the time they had, he'd already moved past them. Darting from left to right, he moved through the meager blind spots and the small opportunities where he was allowed a few moments without fear of blistering pain.

A few of the sharp light weapons grazed his shoulder, his spine. One went right through his fluke. But still, he pushed forward. He was the only one crazy enough to do this and the only one they could actually spare if something went wrong.

But he wanted to prove that even if he was broken, he was still worth something. He could still do...

This.

There was a small tube he'd noticed from his great distance. It seemed that some water went in and out of it, a filtration system, perhaps. He'd seen them before in Beta and had destroyed quite a few of them in his time. If he could fit through it—which was a big if—then maybe he could get into the city.

Swimming past the last set of lasers, he shoved himself against the end of the tube. There was a metal grate over it, but that was easy enough to wrench open as a laser struck him. Baring his sharp teeth in a snarl, he wriggled his way into the tunnel and disappeared from the sight of the lasers.

And just like that, he was in.

Turning to look back where he'd come from one last time, Daios tried not to hear the screams of all those he'd left behind following him into the pipes.

Chapter 2

Ace, I'm a little busy."

"Message received. Information has been acquired."

"Negative," Anya replied as her droid relayed the message through the lens currently on the table. "Not until I finish the new upload. You can provide the information later."

Another message came through, this one underlined in red. "Urgent."

"Of course it's urgent," Anya muttered. Using the pliers in her hands, she peeled open the small panel on the bottom of her droid. It was a very old model, not one that was even made these days. Her father liked that it was almost impossible to reprogram the damn things, though, so this was the one she was given.

But Anya had figured out how to reprogram it, even after the technicians continued to fiddle with the electrical panels. The poor thing was little more than legs. Sometimes she thought it looked like one of those deep sea squids. Just a bulbous head, about the size of a clementine, with a screen on the front that projected adorable blinking eyes. But the four legs were meant to wrap around someone's head.

The intended design of this model droid had been for magnification. Engineers sometimes used them, but mostly she'd heard of them being used in artisan work. Jewelers would use the screen to magnify the tiny settings, making it easier for them to complete their crafts.

Her father had her droid reprogrammed so Anya could interpret what people were saying. After the accident, it had been more helpful than any of the doctors she'd seen. At least he'd done that.

The tiny panel finally came off. Switching her pliers to a needle nose pair, she finally pulled out the little chip the technicians had installed in her droid. They always did this. For some kind of safety reason, apparently, but she knew the truth. They wanted to spy on her, and she wasn't going to have it.

Yanking out the chip, she pulled out her own from the drawer where she had about thirty all reprogrammed already. They did this every single month, and every time, she changed out their chip with her own.

Inserting it very carefully, she closed the panel back up and then slowly stood the droid back on her feet.

"How's that, Bitsy?" she asked, gently patting the top of the droid's head.

Its eyes fluttered a few times, blinking rapidly before it picked up a leg and waved at her. She could just barely see a message flash in the lens that it held in one of its legs.

"More like myself."

That's what she liked to hear. The droid was her best friend, and really only friend in this place. Anyone else she trusted, like Ace, wasn't in Alpha.

"Bitsy, send a message to—" She froze, staring into the reflection on Bitsy's glass. There was a person in her doorway. Someone standing there like they were listening in on what she had to say.

Whirling, she realized there were actually two people in her room. The first one must have just walked in, although the woman wore a surprised expression on her face. A maid, Anya thought. Or something like that. She'd only seen the woman around a few times before now, but she held a stack of clothing in her hands.

Now, looking right at them, she could make out the muffled sounds of their voices. She just hadn't heard them over the music playing because Anya liked to have background noise whenever she was alone. Otherwise, all she could hear was the ear-piercing shriek of her tinnitus acting up.

She could read the lips of the closest maid saying, "So sorry, miss—" but then the woman turned her head to the other and all the words were lost.

"Damn it," Anya muttered, reaching up to situate Bitsy on her head and dropping the lens down over her eye. She'd missed some of the words, but they flew immediately on the screen in front of her left eye.

"—said to get you dressed. These are the clothes he picked out, Miss Anya."

Taking a deep breath, she remembered that tonight she was supposed to accompany her father to a benefit supper. All the rich and famous people would be there, which she supposed she was a part of. Just look at her room.

Anya wasn't allowed anywhere near the edge of the city, so her father had given her the best room he could find that was in the interior. Golden walls carved with gods and goddesses, although they had always seemed very intimidating to her. Her bed was a massive round monolith. The headboard was poured to look like a golden seashell with an inlaid mother-of-pearl on the inside. The tiny mosaic chips were so meticulously placed, it looked like her father had actually found a seashell this large.

Of course, her floors were all carpeted with thick, plush material that had come from Above. Quite literally. She even had a record player from Above that her father had spent someone's yearly salary to get. But he wanted her to have all the nice things possible. Even the bathing room with its saltwater pool that was supposed to help with her therapy somehow.

She thought it was all trying too hard. She'd lost her hearing, not her mind.

Rubbing a hand over the free side of her face, she nodded before gesturing for the clothes. "I forgot. Let's see what he picked out for me."

What she really wanted to do was complain about how her father seemed to think she was nothing but a doll for him to dress up. He always sent her an outfit before any function. He told her exactly what to wear, how to wear it, and how long she would be wearing it for. He told her where to go, what to eat, even how to act. And all of this had come after her accident.

Gritting her teeth, she moved behind her ivory partition to slip out of her much more reasonable clothing and pour her body into what her father considered appropriate for the daughter of the General.

It was a nice dress. Nearly a perfect match for her blonde hair, a pretty yellow pattern with a sensible straight neckline. The bell skirt swirled around her waist and tucked in her shape very nicely. But it was just slightly too tight around her ribs, and every breath was a reminder that she couldn't breathe. Not in this dress, and not in this city.

"You look pretty," Bitsy said, the words flashing in front of her eyes. At least that sentence took over how she felt when she looked in the mirror.

Sighing, she pulled her hair back into a sensible twisted bun and then stepped out into her room. She had thought maybe the two women would leave, but no. Of course not. They were still standing right where she had left them, ready to accompany her.

To literally walk her to the benefit supper because no one trusted her.

With the two women on either side of her, she left her private quarters and made her way out into the madness of the street. She lived on her own, at least. It was the first and last argument she'd won with her father. And perhaps that was because he had installed so many people around her that it was almost like she was still living in his house.

The streets were busy today, though. All the stone paths were filled to the brim with men and women wandering around. Some people were shopping, and their shopping center really was beautiful. The intricate carvings made it seem like they were inside of a honeybee hive, all the windows each delicately set up with all the artwork and glass blown creations that existed in Alpha.

Everyone wore their best, but when didn't they? Flashing colors of gemstones burned through her eyes, even as Bitsy tried her best to keep up with the conversation. Words ran in streams down the lens, too fast for her to really read any of them, other than to catch singular words.

"Bitsy," she muttered, hoping she was quiet enough for the other women to not hear her, but also not sure how loud she was talking. "Can you stop that?"

The flashing words appeared in all caps, as Bitsy always typed. "You sure?"

"For now."

The words disappeared, and she was blissfully unaware of everything around her. The hum of conversation all turned into one tone, nearly impossible to tell who was saying what. It was like she was underwater, everything muffled and jumbled together.

They walked through the crowd, and she nodded and smiled whenever someone caught her eye. But eventually they made it to the banquet dinner where her father had insisted she go. It was mostly held in the front yard of a rather large estate that looked to be made entirely out of white marble. The tall pillars went up two stories and then flattened out onto the roof that she happened to know was filled with a garden.

A politician lived here. The man and his wife were usually quite busy making new laws and passing bills that all the citizens of Alpha had to follow. She was quite certain they had something better to do than entertain more rich and famous.

Instead, they were all out here. In the front yard, where there was yet another garden and a beautiful tea setup with white tables dotting the grass. Over done, really, considering all the people invited were likely in heels or their best garb. They likely sunk heel deep every time they took a step.

Her father was in the back corner, surrounded by a crowd of people. At one point, he was a handsome man. But years of stress had worn down his body. Where he used to stand tall and broad, now he was starting to curve in on himself. He refused to carry a cane, or even try to ask for help, though. He had to look the part.

One of the maids told her that her father wished to speak with her— with her face turned away so Anya wouldn't have known what the other woman had said if not for Bitsy—and then pointed at the man of the hour.

Frowning, she stalked across the grass. Thankfully, she hadn't changed her shoes this time. Neither of the maids had noticed she had on her comfortable white flats.

They were the first thing her father noticed.

His nostrils flared in anger, and she saw him excuse himself from the crowd. That stomping walk definitely meant he was mad at her. Even if she hadn't noticed the way his shoulders were much more square, or how his eyes had narrowed in that glare that he saved just for her.

"What are you wearing?" he said, his mouth warping around the sound so she could only assume he hissed the words.

"Bitsy, turn translation back on," she said, certain that she was a little too loud. "I'm sorry, Dad, what did you say?"

Again the nostril flare. Again, the pinched lips that surely meant he was about to explode. "I said, what are you wearing?"

She liked to remind him whenever she could that she'd lost her hearing. It was, after all, his fault. And the man had been exposing her to situations that made her uncomfortable ever since.

Oh, his poor baby girl was surely too fragile to do things on her own. That was the excuse he always said. But it wasn't for that reason. No, he wanted to keep her under his thumb because he didn't trust her.

The old man was far too observant.

"The clothes you sent me," she replied.

"You are wearing flat shoes!" Bitsy underlined and made the words shake in red.

Then her little droid added in blue, "Heavens forbid!"

It took everything in her to not grin. "Sorry, I won't do it again. I must have forgotten."

"Just go and talk with the Harpswells, would you? They're waffling on the deal, and I need them to sign the paperwork to build the next service center on the eastern promenade." He pinched his nose between his eyes, exhaling and pulling that mask back over his features. "Be nice."

With that last warning, he turned toward his crowd of adoring fans and opened his arms. Considering the muffled noise that then disappeared into nothing, she could only imagine they were cheering him on.

Shaking her head, she grabbed a glass of champagne from a waiter walking past, and she started toward the Harpswells. But then she was stopped by a middle-aged woman Anya thought was part of the family who ran the artist's guild. Or maybe she was just on the board. She couldn't remember.

"How are you doing, dear?" the woman said, her mouth becoming pinched. The wrinkles on her forehead deepened. Not a good look considering her pale hair had turned the color of sickly straw.

"I'm fine, thank you." She really needed to get past this barrier of a person. Obviously, everyone knew she was fine. Anya hadn't even hidden in her room recently, so no one could say she had been sick.

She side-stepped around the woman, only to have her mirror the movement. That pinched, wrinkly mouth said, "It's just that we worry about you. Since the accident."

Anya reached up to tap Bitsy's glass, only to have the droid add on the screen, "That's what she said."

"The accident that happened years ago?" she asked for clarification.

"Yes." The woman's eyes flicked to her ears and back. "Do you mind if I ask you some questions about it?"

Of course she minded. She wasn't a doll for them all to pass around. The rumors could fly about what happened ten years ago, but she'd like to leave it in her past. Especially when she had stuff to do, like go and talk to the Harpswells. Already her father was glaring at her. The Harpswells were looking at her surprised as though they couldn't guess why she wasn't right next to them. And this woman sidestepped with her again to ask more questions.

She couldn't really hear the woman. It was all just blended together, and Bitsy was making snide comments on top of what the woman was saying, which made it hard to guess what was actually being said. Most of the time Anya could match the lips to the words, but she was so overwhelmed and everyone was looking at her like they were expecting something to happen.

Suddenly, she felt like a songbird her father kept in a cage and only let out for his friends to ogle.

"Fuck this," she muttered.

"Pardon me?" the woman said. Or at least, Anya thought that was what she said. The woman had turned at the last second, making it hard for her to read her lips.

"You're pardoned," Anya replied, and then brushed past her.

She wasn't going to stand here and be the performing monkey for them all to look at. Her father could be angry at her, put her under house arrest, whatever he wanted to do. She needed to breathe and she couldn't breathe here.

Stepping into the house, she made her way to the very back of the building where no one would be. Anya ignored everyone milling around and socializing, pretending she didn't notice when someone lifted their hand that they wanted to speak with her. And then finally, blissfully, silence. No noises, no words or tones that garbled together, just nothing.

Pressing her back against the pool room's door, she blew out a long breath. This was a pretty room, at least. The pool was large enough to do laps in, and deeper than she was tall. And Anya wasn't a small woman. There were benches all around, and small areas that dipped into the stone floor that were filled with pillows. Maybe a spa area, if she squinted her eyes hard enough at it.

"That didn't go well," Bitsy remarked, the words flashing over the pool.

"I know," she replied. "Trust me, I know."

"She's going to talk."

"I know," Anya expelled a breath. "I know she's going to talk. They're always talking about me. No one in this city knows what privacy means."

Stomping over near the pool, she settled down on a bench and touched her finger to Bitsy's screen. "Make a connection with Ace, please."

"Here?" The glass glitched out a bit, showing a patchwork of squares before her droid settled again. "You're sure?"

"I'm sure Bitsy." Sighing, she frowned at a few ripples in the pool and looked around to make sure no one else was in the room with her. But she was alone, she was sure of it. "Connect with Ace."

Chapter 3

For once after his injury, he was glad he only had the one arm. The pipes were tight, and slithering through them was grueling work at some points. For the most part, he was able to move through them fairly easily, though. There was enough space for his tail to flick him forward. With one arm raised to guide him through the darkness, and the other shoulder bent down, he could slide into their world far too easily.

These achromos. They were always so certain that they were protected and safe in their little bubbles, but they were not foolproof.

He had spent too much of his life learning how to fight them to not know their weaknesses. And hubris was the greatest weakness they had.

Finally, he saw a small light at the end of the piping. He'd traveled through this section for a while, mapping it out in his mind as he took only rights to ensure that he knew how to get his way out. The last thing this mission needed was for him to get stuck in the piping system with no idea how to get out.

He kept the fears at bay. But the voices constantly whispered in his mind. At least there was no one else for him to kill here. At least he couldn't harm anyone else if he was the only one who ended up dead.

Maybe he deserved to end up dead, just like all the other People of Water who had suffered the consequences of his folly.

Breathing slow and shallow through his gills, he conserved his energy in case something else happened. But strangely, these pipes led straight toward a light that flickered at the end of the tunnel. That golden light called out to him, even if he was quite certain it could be his end.

These achromos didn't see the world the way they should. All they saw was something to plunder, and he could only imagine their homes were dismal and disgusting. He liked to think they lived in caverns like eels, staring out from their dark homes with beady little eyes that watched for the slightest glimpse of a weakness in anything approaching them.

But as he stuck his head out of the piping that led into a massively deep structure, he was speechless as he realized everything above him was beautiful. The ceiling held the image of clouds, so detailed and streaked with pinks and reds that it was almost as though he looked up at the actual sky. He'd only seen the surface a few times in this life, but it had looked like this.

And the strange pool he was now in was decorated as well. There were chips of glimmering gemstones all around the bottom. Those gemstones caught in the golden light and flickered against the wall in a thousand rainbows that danced everywhere his eyes looked. Even the walls of the pool were smooth to the touch when they shouldn't be. They couldn't be.

Rock wasn't smooth. Not like this.

He reached out with a clawed, webbed hand and gently patted the edge. It really was lovely. It made him hate them all the more. They hoarded this wealth to themselves when his people might have used this to make more comfortable homes for themselves.

A low rumble vibrated through his gills as he moved all the way out and approached the surface.

Breaking the water line, he kept most of his body underneath it, but lifted his gaze. Blinking the water out of his eyes, he was surprised to see even more wealth here. Gold poured from the ceiling above him, and the benches were made out of a pure white substance that he'd never seen before.

He pulled himself out of the water a little farther, lifting his head up as he searched for anyone in the room. And for a moment, he thought he was entirely alone, until someone started speaking.

Daios ducked into the water again, his hearts racing as he worried that there would soon be screaming. The sound was almost similar to screaming. The cries of the achromos were terrible, and he knew that they summoned others with that horrible squawking sound.

But the sound continued on and on, almost as though this was intentional. As though the person didn't realize that they were screaming.

Frowning, he allowed his ears to pop above the surface again. And yes, it was similar to screaming, but nowhere near as loud. The pitch continually changed up and down, some of it quiet and some of it loud. Then he realized where it was coming from.

A woman sat in the corner, something in her hands as she waved them in front of her in a graceful dance. Her fingers flew over the air before her, as though she were playing some instrument he could not see.

Her golden hair fit in with this place, just like the yellow dress she wore. But it was her hair that he could not stop staring at. It was so... elegant. A smooth waterfall of golden color that was pinned in place with some claw shaped device that held all the locks where she wanted them. But he wanted to rip that out of her head. He wanted to see the shiny tumble and to feel if it was as smooth as it looked.

His fingers spasmed in the water, a strange reaction considering he also wanted to kill her.

She was too small for him to be interested in. His hearts did not beat for someone that would break the moment he first touched them. Not to mention she was so perfect. A little golden statue hidden in the middle of her golden city. So pretty and perfect and wrong for him.

A monster would leave smudges on something so lovely as she.

Besides, he hated her kind. And he was going to destroy them from the inside out. She would never see him as anything other than a nightmare, nor should she.

For now, he would know that this pool was a start. He should return to his people and let them know he had found a way into the hidden city. He could get them into Alpha, which meant he could likely shield Mira and bring her all the way here. Then she could steal some of their coverings and make her way into the city. From there, she could hopefully find the General's daughter.

That was who they were looking for, after all.

The door to the room opened, and he ducked back into the water with a soundless movement. He barely even saw ripples as he sank back toward the pipe that would lead him out of the room.

But this person spoke clearly, loudly, and succinctly. He could hear this woman's voice all the way through the deep water and to the pipe that he had almost finished backing into.

"Are you quite done?" the woman barked, her voice piercing even from these depths. "The General would like to see his daughter making rounds, and if you're unwilling to do that, I'm sure he will happily have some words with you."

The General's daughter?

Daios suddenly turned his attention to the surface again. Though slightly warped through the surface, he could see the new woman standing there with a frown on her face. But more importantly, he could see that the golden-haired woman had not responded.

"Hey!" the woman said, much more loudly. "Would you look at me, please? Clearly you cannot hear a damn thing I'm saying."

There was a longer pause, but the General's daughter still did not look at the woman.

"Absolute nuisance," the woman muttered, stalking away.

But as the door closed, clicking shut, he could see the General's daughter look to the door. What a strange woman to pretend that another person wasn't even in the room. But then she turned her attention back to something floating in the air that didn't exist.

Interesting, he thought as he returned to the surface. Curiosity burned in his chest. Why did this woman have so much power over others that she didn't have to respond?

He crested the surface again, moving slightly closer to her. Enough so that he could reach up with a webbed hand and grab onto the edge of the pool. Still, she did not move, didn't respond, didn't even see him. For the daughter of a warrior, she didn't have a lot of self preservation. She should have felt his gaze on her or something of the ilk.

His fingers accidentally brushed against a silver container that clanked as it fell against the lip of the pool. The high-pitched clamouring echoing through the room. He froze, already halfway out of the water at this point. She would soon turn to the sound, see a monstrous red beast coming out of the pool, and then she'd scream.

A sound erupted from her mouth, and the sound made him flinch. The scream would surely warn all the other achromos that an intruder had finally broken through their defenses...

Except, it was the same off key sound she'd made before. A terrible sounding voice, but the more he listened, the more he realized she was attempting to sing.

What a grating voice, but she was clearly enjoying herself. And she hadn't heard the sound of the pot. He looked at the metal, frowning as though maybe he'd only heard the sound in his mind. But the metal had sunk down to the bottom, soap floating up and bubbles floating on the surface. He'd only seen Mira use this awful substance, and it stuck to his gills in the most horrendous manner.

Glancing back at the woman, he felt something in his chest click.

For whatever reason, she was unaware of her surroundings. Clearly, she could see. Her fingers flew in front of her as only a person who could see would do. Could she not hear?

Narrowing his eyes, he tested this theory. As strange as it was, there was a thread in his chest that screamed for him to know more about this woman. He needed to understand her. Why? He had no idea.

Daios knocked off another of those metal containers, listening to it clink and echo as it tumbled across the strange texture of stone and then fell into the pool. Nothing. No reaction at all.

It made him brave. Her lack of reaction only made him want to test this even more. Perhaps that was what made him so unfit for this mission. After all, he was supposed to find a way in and then report back. There should be multiple People of Water wandering through the pipes right now, seeking out the best way to kidnap this woman who fate had handed to him.

But all he had to do was reach out. He could grab her by the waist and yank her into the water with him. But she was still an achromo. Still a monstrous being who he had fought against his entire life. The thought of connecting one of his longer tentacles to her throat? To create that connection so he could breathe for her underwater?

It made him want to vomit.

Still, he couldn't stop himself from pulling his giant body out of the water. Using his one arm, he lurched forward until he was right behind her. Only his fluke remained in the water, and he knew that this put him in a precarious position. If anyone walked in, they would see him here. They would scream and he would have a hard time getting back in the water before they all arrived with their blisteringly hot weapons that would rip and tear through his body.

But he wanted to know. He had to know.

Daios watched his arm as though it belonged to a stranger. One moment, he was coiling his tail underneath him so he could loom above her. And the next, his good arm was reaching out toward her hair. Carefully, so delicately that surely she wouldn't feel anything at all, he reached for the clip.

She wore a clear square over one eye, and he could see through it from this angle. She saw something far more than just the world in front of her. Every hand flick was moving something in that glass. Messages, perhaps, but it looked more like a map. Like someone had sent her a map, and she was looking through it at the best way to do... something.

So, this little creature had more plans than he had expected.

Perhaps he had been foolish to think she would be easy to capture. She was still the General's daughter after all.

With a quick snapping movement of his claws, he untangled the clip from her hair and launched himself back toward the pool. But he still watched, and all he saw was the slow motion waterfall of her hair falling out of its confines. He'd been right. It was smooth and so soft as it had fallen across his webs with the barest of touches. Like the finest material he had ever seen in his life.

A precious, golden waterfall that made every muscle in his body tense. He told himself it was because he had to rush away from the stupid thing that he'd done and that she surely would call for reinforcements.

Because she whipped around so quickly that he almost didn't get out of her way before she saw him. Maybe she did. Maybe she'd have the sense to realize that a dark figure had been directly behind her, and all that remained was the splashing edges of the water and the waves that billowed onto the floor from where she stood.

He'd already darted into the pipe with her clip in his hand and his hearts thundering in his chest. Stupid. What a risk. She'd probably go into hiding now after she started screaming, but... she didn't.

Daios hesitated, then turned at one of the connectors where he could squeeze his body into a "U" in the tight fit. He couldn't leave. Not when she hadn't reacted the way he'd expected. So he returned to that golden light and peered through the water to see her standing there. The water was still rioting from the massive length of his body, disturbing it, but she wasn't screaming. She was just standing, staring at the water like she'd seen a ghost.

Maybe she had.

Daios bared his teeth in what he was certain was an evil grin. She had no idea that he was coming for her.

A part of him he didn't recognize unfurled in his chest. A demon, surely, because it whispered words he'd only heard in the darkest times of his life before.

"Hunt her," it growled in his chest, rumbling through him until he felt his gills vibrate with the sound.

The woman above him stumbled back from the pool at the sound. Maybe she hadn't lost all her ability to hear. Or perhaps she recognized the feeling that she was suddenly prey.

A predator had entered her home. Now he wanted to see just how easy she was to hunt.

With that feral grin still in place, he tossed her clip out into the center of the pool and waited.

Chapter 4

nya had no idea what had just happened. Her hair had fallen out of its clip and she swore she had felt something very cold radiating against her spine, but that was... insane.

She would have known if someone came into the room. She'd known when that ridiculously rude maid had come in. And she'd heard what the woman said. She had the glass over her eye, and Bitsy was very good about translating any sound that happened around her. So, of course, she knew that her father wanted her to go back and entertain people.

She just didn't want to go back.

Anya didn't think she should be required to do anything she didn't want to. Her father could entertain his guests on his own, without her, and he would be absolutely fine. But god forbid she deny him anything! She was his pretty little songbird. She was supposed to sing when he told her to sing.

He argued it was to keep her safe. She was in danger wherever she went, and he was the only person who could keep her safe.

This was the first time in her life she'd wondered if he was maybe right.

Her heart raced in her chest, thundering against her ribs until she wondered if it was possible to die from fright. Bitsy kept flashing a message in her eye piece but she didn't have the faintest idea what it said because she just couldn't get herself to read right now.

She had been alone in this room. She was certain of it.

Hadn't she?

What if she hadn't been alone? What if someone had walked right up behind her and she had no idea? All she could think was that her father had enemies. What better way to get to the old man than by killing his most prized possession?

But as the water slowly stilled, she could see there was nothing in there. There was no one in the room. Her panicked gaze flickered over everything before she settled on that truth. She was alone. She had been alone.

Something in her whispered that she'd seen something reflected in Bitsy's glass. An impossible thing because her mind couldn't conjure up the details of an undine that perfectly. She had only seen the drawings of them on that fateful day when she'd lost her hearing, and even then, it wasn't like she could remember it all that well.

No. There was no undine in the city. That had never happened before and it wouldn't happen while she was alone here.

Then she read the message that Bitsy kept flashing in front of her eyes.

"There is someone here."

Gulping, she shook her head. "No one is here, Bitsy. You can see that as well as I can."

But again, her little droid was always the argumentative one. "No, someone was here."

"The maid came in and out."

This time in dark red, underlined, with wiggling text so it looked like the kind of message a serial killer would leave on a mirror. "We are not safe."

Anya told herself that the droid was overreacting. They'd both had quite the fright, and it still felt like someone was looking at her. She swore she had sensed eyes on her the entire time she was in here, but she was also talking with Ace and figuring out a plan to get people into Alpha. They had a plan to destroy this place from the inside out, so of course she felt like someone was watching her.

If anyone caught her talking to someone off Alpha, then they would send her in for questioning. Let alone if they got their hands on Bitsy and saw the schematics that she was sending to someone off station.

But there was no one in this room. She was just paranoid because she was doing her work out of her room, and her clip must have just... flung out of her hair. That was the only explanation she could think of.

Reaching up, Anya ran her fingers through the strands. "Maybe the clip had too much strain on it," she muttered.

Bitsy's reply flashed loud and clear. "You've used that clip a hundred times."

She had. It was her favorite because it had been her mother's. It was the only thing she had left of the woman that gave her life, because her mother had died in childbirth. Unfortunately, she'd left Anya alone with a tyrant for a father.

Pinching her nose, she took a deep breath. "Do you see where the clip went?"

By the time she opened her eyes, Bitsy had circled an area in the pool. Because of course her clip had flung off so far that it was now deep in the water. She couldn't leave it there, though. It was the last bit of her mother, and Anya would do insane things to keep it.

Looking around for one of the pool nets, she groaned as she realized no one kept the nets around their pools in this section of Alpha. There was likely some kind of cleaning house nearby where they kept everything. But if she stepped outside like this, then she would be swarmed by people. And she had no idea how much the salt water of this pool was going to ruin her mother's clip.

"Fine," she muttered. "Two birds, one stone."

"What are you doing?" Bitsy asked.

"I'm going to get my clip back. And I'll be soaking wet, so Dad will send me right back to the house to get changed. And then I will decide that I won't come back. Easy. I don't have to go to the party, and I get my clip back."

"This is stupid."

"You're stupid," she replied, before yanking her dress over her head. She took Bitsy off as well, setting the droid on the ground even though she knew it was probably making some kind of noise in displeasure. The little thing was already rocking back and forth like it wanted her to pick it back up.

But she needed to get that clip, and she refused to let fear control her. She had let it control her life for years after the accident. She wasn't a little girl anymore, and she was braver than she was back then.

In nothing but her bra and underwear, she dove into the pool. She'd been swimming her entire life, and she found it as easy as breathing. At least without currents. From what she'd heard, it was harder to swim outside of Alpha than it was within it.

Diving all the way to the bottom, she grabbed the clip and turned her body to kick off from the floor.

But then she noticed the fin. It was a delicate looking frill, just barely sticking out of the pipe that brought fresh sea water into the pool. Though mostly gray, she could see fine filaments of red running through the thin membrane. It was beautiful, a rare color in these parts. But then her gaze followed that fin to what it was connected to, and she felt her heart stop beating.

A monstrous creature lurked in that pipe. An almost human face stared back at her, glinting fangs flashing in the meager light. Though his nose was flat and his jaw broad, he wasn't remotely like anything she'd seen before. Red edged gills framed his face, but long dark hair tangled around his features in matted strands that looked almost like tentacles.

But his eyes... Oh, those black eyes saw straight into her soul. She barely had a moment to realize that his black hand, webbed and tipped with deep red claws, was gripping the edge of the pipe. He could so easily attack her. She couldn't even see how large he was, or guess how fast he could move, because he was deep inside the shadows of the pipe.

If she peered a little closer, all she could see was the faintest outline of a muscular chest, and that was... disconcerting.

Belatedly, terror struck her hard in the middle of her body. She felt a bit like she might vomit until the warning bells screamed in her mind that she had to run. Flee. Hide. This creature would eat her alive. Those fangs could tear her flesh from bone so easily she might not even feel it.

Kicking her feet against the bottom of the floor, she launched herself up to the surface. Run. Hide. Flee. All of those words and more kept replaying in her head.

There was an undine in her home. Alpha was supposed to be impossible for anyone to get in or out of. She knew it was. She'd been working with Ace for years on a way to get someone into Alpha without her father knowing. Yet this undine was right in the pipes.

In the very foundation of the city.

Breaking the surface, she sucked in a panicked amount of air, as though that might help her in the slightest. She was going to die. Any minute, she was going to feel those sharp teeth clench around her ankle and drag her back into the depths. Soon the pool would be filled with the billowing blood exiting her body and no one would even know that she was dying.

She should scream for help. Someone might come running if they heard her, but right now she couldn't force herself to even make a sound. Or maybe she was making noise and she just couldn't hear the pitiful whines that surely... surely...

Grabbing onto the edge of the pool, she hauled herself out of the water and spun around. Like she had a shark chasing her and if she placed a well-aimed kick, that would make it leave.

But there was nothing in the water. Not at all.

Still breathing hard, her eyes wide in horror at what might have just happened, she reached for Bitsy.

The droid crawled onto her head with words scrolling past her vision so quickly she almost couldn't read them.

"What were you thinking? What is in the water? Did something try to grab you? I told you we weren't alone. Why don't you ever listen?"

"There is something in the water," she gasped, her eyes still locked on the waves she'd caused as she tried to escape it. "It's an undine."

There was a long pause as the droid took in what she said, and then there was the strangest response from the little droid, who had always been more afraid of living than it was of being decommissioned.

"Can I see?" The words vibrated with excitement.

"What?" she gasped. "No, you cannot see. Are you insane? That thing could kill me in an instant."

"Anything could kill you in an instant. That noise bomb you picked up that destroyed your hearing could have killed you, too. But you still picked it up. You've always been an adventurous person, Anya. Now let me see the undine."

It was one of the longest messages Bitsy had ever played in front of her eyes. The robot was usually quite succinct, even going so far to shorten what people were saying. Anya had a feeling the droid was a rather lazy worker, but that's what she got for giving the AI its own personality.

Sighing, she shook her head. "I don't think I can get back in the water."

"Sure you can."

"It's not a good idea, Bitsy! I'm already so out of breath, I don't think I could stay under the water for more than a few seconds."

"Try."

Blowing out a breath, she told herself she could do this because there probably wasn't an undine under there after all. It was just a figment of her imagination. A fish stuck in the filters that she'd thought was a massive creature.

No one could get in Alpha without her father knowing. Alpha was the safest place in the ocean for humans, and had been for almost two hundred years. The city was a prison as much as it was a home.

She slithered back into the water, her eyes on the pipe like something monstrous was going to burst out of it at any moment. But nothing moved. The fin she'd seen before wasn't there either.

"Well." Bitsy said as she sank into the water. "That's incredibly disappointing."

If they'd been in the air, she would have muttered something about how the droid was doing fine underwater, which she didn't think Bitsy's model was rated for. And yet, the deeper she dove, the more it seemed like her heartbeat stuttered.

Because there was something in the darkness of the pipe. Even as her ears popped and her tinnitus screamed so loudly it made her wince, she could only focus on the shadows that moved in an undulating pattern.

First came the clawed hand. The red-tipped fingers that curled around the edge and then... then it was the rest of him. Or at least, the rest of him that she'd already seen.

The broad shoulders that barely fit in the pipe. Those soulless black eyes, and the terrifying grin that made her think of monsters in her closet when she was a little girl. He was everything that she'd been terrified of when she was a child. Right here. Right in front of her.

"Oh," Bitsy said, the word even wobbling in her vision.

But then the undine reached out that hand. The light played through the webbing, and she realized it was very delicate and thin between those deadly fingers. Delicate and so... pretty.

Maybe he was magical. Maybe he cast a spell on her. Because the only logical thing to do in this moment was to kick back off the floor and run. Or maybe to scream so hard that bubbles came out of her mouth, obscured her vision, and then he drowned her.

Instead, she reached out a shaking hand and mirrored his movements. Her fingers gently skated over his. She could feel the claws that could tear through her flesh. But he stayed eerily still as she traced her fingers down his, to the webbing that felt like velvet, to his broad palm that was dotted with so many scars she couldn't begin to count them.

He was warm in the cold water, when she could have sworn he'd been behind her and radiating an ice cold sensation down her spine. But he didn't move now. He just watched her, his eyes shifting to look at her hands. At least, that's what she assumed he was looking at. It was hard to tell with that otherworldly gaze.

Black eyes. Completely black without a hint of white.

He was here. And she was touching an undine. Her hand looked so small next to his.

He was patient with her, just letting her stroke him while his fingers remained spread wide. But when she looked back at him, she could see that the gills around his neck had flared out wide. They shuddered in the water, gently fluttering with movement that made them look almost graceful. She hadn't thought she'd ever describe an undine with those words. And, she supposed, her first impression had been terror.

But now, she looked at his face and wondered if there might be some beauty in those angles after all.

Her lungs spasmed, and she curled in on herself with the sensation. This was her last moment before she didn't have enough time to get to the surface. Looking up, she moved to kick off from the bottom only to feel a clawed hand palm her waist.

Eyes wide, she looked down at him to see he'd come partially out of the pipe. His hand was so large it spanned her waist from the middle of her ribs all the way down to her hip bone. Those claws were delicate though, carefully making sure not to break her skin as he palmed the curve just under her heartbeat.

Then, when her wide gaze flicked to his, he pushed her up. Toward the surface. A powerful shove that had her rocketing toward air. Spluttering, she looked back down to see that he had really disappeared from the pipe this time. At least, she thought.

An undine had helped her swim. He'd potentially saved her life.

"What the hell was that?" Bitsy asked.

Anya really didn't have an answer.

Chapter 5

Why hadn't he grabbed her? She was right in front of him. She'd touched him.

He could have grabbed onto her at any point, yanked her close to him, and then dragged her into the pipes. It would have been easy. Too easy, the more he thought about it. She was so weak compared to him.

But her fingers feathering over his had made him feel... something. Daios wasn't sure what that meant. His hearts had slowed down for a bit. All that rioting chaos calmed. He'd held his breath while she touched his fingers and he swore there was something going on with his gills that had never happened before.

There was no chance that he'd fluttered for her. He'd seen Arges doing it for Mira. It was always embarrassing to watch his brother so affected by the woman's mere presence. It made him uncomfortable.

No female had ever wanted to pick him. He was too large for their offspring to be easy births, and too aggressive to battle in the mating dance. He had already resigned himself that fluttering was foolish for anyone.

Daios had fluttered only for two other women. One of them, Melete, had saved Mira after she'd been taken by Beta. The other was a female who had left their pod a long time ago for another, much smaller and more manageable male. She had proven to him that he was unwanted and could not change the physical state he was in.

And that state had only gotten worse in the recent months.

Scraping the stump of his arm perhaps a little too hard against the piping, he paused at the opening to the sea. Something in him screamed that he had to go back. Some primal part of his brain shouted and raged against the cage he had tried to put it in. He had to return. He had to make sure that she was safe because no one could keep her safe better than him.

But that primal part of his brain had been the one to lead him to trouble before. That was the same part of his mind that had said he should protect his people. The achromos were easy targets. He could take down their city if he just attacked it the way he had planned.

So he did not trust that primal part of his mind, even if it screamed and clawed and tore at his insides while he darted through the pillars of pain. It didn't matter in the long run. He couldn't trust himself.

Still, her pretty sea-blue eyes haunted him until he paused at the rendezvous place where he and Maketes were staking out the city. He could still see her eyes. His fingers could still feel her, trailing her fingers along his webbing like she wasn't tapping her way through his carefully laid defenses.

Silly thoughts, and he had to remind himself that they were. Even if every fin on his body stood out and shuddered. Even if his tail had already turned him to look back at that glass dome that kept her imprisoned.

Where did she live? Somewhere pretty, like her. She was too delicate and too quiet for her to live in hardship. If she was the General's daughter—and he had no reason to think otherwise—then she was likely one of the richest people in that city. She'd have plenty of food and water to drink. Plenty of options for someone to look out for her.

Still, his mind roared that he would bring her better meat. There were more nutritious options in the sea, and her people clearly were not feeding her enough. She was too thin. Too delicate.

Easily crushed by anyone who might want to hurt her.

Frowning, another thought flashed in his mind. Was she mated? Did she have someone who already fluttered for her and made her smile?

A white hot rage flowed through every inch of his body. He was glowing, bursting into a bright red while every bioluminescent dot on his form flared with rage. He could see the light reflecting on the sand around him, the waves of color rotating on the ground.

"So I'm going to guess you found something?" Maketes's annoyingly amused voice broke through the anger. "You look upset."

"I found her."

"You found an entrance to the city? That's fantastic."

"No, I found her."

"How many of us can fit through, do you think?" Then Maketes blinked a few times. What Daios had said twice now must have finally gotten through his skull. "What do you mean, you found her?"

"I assume most of us could fit through," he murmured, his eyes never leaving the city. "The pipe system is tight for me, but smaller males would have no issue. Perhaps a band of us could fit through together, but the city is massive. Even larger on the inside than it looks from here. It wouldn't be safe to send more of our people through."

"I think that's the most you've ever said to me in one sitting," Maketes muttered, before he swam in front of Daios.

It didn't escape his notice that Maketes left a decent amount of space between them. He wouldn't have advised anyone to get close to him right now, either. The colors rioting up and down his body were a way for his form to tell others that he was in a dangerous mood. The kind of mood that would have him reaching out for someone's neck and snapping it just so he could feel something.

Maketes cleared his throat, gills vibrating with the sound. "You found her?"

"I did."

"Why didn't you grab her? Were there a lot of people around her? Probably. The General won't give us an opportunity to grab her that easily, damn it. We're going to have to send in more than just you if that's the situation. We can't just let her stay there, and Mira is adamant that taking his daughter is the only way to get the General to listen to us."

Daios was already tired of his prattle. "She was alone."

Maketes stared at him for a few moments, his mouth open and blissfully silent for a few heartbeats. "What do you mean, she was alone?"

He grunted in response, already done with these questions.

"She was alone?" Maketes shifted closer, freezing at the growl that rumbled through Daios's chest. "Then why didn't you grab her?"

"Just didn't."

"But why?" Tossing his arms up in the air, Maketes spun in a dramatic circle before facing him again. "And don't give me some lie about how it was too dangerous. You were in the pipes. We know how to give them a way to breathe underwater. You could have snagged her and you didn't!"

Slowly, he turned his head to focus on Maketes. Perhaps something in his dark eyes was enough to threaten the yellow-finned brother who was too talkative for his own livelihood. "Wasn't the right time."

"It wasn't the right time," Maketes repeated, although his words were mocking. "We're back to that, are we? When is the right time going to be?"

"Don't know."

"Ugh!" Maketes kicked his tail up and floated down onto the sand. With his arms crossed over his chest, he stared up into the darkness above them while muttering, "This is why I didn't want to take this job. I knew without a doubt that he was going to be a problem. I told Arges, I'm not the person for this job. If they wanted Daios to be controlled, they should have sent someone bigger. And who was right? Me. I was right. No one's going to give me credit for being right, so I'm giving the credit to myself."

Daios watched him and felt the lights of his body flickering. Amusement replaced the anger that was so hard for him to think through. "You were right."

"Of course I was right! I'm always right, and no one ever listens to me before the start of anything. You know—" Maketes paused, then looked up at him with his mouth again wide open. "Did you just admit I was right?"

Daios nodded.

"Well... That's awfully remarkable, coming from you."

With a shrug, Daios slapped his brother with his tail and then used his much larger blade of a fluke to shove Maketes upright. "Go tell the others that I've found her."

"What about you? You're supposed to be the one making the report. You haven't told me anything about your interaction with her or how to find the girl. There's no report for me to give other than you grunted at me and said it was done." But Maketes was already moving away, already moving even while he argued that he shouldn't be.

"Just tell them I have it handled."

"So you're not coming back with me?"

Daios had thought he was going to. Everything in him shouted that he should. He was rebuilding his relationship with Arges, and every moment that he did something like this was another moment when he was failing his clutch brother. But... something in him also said that he couldn't leave right now. He had more to do.

"I'm busy," he replied, his gaze back to the city. "Tell them I'll return with her when I'm ready."

That stopped Maketes. The currents played through his brother's long hair, coiling through his gills and filling him with purpose. Daios missed that. He missed the moments when the sea had given him its approval. This moment felt like one of those times when the sea approved of his choice, though. It wasn't giving him too much attention, likely because it hadn't entirely forgiven him for all the death yet. But he was taking the right steps to getting back into its good graces.

Sighing, he waved a hand at Maketes when his brother didn't respond. "Go on."

"You're not going to hurt her, are you?" Maketes asked, his voice very low and very quiet. "We need her alive, Daios."

"I'm not going to hurt her." The growl that came after those words startled even him. He pressed a hand to his hearts, trying to still the anger that writhed inside of him at the mere thought. It was wrong. It was disgusting to even react to an achromo like this.

"Then what are you planning to do?"

"I don't know." He wished he had an answer to that himself. All he knew was that right now, he had…. feelings that he couldn't explain. A sensation in his chest that wouldn't go away and a strange need inside himself that had him stuck in this spot.

Maketes moved a little closer, flicking his tail and keeping himself lower than Daios's vision, so he didn't seem like a threat. "Are you making decisions based on instinct right now?"

"You could say that."

"This is going to get real complicated real quick," Maketes muttered before blowing out a mouthful of bubbles. "All right. Just don't get caught and die, would you?"

"I don't intend to."

As his brother disappeared into the darkness, he told himself this was good. He worked better on his own, when there was no one else to risk. But turning back toward the city, he already knew that there was a long way for him to go. He didn't know where she would be again. Surely there were plenty of other pools, but which ones would she be at, and how could he guess when she would be there?

What had the other achromo said? He tried to remember what the other female shouted while she tried to scold the golden one. Something about her father and other people to speak with.

A gathering then. The achromos were not so different from his own people in that way.

He'd have to go back into the city. She obviously didn't live in that strange pool room, and likely only visited it when her father wanted to show her off. The General's golden daughter, a precious gem to show all of his friends. But considering how she did not go to see her father, he could only assume that meant she wasn't anywhere near as close to the man as others thought.

This was good. He could get her away from the city faster if she didn't fight.

What would he do with her after he'd gotten her away? He had no idea. But like Daios had told Maketes, he was running with his instincts. He didn't have a choice for another way.

So Daios launched himself toward the city again. It took him the better part of a week, perhaps even longer to map out the city. He'd gone through every pipe, every tunnel, every pool. And when his mind was near full to bursting with information, he would return through the pillars. His body was decorated with healing scab wounds by the time he got back to his map that he'd made out of stones on the sands.

He could map this city out by himself. Even if that meant he was lacking some of his fin, because he kept getting sucked into sharp vents with spinning metal pieces that sliced through his fluke. One had even gotten his elbow when it had turned on and surprised him.

But blood was something he could lose. He wasn't afraid of pain or what would happen to him if he was caught. He had to keep going because there was a little female in this city that was without him. And when he was finished, he would find her again. He would map out this city until he knew as much about it as he could, and then he would make his attack.

The day that he finished, he could almost taste blood in the water. His gills flared wide, the fins around his face fluttering with the realization that he'd done it. He knew all the places where they traveled. He knew every pool and every pathway in this city. At least, all the ones that he could reach.

Daios had stayed in the water. He hadn't been caught by anyone or anything as far as he knew, although he was certain the achromos had noted the amount of time those pillars had gone off these days. He could only hope that they were so foolish that they thought it was a migration of some fish passing by their home.

Regardless, it was time. He could find her now. And he already knew where she was.

Every gill and fin on his body fluttered, flaring wide around his body until he knew he must look even more monstrous than ever before. But he was ready to see her. To impress her. To take her away from her home and fight off anyone who tried to keep her from him.

He told himself he was ready. He would bring her somewhere safe. Somewhere much better than Alpha. Then he would feed her. He would prove that he was a good hunter who could provide for her.

Beyond that, Daios didn't allow himself to even think what might happen. The thoughts made him a little uncomfortable, and it felt like he was a little unpredictable even to himself.

That little achromo was his, though.

And now he was going to take her.

Chapter 6

He was back.

The undine.

Anya sat at her dressing table, staring into the mirror where she could see the sudden ripples in her pool. That was all she could see, and hopefully that was all the cameras saw as well.

Her father had been in his "war room" for days on end with some of his other advisors. Apparently they were concerned about the undine problem. They were certain the creatures were getting ready to attack Alpha, but they wouldn't tell her why they thought so.

Thankfully, Bitsy had yet to go in for her checkup, and therefore was capable of hacking into her father's system. With that little lens over Anya's eye, they had both searched through the videos from the exterior of Alpha. And she'd watched the same undine she had seen sneaking through the pipes day after day.

Sometimes hour after hour.

She'd watched those videos more times than she wanted to admit. There was a certain power in his body as he blasted through the water.

Sometimes she could see the lasers hit his sides as the command center sent the message to kill. Those pillars each contained an AI of their own as well. They scanned his body, providing more information than she thought the undine would want them to know.

He was larger than most males they had seen. Sixteen feet from the top of his head to the bottom of his tail, and broad across the chest. The AI had also noted that while he was faster than the others, he turned slower. It had been learning his movements and patterns every time he went by the pillars. But for some reason, even the AI couldn't track him.

He was changing his patterns, she realized after watching the third clip. There was enough time between his visits that it was clear to her he was watching the pillars. Perhaps he saw the lights on the top that blinked when something got close to them. Or maybe he was watching the animals as they approached her city. She had no idea.

But watching him struggle over and over again, it made something in her feel hope for the first time in a very long time. This undine hadn't killed her. He hadn't even grabbed onto her, so that had to mean something, right?

He was still trying to get into the city. He was still doing something because he slipped into the pipes where the AI couldn't see him anymore.

And this was the third time she'd seen him in her bathing pool.

Wrapping her shawl tighter around her shoulders, she gently pulled Bitsy off of her head. "Take care of the cameras in the bathroom, would you?"

The little droid bounced up and down once, twice, three times, and then skittered off into the bathroom. She could only imagine what Bitsy would do. Generally, her droid was good about taking orders.

Especially when it came to the cameras. She made very quick work of the frustrating recorders that were in every part of her room. But right now, she needed her bedroom cameras to stay on.

None of them had a good angle of the bathroom, for privacy, because only certain people were allowed to check in on her in the bathroom. Her father was a jealous man, at the very least. Overprotective of his daughter, he didn't want any of his men peeking in on her when they shouldn't.

She'd never been more thankful for his boorish nature.

Anya had thought maybe the undine would return today. He seemed to come in patterns of threes, and it had been three days exactly since she'd seen him last. She had no idea how he knew where to find her, but it seemed like he always knew where she was. The first time she'd seen him in her neighbor's house after she'd taken a swim in her friend's home. The second time, she'd seen him here.

And now he had returned. At least, she had to hope it was him. The water moving like that wasn't normal. Bitsy would overlay the cameras with a picture of her bathroom with no one in it. It would take a while for anyone to review the footage, so she could only imagine they would see her walking into the bathroom and then give her privacy as long as she walked out at the right time.

Even if they did check the cameras, she was hoping they wouldn't notice that the image didn't quite move the way it should.

Blowing out a breath, she brushed her hair back over her shoulder and then nervously tucked it behind her ears. She had no way of knowing what this undine wanted. But she was curious enough to entertain him.

Clearly, a creature with this much dedication had something to say. Anya liked to think they were smart enough to... well, at least talk?

But maybe they didn't, and that was okay too.

After all, she knew what it was like to not have the same ability as everyone else.

Padding to the entrance to her bathroom, she paused. The people watching the feed into her room needed to believe that she was going to be in the bathroom for a while. If she wanted any sort of information from this creature, then she would need to time this correctly for them to interact.

What would Ace do? Her contact in the other station—she still had no idea where Ace was located—seemed to be far braver than her. They would say something like get all the things she could possibly need and lie through her teeth. Put on a performance that would last a lifetime.

That's why Ace had always called her the Queen of Hearts. She was supposed to be the most believable liar there was, at least that's what Ace always said. Anya was the person everyone wanted.

Snorting, she walked back to her table and grabbed an armful of bath products. She knew for a fact no one that watched her feeds would think twice about the amount of items she carried. They would think the spoiled brat was going to take a long bath and pamper herself.

The moment she walked through the bathroom, she dumped her armful of stuff on the floor.

She could already see him. The dark fringes of his fins were sticking out of the pipe that led into her private bath. And if she peered a little harder, squinted her eyes to see better, she could see there was a face looking at her through the water.

It really was him. Not that Anya had a lot of experience with undines, but she assumed she would be able to recognize this one no matter where he was. Those scars decorating his shoulders, the dark glint in his eyes, all of it hinted at a man possessed by a plan and barely leashed rage.

Maybe that was what called to her about him. He was angry, and she was angry, and maybe two monstrous people were supposed to find each other. They'd either end up like a bomb or they would fizzle out beating against each other's rage.

But right now, she was the one with a plan.

Crouching at the edge of her pool, she patted her hand against the tile. "Come up here."

Bitsy hit the floor on the other side, racing across the tile with her little spindly legs moving almost too quickly. She leapt up onto Anya's shoulder. Tiny pinpricks of metallic pain followed the droid's sudden rush before she wrapped herself around Anya's head and immediately put the lens over her eye.

Words vibrated around the image of the undine in the pipe.

"Danger. Undine. Do not approach."

"Oh now you're afraid of the undine? You were the one arguing to see him just a week ago," she muttered, before patting her hand on the tile again. "I'm just going to get him to come up here so we can talk."

"Talk?" Bitsy said, the word vibrating with anger. "How do you expect to talk? He is undine. You are human."

She wasn't really sure. But something told her this undine was coming to the city for... her. And she wasn't sure why that was.

He seemed to think the same thing. Because with one more pat, she'd already convinced him to come out of the pipe. With a sharp inhalation, she got her first good look at him.

The AI had captured images of him swimming, but he was always a darting shadow in the dark waters, barely a hint of what he might look like. In person? The undine was enormous.

She hadn't realized how large sixteen feet was until she was suddenly right in front of it. His broad, blunt features were creased with a frown that should have sent her running back into her room or perhaps sent pee running down her leg. His long hair tangled around his face, falling to his wide shoulders in a waterfall of darkness that almost distracted her from all the muscles that were laid out in front of her.

"Oh boy," she muttered. "You're really big."

That was the first thing she said? She sounded like an idiot.

His skin was a very strange color. Gray, with dark stripes starting at his collarbone and plummeting down to join the darkness of his tail. And the red streaks! He had glowing red streaks running up and down his tail, disappearing into the water where the rest of him was coiled, some of it still inside the pipe, and it seemed like he was already taking up her entire pool.

But then she noticed his arm. Or rather, the lack of it. One arm was big and strong and had so much meat on those biceps her first thought was, "Bite". The other? It had been cleaved clean off, right in the center of where his biceps would have been.

Anya schooled herself to not stare. A missing arm wasn't all that surprising, considering he lived out in the ocean. He could have lost it to a fish, or a squid, or a shark. There were whales out there that were rather large as well, and aggressive if the rumors were true.

But then her eyes wandered to the missing appendage one more time, and she recognized burn scars that moved up nearly to his shoulder.

The limb had been burned off. Or rather, it had been shot off. Her kind were the only ones who were capable of doing that.

Her eyes flicked to his black ones, unmoving and dark, as he met her gaze. "I'm sorry you had to suffer that," she said quietly. "I know the pain of losing something that was once a part of your body, and I know it's not easy."

At her words, he leaned a little closer. A flick of those fins at his hips and suddenly he was right in front of her. His hand braced against the side of the pool, right next to hers, and he was so close she could see her own reflection in those dark eyes.

But then he opened his mouth, and he spoke.

Bitsy sent red warning exclamation marks dancing all over the lens, but Anya didn't read a single one. She barely even noticed the exclamation points because, as he backed up, those words echoed through her head.

She could hear him.

Holy shit, she could hear him.

Reeling from the sound of his deep, echoing voice that was so gravely it sounded like the burble of water passing by the glass, she blinked as he moved away from her. He sank a little deeper into the water, his eyes on her a little too sharp.

But she could fucking hear him.

Not a mess of overlapping sound or the knowledge that someone was speaking, but not having the faintest idea of what they were saying. His voice was so deep, she could only compare it to the sound of water underneath ice. A boom of sound that she'd so rarely heard since her accident. Loud, echoing, and so incredibly deep.

It was stupid. It was risky. It was taking her own life in her hands and thrusting it at this monster who had just showed up in her pool one day. But she suddenly launched herself into the pool.

Anya wasn't even sure what was going through her head, other than the thought that she had heard him speak. That she could hear the tones of his voice and it had been such a long time since she'd heard the clipped movement of words. They'd been muffled for so long and she had resigned herself to never being able to understand what someone was saying, so her mind just sort of... fractured.

She'd met with the doctors. She'd met with other people like her, but so few of them were injured after they had fourteen years of hearing. Most of the people she knew were born deaf. She wasn't born like this, and she wasn't entirely deaf. She existed in a world between two peoples and...

Oh, she had missed hearing someone talk.

The water struck her a little too hard. Maybe she'd belly flopped, but then suddenly there was a massive hand around her waist again. The same way he had pushed her up and out of the water the last time.

Webbed fingers held onto her suddenly clinging clothing, the claws scraping against the lace of her shawl. And none of it mattered.

She braced herself against his chest, her hands on either sides of those blocky pectoral muscles where she could feel two hearts beating just slightly out of rhythm with the other. He stared down at her with wide eyes. Maybe she'd shocked him. She had no idea. All she could focus on right now was the feeling of that massive hand spanning her waist, his fingers just slightly moving against her back. And it was... nice.

Not as scary as she had thought it would be, at least.

Licking her lips, she told herself not to do it again as she noticed his gaze followed that movement. "I can hear you speak," she whispered. "I... Just do it again. Please?"

He frowned down at her. Maybe that should have been intimidating, but the gills around his neck flared suddenly and all she could think was that they were pretty.

"Say something," she whispered, her words a little close to begging. "Please."

He said one word, the guttural tones breaking through the injuries in her ears and she could hear what he had to say. It was loud, probably louder than was safe for her to be around. He might even be injuring her further, but oh... Oh, the sound of a word.

"More than one." Anya's eyes fluttered shut, luxuriating in this moment.

He said two words.

She peeled one of her eyes open, frowning at him in disapproval this time. The undine was toying with her. He was...

Responding to every single word she said, like he understood what she was saying.

Anya froze, and suddenly all of this came into very clear focus. She was in the middle of her pool with her arms hooked over his neck. Her legs dangled in the water from where he held her up, but that massive and muscular tail brushed between her legs every time he flexed his muscles to keep them upright. His arm was around her waist, his massive hand wrapped around her back, but his fingers were eerily close to her breast. She was close enough to his mouth to kiss him.

And the undine understood what she was saying.

Chapter 7

Daios liked the sound of her voice. It was a little rough, a little raspy, slightly off key—just like her singing—but it was pretty. Prettier than he'd expected. He must have heard her talking in their first encounter, but he couldn't for the life of him remember it.

Maybe that was because he wanted to remember this as their first meeting forever. With her pressed against his chest and all that long, lean body at his mercy. He'd swallowed hard the moment she'd leapt into the water. Her awkward limbs flailed, and he was reminded again of her swimming.

She was a terrible swimmer. She used her arms far too much, and there wasn't enough movement in her twin tails.

Legs, he reminded himself. Mira called them legs.

Either way, she wasn't very good at swimming. She was so slow, so weak, and now she splatted into the water like an overdramatic whale rather than the graceful dive of his people. He'd be afraid she couldn't swim at all if he hadn't already seen her survive the water, even if that was only for a few moments. Still, some part of him needed to hold on to her and so he... did. He grabbed her by that tiny waist and banished the thoughts inside him, screaming for bloodshed and violence.

Rip her apart, the voices in his head whispered. Tear at her soft flesh and see what redness she hides beneath. See if she bleeds like you want and makes this pool run red with her blood.

But even as his claws curled into the fine woven covering she wore over her skin, he found that he couldn't. Even if he had wanted to harm her, his body wouldn't let him. He wanted to dive away from this place with her, yes. He wanted to press his face against the soft curve of her neck and draw her underneath the water with him.

What would she smell like? What would she taste like as he drew her into the haven of his arm?

He already knew her scent, just barely. There was a hint of her in the pool. A vague citrus flavor like the rare underwater pods that grew in the depths. The faintest hint of sunshine in her scent, even though he knew that wasn't possible.

She was a grotesque monster. He'd hated her kind his entire life.

So why then did his fingers press against the lean lines of her back and why did he want to run his hand up her muscles? She felt so delicate in his arms, so easy to hold against him.

And she wanted to hear him speak. She wanted to hear his voice, and he wondered why that was. He had thought perhaps she couldn't hear. But now he knew that she could hear him.

"Hello," he said when she asked him to speak again.

It made him feel foolish. But he'd never been one for talking. He didn't know what to say to the opposite sex. Never had. He barely knew what to say to warriors. Daios communicated in grunts of approval or disapproval.

But then she let those strange eyes drift shut, and those dark eyelashes smudged her cheeks. When she asked him for more words, who was he to deny her?

"I am Daios," he replied, because what else was he supposed to say? He didn't know what to do with someone like this. She clung to him like some of the cleaning fish that followed him when he swam through waters that were closer to shore.

And when she peeled one of those strange, pale eyes open to glare at him, he almost grinned at her. She was a monstrous little thing underneath that strange exterior. Or she was insane. One or the other.

He wasn't sure which was better. Part of him wanted her to be insane, because no achromo should so easily throw herself at what was a terrifying creature from the depths. If she was lacking in sense, at least then he knew that he should expect the unexpected from her.

But if she wasn't senseless? If this was just a strange moment between the two of them where she had decided she wanted to touch him?

Daios wasn't sure he was prepared for that.

Then she stiffened in his arms, and he knew it was the former. She hadn't been thinking, and she had thrown herself at a dangerous creature. Perhaps it was the sudden realization she was in the grasp of a deep sea beast who could speak that frightened her so much. Or perhaps she was so disgusted at herself for touching him that her entire body tensed.

It was easier to think of her as what he knew of achromos. It was easier to swallow when she stiffened and then gently placed her hands against his chest with a soft shove.

She stared at him, her eyes widening as they both looked at each other. He couldn't guess what was going through her head. She had so many expressions, and he didn't know what a single one of them meant.

"Blink once," she whispered.

Why she would have such a strange question, he had no idea. But Daios didn't mind entertaining this small achromo, even though he knew it was a danger. He had a reason for being here, and that was supposed to be kidnapping her.

But... she'd asked. He blinked once.

With a small scoff, as though she didn't believe that he could understand her, she cockily tilted her head and said, "Okay, smart guy. Blink twice."

He didn't see any harm in this strange game. So he did.

She hissed out a long breath, one that would have been a sign of anger in his people. But she didn't look angry. He'd seen Mira's brows furrow and her face turn red. This one was not doing that. Instead, her eyes widened and her face paled.

"Can you understand me?" she whispered.

"Yes," he replied with a nod.

Apparently that very achromo-like response was the one that made her afraid of him. Her legs kicked against his sides, and Daios knew this was the moment he needed to take control. But again, he couldn't do it.

Maketes would have laughed to see the fearless warrior cowed by a woman only a fraction of his size. He let this little achromo wriggle herself out of his arms and launch back to the safety of her strange home.

Daios even let her get out of the water, not that it would save her from him. He could grab her at any moment. He could launch himself out of the water as well, and his reach was longer than hers. Even if her small pool barely contained him.

At least it was deep. Otherwise, he feared he might not be able to breathe through the gills on his ribs.

She spun around, the wet ends of her hair slapping against her cheeks as she turned. "You can understand me."

A low rumble started in his chest. This was getting ridiculous at this point. "Yes, achromo. I told you already."

She blew out a long breath, then pressed her hand to her chest. The strange being she wore on her head made a soft chirping noise, and then it held a piece of glass in front of her eye again. What was that creature doing?

He could see her eyes moving as though she were looking at something he couldn't see, and it made him uncomfortable. This situation had to be controlled, and he was not in control right now. Daios preferred knowing everything that might happen in any situation. Knowing everything was his safety net.

With a soft growl, he lunged forward. The little achromo had no time to react before he had already plucked the droid off her head. It was built a little like Byte, and he still hated that strange box that Mira carried around. This one had spindly legs that tried to stab into his hand as he lifted the glass up.

Writing?

Mira had shown him a book before, and she'd written words on the sands. He wasn't particularly good at reading their language, but he knew the word "Danger" after Mira had written it so many times.

That made him grin. Wide and feral and probably everything she'd seen in her nightmares. She certainly went white as the pale underbelly of a fish. But then he handed the droid back to her, still in one piece.

He hoped she realized what an exercise in personal strength that had been. It would bring him much satisfaction to feel the droid crushed in his grip.

She took the metal spider back with delicate hands, so small compared to his own, and he hated how intrigued the size of them made him. He wanted to hold her short little fingers, and what a curious thought that was. He'd never wanted to touch an achromo. If he was being honest, he had little interest in touching his own people, either.

How strange that he looked at this one and wondered how soft her skin would be if he ran the back of his finger down her cheek. He could see the fluttering of her pulse on the side of her neck, and he wondered what it tasted like.

A small part of him sent off warning signals, screaming that he shouldn't want to know what she tasted like. Maybe there was something wrong with him, because what if he wanted to eat her? His fangs would so easily tear through her skin. He could hurt her like he had hurt everyone else, and he'd already thought about her blood. Daios made mistakes. That was his fate. He fucked everything up. Why did he think he wouldn't hurt her?

He swallowed, suddenly afraid of what would happen if he stayed any longer. So instead, he held out his hand, which contained the small chip she was supposed to affix to the side of her head. Mira had given it to him. Once he had kidnapped her, he was supposed to put it on the head of the General's daughter. Ignore the pain it caused her, and bring her to the others.

She looked at the chip, then back up at him. "I can't install that. It goes directly into the cochlea, but mine is damaged. It can stick into my ear, but it won't work. I'm not... I can't download any translation chips." She turned her head, showing him the blank space behind her ear. "I had to have mine removed after the accident. Those devices translate the words using tones we can hear, but those are the tones that I can't hear. It doesn't work in any other way. It... it can't."

Well. That was going to complicate things. How was he supposed to communicate with her, then?

He looked down at the chip in his hand, at a loss for what to do. The voice in his head that warned him about wanting to hurt her, suddenly started whispering that this was wrong.

He would be taking her into a world where she would never understand anyone else. She already had admitted there was something different about her hearing, which meant communication must be difficult for her to begin with. If he took her with him, then he was condemning her to a life of silence. Not just underneath the sea, where all sound was muffled. But completely and wholly silent.

Those delicate fingers brushed against his. She plucked the chip out of his massive hand and held it out to the robot at her head. "Bitsy? Hold on to this for me, will you?"

He watched the robot take it, his eyes narrowing in distrust. Another robot had created that chip, but he was uninterested in any of their kind. They were unnatural and untrustworthy.

The achromo licked her lips, and his eyes immediately zeroed in on the movement. Every time that little flicker of pink appeared, he wanted to know where it came from. What other differences there were.

And if she was pink in other places.

"I saw the security footage of you coming into the city multiple times," she said, her voice almost too soft to hear. "Do you know they are tracking you?"

He shrugged. Let them. Once he was inside the pipes, they were blind.

"They're going to put droids in the piping system. Or they're going to flush it. They'll remove all the water from the city for an afternoon, probably. You'll be stuck wherever you are, and then they'll send the clean-up crew. Those droids will slowly take you apart, bit by sawing bit." She took a deep breath when he puffed up. "I know you think you can fight them, but there will be hundreds. Too many to destroy."

Though his chest puffed up even more, he had to admit that didn't sound like an ideal situation. His spines slowly rose on his back, even the ones along his arms. If he had to fight his way out of here, then he would. Daios didn't mind fighting. But he had a feeling this little achromo would not like to see what he could do with this massive body of his.

She should have been afraid of him. The sight of his anger was enough to startle most people, even his own kind. But instead, she bit her lip and just looked at him. Regarding the anger as it rose like she was watching water boil.

"If I'm guessing right, you're here for a reason."

He nodded.

"For me?"

He lifted a hand and tilted it side to side. He was here for her, yes, but they really wanted to strike at her father. They needed a chance to prove that his people would fight to the bitter end against the achromos if required. His people would be left alone, and they would take their sea back.

She licked her lip again, that aggravating movement stealing his mind until she spoke. "If you are here to take me away, then I want the same thing."

For a moment, he was tongue tied. What did she mean she wanted the same thing? Surely not. She was the General's daughter. A paragon and figure of this place. Everyone knew that she was the General's golden child, according to Mira.

She must have seen the confusion on his features. "I will explain everything if you can get me out of this city. Can you do that?"

He nodded, reaching for her. This had played into his plan so well, he almost had a hard time believing it.

But then she took a step back from him, shaking her head. "In a few moments. Can you wait here for me?"

If no one knew he was here, then yes. But he frowned and then looked pointedly up at the cameras on the walls. He knew that Mira had told him there was a tracking system throughout the entire city. They would know he was here soon enough. They had every time he'd come up to the surface. He only had a few moments before people were about to swarm this room. Surely she knew that?

She tapped the robot attached to her head. "Bitsy already took care of the cameras. As long as you stay in the pool, then no one will know you're here. Just... Give me a bit to get ready."

And so he waited. Watching as this strange creature backed out of the room and walked into the other. All the while, he wondered just what he had captured.

A delicate golden fish? Or a shark in these strange waters?

Chapter 8

She had so much she had to get. And Bitsy was shrieking in front of her eyes, "Do not do this! What are you thinking? No. No. No."

And then it was just "No" repeated until she ripped the lens away from her eyes. "Bitsy, stop panicking."

The leg holding the lens slammed back down over her eye. "No. Danger. No. Stay."

"Bitsy, I'm going to put you in a waterproof box, okay? I know you got wet in the pool, but with the pressure down there, we don't know that you're going to survive. The box will be dark, but I will take you out of it as soon as we get somewhere safe."

The droid flailed its arms the moment she opened the box. But Anya had been preparing for this exact moment for months. Even if Ace was unaware of it, Anya was ready to leave. This place was a prison. It would be so much easier for her to get out of this area and then they could take it down from the outside.

"I know the plan was taking the city down from the inside out," she said, feeling like her throat was closing up as she placed the droid inside the box. Bitsy's hologram eyes blinked up at her, wide with simulated fear. "But I can't stay here. This is an opportunity I have to take."

She'd been trying to figure out how to escape on her own. It wasn't likely, though. Her father had people at the front of her door all the time. Hell, even her neighbors were watching her on a regular basis. There was nowhere she could escape to and no one she could go to for help.

This undine had no idea she was going to use him to her own advantage, but did it matter? He wanted to get her out of here, too. She didn't know why, but that was a risk she was willing to take. She wouldn't be here if she went with him. And that was good enough for her.

Rushing into her closet, she yanked out her wetsuit. It was rated for waters this cold, although the pressure would likely mess with her. She thought she had...

Grabbing the device her first doctor had given her, she shoved it into her ears. They weren't going to be perfect, but it helped regulate pressure in her ears after the accident. The plugs should help while she was diving.

She ducked behind the partition and hoped this would look at least a little realistic. Tossing the shawl over the edge, she worked the wetsuit up her body. It was hard work. The damn thing was tighter than she expected. But she got it on, eventually. Then she tossed her pale green sundress over it.

Her arms and legs were still visibly different, but she thought if she tossed the shawl back over her shoulders, the wetsuit might look like leggings to anyone watching her. Poking her head out, she thought maybe she was ready. Maybe...

Her door opened, swinging wide enough that the movement caught her attention. Wide eyed, she looked into her bathroom.

The undine was still there. He had his forearm on the cold tile of her floor, his chin propped on a closed fist as he watched her. Those black eyes didn't miss any details. He saw the wetsuit underneath her clothes. He had to know what the plan was.

Her father stood in the doorway, hesitating as he noticed she was behind the partition. She read his lips as he said, "We have to talk. Get decent. I'm giving you three minutes, girl."

The door closed, shaking the wall beside it so hard that a picture fell and shattered on the floor.

"Shit," she whispered. Or at least, she hoped she whispered it. Waving a hand at the undine, she tried to get him to understand that he needed to go.

He lifted his head. The gills along the sides of his neck flared. She was suddenly shocked to see... lights. Glimmering red lights burst into brightness around his face and down his chest.

The undine could make himself glow.

Her mouth dropped open as another painting fell onto the floor, she assumed because her father had knocked again. Right, she couldn't stand there looking at what was quite possibly the most amazing thing she'd ever seen in her life. She had to take care of her father.

Whining, she could feel her throat vibrate with the sound. Tucking her shawl around her shoulders, she lunged for Bitsy's box. She took the wiggling droid out and forced it to wrap around her head. Messages flew so fast she almost couldn't read them.

"Your father. Anya. More danger! We are in trouble!"

"I know, I know," she muttered, closing the box and then rushing for the bathroom. She didn't have a door for the damn thing. Her father said it was just in case she slipped and fell in the bathroom and someone had to save her. She knew the thin beaded curtain was only there to give her a semblance of privacy, though.

Yanking it shut, she turned toward the door and took a deep breath.

Acting. She could act like nothing was happening and there wasn't an undine in her bathroom. As long as her father didn't look between the beads, he might think everything was okay.

Other than the wetsuit she was wearing underneath her dress. Because that was... normal.

Breathing in a slow and steady breath, she answered her door.

Bitsy had two columns of text flying by her eyes. One was what her father was saying, although she could easily read his lips. Anya was so familiar with him, she didn't need to be wearing Bitsy at all.

"What took you so long to answer your door, girl?" Her father's eyes swept up and down her body. "And what the hell are you wearing?"

Meanwhile, Bitsy had added, "He knows! He knows something's wrong!"

She didn't have a second to mutter that her father had no idea what was happening. Even if the meddlesome man did sweep into her room like he knew she had an undine in her bath.

He didn't. He couldn't. Bitsy was very good at dismantling the cameras, and besides, who would dare watch the General's daughter bathe? No one knew there was an undine in her room.

Not even the man with all the eyes and ears of the city at his disposal.

Her father's gaze swept over her room before landing on her. She was always shocked by how old he appeared these days. With his bent spine and wrinkled features, he hardly looked like himself at all anymore. She'd even asked recently if he was feeling okay, but that hadn't gone over well at all. He'd yelled at her for the better part of ten minutes, even if she couldn't hear him.

Even though he was turned away from her, Bitsy still ran his words over her lens.

"I'm sure you've heard about the security reports lately."

"I have." She tried to move so she could see his lips, but her father knew what she was doing. He didn't like that she analyzed his face, his words. He didn't like her looking at him at all, really. Which made this all that much more difficult.

"Your security detail is going to be tripled. I want nothing threatening your safety, do you understand?" He turned toward her then, the false worry on his face almost comical. "We can't have the songbird of Alpha getting harmed, can we? Not after the last... mishap."

Because that's all his worry ever was. His image. His city. They couldn't trust a man who didn't even keep his own daughter safe. Let alone have her injured twice. And if he didn't know how to take care of his children, then he certainly couldn't take care of them.

An image. That's all this was about. And that meant she had to play her part.

If that didn't cut right through her heart, she didn't know what would.

Sighing, she nodded. "I'll stay in my area of the city then."

"You'll stay in your room until we've caught this monster. Once it's dead, then we can talk about letting you out again." He reached for a lock of her hair, gently twisting it between his fingers. "My greatest creation. It's such a shame you listen as poorly as your mother."

What was she supposed to say to that?

Her mother was apparently a paragon in this city. Everyone always told her how much Anya looked like her mother. How everyone had always loved her mother. That if only she was a little more graceful, she'd have been the spitting image of the woman that had made all of Alpha fall in love.

But her father? He hated the mere mention of the woman. If anyone even brought her up in front of the General, he lost his mind. He grew red in the face and that vein on his forehead popped out far more than usual.

Anya didn't even know her mother's name. It was like he had scratched it from the history books and terrified anyone who thought to maybe mention her name to her daughter. Not that her father ever went by 'Jonathon'. He went by 'General'. That's the only thing that anyone ever called him.

She stood there, letting him tug on the lock of her hair before he started back to the door. His words flashed in front of her eyes.

"Just try to be good for a few more weeks, would you? Can't have anything happening to my daughter. The undines would tear such a little thing apart."

Then Bitsy added, "He's an ass."

It took every bit of her willpower not to laugh at that.

The General turned around and frowned at her expression. "And stop dressing like that. You look awful."

The door closed, and she stuck her tongue out at the flat panel. For good measure, she also flipped it off. At least her back was to the cameras and no one would see her small act of rebellion against the man who kept her under lock and key.

Spinning, she rushed toward her bathroom and ripped the beaded curtain open.

No undine.

Not even the faintest stirring of water that would suggest he was still here. But she walked up to the edge all the same, peering into the water where the pipe came into her pool. She still had the hope that maybe, just maybe, he'd waited for her.

He hadn't.

"Damn it," she muttered. "That might have been my last chance."

"Safer here," Bitsy flashed, the words then outlined with a growing heart that popped at the edges of the screen. "We stay safe!"

"I don't want to stay safe here. That safety is a lie. There is only a cage that I need to get out of."

Maybe there were other options, though. Now that it was in her head, it was all she could think of.

She didn't want to stay under her father's thumb for the rest of her life. She didn't want to help Alpha be this paragon of a city where only the rich lived. And she sure as hell didn't want to be the figurehead for all the people to look at and say, "Wow, I want to be just like her." Not when she wore the chains of an entire city around her neck.

"Bitsy, try to connect with Ace."

Bitsy repeated Ace's name in bright yellow.

"Yes, contact Ace. And do you still have that translation chip he gave you?"

Sitting down at her desk, she took the little droid off her head and let Bitsy splay out on the table. Obviously, the droid knew what Anya wanted to do. Bitsy stretched out her spindly legs and got comfortable while presenting the underside of her unit.

The lens she laid flat out on the desk so that Anya could still see it, even while fiddling around.

Her message was almost immediately received. "Queen of Hearts?"

"Hey Ace," she said, pulling out all of her tools. "Any chance you know how to add a translation chip to a droid model Terra Lingua 4275?"

There was a long pause before more words appeared. "No, but I can find out. How soon do you need the information?"

"As soon as possible. I've got the droid open right now."

"Let me get somewhere private and then I'll figure it out. Why do you need this information?"

Anya had always trusted Ace. Since the first message had shown up on her lens and Ace had told her they weren't a threat. The message had been sent in the hope that Anya might help them, and the rest was history.

They'd talked hundreds of times since. She knew that Ace was in another city, and that Ace had spent most of their life trying to figure out how to take Alpha down. Together, they had come up with a plan that was foolproof. Get someone into the city. Hack the systems. Spread all the terrible information about her father that they could.

Once that was finished, they could throw up their own candidate to replace the General. Someone who wasn't the head of the military. Someone who wouldn't take every problem and answer it with violence or death. That was the only way to heal what had been broken. They were both sure of it.

But she wasn't sure what Ace would say if Anya said she was trying to speak with an undine. "Might be nice if we had a code. I found a new translation chip, not sure what language it is. But if I install it, no one will know what we're saying to each other.."

"Smart."

"Yeah," she said quietly, popping Bitsy's bottom off and exposing all the delicate wiring inside there.

She wondered what was going through Ace's mind. Did the other side of their operation believe her? Then the guilt set it, sinking into her gut like a fist wrapped around her intestines. They had a lot of plans and it might be harder for her to help make sure those plans happened if she wasn't here.

But if she was here, she was risking her life. At any point, her father could figure out what they were doing. He could catch her, and then she'd really be in a cage. He'd only let her out to see the fake sunlight when he needed her to parade in front of his people. Other than that, she worried what her life would be like.

"Good for you." The words danced over the screen. "I was wondering when you were finally going to grow some balls."

A bright grin spread across her face. "Well, I had a good mentor to teach me how to be brave."

"You'll make me blush. Stop."

"It's the truth, though. I don't know what I would do without you."

Another long pause before Ace said, "Enough mushy shit. I figured out how to hack your droid's translation chip and add that new one. You want to know how to do that or what?"

Even if the undine never came back, she wanted to know. Because Anya wanted to know how to do everything that would make her father angry. Lifting her tiniest pair of needle-nose pliers, she replied, "Yeah. Let's do this."

Chapter 9

So that's going to be a problem," Maketes muttered as Daios joined his brother again at their rendezvous point.

Daios filled him in on everything that he'd discovered. The lack of their ability to communicate with the General's daughter. The pipe systems. He showed his brother the map that he'd drawn, and told him of her threat that he would end up stuck in those pipes while hoards of robots descended upon him.

"Which part is going to be a problem?" he muttered, staring down at the map with a trouble expression.

"All of it."

"Which part the most?"

Maketes shrugged. "I mean, we can get over communication issues. Mira and Arges did in the beginning. We'll figure that out. The main problem is getting her now. How did you not realize they were watching you?"

"I knew they were." Daios stared at the stones on the sand, trying to will the solution to appear before his eyes. "I am uncertain what is the best way forward now."

"Why aren't you panicking? You should be panicking. You've seen her multiple times now and each time you failed to get her. Now there is no way for us to get in, and we're all screwed."

"What is that word?" He finally looked up from his project to frown at the yellow-finned pod mate. "Screwed?"

"Ah. It's something Mira says when there is no winning the situation." Maketes scrubbed the back of his neck. "I think I used it right."

The yellow glow from his body turned a sickly pale, as it always did when Maketes felt embarrassed. His brother had never gotten very good at controlling his colors.

Daios sighed. "There is nothing wrong with how you used it. I'm certain."

And there it went. All the colors turned bright yellow as the sun, just as it always did when his brother was reassured. "That's kind of you. Anyway, I thought you'd be more angry at me than you are."

"Why would I be angry at you?"

Then he smelled it. Or rather, them. The scent on the current was not one that should be in the ocean. At least, not this part of the ocean. Baring his teeth in a snarl, he cast his gaze behind them, where the darkness slowly parted around two figures. One he knew as well as he knew himself, the electric blue of his body lighting up the darkness of the ocean. The other was connected to him by a cord, her red hair as dark as blood in the dim light.

Mira and Arges.

He wasn't comfortable around her yet. He'd tried to kill her multiple times, and he was certain she'd never forgiven him for that. She shouldn't, anyway. The cruelty of his nature had nearly ended her life, and she had every right to hold that against him.

He preferred it that way. At least if everyone thought he was the villain, he could take the attention away from anyone who messed up as well. His broad shoulders could hold their hatred, and they could forgive others.

It was his place. And he intended to keep it that way.

He waited there, his hair floating and coiling around his shoulders as his clutch brother joined him. With a nod to his brother, and a slight tilt of his head to Mira, he pointed to the rocks. "I know where to go."

"Maketes already filled us in on that this morning." Arges narrowed his gaze. "I assume there is yet more information, now that I see you are here again without the woman."

He stared his brother in the eyes and hoped that he wasn't giving too much away. He had no intention of telling Arges anything, even though he knew his brother would most certainly try to get it out of him. And would likely succeed. They knew each other too well, and Arges knew when he was planning something.

Mira narrowed her eyes before turning her attention to Maketes. "What changed?"

Maketes might be their pod mate who enjoyed his fun, but he knew how to stay out of a fight. He held up his webbed hands, fingers spread wide, and shook his head. "I'm not getting in the middle of this. He's the one you gave the mission to. I'm just here to babysit."

"What does that mean?" Daios growled.

Sitting on babies didn't sound remotely close to what Maketes was doing here with him. Yes, his brother was watching him to make sure there were no surprises, but that was all it was.

Maketes only grinned and shrugged. "It's another term that Mira uses. She knows what I mean."

"It means he's watching over you because you cannot watch over yourself. Like a child," she said, her voice turning gritty with anger. "So what changed? I can see something has happened and neither of you wants to tell us."

He'd admit he was impressed by her ability to see straight through them. Arges had picked a rather terrifying shark of a mate, and that was the only way she would fit in with their people. Though there were some who were still very hesitant about her, a majority of the People of Water had accepted her. After all, she was Arges's mate. And they loved Arges.

Baring his teeth in a wince that likely only his brother would recognize, he turned back to the stones. "There are three entrances. The achromos have been watching me go in and out, unfortunately, which means I will need to be quick about this. The one you sent me to steal away has informed me that they will drain the pipes soon. Closing the city off from water for an undetermined amount of time."

Mira joined him, looking down at the stones with a frown. "Unless they have a considerable store of fresh water somewhere, they can't cut off the entire city from water. Humans need that to live."

He shrugged. "It is what she told me."

"You have spoken with the General's daughter?" Arges swam to his other side, his fins scattering sand over the stones. "Why did you not take her when you had the chance?"

There was a muffled laugh and cough that came from a short distance away, and Daios glared at the yellow finned brother who knew better than to snicker at times like these. "Yes, I have spoken with her."

"And why did you not take her then? You knew what you were there for."

He met his brother's gaze and knew that perhaps something passed between them that he didn't want Arges to know. Not just yet, at least. His brother's tail came around his, shoving him away from the other two.

"Come," Arges said, his voice low and guttural. "We need to talk."

What Daios did not expect was for Arges to hand Mira off to Maketes. Even she looked surprised, but quickly disconnected from Arges and took Maketes's offered tendril. All People of Water had this tendril, though its purpose had long been a mystery. Daios had one. All of them did. The tendrils were a part of their bodies for which they had no explanation, until Mira.

Once Arges was satisfied that his mate was still breathing, they took off closer to Alpha. The two of them settled into the sand on their bellies, watching the city move, and the pillars flare bright and hot as fish swam too close. They'd done this a hundred times in their lives, but their ease together was not the same. Never would be after what had transpired.

"You are different," Arges finally said. "You have a purpose, it seems, and I don't think it was the one we gave you."

Again he winced, his teeth bared to the icy sea before he replied, "I do not know what it is."

"I can see it in your coloring, you know. Your body is making decisions for you, is that it?"

He'd tried to understand what was happening for many nights. Daios had hardly slept as he tried to convince the urges to disappear. After all, he had a mission. This woman had to be delivered to Arges and Mira. That was the only choice.

But again, even the thought made something in him rebel. His entire body tightened, seizing against the very idea of bringing her to their home where he knew others would take her away from him. She would be in that pod with Mira. He would be able to see her every day and not do... something that his body seemed to understand.

"I never thought it would happen to you," Arges said, his eyes following the trailing red lights that illuminated Daios's entire body. "Of all our people, you hate them the most."

"I have the most reason to hate them," Daios replied.

"After all that you have done? I think you may be right."

How did he tell his brother that he could still hear all the people he had failed? All of their people who had died because of the achromos? He still dreamed in bright flashing lights and blood coating the water. His arm still ached when he woke, a constant reminder that no matter what he did, no matter how much he paid for his penance, he had still led them to slaughter.

Then he blinked, and he could see them all again. Floating behind Arges, this time a delicate tail with holes all through the fluke, just drifting through the sea. A tail that had once belonged to someone so wonderful, even if he hadn't known them. All of his people were special in their own way, and he had ruined so many of them.

"Daios," Arges said, drawing his eyes back to his brother even though he could still see the carnage behind him. "What are you planning to do with her?"

"I do not know."

"Are you going to bring her back to the pod?"

"No."

"Will you harm her?"

As much as he wanted to kill her and end his own suffering, he wasn't certain he could bring himself to do it. Something deep inside him rebelled at the thought of her coming to harm, and that was as much a warning sign as anything else.

He sneered before replying, "No."

Arges slowly nodded, his gaze returning to the city as though he might be able to see her from here. "They are delicate. Keep an eye on what she eats and drinks. Make sure she is not in the water for too long, because it is very cold for them."

"I have seen you with Mira."

"You don't know what it's like to have one of them as a mate. The constant fear that they will die on your watch. The nervousness that comes with knowing anything could kill them. They have no natural way to protect themselves and they are being forced to give up their world due to our own desires for them. It is not easy." Arges cleared his throat, his eyes still not on Daios. "I don't think you're ready for what it will make you feel."

Neither did he.

Wait. No, he didn't want her as a mate. That wasn't what this was. It couldn't be. His body was his own to control and tell what to do, and he would not let biology make his choices.

"I am not keeping her," he growled.

"Really?" Arges replied with a laugh. "I see the way your body is reacting to a single word about her. You're going to keep her, Daios, and it won't be easy."

"I have no interest in achromos." He spat the words. "You fell to that folly. I will not."

"So many words to defend a male who has already lost the fight." Arges pushed his hands on the sand, sending his body careening upright. "Bring her somewhere safe for a time. Do whatever it is that you need to get this out of your system. But I know you, brother. I know you well. You can fight against this all you want, just as I did. But soon enough, you will find yourself completing the mating rituals."

Curling his fist in the sands, he told himself he wouldn't. But he already knew that was a lie. Some part of him wanted to keep this little gemstone he'd found in the depths of the ocean. It was a covetous need inside of him, a flexing beast that writhed in his chest and pushed his body to do things he did not understand.

"I do not want her," he said, looking up at his brother, who floated in the dark above him.

A few flickering blue lights glimmered along Arges's tail. Then Arges looked farther off, at Mira and Maketes where the two of them were arguing about some form of the achromos language, most likely. Those lights flared brighter for a moment before he got them under control.

"Neither did I," Arges murmured. "I did not want her, and she did not want me. But the longer I was with her, the more I realized there was a strength in her heart that I admired. A kindness in her soul that I did not have. A wit in her mind that matched my own. She was unexpected and resilient in a way I had never attributed to their kind before."

"I know your respect for her." He really did. Daios just didn't see the achromo the way his brother did.

"Then you will soon find you see something in this human that you did not realize. And by then, it will already be too late for you. Just as it was for me." Arges slapped his back with the flat of his tail. "Good luck, even if I don't think you're cut out for this. Just keep her alive. Yeah?"

"I will," he grumbled.

"From your mouth to the ancient's ears. Let them punish you if you fail us all again."

The words echoed in his mind long after Arges gathered Mira up. He could tell the achromo was staring at him. Her gaze was like a physical touch that lifted the deadly spines along his back. He wished he could send them out into the sea like daggers, just to give him a small moment where he could feel as though he was at peace.

Instead, he laid there in the sands. His gaze never leaving the city of Alpha, but he didn't see the city. Instead, he saw bodies. He heard the whispers of the dead in his ears.

Even his brother didn't think he could keep a measly little achromo alive. Even his clutch mate, the one who had shared an egg with him, believed he was too careless to keep someone else alive.

His touch was death.

His body was made to be a weapon or a shield, nothing more. A destructive tsunami that killed any and everything in his wake.

The water stirred beside him, and Maketes paused beside the rise. "I'm returning with them."

He grunted.

"Arges said it would take you a little longer to get her back? He made excuses for you, although I don't think Mira believed them. Soon enough, you'll have to deal with her."

Another grunt. Let the achromo try to stop him. He was not afraid of Mira.

A small current kicked up, as though Maketes was leaving. But then he heard one last thing from the yellow finned brother.

"There is an abandoned facility nearby. The achromos never go there anymore. I explored it a while ago, and there is still air if she needs it. Of course, there are only so many pockets that I've seen but... Well, I think it will be a good enough spot. It's closer to the ledge. Big drop off. You can't miss it."

He knew the general area of which his brother spoke. It was easy enough for him to find, even if it would be a terrifying swim for her.

He had to shake the thoughts out of his mind. Why did it matter if she was afraid? He was taking her away, and this was about getting rid of these urges. Not indulging them.

At least, that's what he told himself.

A mask thudded onto the sand near his shoulder. "Mira left this for her. I almost didn't give it to you, since I think you should at least try to make a connection with something else living. Still. I'd feel bad if you drowned the poor thing because you refused to breathe for her."

He waited until Maketes was gone before he curled his fingers around the straps of the mask. He wasn't doing this to convince her to be his mate. He hadn't tried to do that in years and had told himself he'd never do it again.

But he couldn't make himself let go of the mask.

Chapter 10

She'd never had so many panic attacks in a row.

Her father had put so many people around her house, she felt like she couldn't breathe. Anya had only seen this many people all constantly walking by her door when there was a festival going on in town. But now? It felt like every time someone walked by her door they were pausing to listen in on what she was doing.

The cameras kept moving. Even when she was sleeping, she would hear them shift and creak as someone constantly monitored her.

Bitsy had to fix the ones in the bathroom almost constantly. She didn't want anyone to realize that she could tamper with the cameras, which meant every time she went into the bathroom, Bitsy had to go first. They had to make it believable that she was still moving around.

She couldn't talk to Ace.

She couldn't do anything other than try to pretend she had a routine that didn't involve everything else she usually did. All she could focus on was that they were watching her. And that no matter what she did, she had to suffer through that.

No one was coming to save her. Not the undine. Not Ace. No one.

And now, Anya couldn't even save herself.

The operation that she and Ace planned had already fallen through. Just a few days ago, she'd gotten the message through Bitsy that the agent they'd chosen to hide out in Alpha while their ship left had failed. Her father's guards were so amped up about this stupid undine coming in and out of the city that they'd made all the other security measures intensely heightened as well.

The young man had been caught and executed on the spot. Anya couldn't help but feel like that was her fault.

She had no control over the undine, but she might have stopped the creature from coming into the city. Maybe. If she had been with her father when they'd discovered the unregistered young man, maybe she could have begged for mercy.

Not that it would matter. Her father had no mercy to give.

"You need to breathe," Bitsy said, the words flashing bright blue on the screen. A small drop of water, cartoonized, so she knew it was Bitsy, followed the words.

She did need to breathe. But really, the only thing that would make her feel better was getting out of here. She didn't want to stay like this anymore. She was being crushed.

Every breath slowly calmed her, though. Wandering into the bathroom, she sat down next to the pool. Soon enough, someone would be knocking on her door to remind her that the pool wasn't safe to sit next to.

There was always someone watching the screens now. Even if she had Bitsy change them over, someone would come over to fix the cameras. They'd done it twice now. If she wasn't careful, she was going to have to... to...

"Is that a crab?" she whispered, so the cameras might not pick up on her question.

Bitsy circled the rather large crab on the bottom of her pool and surrounded it with red exclamation marks. "A crab!"

"A crab," she repeated, leaning a little closer to the water. "What is a crab doing in my pool?"

Sometimes sea creatures wandered into the pipes, but never had they made it this far. There wasn't anything for them to eat in there, and of course, there were the vent systems that they usually got caught in. What in the world was a crab doing in her pool?

But then she peered a little closer and could see there was an etched wave on the back. Someone had carved the shell of the crab. A symbol that she thought maybe was meant for her.

"Bitsy?" she breathed. "I think it's time to get in your case."

The crab looked up at her and rubbed its claws together. She didn't know what that meant, but if she pressed her fingers against the side of the pool, she could almost feel the vibration. The faintest shake of clicking that echoed through the water.

"Don't run," she muttered to herself as she walked into her bedroom. "Don't give them any reason to—"

"Someone is knocking," Bitsy interrupted, with an arrow pointing toward the door. "Answer it."

She immediately opened the door, stopping the man mid knock. He dropped his hand quickly, his eyes moving over Bitsy before he nodded. "Good, you're wearing that. Your father wished me to remind you that you are not to sit by the pool. If you continue to do so, we will close it off from your quarters."

Anya didn't care what he was saying, but she pretended to read the words flying by as he said them. This man didn't even try to slow down what he was saying, so she could read the words. He just spat all the sounds out, gave her another nod, and then turned to walk away.

"Rude."

She must have said the word too loud because he turned around, only to have her slam the door in his face. She didn't care. This was a sign, she was certain of it.

Taking Bitsy's carrier behind the partition with her, she yanked her wetsuit out of her closet. This was the only area where there wasn't a camera pointed at her. Of course, if she didn't hurry up, then someone would be knocking again to make sure she was okay. And the microphones in here made it impossible for her to talk to Ace. At least, not easily.

So she took Bitsy off her head and gently placed the little robot inside her waterproof carrier. Dragging a finger down its side, she booped it right on the screen where those big eyes stared up at her.

"Trust me," she whispered, hoping the camera wouldn't pick up on her words.

It took forever to yank on her wetsuit, and the entire time she had to talk herself into this crazy plan. After all, a crab with a strange marking wasn't all that much information to go on. It might just be a coincidence.

What was the likelihood that undines had some kind of connection to the sea that humans couldn't understand? Very slim. She was likely going to get herself locked up while her father emptied the entire city of water because of his stupid daughter. She'd be blamed for a lot more things to come than just what she was doing right now.

Risky. All of this was risky.

This might all be something she'd made up in her head because she was so desperate to get out of here, but... She wasn't going to stop. She had to try.

Wetsuit on, green dress over it to give her a few extra moments, she picked up Bitsy's sealed case and took a deep breath. No running. She could only run once she'd crossed over to the bathroom. So she waltzed through her room like it wasn't suspicious that she was carrying a case and wearing strange leggings underneath her dress.

All she had to do was get to the bathroom. Then she could… bolt.

Her foot crossed the threshold, and she ran for the water, hitting it with a sharp slap. The icy temperature stole her breath, and she had to swim back up to the top to fill her lungs.

Fuck, it was so cold. So much colder than it should have been, which could only mean that her father was moving forward with his plans to drain the city. The water was straight from the icy depths of the ocean, and not filtered. That's how the crab got in here.

Taking one more deep breath, she sank underneath the water and made her way to the pipe. The crab was still on one side of her pool, and another was waiting at the opening of the pipe.

But it was all darkness beyond. No undine. No one waiting there to steal her away like some villain in a fairytale. There was just her, staring into a pipe with her droid case in hand.

What did she do? Was she supposed to go back up into her room and somehow try to argue that she'd fallen? She very clearly hadn't fallen into the pool. Her father was going to take her apart for this.

Kicking back to the surface, she took another deep, steadying breath. The water wasn't so bad now, or maybe she was just turning a little numb.

Whatever the reasoning, it made her feel a little crazy. She looked at the door where she knew someone was about to knock or bust in without asking, even though she couldn't hear them. And she felt the pressure of living like this bear down on her shoulders. She couldn't handle it anymore.

Undine or not, she wasn't going to stay here any longer.

Taking another deep breath, she headed back to the pipe. The other crab in there looked at her with something she assumed was surprise and started rubbing its claws together even harder.

Anya shoved Bitsy's case in front of her and then dragged herself into the pipe. Maybe her father would empty it while she was in there. Just the thought made a bubble of insanity pop in her chest, a little giddy whirl of madness. She was small enough to be thrown out the other end of it into the sea. She'd probably die. But what an adventure.

Using her arms and legs to haul herself and the case forward, she made it all the way into the pipe and to the first fork. There were four pipes here, three directions other than the one she was already in. But when she looked, there were crabs in all of them. She could just barely see two of them from the light in what must be other pool systems. The darkest pipe, though, she could feel the faint thrum of another crab rubbing its legs.

The creaking, gritty vibration sent chills down her spine. Or maybe that was the feeling of her air running out.

Still, she turned to the right and followed the sensation into the dark, even as her lungs screamed. Even as the darkness settled around her, cloying and sticky. Everything suddenly pulled at her mind. Whispering that she'd made a mistake, that she was going to die down here and no one would know.

She'd trusted a dream. An undine that likely hadn't even existed and here she was, too far away from her own pool to make it back. She was going to drown. What a terrible way to die when she could have chosen to stay where she had been. Safe as a songbird in a cage.

Everything in front of her turned red. At first, she thought it was the security system. Her father must have already gotten the news that she'd plunged into the pipe system and that could only mean he was about to turn all the water off. It wouldn't save her, but it would kill her very quickly, and maybe that was his game.

Then she realized it wasn't a light above her head. It was many lights, all glowing from a body that reached for her.

A sharp shriek erupted from her mouth, expelling the last bit of her air. She had hoped he would be here, and still, all her mind saw was a clawed hand and sharp teeth flashing in a rhythm of red lights that spelled her doom. Even if she was going to drown, she still was terrified of the monster that suddenly took up the entire pipe with the massive length of his body.

He didn't react to her scream. Instead, he pressed something against her face. It was cold and hard, and for a moment she wondered if he was trying to kill her. But he'd never tried to kill her before and—

He hit a button on the side and suddenly all the water around her mouth disappeared and she could breathe.

Sucking in as much air as she could, Anya's heart nearly beat out of her chest as he affixed the apparatus around her head. So gently. His claws never once caught in her hair as he strapped it behind her ears and then made sure it was fitted to her mouth correctly. He waited until she was breathing slightly normally before he started to... back out of the pipe system.

He planted that webbed hand against the smooth metal and shoved himself backward. It looked awkward and uncomfortable. He didn't even look up at her, just kept moving as she followed him.

There were more crabs. Everywhere she looked. Crabs with carved waves on their back, a symbol she could only take to mean the ocean itself. He had sent her a message with crabs.

And she'd been right. He was coming for her.

Adventure and hope burning in her chest, she moved after him. Once he realized she could move faster, he did too. She wasn't sure how he was slithering so quickly with only one arm, but she couldn't think about that too much right now. They only had so much time before...

He froze. The undine looked at her, then down the pipe to the right of them. He leaned forward and shoved her hard, back into the pipe that she'd just crawled through. Then, with a surprisingly quick movement, he turned his body around. Wriggling and writhing so hard that blood plumed from a wound across his back and then suddenly his tail was right in front of her. He hit the bottom of the pipe a few times with it.

She wasn't sure what he wanted.

Then he hit it again, not moving.

Did he want her to... grab his tail? For what reason?

Anya didn't want to argue with the undine who was saving her, but she did think this was mad. Grabbing onto a spine just above the fluke, she adjusted her hold just as he launched forward.

They were flying through the pipe now. And she realized that he had been moving very, very slowly for her. Because now they were moving so quickly that she didn't even have time to see the bubbles coming out of the mask he'd attached to her face. The mask she hardly had time to question before she heard the rumbling he must have heard before.

Her father was making good on his promise. He was draining the pipes.

Suddenly, pressure pushed behind them. Air flooding through the system and shoved everything inside the pipes. If the water didn't push them free, then soon enough they would be trapped. They weren't going to make it out because how were they going to get out of the opening into the sea? She didn't even know if they were close to it.

Just as suddenly as the pressure struck her ears, the ringing of her tinnitus turning into a sharp ache, they were suddenly free. She almost heard the sharp pop as they tumbled out into the vast beyond.

She only had a moment to listen to the absolute silence of the sea. Even the ringing in her ears ceased as she looked into the utter nothingness that surrounded them.

And then her eyes found the undine who stretched out to his full height. She had continued to tumble away from him, rolling across the sand until she finally stopped moving. Lying on her back on the ground, she looked up all those strong, flexing muscles. The rolling peaks of his abs, the flat planes of his pecs, the absolutely stunning arm that was splayed wide at his side to stop his movement. And all those brilliant lights, glowing red and evil as he loomed above her. The spines on his back were raised high, she could see it almost like a dorsal fin at his back, they were so large.

The red light cast shadows from underneath his face, turning him into a villain of a story that she might have dreamed up. But then he reached for her and she didn't scream. Didn't even have the feeling that she needed to. She should have been terrified. Instead, she took the villain's hand and clutched Bitsy's box close to her chest as he gathered her tenderly in his arm.

That thick arm bracketed her back, and his strong forearm flexed against her side. He planted his hand flat against her belly and suddenly they were moving again. Rushing through the pillars that kept her city safe.

With her chin on his shoulder, she watched Alpha disappear behind them. Her home was gone.

But her heart was free.

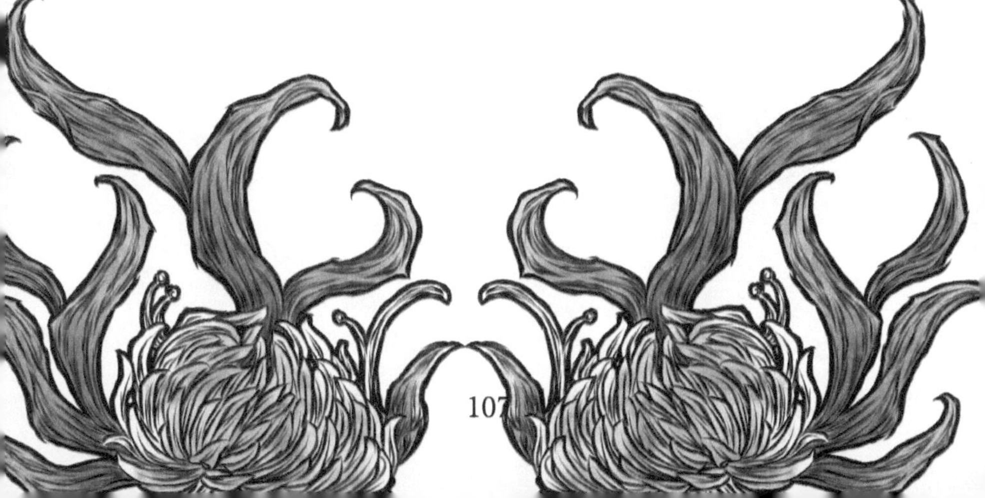

Chapter 11

Now that he had her, he had no idea what to do with her.

Daios had known it would be difficult to get to her. He'd been watching the city for some time, and he could see that there was significant movement within. All the pillars that shot those horrible, painful lasers were fired up and at the ready. He'd had to be quicker than he'd ever been before he reached the pipe.

But he had. And then he'd expected her to have moved until he heard the grating sounds of the crabs talking. So they'd found her, at least, even if that meant he had to go deeper inside the city than he wanted.

What he hadn't expected was to find her halfway there. She'd gone down three tunnels, following the crabs like a madwoman before she came upon him. Immediately, anger had flared so hot and powerful that he hadn't been able to control the lights of his body.

What if she had died? Drowned? What if he was just a few moments late, and he'd found her dead body? She would have ruined the entire mission. Again, the anger pressed against his throat and he wanted to hurt something. He wanted to grab onto the nearest deep sea squid and fight until there were little sucker marks all over his body and he couldn't see through the cloud of ink.

But he didn't want to hurt her. And that was curious enough on its own.

He didn't mind that she was pressed up against him, nor did he mind that her tiny little fingers gripped his shoulders. Even the one that was close to his missing arm. He wouldn't mind all that much unless she moved it lower. Which she didn't. He wasn't sure if that was because she was disgusted by the missing limb, or if she was just terrified.

He didn't think she was terrified, though. Her legs looped around his hips, right where his lower fins grew. Her tiny feet, as Mira called them, were covered in some kind of strange material, but they kicked against the back of his tail whenever he changed directions. The box she'd brought was between them, or he would have focused on her heartbeat.

Instead, all he could think about was that she was wrapped around him. Her warmth pressed against him as he swam, and—for fuck's sake—was that his fins fluttering against her thighs?

He tamped down on the movement immediately, a low growl starting in his chest with disgust at himself. He could not, would not, flutter for an achromo. Daios was not trying to impress her, and he did not want a mate.

Or perhaps, something deep inside him whispered, he did not think a mate would want him.

He started toward the achromos old lair, and then he realized she was talking. The mouthpiece makes it so quiet that he couldn't hear her, and she already spoke so softly.

He leaned down to hear what she was saying. "One, two, three, four, five. One, two, three, four, five."

Rhythmically, she counted. Over and over again. He tilted his head, apparently seeing better in the dark than she did. Her eyes were squeezed shut underneath the goggles attached to the mouthpiece. Her lips moved, and as he watched, her pulse sped up. The rapid beat in her neck was concerning enough without her ribs moving like that, almost as though she were hyperventilating.

Was she afraid? Had he done something? Daios didn't know what would make her afraid if she hadn't minded fleeing the city. She'd already been in the pipes when he found her! Clearly, she wanted to leave.

He wasn't so much a monster that she would fear him as they fled. Was he? Was the sight of him the problem?

She must have felt him straining to see her, because she opened her eyes. But she didn't look at him. Not exactly. More like over his shoulder.

"I'm sorry. I don't like the dark," she whispered. "Counting helps keep the panic attacks away. I'm sorry."

"Why are you apologizing for something you cannot control?" he grumbled, but then realized that his low tones and raspy voice were more likely to add to her fears than assuage them.

Sighing, he shifted his grip to palm the back of her head. Carefully, he turned her skull, so she was looking at the part of his neck and shoulder that weren't damaged.

It took a lot to control the colors individually on his body. When he was younger, he'd been obsessed with trying. Their mother had always laughed at his antics. She'd claimed only octopi were so talented, and no undine were good enough with their colors to do what he was attempting.

He'd mastered it, though. So, in the same rhythm she'd been counting, he focused on the lights while they swam. One, two, three, four, five. All the way down his neck. Then again, to the peak of his shoulder. More down his bicep. Then he made the lights turn and go back up the same way.

She couldn't see him very well, although likely better than she had before, but he could see her. The trembling that he'd noticed almost disappeared entirely. Her eyes followed the lights up and down. Over the repeating pattern until he felt her tension ease. It just melted away until she was pliable in his arms once more.

He kept the lights going as they moved through the water, although Arges's concerns were suddenly blasting in his head. Achromos got cold, his brother had claimed. Often. So he needed to keep her warmer. That would be easier with two arms, but she was so small compared to him. It was fairly easy to do with one as well. He tucked her closer to him, shifting his grip to fit her feet into the fins at his hips.

He was grateful she couldn't see his face. The grimace he couldn't control at the soft touch of her feet sliding against the sensitive fins would have scared her even more.

They were making good progress, at least. He didn't want to stop swimming at this speed until he found the facility. Her father had seen them leave. He was certain of it. Which meant there would be ships coming after them soon enough, likely there already were.

Then he was faced with a new obstacle. He paused in the water, more upright than he had been before. Her legs curled a little tighter around him, and she craned her neck to look at where they were. Not that she could see much.

There were lights in the distance. He had really hoped they would avoid being followed. He was a small speck in the ocean compared to the massive ships her father had, but unfortunately, it appeared the General had more resources at his disposal. That made it difficult for Daios, even more than the obstacle that now laid out before them.

The red coral bed was famed for its danger. When he was nothing more than a pup, he and his friends used to see if they could swim through it. His first jagged scars were from this place. They looked like fingers reaching out toward him. Fingers dipped in red blood, begging to drink more from their flesh.

He found himself flaring brighter for her to see what he was looking at. Maketes had thought that they would go right over this deadly coral bed, but he had forgotten that there would be people chasing them. Which meant, unfortunately, he had a choice. He could go through the jagged, spindly red coral that would slice through his scales if he made a mistake, or he could swim above them and chance her father's ships seeing the direction he swam in.

He tensed as she reached out, running her finger along one of the nearest coral pieces. Daios hadn't realized they were quite so close to them.

"These are sharp," she said, her voice muffled and low.

Releasing his hold on her waist, he trusted her to hold on to him as he grabbed her hand. Gently, he forced her to let him look at the tiny finger that had been in so much danger. No wound, at least.

He pressed her hand between them, tucking her arms against his chest. "You stay very still," he said, trying to keep his voice low, so she knew how important this was. "I fear there are achromos following us."

The words were probably ridiculous to say to her. She was an achromo, and of course she knew her people were going to follow them. Not to mention she had no idea what he was saying.

So he gestured toward the lights, moving his hand as though it were a ship through the water. Then he reached for one of the corals, flaring red even brighter so she could see the plume of blood that immediately erupted from his skin at the barest touch.

He would keep her safe, he tried to mime to her. He would take the wounds for her.

Daios didn't like the thought of her bleeding. He didn't want to see those red ribbons stretch from her skin as they moved through the sharp red coral bed. Her blood would likely taste sweet, and he didn't know how he would react to that. Not when all he could think about was a sea turning black with blood and all the people he had lost. All those souls that blamed him for their deaths.

Cool fingers touched his face. The strange texture of her gloves didn't change the calm that descended upon him as she ghosted those fingers over his forehead. She smoothed the creases there, her touch lingering a little longer than it needed to.

And then his little witch of a woman whispered, "We can go through the coral. I'll keep my arms tucked in tight."

He could almost hear the ships now. The strange metallic hum of their movements through the water and he could certainly smell the oil in his gills that only those machines put out into the ocean.

With a sharp nod, he descended into the madness with her. The sharp spines cut into his back, slicing through his arms and shoulders as he pushed them into the only opening he could find. All he had to do was get to the bottom of this coral and then there should be space for them to swim.

All throughout the struggle, she remained still as stone in his arms. He gripped her around the waist, holding her spine in his one arm as he used his entire body to break through the coral. He would be her shield if that kept her safe.

Finally, he broke through to the bottom. There was enough space here for him to swim, and for him to keep her away from those sharp pieces. If anything stretched too close to the silty sand below, it would cut only him.

Until he smelled her blood.

He dragged the scent deep into his gills, feeling it flutter so soft against the edges of his rib gills and then he could taste her on his tongue. Metallic and oh so sweet.

His first reaction wasn't one he was proud of. He wanted more of it. He wanted to sink his teeth into the graceful column of her neck and make more of that sweet scent plume in the water so he could drag it into himself. But then he hated the thought of hurting her. He hated that she was hurting now.

Tugging her in front of him to unfurl her body, he started looking for the wound. There wasn't anything on her arms and hands, but of course he knew that. She had her arms tucked in to him. So maybe it was on her back. He spun her around, ignoring that she had started speaking. He had to find the wound. He had to make sure she wasn't going to bleed out on him.

He'd promised.

Daios had promised he would keep this one alive. But the luck that followed him was so evil that no matter what he did, it felt like he was killing everyone and anyone that meant...

She tapped her fingers against his shoulder as he turned her, looking again for the cut that would dare to mar her flesh. Then more tapping, rhythmic movements that brought his attention to her face.

"The lights," she said, her voice little more than a whisper. "You have to turn off the lights."

She'd been touching her fingers to every single light that was flashing on his skin. Like she was trying to cover them up with her fingers, or that perhaps she thought her touch had turned them off. And when he finally pulled himself out of that dark place and realized the risk he was taking, Daios allowed them to sink into darkness.

It didn't matter where she was cut. Clearly she wasn't so injured that she risked death, and the ships were bound to be close to them now. Too close.

He pulled her against him again, holding her tightly against his twin heart beats as the strange ships moved over their heads. The silver bellies glowed, and he could see their insides through the glass panels that separated the sea from the creatures inside. Giant beams of light moved in front of the ships. They were searching for the two of them, and if he wasn't careful, they would find them.

Nearly vibrating with anger, he drew her closer to him yet again and tucked them flat against the ground. The red coral and dark earth would hide his body, but her silver wetsuit would stand out just as much as the ships did. So he had to cover her.

At least, that's what he told himself. He said that he was only covering her so that he could keep her safe for a little longer. He refused to admit that her tiny hands pressed against his bare skin twisted something inside him.

Then she started tracing circles against his chest. The circles became patterns as they waited for the ships to stop their search. Patterns he had no idea how to decipher, but fuck.

It felt so good to have someone touch him.

He couldn't remember the last time someone touched him just to touch him. He'd always spent such a large portion of his time alone, and when he wasn't alone, he was fighting. That was it. He had nothing else in his life until this little beast was forced onto his path.

His tail shifted in a current that he had never felt before. It was like someone placed a cool blanket over his shoulders, wrapping him a little tighter, and he had to wonder if this was a goddess of the sea. If she was telling him, this was... right. That after all this time of fighting, he had finally been given something soft.

But she needed to stay alive for him to keep her.

So as the ships turned to go in another direction, he swam with her in his arms. Underneath the sharp spines that bit into his back and shoulders and tail. He would bleed for as long as it took to get them out of here.

It was a long time. But he finally broke free from the coral to a rare sight of the sun above them, a blessing so he did not have to suffer more wounds. Carefully, he took her to the abandoned facility that Maketes had spoken of. Though there were no lights to be seen, it looked like it was intact.

As he swam by a window, he peered into the shadows beyond and could see there was air in there. Hopefully breathable air for her, but at the very least, something had to be working.

Now he just had to find a way in and to force himself to let her go. Which, he was finding, would be harder than he anticipated.

How to get in? He wasn't sure. There weren't a lot of openings in the achromos builds, and he could only imagine it would be complicated.

A soft tap had him looking down at the little creature in his arms.

"Lights?" she asked. "Can you make the lights?"

"Are you afraid again?" he asked, his voice a low rumble in his chest.

At her shiver, he sighed. Of course, he had to be thrown in the direction of a creature who was terrified of the dark. She feared so many things, likely, that he would have to spend the rest of his obsession catering to her every whim. She was weak.

But he still started with the rhythm of lights that went up and down his shoulder, trying his best to ignore the way her fingers tapped each one out of existence before he let the next light illuminate.

Chapter 12

She'd underestimated just how *dark* the sea was. Anya had looked out at it through Alpha's glass dome for her entire life, seeing only darkness beyond the artificial lights. She had known that it was pitch black out there. The city of Alpha was built so deep that no light could penetrate their city from Above. Not that there was any light to come through.

But she hadn't expected the darkness to affect her so much. Apparently, she'd never seen true darkness.

It had pressed down upon her out here. The weight of the dark felt worse than being blind. She'd always thought losing her sight would be harder than losing her hearing, likely because she knew what it was like to lose one of her senses. But this was... heavy. So heavy.

Anya could feel her heart beating harder. She was more aware of her body and every ounce of blood that pumped through her veins. She could feel her breath coming in and out of her lungs, entirely reliant on a device that she'd never seen before.

All of it gave her mind time to turn and rumble and boil with the fear of what she had done. She'd been so desperate to be free that she hadn't realized that it meant trusting her entire life in the hands of an undine. A creature who her people had fought against for years. It was a risk she had thought she was ready to take.

Until the cold depths of the sea swept her away in his arms.

But he had sensed it. Or perhaps he had known that she would be afraid. She wasn't sure. One moment she was counting under her breath and the next, he'd lit up.

She didn't know if he was aware that red was a warning sign to her people, and the red light wasn't immediately helpful because it sent messages to her mind that she was in danger. But then she noticed the pattern. How he was lighting up specific parts of himself for her to count, in the same rhythm that she'd been counting.

This monstrous being who had crept out of the sea had wanted to keep her calm. He'd panicked when he'd thought she was hurt, and that was the only explanation she had for the way he'd acted after they'd gone through that sharp coral. Even though he had been the one to be nearly ripped to shreds.

Even now, her fingers touched the edge of a deep gash left behind on his back. There were plenty of them. She didn't know where to hold on to him that wouldn't hurt, but he didn't seem to notice. He moved through the water like it wasn't a problem that he was bleeding.

Swallowing hard, she told herself that he was a monster. It didn't matter that he had spoken more to her in body language than anyone else had in her entire life. He cared that she was well. And he was willing to do whatever it took to make sure that she stayed safe.

Fuck. She liked him. He wasn't just a monster; he was becoming a real being to her, and that was dangerous. He was the means to an end.

An escape from her city and she was going to get away from him the first moment she could so she could reunite with Ace.

Her heart sank into her stomach when the light of his body caught on the edge of an abandoned research facility. She'd heard of this one before. It had failed in a few key wings of the building, and the flooding had made her father order everyone home. It should still be liveable, though.

Damn it. He was bringing her somewhere that he deemed safe enough for her to be in. Why did he have to be thoughtful? Why couldn't he be the murderous creature that her father claimed all of his kind were?

They took a while to circle the entire building before he decided on a place to swim inside. There was water damage galore. She could see where the pressure had caused one of the walls to cave in. The puncture looked like a giant creature had plunged a talon into the side of the building, even though she knew that wasn't... possible.

Was it?

Anya swiftly realized she knew nothing about the world she had just tossed herself into. And the deep sea was more terrifying than she had originally thought.

But maybe it was a little less terrifying with his arm wrapped around her and all that power between her legs. She felt her cheeks heat beneath the mask as she realized just where those thoughts were going to get her at the same time he surfaced in the air filled room.

Time to get away from the Stockholm Syndrome that was setting in way faster than she'd thought it would. Scrambling out of his arms, she half crawled up the broken metal floor and into the air beyond.

This she could do. This was air and home, and she knew how to wander around places like this. Ripping the mask off her face, she ignored the angry growl that rippled from the creature behind her.

Taking in a deep breath, she was relieved to find that most functions of this facility were still online. Obviously there was power if there was air.

"Computer?" she called out, her voice a little raspy. "Report."

Crawling a few more steps, she pulled Bitsy out of her box. The little robot blinked a few times, looking for all intents and purposes like it was waking from a nap. Though she knew that wasn't entirely how it must have felt. Still, she put the little droid onto her head.

Bitsy put the words immediately on the screen, a little warped as she projected the words coming out of two speakers, but not at the same time. "Life support, online. Messaging function, online. Research facilities, damaged. Living quarters, damaged. Generators, online. Air compressors, thirty-two percent."

"Damn it," she muttered, pressing her hands a little more firmly into the metal floor. She'd have to divert some of the power to this room. She'd hoped the generators would be outputting more electricity than that, but she assumed that meant quite a few of the generators were either no longer functioning, or that there was significant water damage in that room, too.

This was liveable, for now, but not forever.

"Bitsy, can you hack into the system?"

The droid gave it all a once over before the words flashed. "Of course."

"Good. We'll need to shift all life support to this sector and try to divert whatever power we can without letting my father know we're here. If we can get into the system correctly, then we should be able to message Ace as well."

Desperately trying to ignore that the undine was still right behind her in the water, she scanned her gaze over what would now be her home. A giant wall of windows made up an entire wall, but they revealed very little beyond ten feet. The murky water was only barely illuminated by the meager light of the consoles beneath the windows. The floor space was maybe fifteen feet wide before it hit the water that curled icy tendrils up into the air. Even her breath frosted with every exhale, and she could only imagine if she didn't have her wetsuit on, she'd be freezing.

Currently, this room had no doors that were open to any other part of the facility. The drain doors were sealed shut, and when she leaned to look past the wall of windows, she could see both hallways on either side were filled with water. So she was stuck in this room, for now, until Bitsy could hack into the system and drain the water out. At least then they could maybe see what they were working with.

Scrambling to her feet, she bit her lip and took another step into the room. Red lights blared all around her and she could feel the reverberations of some kind of alarm. She couldn't quite hear it, not really, but there was definitely the sensation that there was noise just out of her reach.

A hand grabbed onto her ankle and yanked her back into the water.

With a yelp, she hit the icy water hard. It flooded up her nose, and all she could feel was the burn of salt as she came back to the surface, gasping in air and trying to clear out her nostrils.

"What the fuck," she muttered, but had a feeling she might have shouted, before that hand slammed the mouthpiece over her face a little too hard, and then yanked her back underneath the water.

The undine had his hand wrapped around her ankle, and he was dragging her into the depths. She couldn't tell if the red alarm from above was turning him red, or if his own colors were flashing in answer to the colors above them. Either way, she was pissed.

Kicking out with her other foot, she slammed her heel into the hand holding onto her ankle.

He released her, but turned with a glare and flared fins around his body. She was stunned by how massive he was. Would she ever get used to that? Probably not. Especially not with his teeth bared like an animal and all that anger rioting through his body like a tsunami just waiting to sweep her away in the sheer power of his emotions.

But she would not be dragged around like luggage while he tried to get her to go somewhere else.

"I'm staying here," she said, flexing her stomach to force the words out louder. "Here is safe."

Those sharp teeth gnashed at the water as he mimicked biting. "Stupid achromo. Nearly got herself killed."

The words flashed in front of her eyes, and it made her pause. She hadn't realized Bitsy had downloaded his language yet, but apparently she had. The sassy little droid had chosen a vivid pink color for his words.

"What did you say?" she asked, her voice little more than a whisper.

He cupped a hand behind what she assumed was his ear, and also a handful of gills at his neck.

"This is so fucking frustrating," she swore under her breath before squeezing her stomach to try to shout. This time, she used her hands as well, signing to him, "What did you say?"

He watched her hands moving, his gaze narrowing before she swore she saw his hand move in a similar way. But then he growled low under his breath.

"Come," he growled, the word ripping through his throat. "We are not safe."

"I can understand you." Her hands flew with the words, probably too fast for most people to even decipher, but she was so excited. "I can understand what you're saying! And I can hear you. I can…"

The deep rumble that came out of the undine in front of her wasn't a word. It was an expression of frustration and anger and… desire. Or at least, that's how she took it. Stupid. Stupid thoughts that had no place here. It didn't matter if that's maybe what he sounded like when he was in the midst of…

He made the sound again, and it shook through her entire body, sending a zing of electricity from her chest all the way down between her legs. She pressed her thighs together, trying her best to not think about that sound and what it did to every hair on her body that wanted to raise.

He lunged for her, or rather, flicked his tail so hard that he was right in front of her again. She flinched, expecting him to grab her and drag her deeper into the depths with that clawed, terrifying hand.

But he didn't do that. Instead, he touched the back of one of those black claws to the side of her throat. She could feel the smoothness of it. The edge caught on the glimmering red lights that refracted along the churning waves above them, and from his shimmering body that had yet to stop glowing like some strange electric eel.

That deep, deep voice dropped even lower. The sound was something she didn't even hear. She felt it deep in her chest, rattling her ribs. "We go," he said, the words flashing all around him. "So that I can keep you safe."

Tears burned in her eyes and she didn't know why. She'd been protected and cared for her entire life, hadn't she? Her father and everyone else had always made sure that she was safe.

But they had never made her feel like this. They'd wanted her to stay where she was so they could watch her, control her, manipulate every move and then use her to their advantage. But this undine? He just wanted to keep her safe.

Such a simple thing to say, and yet she felt like she might never recover.

Nodding her head, she sniffed hard, so she didn't get all snotty inside of the breathing mask. "I'm safe here. I promise."

He shook his head, pointing up at the red lights with a clawed finger. "It attacks."

She grabbed that clawed finger, some madness in her telling her to reach out and touch him. Maybe she had some insane feeling that she could help him relax just by touching him, and that was stupid. She was stupid for even thinking she could grab onto his claw and that he would listen to her.

But she saw the way his eyes widened. In shock or anger, she had no idea. He stared at her hand wrapped around his finger, and every single part of him froze. Like she had stopped time.

All his gills didn't even move, and she thought maybe they had to move for him to breathe. He just stared at her hand wrapped in his, and then, just the barest movement. A fluttering at his neck, in what she thought was his gills. It made the delicate membranes there look almost pretty. Just the barest of fluttering, a little wrinkle of silk that attached to his neck.

He swallowed hard. Then those black eyes turned to her.

"It's not attacking," she said. Those eyes made her feel pinned, like a butterfly stuck to a board. "It's a warning system. I can turn it off."

"Explain."

"It's in the entire facility. Anyone not authorized to be in an area will set off an alarm system. It's a safety measure."

"Then turn it off." But he didn't move. He didn't seem to even breathe as she gently released his hand and turned back to the room.

Using her arms and legs, she moved through the water with ease and then took Bitsy off her head. The little droid ran for the middle control panel, attaching herself to the electronics there and setting to work.

She could feel the pressure in her head lessen, which she assumed meant the sound was off. And then the red lights stopped swirling as well. Her tinnitus flared immediately, likely the pressure changes that meant the room was finally safe for a person to be in.

With the ringing in her ears, she hauled herself out of the water and said, "Computer, change all life support to — Bitsy, where are we?"

Her droid bounced up and down, usually a sign that she was going to take care of the situation so Anya could turn her attention to other things. She spun around, ready to argue more with the undine, even if she couldn't understand him without her droid.

But he was gone.

There was nothing in the water, no dark shadow, nothing but a murky grey mess and white caps of waves still lapping at the metal floor.

"Shit," she muttered, before staggering over the consoles and sitting down in front of Bitsy. "He's gone."

Her robot wobbled up and down again.

"I wish I had brought more things." She looked down at the wetsuit, blowing out a long breath. "This needs to be dried, and I can't just stay in a wetsuit the entire time I'm here."

Bitsy lifted one of her legs out of the console panel and pointed to the right. In the corner, where a few other wheelie chairs had been shoved, there were a couple boxes with the big label, "Emergency supplies."

"Perfect." Staggering once more to her feet, Anya told herself she could do this without the help of a confusing, too handsome for his own good, undine.

And it was really messed up that she had to tell herself that he wasn't handsome. He was a monster. An undine. Not even her own species.

A whisper in her mind said, "Yes, he is. But you still like him."

Chapter 13

He raced away from that room and the confusing feelings that it had wrought. When those lights had turned on and the screaming started, he was certain he had delivered her into the mouth of a monster. She hadn't even reacted, and he realized she couldn't hear the sound.

She didn't know she was in danger. His little achromo had no idea that she was in so much danger that he had to save her. So he'd grabbed her, yanked her into the water with him so they could both flee. He'd make the journey more comfortable for her after he got her out of danger.

Until she'd kicked him between his webs so hard that he felt the shock of pain all the way up to his jaw. He'd turned on her, enraged that she would fight him on this, only to find that she was already glaring at him like he was the problem.

Him.

The one who was saving her.

Then she'd explained everything that was happening and he'd felt like an idiot. Of course, there were alarm systems in this facility. He'd seen the alarm systems in the other cities and had suffered through the loud noises and the red lights before. He knew exactly what to expect when the achromos realized there was an intruder in their home.

Then she'd touched him again. Again.

After everything she could see of his body, and what he was lacking, she had still touched him. She'd grabbed onto his claw and he'd been struck by how easy it would be to harm her. All it would take was a single twist of his wrist, a turn in the wrong direction, and she'd be... gone. He could cut through all that delicate flesh and rend it right to the bone. She would bleed out before anyone could stop her.

And those thoughts had terrified him. More than he had ever been terrified. Because with those thoughts came the knowledge that he had never been very good at not hurting people.

She was so small and delicate. So easy for him to hurt and he didn't want to hurt her. He shouldn't want to mate a weak creature. He should search for the strongest, the most powerful, the best. Someone he couldn't best or overcome in a fight. The People of Water valued strength, not delicacy.

So while she turned her attention to stopping the alarm and freeing them from that gods awful noise, he'd fled. He couldn't look at her when he feared what he might do if he stayed for even a moment longer.

What if, for the briefest of moments, he fell to weakness like he had before?

Daios had spent his entire life knowing that he was a weapon. He was proud of the danger that his body posed for almost anyone who was around him. That was his role.

Now, he knew exactly the loss that his body could bring as well.

And it plagued him until the very end of the world.

Darting through the water, not toward the sharp coral, but out into the abyss beyond the ledge, he dove into the darkness. Trying to escape the madness, the horrors of his memories, and the fear that he would do it all again. But he'd learned a long time ago that he could not run from those thoughts. They chased him into the darkness.

Breathing hard, his chest moving up and down and his gills flaring wide as though there wasn't enough oxygen in the water around him, he reached the very bottom of the abyss.

There were deeper parts of the ocean that he'd been to before. But down here, even though it wasn't the deepest, there was still a silence in the pressure. It let him think. It let him breathe.

Slowly allowing his body to illuminate the water, he got his bearings. The silt down here had been disturbed by his mad dash into the depths, so it was hard to see much farther than a hand's distance. Everything was red, though. All the dust, all the particles, all the nothing that surrounded him.

Turning in a slow circle, he let his gaze float through the water. He was alone. Finally. He could be free of the worries because there was no one down here with him.

Until he turned in a full circle and came face to face with a rotting corpse.

The undine had been pretty, once. She had been one of the few that Daios had thought he might like to mate. He'd even fluttered for her before, although she had turned him down. Daios was too big. He'd make children that need larger purses, and therefore were harder to birth. And even then, what use would he be to them? The females of their kind were supposed to be bigger, and he'd never met one who was larger than him.

He knew she'd been in the group of fighters with him who had attacked Beta. He'd watched her rush to the forefront, the first of his kind to meet the weapons that the achromos had never shown them before.

And then he'd watched her die. He'd watched as the bright fire had burned through the sea, an impossible nightmare as it struck her in the chest. There were many who fell with her, but she was the one he remembered most.

"Hamartia," he whispered, lifting his hand to ghost it in front of her face. "I am so sorry."

She'd been so beautiful in life. But death had rotted her. One of her eyes was missing, and the pale blue of her coloring was nearly gone. Gray flesh sagged around wounds through her right cheek. She did not look like the beautiful visage he remembered. And the more he stared, the more he feared that he would never remember her powerful beauty.

That rotting mouth fell open, and to his horror, the gills along the sides of her neck flared in with a breath. "You killed me," she said, her voice little more than a death rattle. "You left me there to die."

"I would never have brought any of you there if I had thought for a second that I would lose you."

"You knew. You just didn't want to listen." The dust swirled around her body, and he could see the ragged hole in her chest where her life had leaked out. "And now you will kill another."

"I don't want to kill again," he desperately replied. "I know now the price of my hubris and I don't... cannot suffer this again."

"You have stolen yourself a mate," she said, her one remaining eye rolling in the socket. "You have taken her and tried to forget what you have done. You think you will find a haven in this creature who will see you as nothing more than a monster?"

A flash of light in the distance parted the dust. And then he saw them. Bodies raining down through the water, all limp and revealed only in the bright flashes of light. The achromos? Had they returned for him? Had they finally hunted him down as their greatest beast to destroy?

He was the monster who had attacked their city, and the monster who had failed. Fleeing from them as his brothers had dragged him into the depths while all the others fell.

A rotting hand grabbed onto his chin. He could feel the brittle tips of her claws, and the lack of webs that were the first to rot from her body. Daios couldn't breathe as she dragged his face closer to her, forcing him to look at the nightmarish features that remained. There was nothing left of her. Nothing of the woman he had found so intriguing.

"You wanted me," she hissed. "You would have taken me if I had given you the chance. I was the greatest of my clutch, the strongest and best hunter of our pod. And you think an achromo can replace me?"

"I don't want her."

"But you do. You've already fluttered for her. Your body has betrayed you, warrior, and it makes me sick." She tossed his head to the side so hard it felt as though she'd struck him.

Frozen with his head turned away from her, he squeezed his eyes shut. "This isn't real," he told himself. "This is all in your mind."

"I am not real?" her voice still cackled, and then he heard her snarl in his ear, "I promise you this, Daios the Destroyer, you will kill her just as you have killed all of us. You are a monster, and you are unworthy of anything but the depths of the sea."

Hand clenched into a fist, his entire body shaking, he felt a single word snap out of his mouth and thrust into the sea. "No!"

The word echoed as he finally opened his eyes again. Spinning right and left, he searched the dust for the corpse of the life he might have once had. But there was nothing and no one to be found in the red tinged light. Nothing at all.

He was alone. As he always was. And as he was cursed to always be.

But he couldn't get his breathing under control. He didn't know what this feeling was. Pressing a hand against his chest, he tried to rub at the uncomfortable ache beneath his ribs. Both of his hearts were racing and he couldn't get them to slow. No matter how hard he pressed his hand against them or how many breaths he took through just his lower gills. He was... Something was wrong.

Daios tried to take a deep, long, steadying breath. But it rattled as that wrong emotion made it hard to take a breath in without stuttering. His jaw shook, chattering as he stayed at the cold bottom of the sea where there was no one and nothing but him.

At some point, it felt as though the current had grabbed onto him. The sea herself shoved him away from the muck that was seeping underneath his scales and clogging his gills. She tossed him upward, toward something. And so he rode the current. He allowed her to carry him away from that place, even though he knew she had not forgiven him for what he had done.

The sea moved him higher into the water, much higher until he saw what it wanted. There was a small school of tuna. Already picked apart, it seemed. There were too few of them, or perhaps they had been sliced away from the rest of the group. He was high enough that light speared through the sea, and he could watch the silver flashes of their bodies as they spun and turned away from him.

It was beautiful. He thought, perhaps, the sea wished to remind him that no matter what, there was still life in the water. There was still a reason for him to keep fighting, even if it felt like there wasn't.

Bowing his head, he murmured, "I honor your reminder. The darkness and the depths do no favors for my state of mind. I should not seek out the shadows when there is so much to see in the light."

But then he felt the current nudge him again, closer to the tuna. Again and again she pushed until he realized she wanted him to take one of the creatures for himself.

Sighing, he shook his head. "I have no wish to cause more death. Not today."

Another nudge, another push.

The sea was insistent, it seemed. One of those tunas was for him, although he could not understand why she would wish for him to take prey that large. He certainly couldn't eat all of it himself. He couldn't...

The achromo.

The sea wished him to feed the achromo.

"No," he snarled, baring his teeth in denial of the order. "I've already stolen her. I will not and cannot feed her. These are mating games you wish me to play and I do not want to play them."

This time he was shoved so hard toward the tuna that they scattered. And then the current disappeared entirely, as though the sea was warning him that he had been out of her favor for a very long time. He'd fought against everything she'd thrown his way in punishment, and she was giving him a chance to get back in her good graces.

Darting forward, he looped through the currents and circled the tuna. They were large beasts and fought back harder than most. But it took little for a creature like him to cut one down. With a flick of his tail, he sliced through the water. He could change directions faster than they could, and the sharp claws at the end of his hand cut through their flesh too easily.

The tuna he caught up with flashed silver, then red. The ribbons of blood caught his eye. Daios forced himself to remain in the present, though. He felt the current that suddenly caressed down his sides, toying with his fluke as he caught the dead creature up in his arms. He was not alone, not right now. The sea was with him as he felt around for the nearest current.

Like magic, it caught him up in her arms and drew him down into the depths again.

He'd forgotten what this felt like. The sea always made him feel weightless, but this was effortless. With their goddess on his side, drawing him where she wished him to go, he was invincible.

He saw the facility right in front of him again. And he knew there was another within. A woman who waited for him. An achromo who made him feel things that he shouldn't feel and made him so afraid that he would do something wrong.

Every part of him was made to hurt every part of her. And here the sea was, pushing him to feed her. To care for her. To do whatever it took to keep her alive and tie them together even more than they already were.

He didn't even know how long he'd been gone. He wasn't sure if she wanted to see him or even if she would stop doing whatever it was she was doing. The water was suspiciously murky and all the dust had been stirred up around the building. Daios couldn't even see through the windows the particles were so thick.

He had to imagine that meant she was doing something. What she was doing? He had no idea. And he certainly didn't trust it.

Swimming into the room where he'd left her, he poked his head up to see that the door to the right was open, the hallway somehow drained. And though perhaps that was a good thing—she did need to spread out, most likely—he also feared what that meant.

Heaving the tuna out of the water, he let it flop onto the smooth floor while dragging himself halfway out of the water. Leaning to the side, he stared down the hall to see what his achromo was doing.

What he saw made all the air wheeze out of his lungs.

Skin. Smooth, unblemished skin. And all he could do was freeze in place as his gaze trailed down the shadow of her spine.

Chapter 14

She hadn't expected him to leave her alone for such a long time. But it gave her plenty of opportunity to look at the research facility he'd brought her to. Though the place was running low on power, it hadn't been abandoned for that long. There were useful power stores that could be diverted, and oxygen that would keep her alive for a while yet.

Bitsy did the work she was required to do. Ace had sent them a download a long time ago for hacking, hence the ability to hack cameras. Apparently, there was some information in that download as well about manipulating a system such as this.

According to her little droid, the AI functions on the ship were simplistic, outdated, and run down. If that was said with rather sarcastic italicized words, then Anya ignored the sass. She figured Bitsy deserved it after surviving their plunge into the depths of the sea. Such was a traumatic event that the droid would not let her forget.

Together, they worked to get the facility back semi-online while also still not allowing the AI to send off any warning signals back home. If anyone at Alpha figured out that a long dead facility had just gotten back online, they would send someone to check what was going on.

And that was something to avoid.

The emergency supplies had a few things that were helpful. A medkit, which she moved somewhere safe just in case they needed to use it for someone's injuries. A droid that had died a long time ago, the battery running out with no access to electricity. Three old tins of food, as well. But no clothing. So she was forced to shiver as she tried to keep herself warm in the icy building.

"What do you think?" she muttered, looking over the console panel Bitsy had lit up. "Can we get the tunnel to the left open?"

Bitsy had left the screen on the console table with one leg connected to it. Words scrolled across the glass. "Maybe."

"Is it functional?"

"Maybe."

"These are not answers, Bitsy. I need a report that's useable, not just a maybe."

Exclamation points jumped all over the screen. Clearly, she'd made her droid angry again, but that was just the way of it. She sat in the wheelie chair, trying not to be overwhelmed by the dust in front of the window. She was used to Alpha, which had miles and miles of clear ocean surrounding it. The pillars had always lit up some of the sand, and of course, the lights from the city itself spread like a beacon. She had watched bubbles move over glass for her entire life.

Here? The bubbles were even murky and filled with dust. Every time she thought maybe she caught movement, there wasn't anything at all. Just a whole lot of dust that could hide almost anything out there.

For a second, she thought she saw teeth. Just a wide open maw of a mouth, grinning at her through the window because it knew she couldn't see.

Trapped. Oh, she was so trapped in this place and she wouldn't even know if something was coming at her until the very last second. She could feel her heart beat kick up as it got a little harder to breathe.

Rubbing a hand over her chest, she stood and paced. "Bitsy, we have to get more room in here. I can't stay like this for much longer. I'm losing my mind."

She didn't even look at the screen to see how her droid replied. She knew what Bitsy was going to say.

This is nothing different than her room at home. Her father had her cooped up in that room for weeks on end, and she hadn't gone as stir crazy as this. Or hadn't panicked, at least. This room was the same as all the others she'd been in for countless times in her life. She could manage this.

Still, she didn't know how to sit still or even how to breathe like normal until she saw more exclamation points come across the screen. Jolting forward, she grabbed onto her droid at the same time Bitsy exclaimed across the lens, "I did it!"

"You did?" she breathed, craning her neck to peer down the tunnel.

And she could see it. The water was draining and there were plenty of buckling joints all around it that she knew someone else might have heard it. The building was shifting and moving and finally, finally, the door opened.

A rush of water erupted into the room, sliding toward the opening in the floor. A cold blast of air followed, smelling like seaweed and rotting fish, but it didn't matter. Because at the end of that hallway was another room. And she didn't care what that room was as long as it was more space.

Rushing forward, she tested her foot on the floor of the hallway into the other area. It had been filled with water, after all. The last thing she wanted was for the rusted out floor to give and then she'd been stuck in that murky water. Already she could easily envision how hard it would be to even find the facility. Her eyes would burn with the smarting of dirt and the saltwater that would make the light seem like it came from the wrong angle.

She'd drown. And even though she'd lived her entire life in the sea, Anya was just now realizing how terrified she was of it.

The floor held, though. As she skittered across it into the other room, she was surprised to find it was one of the few living quarters. Popping Bitsy back on her head, she started through the room and peered at all the details.

"I turned life support back on for this room only," Bitsy said as Anya turned toward the bunk beds on the wall.

There were four of them, each one made of steel that would last for centuries down here. Clearly there hadn't been any water in this room, because the blankets were still on the bed and they didn't look too worse for wear. Other than the dust, of course, but even that was minimal.

To the right, there was a small plastic card table that had seen better days and a lot of cards thrown around it. Bitsy highlighted the cards. "Look! Entertainment."

She shook her head, trying hard not to snort at the joke. There was a wall of lockers as well. Even if this space was limited, it was something.

Anya opened the lockers first and ran her fingers over the ancient photographs inside the first one. The man looked friendly with his arm around another man, younger, who looked just like him. There wasn't much left in this locker other than an emergency gas mask, which she supposed would be useful.

She closed it, feeling the angry way it fought back against her hand. She remembered when she was little there was a sound to that, but she'd long forgotten what that sound was.

A shame, really. She had a feeling the sound might have jolted her out of the fear that she was going to find a skeleton in one of these lockers.

Blowing out another anxious breath, she opened the next one. This one had drawings on the inside. Clearly done by a child, they were so thickly attached to the door that it almost created another stiff layer. With a soft smile, she looked in and let out a sound of surprise.

Clothing. The suit was old and smelled like mold. It had the Alpha seal on the breast pocket, a winged bird with the sunset behind it. The gray color wasn't flattering, and it was a man's size so it would be baggy in all the wrong places and tight in others, but at the very least, it would keep her warm in the cold facility.

Finally. She had something useful. She'd been a little afraid she was going to have to peel off the wetsuit and wrap herself in a blanket while hoping she didn't lose her toes.

Peeling off her wetsuit, she worked it down over her shoulders and had to take a breather with it stuck around her hips. Her bra was so stuck to her skin it was almost gross. So she quickly took that off as well, even though the icy temperatures turned her nipples to diamonds and made her skin so goose bumped she swore it was going to stay that way.

Hissing out a long breath, she started in on the wetsuit again. "Heat, Bitsy? That's kind of important."

"The heat is on."

"It's clearly not on. Do a scan."

The little droid scanned before teeny, tiny words flashed on the lens.

"Bigger."

The words only got marginally larger.

"Bitsy, you know I can't read that," she grumbled as she yanked the damn wetsuit down over her hips. Breathing hard and bending at the waist, she worked it down over one of her legs. "Make it bigger."

"It's fifty-two degrees." Finally, the words were big enough to read.

"And I'm in my underwear, still soaking wet," she grumbled.

"Not cold enough to die."

"So, is the heat on or not?"

The words this time were underlined as Bitsy tried to make her point. "Yes, the heat is on. This is the capacity at which the facility can run."

Great. Just great. She was going to freeze her ass off down here, all while trying her very best to stay alive in the middle of the sea. Why had she thought this would be better?

Her skin prickled with the sensation of being watched. Which was crazy. She was losing her mind down here too now. Bending to pull the rest of the wetsuit off her other leg, she struggled to get it off and then tossed the offending suit as soon as it popped off her foot. Even though it was still cold, she was surprised at how much better she felt without the wetness pressed against her skin.

She must have torn a hole in it while they were going through those sharp corals. That's the only explanation for her being wet inside a suit that was rated for these depths.

For some reason, she turned back toward the tunnel and the room she'd originally been in. She didn't know why, perhaps it was some sixth sense because when she looked up, all she saw was red scales.

Red scales that connected to a dark black body and soulless eyes that watched her with a sense of hunger she hadn't seen in them before. His eyes were wide, his claws digging into the ground as he looked her up and down.

With a strange garble vibrating her throat, she pressed the suit against her breasts. He had been looking at her. Staring at her.... wanting her?

No, that wasn't possible. He was an undine. He was probably looking at her body like it was strange and uncomfortable, not intriguing. And that heat in his gaze was just because he was surprised to see her. And the way he licked his lips as he looked her up and down. That was just because he was... hungry. That was it.

But she couldn't help her own reaction to that expression. Clenching her thighs together, she grit her teeth against the unnatural reaction to him, as well. She was human. She shouldn't feel this way about a monstrous creature who had kidnapped her.

Her eyes still skated down the bulging muscles of his shoulders and the powerful flexing of his chest and ab muscles as he braced himself on that single arm. Those abs twitched at her stare, and she swore he flexed them just a bit harder.

Spinning, she turned herself beyond his sight and stepped away toward the lockers. Grabbing onto the fabric there, she shoved herself into the utilitarian body suit, and then grabbed a blanket off one of the bunks for good measure.

But, as she made her way down the tunnel back toward him, she couldn't help but feel like she was putting on clothes to stop herself from feeling anything. It wasn't a shield against his eyes. It was a promise to herself that she was covered, and coverings made it harder for her to want his eyes on her.

Because maybe she was a deviant who wanted him to look again.

Blowing out a long breath, she shook her head before stopping before him. "I didn't know when you were coming back."

From this angle, she was taller than him, but not by much. That massive arm still held him almost halfway out of the water. His serpentine tail disappeared into the dark, dingy water behind him. But from this angle, she was staring down into his face. He was so close she could see the water dripping off his hair and rolling down the mountains of his shoulders, pooling in the hollow of his collarbone.

She wanted to know what that pool of water tasted like.

Damn it, Anya, she told herself. Mind of out the gutter.

He nodded toward something to their right.

"Oh," she whispered. "You brought me a fish."

Bitsy highlighted an area beside her, bringing her attention back to the undine before her. And when she looked, she could see that his gaze was trailing down her body once more. Almost as though he were remembering what she'd looked like without her clothing.

A black tongue darted out as he licked his lips, and she couldn't look away from it. For a second she swore she saw bumps on that tongue, and it took everything in her to not squeeze her thighs together again.

Deviant. Wrong. She shouldn't be affected by a creature who looked like this. Not when she knew how sharp those teeth were and how much he had fought against her own people. He'd killed humans. Probably killed a lot of them. She was an idiot for even thinking....

He shoved himself forward. She watched as that thick tail coiled underneath him so he could loom above her. It was a slow rolling of his body, his face so close to her, and then it was miles and miles of hardened muscles dotted with scars.

His hand came up between them, those claws gently trailing up the fabric she now wore. She could feel the pull of the claw against every single button that it dragged against, each one sending a little popping jolt throughout her entire body as they snapped back against the fabric.

Finally, his claw eased up her neck, feather light and sending more goosebumps scattering wherever his touch lingered. With a gentle tap against her chin, he forced her to look up at him.

"You are pale everywhere," he said, his voice a low rumble that moved through her body with a white hot heat.

"Humans are usually the same color everywhere." She cleared her throat, feeling like it was a little hard to breathe. "We don't have patterns like..."

She didn't finish the sentence, because she'd focused a little too hard on the black lines that went from his collarbone and disappeared into the darkness of his tail. Because within those patterns were the gills on his ribs, and they were moving. Gently. Just a little.

Was being out of the water difficult for him? Could he even breathe?

She meant to ask, but then his thumb brushed over the peak of her breast. A lightning bolt shocked through her entire system, and she couldn't think. Couldn't even move as he did it again.

"Except here," he murmured. "Here you are not pale."

Fuck.

The slickness between her thighs rushed so quickly it was distracting. She had never thought... He couldn't know what he did. He didn't understand that humans were sensitive there.

He was curious about her kind, and the touch to him must be

innocent. She was over thinking this entire meeting, but she had to... to...

Swallowing hard, she nodded, still frozen with his hand against her breast. "Thank you for the fish."

When he didn't reply, she looked up into that hungry expression. His eyes reflected her own features back at her. The black orbs of his eyes showed a woman with bright red cheeks, a blush staining all the way down her throat and hidden beneath the ugly fabric of her clothing.

His claw tugged the lapel of her borrowed suit. "You turn so many colors, kalon. I can't wait to see how many."

And then he slipped back into the sea, leaving her breathless and so red she felt like her skin might melt off.

Chapter 15

Thoughts of the woman consumed him. Even when he wasn't in the facility with her, he couldn't force himself to go far.

Instead, he found himself sleeping just above the building. Suspended and held aloft by the sea, he let his tail drop to keep him still. And even in his dreams, his mind was consumed with the image of her.

The flashing of her eyes, bright and warm as she looked at his body. The way her cheeks had turned red with some warning sign that he didn't understand. In the moment, he'd been quite certain the red was likely a mating flush. Perhaps she was receptive to him, but he'd kept his body tilted. The lack of an arm was easy to ignore when she couldn't really see it. When she could pretend he was just holding that arm behind him so she couldn't see the nightmare he really was.

No matter how he tried to twist his dreams, his sleep was always troubled. In the end, she always denied him. Just as all the others had.

He was too big. Too dangerous. He was not a worthy mate and even the achromo knew that.

But he didn't even call her an achromo anymore, did he? Kalon was the name that he'd given her, and now he couldn't get it out of his head. His little kalon, and it made him all too pleased to say the word.

A warmth grew in his chest with every thought of her. Out of the facility, he let all the nervous energy flutter through his gills. The water even turned white around him with the breath that ripped out of him. Even his fluke fluttered for her, like he was nothing more than a child who had seen his first crush.

Daios had never acted this way before. He had to get control over himself. He needed to make sure she didn't have this much control over him.

Why? He didn't know.

Daios needed to bring her back with him to see the others. He needed her to see Mira and for them to explain the reasoning behind his taking of her. That was the only reason he'd been in Alpha, after all.

At least, until he'd seen her. Until he realized that some part of him wanted to keep her and worse? That the sea was pushing him in her direction as well.

It all felt rather fated, and he was overwhelmed. So overwhelmed that it made it hard to breathe in the murky waters his tail stirred up every time he moved.

Eventually, though, he'd gotten himself under control. He would return to his kalon—no, the woman—and he would tell her they were leaving. He would pry his icy claws out of her clothing when he had to hand her over, and then he would not look back. He would give her up, just as he was meant to do. Because that was his role in this life.

He was to sacrifice for others, and then he could truly protect them. Nothing could be more important than his people. Certainly not a mate.

Swimming up to the surface of her facility, he broke through the water, ready to tell her to get her things together.

But she was already sitting in that strange seat that moved all around the room, with her droid perched on her head. Her strange tails were crossed underneath her body, the angles of them looking rather painful. The expression on her face was one of sheer boredom as he first saw her, but all of that narrowed into determination as she caught sight of him.

It made him nervous.

Narrowing his own eyes at her, he opened his mouth to tell her they were leaving.

"My name is Anya," she said, her voice a little too loud for the room.

He froze, incapable of saying anything else. Had he gone all this time without asking her name? Had he spent all this time not realizing that she even had a name? That he could have called her something other than achromo or kalon?

He was going about this all wrong. Here he was, fluttering for her, and he didn't even know her name.

Blowing out a long breath, he stilled his gills and then pressed his clawed hand to his heart. "Daios."

"Is that your name?"

He nodded and watched as she curled in on herself. He couldn't tell if that was relief or not, at least until she looked up at him through the waterfall of her golden hair and smiled.

"It's nice to know you have a name, Daios."

And oh.

Oh.

The sound of his name on her tongue was exquisite. He'd never heard someone say it in those raspy tones, but even more than that, it was the way she lingered over the word. The sound was wrong, like she was trying to put her tongue around the taste of his name and he...

Fuck. He shouldn't be here. Already those gills around his neck were moving, and he wanted to slide back into the water and kill something for her. He wanted to return with blood all over his claws, dripping from his teeth as he presented her with a kill that would show her just how badly he wanted her. No. Needed her. He needed every ounce of her attention. He was greedy for the feeling of her eyes sliding along his skin. And he would lay his body flat on the sands and pray to his gods for years, if that's what it took to feel her touch him again.

"Daios," she repeated. This time she looked at him, and he had to struggle to not roll his eyes back in his skull at the sound of his name on her lips. "I think we should talk."

He could listen to her talk for hours. But he had a feeling that wasn't what she was suggesting.

All he could manage was a low grunt, and then a wave of his hand.

She nodded, her eyes flicking back to her fingers. He watched as she moved them in her lap, curling them together and then untwisting them. "I have not been entirely truthful with you. I know you took me for your own reasons, and I have the suspicion that they are similar to my reasons for wanting to leave. You dislike my father. Is that correct?"

He bared his teeth in a low growl. How was he supposed to tell her how he hated her father? That Alpha was at the top of all the cities that were ruining his home, and now that he knew they were helping to control all of it? He wanted to destroy it all from the inside out.

She observed his expression and then nodded. "That's what I thought. I know you might not believe me, but I feel the same way about him."

She dropped one foot onto the floor, rocking the chair back and forth. The sharp squeal of it filled the room, before he leaned forward and stopped her movements. The strange look on her face had him shrugging.

"Loud," he said, pointing to his ears.

She bit her lip, then rasped. "Sorry. Can't hear it."

With a small nod, he moved back into the water, pleased that she stayed where she was this time. High-pitched noise no longer distracting him, he again waved his hand for her to continue.

"I think it's fairly obvious that my father is controlling. But it went beyond that. He was obsessive about my safety, although only because I had use. I was his songbird, his figurehead, the person that convinced everyone how great he was. The better I was doing, the more of a symbol I became." Her cheeks puffed out before she blurted, "My mother would have been that person if she hadn't died. Instead, I was the person who had to convince them all how great he was. Even though he wasn't."

Something coiled in his chest. It reached through his skin, forcing his hand out of the water. With a gentle touch to the bottom of her foot, he tried his best to show whatever comfort he could. Even if it was strange to touch what felt like bone underneath too thin skin.

At her sharp look, he moved the hand and pressed it against his own heart. "My mother died."

"I'm so sorry to hear that."

He nodded, claws curling over his right heart until he could feel the pinpricks digging into his skin. "The pain never goes away."

Another flash of emotion crossed in front of her eyes before she shrugged. "I never knew her."

He mirrored her shrug, and with a grunt added, "And yet, the pain still exists."

Her lips parted in surprise, and he couldn't stop staring at them. Why were they so pink? He'd never seen that color under the ocean, only when he had gone to the surface a few times. He'd seen similar hues in the sky up there. When the blue above the waves turned to streaks of bright pink and purple before the sun set and the moon rose on the horizon.

"I've been working for years with a group of people trying to take Alpha apart from the inside out."

The words shocked him. He opened his mouth, likely to lecture her on the dangers of such things, but all that came out was, "You?"

That bright red color burned through her cheeks, and he second guessed that the shade had anything to do with mating readiness. "Yes, me. Why? Do I not look like I'm capable of that?"

"But you're so... so..." He looked her up and down before blurting, "Small."

"What does size have to do with anything?"

Suddenly, he was angry with her. She thought size had nothing to do with keeping herself safe? She was so tiny and here she was, thinking she could take on a city as powerful as Alpha. One that he and his people had been fighting for ages. She thought she could do what his people could not?

With a flick of his tail, he lifted himself out of the water. His lunge brought him all the way to her side, where he braced himself against the strange contraption she sat in. Together, they wheeled back until her chair hit the glowing boxes against the glass. There they stayed, with him looming over her while his arm held him away from her.

Trembling with rage, he already knew the lights on his body

danced with his emotion. The red illumination caught on the edges of her face, lighting her up from every angle.

"You think size has nothing to do with it?" he snarled, his teeth snapping in her direction. "How could you keep yourself safe? I see no claws, no teeth, no natural way to protect yourself. Tell me again how you, of all creatures, are able to protect yourself?"

He'd expected her to cower. Most people he tried to intimidate trembled beneath him, shaking as the fear spread throughout their form until they could think of nothing and no one but him. A monster was before her, covering her body with his and threatening her very life. He bared his teeth, slowly moving closer and closer to her face until he could feel the quick puffs of her breath against his lips.

This was what he wanted. Wasn't it? He wanted her fear. He wanted to know what that tasted like as it ran through his gills, because he was certain it would taste like all the other achromos he'd hunted.

But she was... Anya.

Not an achromo he'd been ordered to kill. She was the woman who had shown him kindness, who had no fear of touching him, and the one who had looked him in the eyes and not flinched when he'd done everything in his power to terrify her.

She watched him, her eyes maybe a little wider than they were before. But then her hand lifted, and she placed it where his neck met his shoulder. Just above the wound that had taken so much from him.

"Bitsy," she said, and the name made him realize she was talking to her little droid. "Shock him."

Shock him? What were they about to do? Change their skin into a different color so he was surprised?

But then he felt a zing of pain jolting through his body from where her hand touched him. He winced, even though it was only enough to contract his neck muscles. He moved toward her touch, his teeth bared with anger as he endured her torture.

The pain stopped as soon as it started. He remained where he was, his head turned into her hand as he got himself under control.

"I'm not without my own tricks," she said. "But I do agree that you're more powerful than I am. But you're more powerful than any of my kind, aren't you?"

He winced. "This strength is a curse."

"Is it?" She'd left her hand on his shoulder, and this time her fingers dug into the muscles there. "I wish I was as strong as you. I wouldn't be afraid of anything."

Daios wanted to turn to her and say that he would keep her safe. If she wished to send him out into the world as her weapon of destruction, he would massacre anything in her way.

But those thoughts were madness. They were the sickness that toyed at the edges of his thoughts.

Instead, he leaned down and nipped at the delicate flesh of her wrist. He didn't break through her skin, although he could feel how easy that would be. Instead, he left tiny red marks that dotted all along her arm as she drew it away from him.

Her catch of breath filled him with purpose. Gently, still holding onto her wrist with his teeth, he licked the sensitive skin there. His gaze caught hers as the rough bumps of his tongue toyed over her rapid pulse.

He might not know what the red coloring of her skin was, but she couldn't hide how her pupils blew the moment he made contact. And gods, the way she tasted.

He had to stop before he did something they both would regret.

"You thought to destroy your own father?" he asked, trying his best to get control over his emotions. He could taste her on his tongue. A soft pop of flavor that was earthy and real. "How long was that going to take?"

"Years of my life," she whispered, her wide eyes meeting his. "Many, many years. We planned for a very long time, and you ruined that plan by showing up when you did."

"And stealing you away?"

"No, we had someone sneaking into the city." Again, her breath puffed across his lips. "He was caught because my father made sure there was no one coming in or out of the city while you were somehow sneaking in. But I think this might be even better."

"Why's that?"

"Because now we have you." Her eyes flicked from his, down to his lips, then back up again. "Now we have you, and I think you want to destroy that city just as much as I do. Am I right?"

"If you want to kill your father, kalon, then I will help you kill him."

"My name is Anya," she corrected.

"I know." He forced himself to push away from her, to give them both space to breathe when all he wanted was to taste her again. He wanted to know what every part of her tasted like.

Daios wanted to drag her into the water and taste her through his sensitive gills. But he couldn't. Shouldn't. Didn't need to, because all of this was just the insanity in his head telling him to do something that would lead to the most destruction.

Slipping into the water, he left her behind before he could do something insane. Like lick her from head to toe.

Chapter 16

She dreamt she was back in Alpha. Stuck in her room, just like she always was. The walls were warped though, and it felt like everything was melting into her. Hot, molten drops that clung to her hair and skin, pinning her in place until she couldn't breathe.

The dream shifted, warping, so she found herself walking through the streets of Alpha and everyone was looking at her. Staring. Talking. In her mind, she knew they were wondering where she had gotten off to. Clearly there was something wrong with the General's daughter if she was able to disappear for days on end.

But even in her dreams, she couldn't hear them speak. It was just the low rumble of nothingness that, no matter how hard she tried to hear, she couldn't understand.

Walking through a crowd with no understanding of what they were saying was a dangerous game to play in this place. It felt like they were all plotting against her. They wanted her out of their city, no longer their problem after all she had done. What kind of person plotted to destroy her home? She'd always been a problem, anyway.

In her dream, she walked through the streets and knew that everyone didn't want her there. They wanted a figurehead like her mother. They'd wanted the pretty little bird, caught in her cage, a creature who sang when they told her to.

Everyone wanted the golden child of the General who soaked up all their love and attention and told them in not so many words that she appreciated them. They wanted her to fawn over their generosity and allow them to play with the pretty doll she'd become.

But that wasn't what she wanted. Even as a child, she found their attention to be uncomfortable. She hated how they looked at her like she was a pet for them to indulge with treats and a soft pat to her head.

She was more than that. She'd always been more than that.

Her father approached her, a disappointed expression on his face. But when had he looked at her with anything else?

"Your mother would have been better suited," he said, and she could hear what he was saying. Of all the voices she'd forgotten, the sound of her father's was never one of them. Because he'd said these words before she lost her hearing. He'd said them right before she was the stupid one who had harmed herself so badly that he would never look at her the same way again.

And then, suddenly, she was back in that memory. The worst memory she ever had.

She was so much smaller, standing in front of the door that led to the armory where her father kept all the weapons. He stared down at her and repeated the words that had cut her to the core.

"Your mother would have been better suited," he said, his face creasing in a deep frown that made him appear so much more severe. Every time. "She would have known that even speaking about the undines in public was a foolish move. You have never failed to disappoint me, girl, and that's not something you should be proud of."

She wasn't. But he'd never made her feel proud of herself.

Anya flinched in on herself, rounding her shoulders as his hand lifted. He was going to hit her, like he always did. A sharp slap across her cheek, and no one ever mentioned that there were red marks every time they saw her. They just looked at the General and knew, with blind faith, that he would do whatever it took to keep them safe.

Even hit his own daughter.

The pain didn't come. Instead, the door to the armory opened and a young man froze in the entry way. He looked between her and her father, and she saw the pity on his face. She knew it was meant for her, and that stung so much more than she had expected.

He was handsome. Young. He had broad shoulders and a sharp jaw that she'd always found so attractive. In another circumstance, she might have cocked her teenaged hip and hoped she didn't look like a little tumble weed who had yet to grow into her body.

"Sir?" he'd asked. And oh, she hadn't thought about his voice in such a long time. It was so buttery smooth. The voice of a man who could sing and she would have been captivated by the sound of his words.

"Yes, yes," her father grumbled, leading them into the armory. "Don't touch anything, Anya. For once, keep your hands to yourself."

She'd curved even more into her body with embarrassment. Anya didn't want that young man to think she was a burden on her father. She didn't try to disappoint anyone, but sometimes she was curious and she didn't think that was such a bad thing. Curiosity made her want to see more things. To believe that she was more than just a doll for her father to set up in a corner and for other people to look at.

But then she'd seen it.

The back corner of the room had a table where all the prototypes were laid out. They were... marvelous. Beautiful. They made her want to touch things, even though her father had said not to.

For a while, she curled her hands into fists and promised herself that she would be good. This time, she'd be good.

Maybe she could ask her father's guard, who usually followed her, to bring her back. She could ask questions about the prototypes, what they were, what they were meant to do.

Her father left the room with the handsome young boy. He walked right out, leaving her standing there with her hands twisting in her pale green skirts.

No, they'd been blue. She'd been wearing her favorite blue dress with the white collar and shoes that made her feel taller. Not quite heels, because her father said she'd break her ankle, but they were black and had thin straps that made her feel so pretty.

Her father and the young man had walked out of the room and she had reached for one of the prototypes. They were usually weapons to fight against the undines and any other creature that might attack their city. But this one didn't look like a weapon at all. It was a small silver ball, with colors glowing in between the plates.

She'd thought it looked rather pretty and held it up in front of her face. There was a button on the side, she discovered. So small she might have missed it.

In her dream, she screamed at herself not to touch it. Put it down. Don't be the daughter that your father always believed you were.

But of course, she pressed the button.

An ocean of pain seared through her body. The sound that came out of that ball was so explosively loud that she felt her entire body just... stop working. In one second, she could hear the shrieking rage of her father's newest toy, and the next, nothing at all.

Just a pounding in her skull that was unlike any headache she had ever had, and a vibration in her ribs that she thought might be from the ball itself. She thought maybe she passed out, because she blinked and suddenly she was on the floor. The ball had rolled away from her grip and the first thought she had was that she had to pretend she hadn't touched anything. Her father was going to find out. He was going to kill her if she didn't pretend that none of this had happened.

Scrambling across the floor, she'd reached for it. But it was still flashing that awful red color that she'd seen right before it had made the horrible noise. So she pressed the button again, and the rattling in her ribs stopped when it went blue.

She'd thought everything was fine until she noticed movement to her left and realized that her father's mouth was moving. But she couldn't hear a word he said.

Shaking, she'd lifted her hands to her ears and when she brought them back down, her fingers were coated with blood.

God, she hated this memory. Not because she was ashamed of losing her hearing, but that it was her fault. She'd been the one to hurt herself, and she couldn't blame anyone else. Sure, her father probably shouldn't have left her in a room full of dangerous weapons. She had been a child, and leaving a kid in a room like that was bound to be terrible.

And yet, it was still her fault. She would carry that on her shoulders for the rest of her life.

Slowly, she realized there were fingers running through her hair. Not in the dream, not in that place of pain and memories that made her heart ache. No. There were fingers brushing the snarls out of her hair in the waking world.

For a second, time melded together. She must be back in Alpha, where there was a kinder maid who wanted to wake her out of a nightmare. But these fingers were broader, thicker, and there were delicate claws gently raking along her scalp.

Fingers that couldn't belong to anything other than the monstrous creature who she should be terrified of. And yet, she had never been able to bring herself to be scared of him.

Opening her eyes, she slowly rolled over to see that he had dragged himself out of the water and down the hall. His massive tail was still halfway in the hall, the fluke flat against the floor, with water dripping from the red tinged scales. He'd hooked the stump of his missing arm between the bedframe and the mattress and was gently, ever so gently, brushing her hair with his claws.

Her breath caught in her lungs. She had no idea why he was touching her, only that it made everything in her stop. All the anxiety. All the fear. All the self hatred melted out with the tension in her body as she sank into his touch.

His expression was almost serene as she turned, his gaze on the long locks of her blonde hair. She'd never seen that expression on his face, and it disappeared the moment he met her gaze with those black eyes and realized she was looking back at him.

He said something, sliding back down onto the floor and starting to push himself back with that one arm. It looked awkward and laborious and not at all what she wanted him to do.

"Wait," she said, scrambling to reach for Bitsy and before sliding the lens over her eye. "Wait, you don't have to go."

He was still moving, though, and she didn't want him to leave. Not yet. Something inside her screamed that she wanted to feel him brushing her hair again, and it wasn't fair that he'd stopped.

That touch had brought her out of a nightmare. She didn't feel like a failure when she'd woken. All she'd felt was his fingers and the glorious sensation of being touched.

"Daios, please."

He froze where he was, lying flat on the floor even as she joined him. Anya slipped out of her warm bed and sat down on the cold floor, just staring at him. She didn't know what to say. All she knew was that he had to stay, or all those feelings would come back.

"I didn't know you could be out of the water," she tried, her throat aching with the words.

His deep grunt flashed in front of her eyes, before he said, "That's what you have to say?"

"It seems like a rather surprising detail I didn't know about you, so yes."

Another grunt illustrated by a vibrating mass of coiled lines around him.

He stayed braced, leaning on one arm as all his muscles flexed to keep him upright. She thought, maybe it would be more comfortable if he would just let himself go. He didn't have to angle his body away from her. He didn't have to hide the missing arm he was clearly so embarrassed about.

Instead of saying any of that, or even trying to talk to him, she pulled the pillow off the bed and punched it a few times. Stuffing it underneath her head, she laid on the cold metal floor and wiggled her shoulders like she was getting comfortable.

Words flashed in front of her eyes. "What are you doing?"

"Can you keep brushing my hair, please? It wasn't a pleasant dream and I don't feel like myself." She kept her gaze on the ceiling, hoping that he would move a little closer to her. She'd once gotten a stray dog to take food out of her hand like this before.

Just don't look at the dangerous predator, and maybe it would trust her.

There was the faintest vibration of scales rasping against the metal floor, and then the delicate feeling of his claws running through her hair. "Don't look," he said, his voice a low hum against her ear. "What was the dream?"

Of course, she was going to look when someone told her that. He froze again, his fingers in her hair still. He was stretched out as far as he could get. Flat on his belly, the stump of his arm slightly propping his body up. But his cheek rested against his bicep and his good arm reached all the way out so just his fingers were close to her.

Pillowing her own cheek on her hand, she rolled in his direction. "I'm not bothered by it, you know."

He swallowed hard. "The dream?"

"Your arm." She let her gaze actually go to the end of it, and he couldn't move to hide it. Not in this position. "It doesn't make you any less than what you already are."

Daios winced. "You are one of the few to believe that."

"Do you believe it?"

She watched the emotions flicker across his face. Surprise. Heartache. Shock that maybe he didn't.

Licking her lips, she added, "Why don't you believe it?"

"Right now?" His voice deepened even more, a rumble of some creature in the depths. She felt that dark, deep voice all the way to her very core. "Because if I was whole, I could brace myself above you and still touch you. I wouldn't have to lie on my belly just to feel the softness of your hair."

Oh.

Pressing her thighs together against the sudden rush of desire that went through her entire body, she tried very hard not to think of him braced above her. Those muscles flexing and those sharp teeth bared even though she knew he would only bite her if she wanted him to. And strangely enough, she thought maybe it wouldn't be so bad if he did bite her.

He was odd to look at, but he was... also very thrilling.

Swallowing hard, she nodded. "Ah. I understand."

"I don't think you do, kalon." His fingers moved in her hair, gently placing every single strand in a perfect coil to rest against her neck. "I don't think you could understand."

Whatever madness was between them, she wanted to feed it. She moved quickly, certain he wouldn't like her plan if he knew what she was doing. So with a quick bunching of muscles, she lunged for him. One moment, she was lying in front of him, and the next she'd crawled on top of him.

Daios rolled between her legs, his eyes wide with shock and his teeth bared as though he thought she was attacking him. But his fingers were so gentle on her thighs as he grabbed one with his hand.

Hands braced against his chest, she held herself safely on top of him. It wasn't where she'd thought she would end up. Especially considering he was so big her thighs were stretched a little wider than was comfortable.

And for god's sake, that made her think of things she really shouldn't be thinking of.

It took every ounce of her strength not to moan when she felt the ridged muscles of his upper abdomen pressed against her pussy. She wanted to grind down on him. To feel the undulating power of his muscles underneath her, but that wasn't what she was proving here.

"See?" she said, feeling like her voice had maybe changed a bit. It certainly had come from a much deeper part of her throat. "You don't need to brace yourself over me at all. I can do that for you."

Those dark eyes turned even darker, and she could see the hunger in him. He tried his best to stay still and not move, but that tail lashed behind her once, twice, three times before he stilled it. "And what now, kalon?"

"You can touch me without having to choose if you want to be close to me or touch." She swallowed hard. "My hair, I mean. I quite like it when you touch my hair."

Touch me everywhere, she thought. She wanted him to slide that hand up her side. She wanted to know what would happen if he cupped her breast, or if he would use those claws to rip through the fabric of her clothes.

These were dangerous thoughts. Terrible thoughts. She knew there was probably a special place for deviant women who looked at a monster and wondered what he would feel like between her thighs, but... Fuck. These were where her thoughts were.

His hand moved, but only to cup her cheek and jaw in that massive palm. "So many thoughts running through your head right now. I wonder why."

She couldn't tell him what she was really thinking. He'd... maybe do something neither of them could come back from.

"I just don't understand why you don't like what you look like." She tapped the side of the droid on her head. "I wear this. You're missing an arm. But I don't think less of myself because I can't hear what people are saying."

His brows furrowed. "I have no interest in talking about the loss of my arm."

"I'm not asking how you lost it. I'm asking why you hate it so much."

She was pushing him. Too far, considering the coiled tension beneath her, that only made her think about what it would be like if he was tense for another reason.

The frown on his face was one of his tells, but so were the bunched up muscles of his traps. Anya blamed sleep deprivation for the reason why she wanted to run her fingers over that strange, gray skin and see if it was as soft as it looked.

Instead, she used her fingers for something else. Something to distract the both of them. Flicking her fingers and twisting her hands in a repetitive motion. A word, a name, words that needed no sound.

He watched the movement with narrowed eyes. "I have seen you do this before, but not often. What does it mean?"

"That meant... uh... Big man," she said, her cheeks burning. "Or, Daios. I suppose."

"What is the language?"

"Sign." She shrugged. "It's hard to remember all of it. Like any language, the less you use it, the less easy it is to remember. There are only a few people with hearing issues in Alpha, and most of us have a droid like Bitsy. But I remember a lot of it."

She signed with every word that she said, watching as his eyes flew with her fingers.

He watched every single word with rapt attention before saying, "It is a beautiful language."

Anya grinned. "I think so, too. I like talking with my hands."

"I would ask you to teach me, kalon, but..." He released his grasp on the side of her cheek and lifted his single hand between them.

But no, that wouldn't do at all. She grabbed his fingers in hers and gently lifted his knuckles to her lips. With a soft kiss on the back of those deadly claws, she met his dark-eyed gaze and said, "You can still sign with one hand."

He looked up at her like she'd told him that she could give him back his arm. Or maybe, just maybe, that expression meant that he was grateful to her for not making him feel less than.

She didn't know. All she knew was that it made her squirm on top of him until he grabbed her thigh once more. Those thick, broad fingers squeezed hard before he growled, "Show me."

If she had to spend the rest of the night teaching him the basics of sign, she would. Because right now, in the darkness of this abandoned facility, all she wanted was to spend time with this curious man who had captured her attention.

Chapter 17

He didn't know when he became so comfortable around her. It was probably the first moment when he saw her in the water and realized how weak she was. The achromos were dangerous creatures who could surprise him with their violence. But Anya?

Anya didn't have a violent bone in her body.

Not even when she'd leapt on top of him, and he was quite certain she wanted to hurt him. He had, after all, kidnapped her from her home. He'd dragged her down into the frigid depths where she shivered every night.

Instead, she'd asked him to touch her. Even thinking about it made his cocks press against the scales that held them in place. He'd fisted himself multiple times to the memory of her twin tails on either side of his stomach. He'd felt the heat of her between her twin tails and it...

He couldn't think of that now. Not when he was about to see her again, and he had no way of knowing what he might do. Daios wanted to pull her over him like she'd been before, but this time he wanted to use his muscles to grind up on her. He wanted to yank her into the water and show her why the ocean was so much better than being in the air.

He wanted to taste her. Not just to lick her skin, but to draw her scent into his gills and drown himself in every flavor she might give him.

Stilling his thoughts, he poked his head out of the water and peered into her room. He had a fish in his hands, much smaller since she'd wasted the last tuna he'd brought her. But this time, he'd also been stupid. He'd brought a string of oysters with him. It was a foolish idea. A silly hope that bloomed in his chest and one he crushed just as quickly.

She was sitting in front of the consoles, as she called them, Bitsy in front of her face and a projection out in front of her again.

"No, Ace, you can't go in that way. No, I'm not just saying that. Would you look at the damn schematics again before you just start yelling? Look at it." Her words were flying on the glass after she said them, but no other voice replied to her.

He laid the fish out and then tried his best to quietly set down the oysters, but they clacked together. The damn shells were louder than he wanted them to be, and the droid must have told Anya he was here. She spun around in the chair only moments after the sound.

It didn't escape his notice that she turned with a bright grin on her face. One that made his heart thunder in his chest.

"Ace, I gotta go." That smile shifted into a glare as she turned her attention from him to the glass in front of her eye. "No, I'm not leaving you at the worst time. This is a terrible plan. Come up with something better, and we'll chat again soon."

She swiped a finger through the projection before she looked back at him with that bright grin. "Sorry about that. No rest for the wicked, as they say."

"I don't understand that phrase." He pushed the oysters a little closer to her. "I brought you something."

"I can see." She slid down from the chair to sit on the floor, as she had many times since he'd brought her here. With her twin tails folded, she picked up the oysters. "Am I supposed to eat them?"

"You can. They are best raw."

Her little nose wrinkled, and he was concerned by how much he thought it was adorable. The fondness for her that stretched through his chest was almost painful at this point. Arges had been right, he hated to admit. She'd wriggled her way underneath his skin, just by being herself.

Never in his life had he thought an achromo could treat him like a person. But he supposed Anya wasn't like the other achromos. She couldn't be.

He smiled at her, not even noticing the expression crossing his face before she pointed at him.

"You're smiling."

"I don't even know what that means."

"You know what a smile is." The wrinkles above her nose were now joined by twin dashes between her eyes. A sure sign she was upset with him. "You were smiling at me, but now it's gone."

He tried his best to mimic what he thought she wanted, but even he could feel the bared teeth were more a grimace than a smile.

She shook her head. "No, that's not it. You get little wings around your eyes when you smile."

"Are you saying I have wrinkles?"

"Yes." She grinned, and this time he couldn't help but follow suit.

She stared at him with that goofy expression and he could feel a matching one on his own face. This was stupid. But it sent a thrill throughout his entire body because he kind of loved it at the same time.

He didn't remember the last time he'd been able to just... be. And Anya wanted that. She seemed to like it when he was himself, even if that self was a gruff bastard with an angry streak. She didn't mind that he mostly grunted in response to her questions, even though he tried to answer them.

He was rusty at this. Conversing. Being around other people in a way that wasn't just arguing about plans of attack or a need for violence.

Planting her hand on the floor, she pushed herself a little closer to him. This time, she didn't kneel on those strange tails. She wrapped them around each other with those horrible bones sticking out in all directions.

"Is that comfortable?" he asked before he could stop himself.

She looked up from the oysters she'd brought with her. "Is what comfortable?"

He gestured up and down her body.

She seemed confused before it dawned on her what he was trying to say. "Oh! You mean my legs?"

Legs, right. That's what Mira always called them. He had a hard time thinking of them as anything other than tails, but they didn't work like tails. He knew that.

Frowning, he nodded before reaching out to touch a finger to one of the sharp bones. "They do not seem like they should do this."

"They're fine," she replied with a small chuckle. She dragged the oysters into her lap, the cold water staining the fabric around her limbs a darker color. "I forget we're so different sometimes. I must seem so strange looking to you."

"You are quite ugly." The honesty made her tilt her head back and laugh so hard her face turned bright red.

He didn't mean it to sound as terrible as it did. She wasn't so ugly that he didn't want to look at her, but she wasn't exactly... Well, she wasn't a graceful and beautiful female floating through the water with a long tail and fins that helped her skate through the waves. She was an achromo.

It was hard to get used to.

She stopped laughing, wiping her fingers under her eyes as she gathered up the tears that streamed down her cheeks. He felt a little bad for that, although he hadn't thought it would make her cry. Honesty had always been his greatest weapon.

And now he realized what a weapon it could be.

Grabbing onto her arm, he gently pulled her hands away from her face so he could smooth away the tears himself. They were surprisingly warm on his fingers. "I'm sorry. I didn't mean to make you upset."

"You didn't." She held onto his wrist, that grin not moving from her face. "Laughing sometimes makes me cry. They're tears of mirth, not tears of sadness."

Ah. Well, at least he'd gotten to touch her. And suddenly, all he could focus on was the soft texture of her skin. The way her eyelashes flicked against the webs of his fingers when she blinked, and how soft and plush her lips were, just a hair's breadth away from his claws.

With a soft trailing of his fingers, he released her. Even though he didn't want to stop touching her.

He kept their gazes locked as he slowly licked her tears off his fingertips. She watched every single movement, and he swore her chest didn't even rise with a breath. She just watched him, her eyes slowly turning more lidded as her gaze locked on his fingers.

"You taste like the sea," he rasped. "My favorite flavor."

He watched her throat work in a gulp. He wondered if that was fear or something else he saw in her eyes. It was hard to read this achromo, no matter how hard he tried. She surprised him more than he wished to admit.

Her gaze dropped back to the oysters in her lap, and when she responded, it was with that throaty tone that always made him painfully hard. "Why did you bring me oysters? Just to eat?"

No. Not just to eat, although now he didn't think she should eat them at all. They were delicious delicacies, not to be looked at with a nose wrinkle like they were disgusting.

Sighing, he reached for the strand and plucked one off of it. "Not just to eat."

Using his claw, he balanced the oyster on the metal floor and then wedged his nail inside of it. Anya's hand darted out, holding onto the oyster to keep it steady for him.

He looked up at her with an unimpressed expression.

"It's easier if I hold it for you," she said.

"No, it is not."

"It definitely is." She blew out a breath to move the hair that had fallen in front of her eyes. "You're going to cut yourself or me. Just let me hold it while you open the thing."

Baring his teeth at her, he flared all his fins wide to make himself even larger than he already was. She should have run from him screaming. Instead, she just puffed her cheeks up and squared her shoulders.

Like she was mimicking him.

His fins flattened to his sides with a snap. That was… unexpected, but he supposed she might help him if she wished. "Hold it steady then."

"That's what I thought."

Grumbling under his breath about foolish females taking too many risks, he finally got the damn thing open. He let the shells fall to each side, choosing to ignore the tiny wrinkle of her nose—again—as she looked at the pale meat inside.

"You eat that raw?" she asked, clearly struggling. "It looks so... so..."

"Delicious?" he asked, using his claw to scrape it from the shell. He was a little disappointed it didn't contain what he'd hoped, but it would still taste as good as always. "Nutritious? Like food that is much better than the food I have brought you before?"

"Wet."

He slurped it from the shell before dropping the empty halves in the water. She was right, it was a little wet. Oysters were always soft and tasted like the sea where they grew. These were particularly briny, which he quite enjoyed.

Taking the next one off, he waited for her to balance it before prying it open again. "They are wet, I suppose."

"What do they taste like?"

"Salty."

That damned wrinkle deepened. It made him want to press his thumb there, to ease the tension from her features.

"You're not really making these sound good," she said with a soft laugh. "Wet and salty isn't on my list of things that I like to eat."

He opened the next one a little harder, and his claw thunked against the metal floor. "I am wet and salty."

She blinked, her mind clearly trying to catch up to what he had just said. He wasn't even sure why he had said it. He was wet and salty, but what did it matter if she didn't like those things? Sure, he had tasted her tears. The flavor was still on his tongue as one of the best he'd ever tasted, even better than the oysters he had brought her.

It didn't matter if she didn't like him. He was her captor. He didn't even know what he was doing with her here or why he was keeping her here for such a long time.

It was wrong. He was wrong. Everything about this situation was wrong, and he should...

Her hand touched his jaw, gently stroking down his neck to his gills. "Thankfully, I have no intention of eating you. So it doesn't matter if I don't like wet and salty foods."

Right. He was overreacting.

Grunting, he ran his claw over the oyster to find that there was exactly what he was looking for inside of it. Nerves churned in his belly.

She had no way of knowing that, step by step, he'd been completing a mating process that was as old as time. His ancestors had done it years and years ago. They were the ones who had started this ritual by listening to their gut and the sea who guided them. She didn't know what it meant when he brought her food, or that he had kept her to himself so no other competing males could find her.

The last time he'd tried any of this, he'd been shot down so quickly it had made his gills ache. He'd been told he was too large, too bumbling, and that his hunting skills were lacking. Back then, he'd brought his chosen one a necklace made of bones. The back of it had been a massive shark jaw, and she'd looked at him like he was a fool.

Perhaps he should tell her. He should probably explain why he was doing all this and yet, that same instinct told him not to. Hooking his finger around his treasure, he held it up so she could see it.

A tiny, pale pearl perched on his claw. He had a feeling she would have the same reaction as all the other females before. It was too small, too dull. A pearl like this wasn't nearly enough to impress a female like Anya.

But then her breath rushed out of her lungs in a very long, "Oh."

Anya reached for the pearl, her hand shaking as she took it off his claw. Like she was scared that the slightest breath on it would make it tumble from his grip and she would lose it.

She cradled it in one hand, turning it this way and that in the light. "I've only seen these..." She lost her words, her hands fluttering with movement that was so pretty he forgot it was a language. He should be listening to her, but instead, he was just enjoying the way her hands moved.

He tried to catch what she was saying, but there weren't a lot of words there that he knew. He could only wait until she finally gathered herself enough to say, "This is so pretty. I've seen pearls before. I just... I've never seen where they came from."

"You like it?"

"I really do," she breathed, her voice the tiniest whisper that was so hard to hear. "It's beautiful. Are there more?"

He gestured to all the oysters beside her. "We won't know until we find them."

"Oh." She sniffed hard, and he eyed her to make sure she wasn't crying again. "I feel bad that we have to kill them to get the pearls."

His teeth flashed in a dark grin. "I was going to eat them anyway, kalon."

Her eyes widened a bit, but then she grinned right back at him. "Okay, then. If you're sure."

He touched his claws to his hearts and then gestured to the other oysters. "I am certain. They cannot feel much pain. Now, let's gather you a fist full of pearls."

"Why?" Her gaze searched his. "Why did you bring these to me?"

His mouth opened, the words ready to fall from his lips.

Because I want to keep you for myself.

Because if I keep you, feed you, bring you everything you ever dreamt of, maybe you'll give me a chance.

Because no one has made me want them as much as I want you.

Instead, what he said was, "I wanted to."

Her lips twisted into a little half smile. "A man of many words, aren't you?"

But he knew that expression on her face. He could see the way the half smile stayed, and her eyes crinkled just a little. There was a sparkle in her gaze as she held out the next oyster for him to open with his claw. All of this meant she was amused by him. That she... maybe enjoyed his company.

Daios didn't know what to do with any of that. People tolerated him, they didn't enjoy him being around. He was too difficult, too forward, and certainly too angry for anyone to really want to spend time with.

So all he could do in response was grunt, open the next one with a sharp twist of his nail, and then smile at her chortle of glee.

"There's another one!"

Heart squeezing, he told himself to store this memory away for when he no longer had her. Her happiness was a fleeting moment he would cling to for the rest of his life. He scooped the next pearl out for her, so she wouldn't have to touch the oyster she found so disgusting. "Here you are, kalon. Another for your collection."

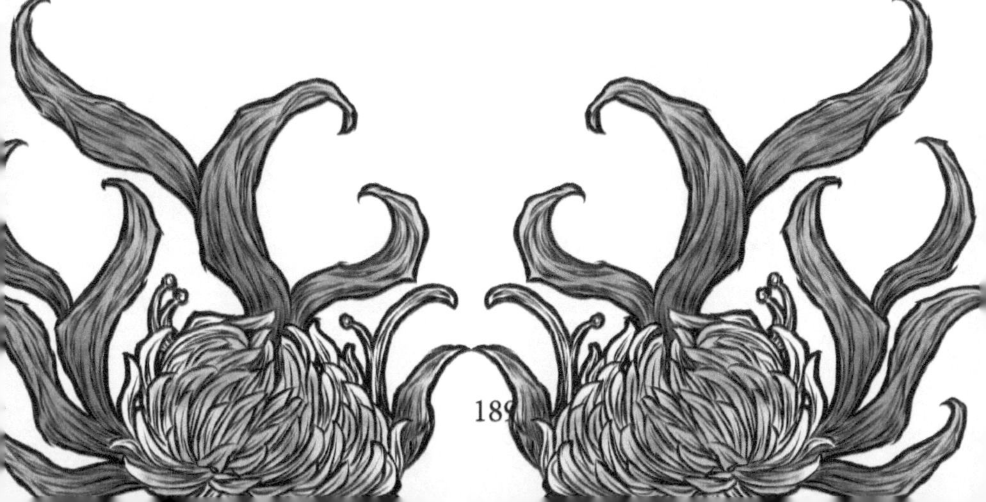

Chapter 18

She'd gotten used to their routines, although she still wasn't sure why she was here. Bitsy had pointed it out multiple times. He'd kidnapped her. Taken her away from the city for a reason, and she hadn't delved into the why.

But did it matter? She was out of Alpha. No one knew where she was yet, and she was able to work with Ace as often as she needed to figure out a new plan. Not that they were getting anywhere with that. Alpha was shut down after her disappearance, apparently, and no one was entering or exiting the city.

"Your father is in a rage," she read on the screen as Ace sent their newest message. "Tearing the whole city apart."

She braced her feet up on the consoles in front of her and wrapped the blanket around her shoulders a little tighter. "Good. He deserves to be a little scared after everything he's done."

"It's affecting our plan."

"What do you want me to do?" She dropped her feet onto the ground with a hard thud. "Do you want me to go back?"

There was a long pause before three little bubbles blinked in front of her eyes. Clearly, Ace was typing. And her little droid thought it was smart to let her know that Ace was typing, then deleting, then typing more, as her partner tried very hard to figure out what to say.

"What do you mean, go back?" Ace finally asked.

Shit. She hadn't told Ace she had left, had she? That was a problem. The lie she'd originally told her counterpart was that she was still in Alpha, but she was safe in a new place where her father couldn't find her. That was easy enough to pretend.

But she couldn't keep lying if they were going to make this work. "Bitsy," she said, pinching between her eyes. "Send Ace my location."

When she finally opened her eyes, there were words hovering in front of the consoles. "Are you sure?"

"Yes, I'm sure. Someone needs to know where I am, just in case something goes wrong."

Bitsy played an animation of an envelope throwing itself into the wind. At least now she knew someone would come to recover her body if she froze to death here. Her gaze caught on movement in the murk beyond the facility. She really wished there was a light out there. Because it seemed like nothing came to this area of the ocean. She hadn't even seen a fish, but she was quite certain they were out there.

Frowning, she leaned forward to stare off into the distance. "Bitsy, do you see anything in the water?"

Her droid turned its attention to the glass even as Ace sent a message through. "What do you mean, you're in the middle of the ocean? Where the fuck are you?"

"An abandoned research facility, I think," she replied, leaning even closer to the glass. "It was one of my father's failed experiments, I guess."

"How the fuck has no one caught you yet?"

"I don't know. Bitsy is using minimal energy and redirected it all. Unless someone is actively looking at this space, I don't think they'll realize I'm here if the energy output is the same."

Of course, it would be nice if she had some heat. She was so tired of being cold all the time.

There was something in the murk, after all. She barely saw the tail that cut through the dust, but she recognized it. The paddle shaped fin with the sharp edges and faint hints of ragged holes could only be one kind of creature that she'd seen in this ocean. And then, as she suspected, she saw the faintest hint of a red flare.

Was he trying to sneak up on her? It seemed like it.

Leaning back, she pretended like she was relaxing again and started talking to Ace. "Listen, there's only so much time I have right now. I'm going to keep looking at the maps, but I still think sneaking into the city and connecting with the database is our best shot. If we can get every screen in the city to tell the story of how terrible my father is, then we've got a start."

"Bloodthirsty, I like it."

"It's revenge," Anya replied. And it was.

For all those years that he made her feel like she was nothing and no one. She would take her revenge on her father even if it made something inside her twinge. Like the undine had said, she mourned a mother she never had and a father who should have been better. The pain never really went away.

The dust outside the window swirled, and a sudden rush of darkness approached the window. At the same time, she stood abruptly and spread the blanket wide around her. Mirroring his movements, she ran for the window with a scowl on her face and the blanket billowing to make her look larger.

Daios paused outside the window, his lights flaring bright and his fins spreading in surprise at her reaction. Clearly, he had been trying to scare her.

Dropping the blanket, she gave him a bright grin and a little wave.

He spread his webbed fingers in a wave as well, frowning at her. He didn't even move until she pointed to the opening in the room that gave him access to her world.

Bitsy flared words in bright red. "Danger."

"Nah." She waved a hand in the air and turned toward the opening to wait for him. "I don't think he's all that dangerous at all."

Her droid was definitely sulking as the undine surfaced. He was still looking at her with that curious expression on his face, one that she might have thought was pride if she didn't know him better.

Plopping down on her butt in front of him, she found she couldn't wipe the grin off her face. "Did I scare you?"

"Not at all."

"You looked a little scared."

Those fins lifted on the sides of his neck and then pressed flat with a hard snap. "I was not frightened."

She shrugged. "Sure looked at least surprised."

"You should not threaten creatures like that, especially when they are larger than you. They may consider such behavior a challenge."

Anya rolled her eyes. "I think nothing would find that to be a challenge. If they're hunting me and realize I'm much larger than they thought, their hesitation might work to my advantage."

A soft sound rumbled through his gills, but then he gave her a reluctant nod.

She shouldn't be quite so happy that she'd impressed him.

Especially when he'd shown up empty-handed today. Usually he brought food or some kind of gift, and now he was looking at her with those deep black eyes, and she had a feeling he was going to tell her something she didn't like.

He opened his mouth, and she rushed ahead of him. Why? She wasn't certain. Only that she didn't want this to end and didn't want to know what was about to change.

"Can I touch you?" she asked, the words falling from her lips before she heard them herself.

"What?"

"Well, you've touched me." Her fingers brushed over the ends of her hair. "And I just... Well, I've never been this close to an undine before. And I don't think I ever will be again once all of this is over."

His brows furrowed a bit, a strangely human expression that made her hold her breath for a few seconds. "You aren't scared of me at all, are you?"

Anya had to bite her lips very hard not to grin. "Not really, no."

"Why is that?" He moved a little closer, enough that she could reach out and touch him if she wanted.

"Well. You've never given me any reason to be afraid of you." She scooted closer too until she could feel the slight chill radiating off his skin.

"I took you from your home."

"Because I told you to." She did grin when he rolled his eyes at that statement. "What? I did! Do you think you could have launched yourself out of the water, dragged me into the pool, and still gotten away with no one running in there with all the guns in the city at the ready?"

With one smooth flick of his tail, he loomed over her. He was suddenly closer, drops of water dripping off his shoulders and onto her chest, seeping into the fabric of the blanket. "Yes. I believe I could have done that."

Oh, she should be terrified. She should shrink into a tiny ball beneath him and pray that he didn't decide to try human flesh.

Instead, Anya found herself reaching up and feathering her fingers along the fins at the side of his face. "What are these?"

It didn't escape her notice that his eyes rolled back in his head. He liked the way her fingers felt on whatever these delicate membranes were. They were surprisingly soft underneath her fingers. And it felt rather natural to slide her pointer finger in front of one, and her middle finger behind it. With only the slightest pinch, she watched as the fins surrounding his face suddenly flared out and started to shake.

His face twisted, and when he spoke, she could feel his words rumbling through her ribs. "Those are my gills."

"Oh." She frowned, her eyes trailing down his muscular neck and impressively broad chest. Faint lines etched along his ribs with the faintest hint of delicate membranes hidden within. "I thought these were your gills."

She reached out to touch those too, only to pause when he grabbed her wrist. Eyes flicking up to his, she swore that hunger was back in his gaze. The webs of his fingers brushed against hers, just as soft as the gills she'd just touched.

"I have two of everything," he said, his voice so low she swore she could feel it deep inside her body.

"Two?" She frowned, looking back and forth between the two sets of gills. "Two lungs then? You're breathing air?"

"Yes."

"I have two lungs." Madness made her press her hands forward, flattening them against the strangely dark chest with stripes down the center from his collarbone all the way to meet his much darker tail.

And then she felt them. Against her palms was the rhythm of two hearts. Slightly off beat from each other. But both of them thundered against her skin, as though he were nervous.

"Two hearts," she whispered, feeling her voice vibrate in her throat.

"Yes." His hand came up to cover hers, pressing her a little tighter against his chest.

She felt like she was missing something, but it was hard for her to think of anything other than the fact that she could feel two heartbeats pressing against her hands right now. He was a medical anomaly. She could only imagine that there were hundreds of scientists who would love to get their hands on him.

How did they swim like they did? How did they withstand the cold and the pressures of the ocean? Did he have air bladders like a fish?

Questions rioted through her mind, but then she looked up at him and her mouth went dry. He was staring at her hands on his chest and she swore that look said he wished she would move her palms. He wanted her to touch him, to know what it felt like, and suddenly, all thoughts of science went out the window.

Sliding her hands up his chest, she watched his reaction. He went so still, seemingly not breathing other than those flared fins that continued to gently shake. She wondered if they made a sound.

Slowly, she reached her arms around him. He stayed right where he was, letting her hug him even as her hands played over his back.

"Careful." Bitsy had to put the words in that garish pink, so Anya knew Daios was speaking. "There are spines on my back."

"What do you mean?"

She'd seen his back, hadn't she? There wasn't anything unusual... But then he turned in her grip, putting a small amount of space between them.

There were spines on his back. They were nearly clear and so easy to miss. But as she ran her finger over one, they popped up at her touch.

There was a membrane attached to those as well. Almost like a dorsal fin that he could flatten at will. She ran her fingers along that deadly fin, trying to not be quite so pleased when Bitsy sent a warning flaring across the lens that he had hissed.

She could see how it affected him. The gentle touches seemed to be his downfall, and she enjoyed touching him like this so much.

With one hand flat against his hip to hold him still, she continued her exploration. Running her fingers all around those deadly spikes, she touched every membrane under each one as she counted them. Twelve deadly spikes. Twelve sharp weapons that ran down the length of his spine.

It took until spine number six for his resolve to crack. He shivered underneath her touch, his muscles twitching and his breath becoming ragged. She could see the way he sucked his breath in through those gills that grasped at nothing because they weren't underwater. His ribs expanded underneath her palm, so quickly it was as if he had just finished swimming the length of the ocean.

She'd had to shift onto her knees, trying to ignore the slick feeling between her thighs and control her own breathing. She hadn't thought she would enjoy this as much as she did. But having him at her mercy? Knowing that he was only holding himself together because he had to?

It did things to her that no man had ever inspired. She was so wet between her legs it was almost embarrassing, and still, her breath caught in her throat as she finished with the last spine at the small of his back.

"So dangerous," she said, hoping that she was even saying the words right.

He turned at the last second, and the smallest spine at the base of his back caught her finger. With a sharp hiss, she drew back in shock.

Bright blood welled on the tip of her finger. It was a small scratch. She doubted it would need anything other than a few moments of firm pressure and it would seal back up on its own.

But he groaned, the sound long and low and delicious as it coiled low in her belly. She hadn't realized how thrilling it was to hear her partner while he took his pleasure. Then all her thoughts scattered as he grabbed onto her wrist and drew it to him.

That long, black tongue came out of his mouth. And she was right. It was ridged. There were bumps all up and down it, little bumps that moved on their own as he wrapped that tongue around her bloodied finger.

"Fuck," she whispered.

That shouldn't be as hot as it was. She shouldn't tremble with need at the sound of his voice and the way that his eyes had rolled closed in pleasure as he sucked the blood from her skin.

This was wrong. She shouldn't enjoy this so much, and neither should he. They shouldn't be entertaining this heat between them, but they were. And she didn't want him to stop.

His eyes slowly opened, meeting hers with her finger still in his mouth. One more warm, wet swipe and he released her.

"I'll return with food for you," he said, that rumbling voice doing all sorts of things to her that it shouldn't.

"You just got back."

"I forgot to bring you something to eat, kalon."

She watched him sink into the water and thought maybe she had imagined it all. Or maybe, just maybe, they'd both lost their minds for a few moments.

And she'd liked it.

Chapter 19

aios darted through the water, a fish tied to his waist for her as his mind rioted.

He understood it now.

He understood what Arges had meant when he said this feeling was all-consuming. That fighting against this connection was a lesson in futility because it absolutely was. With the taste of her blood on his tongue and the feeling of her hands on his skin, he was lost. Completely and utterly.

He wanted to mate her. He wanted to keep her for himself forever. Every part of his body screamed that he needed to consume every drop of what she was and beg for her forgiveness later.

But that wasn't how mating worked. No matter how much he wanted her, no matter how hard he fought for her, the choice would always end in her lap. She had all the power here, and he knew how this story would end.

He was not the first choice. The instinct inside of him to take her and keep her away from the others was to fool her into thinking he was her best option. He was supposed to show her just how useful he could be. All of that was in his blood to keep her away from anyone else that might sway her eyes. But it wasn't fair.

The People of Water did not do things like this anymore. They allowed the females to pick and choose from the smaller amount of males that were available. And he had never been chosen.

She would not choose him either if she could see all the other males. She would eventually greet his pod and set her eyes on someone like Maketes. Someone bright and light and kind.

She never would have let Daios touch her if she knew that there were other options. If there was another person who could sway her thoughts from Daios.

He knew that. She knew it.

And still, he did not bring her back. Because in some fucked up way, he wanted to keep her to himself.

Sighing, he stared up at the entrance to the facility. He knew he was done fighting against this. He wanted to touch her. Taste her. Know everything about her. He wanted to steal what little he could before they were forced to part. And they would be forced. He was certain of that.

Cresting the surface, he searched for her. Like his eyes didn't even see threats anymore, only the hope that she was somewhere nearby. She was sitting in that strange chair again; her legs crossed and her hair wild around her head. Muttering under her breath, she pressed buttons on the console in front of her and then muttered some more when nothing happened.

Setting the smaller, more consumable fish to the side in the water to keep them cold, he flicked a few droplets of water at her.

They soared through the air, farther than he'd expected, and dropped onto the console itself. With a grunt, she immediately wiped away the flecks with her sleeve before realizing where they had come from.

Spinning in her chair, her eyes found his.

"Daios," she said, breathy and far too excited to see someone like him.

But he was the monster who encouraged it.

Nodding at her, he pointed to the fish. He should go. He shouldn't indulge himself like this because he wasn't sure he would leave. He might even beg her to let him touch her, just this once. Just to know.

She took the choice away from him. Suddenly she was right there in front of him, like she always was. Crossing her legs and wrapping that blanket around her shoulders as she started babbling about someone he didn't know and the idea that she had to get into Alpha. She was always working on figuring out a way to take her father down.

He admired her dedication, but right now he couldn't follow a single word she was saying. Not while he was watching her twist her hair in her hands. She wove the strands together, looping and curving until it was in an intricate braid falling over her shoulder.

Then she kept talking, her hands flying, not with words, but with excitement as she rambled about some service entrance that wasn't being as heavily watched as before. All they had to do was get someone on the inside who could attach yet another something into something, and he didn't care about any of that.

Because the strands of her hair were falling out of that twisted braid. She hadn't attached it with anything, so of course they were falling apart. He wanted to wrap it in his hand and drag her head back. He wanted to know what her throat tasted like and if he could feel the beat of her heart against his tongue.

"Daios?"

The sound of his name drew him out of those thoughts. He moved nothing other than his eyes to look at her. "Yes?"

"Do you want to brush it again?"

Surely he hadn't heard her right. Those words were a figment of his imagination and his greatest hope that she would let him touch her. "What?"

Anya's face burned with that red color, and he never knew what it meant. Her words were a little stammered as she said, "You did it before when it was tangled. I was sleeping, then. But it's... Well, it's tangled again and I haven't found a brush in here. I thought, maybe, if you didn't mind?"

He would do anything she asked. If she wanted him to lie flat in the muck while she used those strange tails to sink him deeper into it, he would gladly lay himself in the cold dirt.

With a slight nod, he felt his mouth go dry as she spun around. She used her hands to angle her body away from him, and then suddenly he had all the access he wanted to that hair that had captivated him from the start.

She started talking again, but he wasn't listening. Not when his shaking claws were so close to her hair. He gently touched just the ends, feeling the softness slide through his fingers like water. He'd never seen hair this color, and perhaps that was what had captivated him from the start.

He didn't want to hurt Anya. Not in any way. So he was careful as he started working through the knots. He tried very hard to listen to what she was saying, but he honestly didn't care.

Her plan to take down Alpha wouldn't work. He knew men like her father, because Daios was eerily similar to the man. The only thing that would stop people like them was blood or bartering.

And he held the General's greatest treasure between his claws right now.

She kept talking until he'd gotten most of the tangles out. Now, he could run his claws through her hair with no snarls standing in the way between him and the luxurious texture.

Carefully, he scraped his claws along her scalp. She tilted back into his touch, her words stuttering as he did it again.

He grinned, even though she couldn't see him. She liked it when he smiled, and he hoped she looked up at their reflection in the glass. He was a looming figure behind her, a monster with his hand on her, and she liked it.

He ignored the urges of his own body as he did it again. Running his fingers along her head and then pinching her strands between his knuckles a little harder, so there was the faintest tug as he continued down her hair. He did it again and again until she let out a little breathy moan that had both of them freezing.

But that sound. He wanted to hear it a hundred times. A thousand. He wanted to bathe in the sound until he could think of nothing other than that breathy moan of pleasure that had escaped from her lips without her realizing it. And he knew she hadn't planned for that to come out.

"Sorry," she whispered. "You can keep going, I just... No one has rubbed my head in a long time."

Did she want to brush that away? Flick it with her tails like it hadn't happened between them?

That sudden, dangerous anger rose in his chest. He didn't like that she was trying to hide her reaction from him, even though he logically knew he had done the same only a few days ago when she'd chosen to brush her fingers along the membranes of his spine.

He had no right to demand more from her. No right at all to hear more of that sound, but damn it, he wanted it. He wanted to hear her pleasure, and he wanted... her.

The madness pressed against his mind and he realized that even that part of himself didn't want to hurt her. Not unless she liked it.

He dug his fingers into her hair, massaging her scalp again until he heard the slightest moan again. She was holding back. Trying to keep those sounds from him when he wanted to hear them. He deserved to hear them. He was owed the sound of her pleasure and her pain and every bit of sound in between them.

Her head tilted back as he worked on her head and with a flick of his tail, he moved himself even closer to her. The long, graceful cord of her neck called to him. He... wanted.

The logical part of his mind didn't know what he was planning to do, but did it matter? She was laid out in front of him like a banquet. Her body covered by that stupid blanket that had no right to cover her from his sight.

Leaning down, he pressed his lips to that graceful arch of her neck. He let his mouth linger, and then couldn't stop himself from flicking his tongue against her skin.

Her moan vibrated in his ear as her taste burst on his tongue. She tasted so fucking good.

Warm and sweet, her pulse throbbing against his tongue where her heart raced as though she knew how much danger she was in. No, not danger. He shoved the haze away from his mind to realize she had arched in front of him. Her back bowing, she presented herself to him like she had no restraint either.

A low growl rumbling through his chest. He laved her pulse with his tongue. Slow and methodical, he drew the entire bumpy texture down her neck to her collarbone. Drawing back, he knew his sharp exhale would send cold goosebumps dancing down her flesh. And he couldn't stop himself now.

He'd had a taste, but it wasn't enough. It wasn't nearly enough.

Another growl rumbled through him as he curved his clawed hand around her waist. The blanket still separated them, and he didn't dare move it. The barrier was good. The barrier reminded him that he couldn't go too far with this, no matter how much they both wished for it.

The texture of her waist was so delicate, pushed in as it was. The sensation of her sharp hip bone pressed against his palm, undulating with her movements.

Holding onto her a little tighter, he pressed her head back against his bad shoulder. So she was braced against him as his instincts went wild.

He watched her expression, her mouth falling open as she stared at his webbed hand, moving across to her belly. The softness there only reminded him of how delicate she was, and how easily he could hurt her.

But that wasn't what he wanted. Not when little, soft panting sounds erupted from her lips. Those were good sounds. He enjoyed listening to those breathy sounds, but he wanted her moan.

He let out a little grunt himself as his cocks extruded. He couldn't stop them or hold them behind his scales any longer when she was like... this.

The blanket fell to the side as his hand moved up her torso. He could feel her even more now. The delicate cage of her ribs, expanding and contracting with each ragged breath that she pulled in to ground herself. The way her skin gave underneath his calloused hand. The lush press of her breast against his palm as he finally cupped her, feeling the indents of his fingers as he clutched her maybe a little too tightly.

There it was. The moan that made his hips rock forward and press his cocks against the cold metal. He wanted to feel the grip of her around him. She just arched into his touch, one of her arms lifting to loop around his neck and drag him closer to her.

He brushed his teeth down the column of her throat. His thumb found the peak of her breast, gently teasing it as she writhed in his arms.

They both needed this release that he could give them. Hips rocking, he breathed hard against her throat and knew she could feel the warm breath traveling down her neck. Another moan, this one ending on a plea.

Pressing his thumb a little harder against her nipple, he drew that moan out again. Her fingers clutched at his hair, and madness had him moving his hand.

He spread those fingers wide, sliding underneath the clothing that held her away from him. The soft texture of her skin nearly distracted him until his fingers brushed something warm and wet. Slick skin that had her hissing out a long breath.

He had claws. He didn't know what she liked, but he could feel the softness of her and knew she was delicate.

Arched as she was, it was easy for him to settle her on his palm. The webs between his fingers created ridges when his fingers were held closed, as they were now. And another hiss of pleasure made him certain that she liked his touch. She liked it when he slowly slid his fingers against that burning heat at her core.

"Kalon," he growled, the words low and so deep he knew she could hear them. "Move your hips, little one. I want to watch you ride my hand."

That was a new sound. A whimper that made his cocks kick against the icy floor and fuck. If he wasn't careful he could come like this. Feeling that silken skin glide over his fingers as she moved her body like a wave. Undulating and so graceful as she ground herself down on his fingers.

Beautiful.

The tiny moans, the whimpering sounds that stuck in her throat. He watched her in the reflection of the glass. Her head thrown back against his damaged shoulder, one arm cupping the back of his neck. She bit her lip as she desperately ground herself against his fingers and fuck. It was perfect.

He'd never seen a more lovely creature, nor had he ever seen a more lovely sight as when he leaned down and licked up the column of her throat.

"Keep your eyes closed," he growled into her ear, feeling her shudder at the tone of his voice. "Just feel."

He wanted inside her. So badly it ached. But right now, all he wanted was to see her ride his hand and as he growled in her ear, he knew she was close.

Those little red splotches on her cheeks flared hotter and then suddenly her rhythm changed. She was panting now, then holding her breath as she moved a little faster, a little harder.

And he watched with rapt attention as she came on his hand with a long, drawn-out moan that nearly unmanned him.

"Beautiful," he said. "You come so pretty, kalon."

The consoles started going off, the loud shrieking filling his ears just as she let out another one of those moans that made his cocks ache and his spend swell deep inside him. He wanted just a few more moments. A few more seconds where they could lose themselves in each other while he knew that he shouldn't be doing this.

But those loud noises and flashing red lights usually were a warning. And he knew she couldn't hear them.

"Anya," he said, drawing his hand away from her and cupping her chin. He forced her to look at the consoles. "Something is wrong."

It took her a few seconds. Her breathing was so ragged, he feared there might be something wrong with her. But then finally she nodded and lunged forward for the consoles. The blanket fell entirely onto the ground and he sank deeper into the water so she wouldn't know how much he was affected by her. Not yet, at least.

She slammed her hands on a few buttons, curses falling from her lips until the doors to their left sealed shut. Then he heard it. The crack. The rush of water that flowed through the tunnel beyond and into the room she usually slept in.

The loud boom rocked through the entire facility so hard that the entire thing moved. Water rushed up around him, nearly pushing him into the room and soaking her up to her thighs. He stayed right where he was, both of them frozen as the entire facility groaned. The sound was deep and aching, one he was certain she could hear.

They stared at each other, both silent, certain the entire facility was about to collapse.

Chapter 20

Anya braced herself against the consoles and prayed. She hadn't done that in years, but she wanted to make sure that someone was out there looking after her if this whole place suddenly imploded. At least it would be a quick death. Almost too easy, really. Her entire body would just crush into a blood mist and no one would know. Her father had no idea where she was. No one in Alpha did either.

They would just be two dead people in the sea, with only crabs to pick at the watery pieces of what was left of them.

But eventually the shaking died down. The water stopped churning on the other side of the door, and for a moment, she could breathe again.

They'd almost died. Again. It would take only the slightest push of the water or the wrong movement, and everything in this facility would shut down. The water would rush in and there was nothing he could do to help her. Not when all that chaos would likely throw the mask far out of her reach.

The mask.

"Fuck," she whispered, feeling how shaky the word was in her throat.

The mask had been in that other room. She had no way of getting out of here now, and there wasn't any way for him to get another one. At least, not without him leaving for a long time and gathering it up from wherever he'd gotten it before. But that would mean he had to leave.

She had no food. Only a small tool to purify the water that was filled with grit and grime.

Her situation pressed down on her shoulders hard now. She'd been so content with leaving her home and having this adventure for the first time in her life that she hadn't realized just how dangerous this was.

And then there was the shaking in her legs that had nothing to do with fear. The shaking that had come from the mind-blowing orgasm that had almost felt painful against his fingers. He'd barely even touched her, and she'd come like she hadn't in years.

Daios watched her with those dark eyes narrowed, like he was reading every emotion that flickered across her face. She didn't want him to think she was second guessing what had just happened between them. But also she couldn't focus on anything other than the minor shakes that still rattled through this building.

She couldn't stay here. Both of them knew that.

This was only a temporary home for her, and even then, it was still far too dangerous for her to live in much longer. An abandoned facility with holes punched all through it and flooding issues wasn't a long-term place to stay.

What had she been thinking? What world had she created inside her head that this was okay?

Breathing hard, she sat down on the chair and hugged herself as tightly as she could. "I think you know I can't stay here."

He didn't respond, just stared at her like he always did. But she could read him a little better now. She could see the ticking of muscles in his jaw and how his tail lashed underneath the water. Whatever moment they'd just shared crumbled as their world twisted in another direction.

Her breath fogged in front of her mouth, reminding her of another problem. Turning toward the console, she said, "Bitsy. What's going on with the heater?"

Little darts moved on the screen as Bitsy did her best to figure out what went wrong. "Life support is down to ten percent. The heating elements have been damaged in the tube collapse."

"Shit," she whispered, shoving the chair away from the consoles. She barely even felt the movement at her back until someone suddenly reached in front of her and plucked Bitsy off her head.

Her droid!

"Hey!" Anya scolded, before she realized Daios was holding the droid in front of his own eye. From what she could see on the other side of the glass, Bitsy automatically changed the language that was presented. The language of the undines, apparently, had written word.

She couldn't have guessed that.

"Be careful with her." Anya squeezed herself a little tighter before bending to snag the blanket off the ground. It was soaking wet now, no help against the cold. "She's my only way of understanding people."

He nodded, before returning his attention to reading what flicked in front of his eyes. Then he handed the droid back to her. Anya could see how carefully he pinched the delicate robot in his massive hand, barely even holding onto it as she took Bitsy and deposited the droid back onto her head.

Words flickered to life on the lens as he started talking. "Your droid seems to think this place could come down at any moment."

"I agree with her."

"Then we need to move."

"I can't get in the water like this." She waved a hand up and down the suit she still wore, then pointed to the collapsed section of the tunnel. "And my wetsuit was in there. So I'm kind of trapped."

Her heart started up again. It was thudding and lumping in the wrong way as panic set in. She really was trapped. She wasn't going to get out of here alive.

"And the..." Words failed her, so she just waved her hand in front of her mouth. Maybe he would understand because she couldn't focus on making the right sounds for words when she was going to die.

His hand waved in front of her face, but she wasn't looking until she noticed there was a pattern to his movements. They weren't... right, exactly. Not really. He wasn't precise in his sign language, but she could still vaguely understand what he was trying to say.

"Care. Me. You."

Her breath caught in her throat, ragged and raw, as she tried to say, "What are you saying?"

He pulled himself a little out of the water so he could look her in the eye. "I'm going to take care of you, Anya."

Everything evened out. She could breathe again as she locked her gaze with his and took in deep, steady breaths as he did. Slowly. In and out. It was easy to put her trust in him, even if it felt a bit like madness to do so.

Finally, she nodded. "Okay. Okay, I trust you."

"Good." With his shorter arm, he motioned for her to look to their left. "Watch me while I search for the wetsuit. You are not alone."

"I'm not alone," she repeated.

"I will not be far. If this room floods, I will come and get you."

"I can't breathe underwater," she whispered, not sure if he could even hear her words. "I'm not like you."

"I don't want you to be like me, kalon." And for the very first time, he reached for her with that injured arm.

She didn't hesitate. She just walked into him, even knowing that he was wet and cold and that she was already freezing. He pulled her into him, his short arm hesitating only a moment before he used it to pull her into him.

It still felt like a hug. He was so much larger than her, and she didn't care if he didn't have a hand or an elbow on that side of his body. All she wanted was to be tucked into him like this, where she could feel him taking deep breaths. He was alive. He was strong.

And he wouldn't let anything happen to her.

He released her, although she noticed how reluctant the movement was. He didn't want to let her go anymore than she wanted him to let her go.

"Be right back," he said, his voice low and rumbling as he sank into the water and then disappeared.

Anya prided herself on being resilient. That's what had kept her alive so long under her father's thumb, and she would not be any different in this circumstance. She was a capable person who had lived through a lot of hardship. This was nothing different.

And yet she still ran to the window and watched him as he moved through the water. Unlike the time he'd tried to startle her, he kept all of his lights as bright as he could. The red glow penetrated through the murk and the darkness. She could see him the entire time. He was right there, within reach.

It took him a few moments to figure out a way into the flooded room, but then she saw the same thing he did. Structural flaw. There was a huge portion of the metal that had buckled under the pressure. He reached for the warped metal and twisted it.

She didn't know how much strength that took. She should probably be horrified that he could just bend thick metal without even struggling to do so. Instead, she only felt that fire in her burn all the more hot.

He ducked into the room and then she couldn't see him for a little while. That oppressive feeling of death was back the moment he was out of her sight. Which was silly.

"You don't even know him," she told herself, but her eyes never moved from the spot where he'd disappeared. "You haven't talked about who he is or where he came from. This is just... Stockholm Syndrome."

Bitsy flashed a few words. "Are you losing your mind?"

Probably.

She was looking at an undine like he was the next snack she wanted to take a bite out of, so yeah. She was losing her mind. He had saved her life, though. He'd gotten her out of the city and that was all that mattered at the time.

But then he'd brought her food to keep her alive. He'd brushed her hair and touched her in ways that made her burn. She hadn't thought...

None of this made sense. She shouldn't feel this way about someone she didn't know. She'd only recently learned his name. This was insanity. She knew nothing about his people or where he came from.

It was her mind. She was messed up being this deep under the sea and the pressure was getting to her. That was all.

But she couldn't deny that all the tension in her body eased when she saw him coming out of the room with her wetsuit and mask in his hand.

She held her breath until he came back into the room where she stood. The only air left in the entire facility was in this room and they were only at ten percent life support. Soon enough, that air would run out.

He handed her the mask and then yanked himself out of the water. Awkwardly, he propped himself up on the stump that couldn't be comfortable to bear all of his weight, and then started pressing the water out of her suit.

Unfortunately, the mask hadn't survived as well as she'd hoped.

"Bitsy?" she asked. "What's the damage?"

Her droid looked it over before animated tears appeared all over the lens. "Broken."

"Fixable?"

"Not here."

Breathing out a long sigh, she looked over at Daios, who was doing his best to make sure the wetsuit wasn't a total loss. But he didn't know that she was staying here. Forever.

And in her mind, she heard a voice telling her that if she was going to die, she should do so with no regrets.

Squaring her shoulders, she marched toward him with single-minded intent. He glanced up at her approach, but then turned his attention back to the wetsuit. "I do not know how these things work. Is the water going to be a problem? There is little time for it to dry."

Sitting down on top of the wetsuit, she framed his face with her hands and turned him to look at her. He blinked, those dark eyes reflecting the determination on her features.

"Anya?" he asked, his voice low and slow. "What are you doing?"

"Tell me something about you."

"What?"

"Tell me something about you," she repeated. "I want to know more than just that you are my kidnapper. I want to know who you are as a person, not just what you are capable of."

He shook his head. "I don't understand what you're asking. What do you want to know?"

She didn't know. Everything. Nothing. What if what he said disappointed her? What if she heard his thoughts about the world and realized they were so far different that this could never work?

But she supposed it didn't matter, anyway. She was going to die, and he was going to watch her drown.

Swallowing hard, she forced the thoughts away and tried for a smile. "What's your favorite color?"

His eyes moved to hers, and he was so quiet Bitsy seemed to struggle to catch the word, "Blue."

The color of her eyes.

"How old are you?"

"Somewhere in my thirties, I stopped counting a long time ago."

What else did she need to know? "What do you dream of?"

His gaze flicked down to her lips. Maybe she would have missed the movement if she didn't know him so well, but she did. She had come to read this creature as well as she could read herself.

He licked his lips, that black tongue doing more to her than it should have. "I want to find someone who doesn't fear me. I want to know that when I come home, there is a soft place to rest my head, and someone who cares if I had a hard day, or if I am upset. I want someone to take care of, and who takes care of me in return. That is what I dream of, kalon."

Tears pricked her eyes. This sweet, terrifying man had lived a life she couldn't imagine. What had led him to this point? To thinking that it must be impossible for someone to see him as a person and not just a weapon?

How deeply he must have buried this dream to have come so far. She let her gaze wander over the stub of his arm that must be so painful while he leaned on it like that, but he didn't even flinch. He just took the pain without complaint, because he was afraid the wetsuit was going to be too cold for her, or that it wouldn't work right.

He took care of her. No matter what.

And that was why she held onto his jaw a little tighter and turned his attention entirely to her. "I don't want to die with any regrets." She let the words take flight. Somehow, they were all the more true when she could hear them said.

Taking a deep breath, she leaned closer, giving him time to back away. When her lips were only a breath away from his, and she could see the shock radiating through his entire body, she whispered, "And above all else, I don't want to have regrets with you."

Anya leaned forward and kissed him with every ounce of raw and ragged desire that burned through her.

For him. Only for him.

Chapter 21

aios had seen Mira and Arges kiss before. He'd even asked Maketes what they were doing, considering how disgusting it was to watch. Mouths were for eating, nothing more than that. It was sickening to watch the two of them fit together like that. He also thought it was a risk every time they did it underwater, considering Mira couldn't breathe like they could.

All of it had led him to believe that kisses were, unsurprisingly, something that only humans did and that he would never partake in.

But the moment her lips pressed to his, something snapped inside of him.

Like he'd been just waiting for this moment to feel that soft mouth against his. As though the cushion of her lips had unlocked some demon deep in his chest that he had only held barely leashed until this point.

He grabbed onto her, his clawed hand tearing at the fabric of her clothing. He didn't care if it fluttered to the floor because she was suddenly pressed up against him again. He could hear the soft little moan that rocked through the back of her throat and the way she arched into him.

Her hands pressed to his chest, so tiny that even if she tried to push him away, he might not feel the pressure. Her tongue swept against his lower lip and suddenly she was sucking on his bottom lip and all he could think about was what it would feel like if she sucked on something else. But that wasn't done. None of his people were soft like this when they fucked, and not when they mated, either.

Still, he enjoyed the sensation of her softness spreading throughout his entire body. Her hands came up around his neck, pulling him down closer to her while his claws spasmed against her back.

She wasn't ripping at him. Not tearing. Not fighting the way their people would, and he wasn't sure if that was a good or a bad sign. He was floating in a haze of desire and passion, and he felt like he was maybe doing this wrong.

Until he opened his mouth to tell her that, and her tongue swept into his mouth.

Her flavor exploded into his senses. That warm, sweet taste reminded him so much of home. She was a candy he wanted to lick from bottom to top, just to know that sweet flavor that would never, ever leave his memory.

Letting out a low groan, he pulled her even tighter to him. Was he crushing her? Probably. But she would tell him if he was doing this wrong. For now, he wanted to just indulge himself and drown in her.

Her tiny nails dug into the back of his neck and dragged down the cords of muscle there. His answering groan mixed with the breathy sound of her pleasure had all his gills flaring wide. They fluttered, shaking with such intensity he could almost feel the wind of them as his entire body told him to claim, take, fuck.

Anya noticed. Her soft little gasp and the way she pulled back told him she had no idea why his gills moved for her. But her eyes on him... He loved it. He loved it when she looked at him without fear or concern or even disgust, as he had expected her kind to do.

Instead, she just looked at his gills standing on end and the differences between them with a soft smile on her face. "They're beautiful, you know."

He shook his head, not sure if he was denying that anything about him was beautiful, or just that she had pulled away from him.

Her lips were swollen and stained as red as his scales. He couldn't stop looking at those lips and this woman who surprised him so much, when all he'd expected from her was hesitation. But then again, she'd let him touch her. And that memory was burned into his brain so much that he would never be able to forget it.

She took a deep breath, her eyes looking him over, although her gaze always ended on his mouth.

She wanted to kiss him again.

Claws clenching in the back of her clothing, he gave himself a thousand reasons to not tug her back into his arms. She was too delicate. He had no way of knowing if achromos had to rest after.... kissing. He wasn't sure if he could break her with his affection. He should have asked Arges far more questions when his brother had offered his advice, and instead, he was forced to hope she would take the lead.

This was not how a warrior would act. It was how a mate would act, though. The stark difference suddenly chilled his passion and froze him to the very core. He had always been a warrior. Not a lover. And certainly not a mate. He wasn't sure he knew how to be anything else.

She traced her finger over his lips, such a delicate little digit that he could so easily break with just a snap of his sharp teeth.

"Thank you for that," she whispered when he did not reply to her original words. "I didn't want to die without knowing what it was like."

He nipped at her finger, then forced himself to release her. Though his hand trailed slowly from her body to nudge the little droid down her face so she could hear what he was saying. "You are not going to die, kalon."

"You keep calling me that. It's not my name."

"I know it's not your name." He flashed the hand motions that she had given for him. "Big man is not my name either."

She tsked, the sound cut off by a violent shiver that ran through her body. "That's the name I gave you."

"Kalon is the name I gave you." Daios scooped the wetsuit off the floor and handed it to her. "You're going to freeze if you don't put this on."

"But what does it mean?" She took the wetsuit from him, though. At the very least, she was following his directions. "You know the meaning of the name I gave you."

Grunting, he ignored her question and waited until she gave him a look that said she wanted him to turn around. But this time, he wasn't going to listen to her.

He didn't want to turn around. Not after that kiss. Not after hearing her sweet moans and feeling that soft, wet heat. No, he wanted to look, and he wanted her to trust him.

Anya turned the wetsuit this way and that in her hands, her breath fogging in front of her face as she gathered herself. He could tell she wanted to tell him something. She always looked like this when she had something on her mind.

Finally, she blew out a long breath. "You said I'm not going to die, but the mask is broken. Bitsy can't fix it."

When she looked up at him with those sad, blue orbs, he felt like he could have fought off the entire sea for her. Even though he'd told himself he wouldn't fall deeper into this mating madness, he sighed, "That's fine."

"That's fine?" She tossed her arms out at her side, the wetsuit flopping against the metal floor. "I can't breathe underwater, Daios!"

"I know you can't." He reached for her, trailing his fingers down the side of her neck where his tentacle would sink into her skin. "But I can."

"You make no sense," she grumbled. But she still turned her back to him and started yanking off the fabric that hid her from his gaze.

For a time now, he thought he'd imagined how she looked. That those long limbs and shadows in between the muscles of her back had been his imagination. No achromo could ever be pretty. But he was wrong.

All that pale skin was revealed with a quick jerk that showed every inch of her to his hungry gaze. And by all the gods of the sea, was he hungry for her.

Her back would look so pretty, with red lines from his claws running down it. He knew she would welt. He could already see the marks over her hip bones that he'd left just from pawing at her. At the sight of them, he wanted to create more. He wanted to rake his nails down her sides just to see the red lines that would linger for days after he was done with her.

A low growl echoed in his throat as his gaze trailed up to her shoulders. That lovely golden hair swayed against her spine, and he wanted to wrap it in his fist. He wanted to tangle his fingers in those pretty locks and turn her neck to the side so he could bite her. He wanted everyone to look at her and know that she was taken.

That she was his.

But then she bent at the waist and any thoughts completely disappeared from his mind. Those tails. Legs, he corrected himself. A man would commit murder to catch a glimpse of those legs.

Long and lean, he wanted nothing more than to have her straddle him again. This time without the layers of clothing that kept the sight of her skin from his eyes. He wanted to wrap his hand around them, to see what it looked like to have his claw points pressing into the tender flesh there. He wondered at the kind of sound she would make when she felt him pressing to the point of breaking skin.

Perhaps he was too violent for most of his kind, but he had a feeling he was the right kind of violent for her.

She looked over her shoulder, still bent down and giving him the most perfect view of her muscular globes that looked like the moon. "Would you turn around now?"

Even to him, his voice sounded hoarse. "Absolutely not."

"Putting on a wetsuit isn't the most graceful process. I know you think I look good now, but I'm about to make a fool of myself."

"I'll watch." He had a hard time believing anything she did would put him off. She captivated him with just a flick of her hair over her shoulder.

Until he watched her put on that wetsuit. And suddenly he knew what it meant to have control, because he nearly burst out laughing multiple times. She shook, shimmied, pushed, and turned bright red in the face as she tried for long moments to get the wetsuit on.

He bit his lips and tried very hard to not say a word as she hopped up and down, only getting the material up a few inches at a time.

Although the movement bounced her breasts rather entertainingly, it was hard to focus on that when she was cursing with every movement.

By the time her wetsuit snagged over her hips, she was breathless and angry. "You wipe that smile off your face, Daios."

He did not.

"I mean it. I will come over there and... and..."

Tilting his head to the side, he gave her a feral grin that usually made people quake in fear. "What will you do, kalon?"

She stomped her little foot, adorably infuriated. "I don't know! I will come over there and do whatever it takes. Now, will you help me, or are you just going to watch me struggle?"

"I was unaware I was supposed to help." He didn't stop grinning as he gestured for her to turn around, and then held onto the limp arm of her suit. "By all means, princess. Allow me."

"Princess," she muttered, yanking him a little closer so her arm was finally in the slot. "You know my father used to call me that all the time? Especially when I complained."

He could understand why. But he didn't want to be compared to that man. So instead, he leaned forward and in the lowest, most guttural tones he could reach, he purred in her ear, "Kalon, then."

The shudder that went through her entire body was all too delicious. But then the entire building gave another groan, and he knew they had run out of time.

"Anya, will your eye piece survive in the sea?"

"What?" she asked, looking over her shoulder with her eyes a little glazed. Clearly she couldn't hear the higher pitched creaking of the building.

"Your..." He gestured over his face.

"Oh. Bitsy?"

The two of them seemed to talk for a moment, words flashing in front of Anya's eyes before she gave him a quick nod. "I guess so? She said she'll be fine, but once we are somewhere dry, I will have to air out her circuit boards. But they should be waterproof. At least for a while."

"Good. I do not wish to damage… her." Even though it felt rather unnatural to worry about something that was made of metal and yet had life. The things he did for this achromo that she would never understand were strange.

Once they got the wetsuit on, he wrapped her in his good arm and slithered back toward the opening. He knew the instant she stopped trusting him. Or perhaps when her survival instinct kicked in.

"Wait, Daios. I can't breathe underwater, remember? I don't want to…"

He pressed his finger to her lips. "I am not going to kill you, Anya. I only wish to take care of you, remember?"

Her wide-eyed gaze locked with his, but then she set her jaw. He knew she was ready, even if she was terrified.

"Trust me."

He drew her into the water with him, holding her closer when the shivers started. Soon she would warm up. His body would heat hers, but for now, she needed to shiver to get her temperature higher. Tucking her underneath his chin, he tucked her against his shoulder so he couldn't see her face. If she balked or grew too nervous, he wouldn't be able to do this.

"The People of Water have always been alone. The achromos, what we call your people, they have always been separate from our kind. But a year ago, a woman arrived. My brother took her as his mate and they have been discovering all the ways that we… fit."

He winced at the choice of words. That was a terrible way to explain this to her, and she likely thought... Well, he didn't want to know what she thought.

Shaking his head, he continued as he lowered her further into the water. The waves lapped at her neck now, and she clung to him as she hadn't when they first fled from her city.

"There are parts of me that can help you." He cleared his throat. "It won't hurt very much, but it will feel strange."

She struggled to pull away from him, but he didn't let her. He couldn't. If he thought for a moment he was hurting her, then he wouldn't be able to do this.

Biting his lip, he whispered again, "I promise it won't hurt."

She wriggled, but he held onto her with his short arm while he lifted the tentacle to her neck. He would make sure she could breathe. That was all he could do for her as they fled from this dying building.

Anya stiffened in his arms as the cord slid into her throat. He could feel the seal was good. They were connected. More than he had ever hoped to be connected to her because right now, he was breathing for her. He drew them underneath the water, pressing a kiss to her lips as he carried her into the depths.

Low and resonating in the water, he murmured, "How I wish I could keep you. But I cannot. No matter how much I want to."

Chapter 22

Anya couldn't stop touching the stinging wound on her neck. Not that it was that bad anymore. Now it was just a bruised sensation in her throat, but there was the very unnerving and strange feeling of someone else breathing for her.

The tentacle appeared to be some kind of tube that allowed his air to transfer into her lungs. Right into the cord of her throat that she normally would breathe out of, but now it was him doing it for her.

And how awful was that? The sensation was terrifying and so unnatural, and yet, here she was. Not struggling, even though she knew she could yank it out.

Like a loose tooth, she had a hard time focusing on anything else. There was a tube in her neck. Daios was breathing for her. They were under mountains of water, and if that tube jostled loose, she wouldn't stand a chance at getting to the surface on her own.

His arm shifted around her back, and then he grabbed onto her elbow and pulled her hand away from the site where the tube was sticking underneath her skin. Apparently, she shouldn't fiddle with it so much. She needed a distraction, or she was going to rip the damn thing out without thinking.

Taking a deep breath, she turned her attention to the words he'd said. What did he mean he couldn't keep her? Anya kept her arm looped around his neck, hugging herself tight to the heat of his body as they moved through the sea.

While they were swimming, she found it hard to say anything at all. The sea ate away at her sanity in tiny little chomps, like they were surrounded by itty bitty deadly fish that wanted her to lose her mind. She hated how little she could see. She didn't have the faintest idea where they were going, or even how he knew where they were headed.

He sure seemed confident, though. But she had a sneaking suspicion that was his superpower.

The longer she was around this strange man, the more she realized that about him. He looked at the world like it had something to give him. Daios took whatever he could from every interaction, every moment. She'd always been afraid to do that. But he just didn't care. He took what he wanted, and he didn't mind that others might not like that about him.

Anya wished, for just a few seconds, that maybe she could be like that too.

His arm tightened around her waist, maybe suspecting where her thoughts had gone, or just knowing that she needed him to. That strong arm bracketing around her back was more than enough to ease the anxiety rolling in her stomach. Maybe it shouldn't be that easy.

On one hand, she realized she knew nothing about the man. Or his species. He wasn't exactly a talker, and that certainly didn't make it easier for her to know any of these things.

On the other hand, he seemed to know her intuitively. Every time she was nervous, he lit up those lights for her to count. When she was cold, he brought her in closer to his heat and made sure all her limbs were appropriately tucked into the warmest parts of himself. Even when she had her eyes open, he would look down at her like he knew she was looking up at him.

She didn't know what that meant. They hardly knew each other, and yet, he knew her.

It was unsettling; she decided. Very unsettling.

But another voice whispered in her ear that this was what she had always wanted. She wanted someone who knew exactly what she needed. Just like she could do the same to him.

She could feel the moment they were getting close to their destination. He stiffened against her, every muscle in his body tensing with either anger or fear. She didn't know which yet. He stopped as the water cleared in front of them, revealing a section of the ocean where a city had been swallowed by the sea.

It wasn't much of a city, more like a town, she supposed. There were at least twenty buildings, all in various states of decay. But it was clearly a town where people had once lived before the sea levels had risen.

She'd seen a place like this before in research articles. A team of scientists from Alpha had come across a similar town. But this one looked like it had been underwater for much longer. Spears of sunlight glimmered through the water, highlighting the broken walls and the shattered glass that was barely visible in the sand that slowly took it all back.

But then her attention turned to something else.

A dome.

A small one, of course. Not even remotely close to the size of her city, but it was a dome just like Alpha. Clearly built by the same person who had designed her city. Even from this distance, she could see there were working lights within it. And there was another undine floating above it.

Or rather, draped on top of it. From this distance, she assumed he was a male, just like the one who had her wrapped in his arms. The flat chest was the only thing she had to go on. But this one was bright yellow instead of red.

The other undine was dramatically splayed out on top of the glass, one hand raised over his head while the other traced something above him in the water. His tail flicked every now and then, perhaps a display of recognition that they were staring at him.

Pressing her hand a little more firmly against Daios's chest, she looked up at him with a frown. "Are we going to your home?"

He looked down at her, and that deep voice boomed through the water. "This is not my home."

Right, the man of few words who so easily misunderstood what she was asking. "Then where are we?"

His eyes met hers, and she knew he wasn't comfortable telling her. He didn't want her to know where they were, or who was going to meet her. Or maybe, just maybe, this was what he had meant. He couldn't keep her, no matter how much he wanted to.

Shit. Was he going to leave her here?

"Daios?" she quietly asked. "Where are we?"

A strange swell of pressure brushed against her side before she realized that something had moved closer to them. It took every ounce of bravery in her not to scream, and even then, she tucked herself a little closer to the wall of Daios before she realized there was another undine in front of them. Another undine who was far too close to her face.

Those black eyes looked her up and down, the yellow around his fins seeming to brighten before he grinned. At least, she thought it was a grin. There were a lot of teeth involved in that expression and they were just as sharp as Daios's.

"So you kept her alive," the undine said, and she was startled to realize she could hear him too. His voice wasn't quite as deep as Daios's, although it was still deep. "I was wondering when we would see the two of you."

"Get out of the way," Daios growled.

"She's got one of your air tubes in her, there's no rush. Why can't I introduce myself?" With a flourish, the undine made some kind of move that almost looked like a bow before he reached out his hand for her to take. "My name is Maketes, little one. Welcome to your new home."

He was almost charming, if he weren't so terrifying to look at. But she wasn't scared of Daios, so she definitely would not be scared of this smaller male.

Reaching out her hand, she let him take her fingers and then press a chaste kiss to the backs of them. A dark rumble moved through Daios's chest and into her torso before the other undine let her go.

"Now, Daios," Maketes said, his voice turning chiding even as Bitsy changed all the words to yellow for him. "You have no say over this one. After all, you were just supposed to bring her here and leave her. Were you not?"

"Careful, brother."

"Brother?" she repeated, looking between the two of them. Confusion wrinkled her brows, and she tried her best to see the resemblance.

It just... wasn't there. Maketes was so much smaller than him, not to say that he was small, but at least a couple feet smaller. He lacked the impressive fins around his waist and the ones around his face were much less prominent. He was very much sleeker, a fast moving creature rather than the bullish one who held her. She'd even suggest they weren't even the same strain of undine species seeing them together.

Were undine genetics really so different?

They both stared at her with confusion on their own features. So she licked her lips and added, "You don't look anything alike."

A booming sound echoed from behind them all. This time, she did flinch. Ducking underneath Daios's chin as she tried to get used to hearing that there were people around her.

Bitsy tossed an arrow up that pointed behind her, as if she didn't know there was another undine who had joined the other two.

Daios didn't turn, but his arm tightened around her a fraction more as if he didn't like the other undine who was interrupting them. It should have been enough of a warning for her to toss her guard up. It was not, unfortunately.

The creature who swam around them was significantly larger than Maketes. He was almost as big as Daios, although she didn't think there were many that could reach the size of the man holding onto her. Blue fins glowed in the light, reflecting the sun beams that seemed to caress his features. His massive shoulders tapered into an attractively narrow waist, but it was the softness in his expression when he looked at her that made Anya relax the smallest amount.

"I am his clutch mate," this new undine said. "Although he has no wish to admit it."

Maketes rolled those dark eyes, or at least, the movement looked like he did. "We all grew up together. Just because I didn't share the same purse as you, doesn't mean I'm any less your brother."

The words were confusing. "Purse?" she asked, glancing up at Daios.

"We..." His brows furrowed. "What are your children birthed in?"

"They just... come out." She gestured between her legs and was glad for the cold water against her cheeks. "Do you mean to say you're birthed in a purse like a shark?"

"The translation through this chip is not perfect." He tilted his head to the side and gestured at his ear with his short arm. "But yes. We are born externally after growth, and then emerge from what you call a purse."

"You just come out?" A shocked almost shout interrupted them.

She looked over at the blue undine, realizing his colors were suddenly vivid. The lights underneath his skin had flared so brightly, it was almost difficult to look at him before he dimmed them.

He flicked his tail, swimming almost too close to her, so he peered down into her eyes. "What did you just say?"

"I don't know what you're asking," she stammered.

"Humans have live births?"

She arched a brow. That hardly seemed like something he needed to focus on, but... "Yes?"

Daios used his shorter arm to shove the other undine away, sending his actual brother careening through the water until he bumped against Maketes. "Space, Arges. You've never learned much about it."

Arges, she thought, stowing away the name for later. They all had such interesting names, but of course they did.

The undines were people. They had a culture and a vast history she knew nothing about. And yet, they acted like the men she'd known before in her life. Shoving and gesturing and posturing all the time until she almost forgot they weren't human. Their relationships were similar. Enough for her to realize quickly that this life might be too easy for her to get used to.

Maketes grabbed onto Arges by the shoulders, spinning him around. "You didn't know that?"

"No, I didn't know that!" Arges ran his fingers through his hair, the long locks billowing around him like a cloud. "Why wouldn't she tell me?"

"Well, I don't know. Maybe she thought you knew that it was... was..."

With a soft movement of the tail between her legs, Daios moved past the other two. Their arguments carried through the water, but the red scaled undine who had her in his arm had no plans to listen, apparently.

"You don't want me to stay and clarify?" she asked, bracing her arms straight against his chest so the current didn't shove her flat against his skin.

"No," he rumbled.

"Why not?"

A slight smirk appeared on his lips, disappearing just as quickly. "I enjoy watching him struggle."

Smacking his chest, she shook her head. "He's your brother."

"And that does not change my enjoyment." He glanced down at her, that expression softening again while he just... looked. "But if you wish for me to turn around, I will."

Unable to hold his gaze, she bit her lip and shook her head. "Where are you taking me?"

He pointed to the dome, and she was so relieved to know she'd be dry soon enough. "There is a woman here. Mira. She is Arges's mate. She was the one who wished for me to find you."

"Is that so? Do I know her?" Anya couldn't imagine why anyone would ask her for unless they maybe worked with Ace. But Ace wasn't someone she had ever met in person, so how would Daios have known to grab her?

"No," he replied gruffly, moving so they were underneath the golden dome and just beneath a moon pool. "You do not know her."

"Then why are we here?"

Anya couldn't be more confused. Especially as he hesitated. Daios sighed, then leaned forward to press their foreheads together. He breathed her in. She could see him doing it, his gills moving and sucking in all the air around her.

With a long sigh, he rotated his head against hers. As if he were rubbing his scent into her flesh. "Don't think less of me, my kalon. Not for this, and not after anything they tell you."

"Why would I think less of you?" Tentatively, she cupped the sides of his neck just underneath his gills. She had to wait for him to exhale into her lungs before she continued. "I may not know you as well as I wish, but my soul knows yours, Daios."

"We will see," he murmured, his voice low as his hand wrapped around her waist. With a soft shove, he guided her toward the surface of the moon pool. "I hope you are right."

Chapter 23

SHe let her leave his grip, and it was one of the hardest things he'd ever done in his life. Him, a terrifying warrior who had spent his entire life defending the People of Water from whatever beast hunted them. Daios had fought sharks with his bare hands. Tore achromos apart with his claws and watched them bleed to death in the waters as giant squid fed upon them. He had fought and battled his entire life.

But his fingers wanted to lock around her tiny form. He hated seeing her rise to the surface without him. He hated even more taking that tentacle out of her neck where they were connected.

He pulled it slowly, making sure there was no pain for her as he did so. And with that connection severed, he knew he should leave.

Now was the time for him to go back to his life before Anya. Most of the others here had set up a temporary home for themselves. Some in the old homes of the achromos, others making nests in the sand with stones that they hauled from all over the seas. But he had done none of that yet.

The only way he felt like he could control himself was when he was moving. So he would let her go into the arms of her own kind, and then he would turn his attention to the next job where he had to risk his life. The next mission where he might die. But that was all right. If he died saving his people, then that was a worthy death.

The watery surface above him reflected the image of Mira walking over to the edge of the moon pool. That achromo would take care of his. Mira was a feisty little thing with more bite than most, but she would fiercely protect those that were hers.

She'd wanted Anya, after all. All of them had. They truly believed that the daughter of the General was the key piece in their puzzle. Perhaps they would ransom her to her father. Or perhaps they would pretend to kill her, so the General made a mistake in his anger. There were many options, and he was certain Arges had already thought about all of them.

"Psst." The clicking noise interrupted his thoughts.

Frowning, he glanced down to see Maketes was poking his head underneath the moon pool as well. His brother stared up at Anya's legs kicking in the water above their heads.

"Is she up there?" His yellow finned brother's eyes gleamed. "Sure is pretty."

"She can hear you."

"I thought you said she couldn't hear?" Maketes's gills flared wide, faking a flutter, although it was almost convincing. "Pretty enough for someone like you or me to find tempting enough. How long do you think it'll take for her to settle in?"

Thoughts pushed through his mind. Maketes might be smaller than him, but that was what all women liked. Smooth scales, fewer fins that were poking out in all directions. Handsome to both achromos and to the People of Water, Maketes was a good mate. No one knew why he hadn't chosen one of their own people for his own, although Daios had a feeling it was that Maketes didn't think he could survive a mating.

Still, it made him uncomfortable. Maketes wanted to give Anya attention, and that made him nervous.

This was someone she could make a life with. Someone who would treat her kindly. Maketes would make her laugh. It wouldn't be so hard for her to feel like she knew him, even though Daios had done everything that he could to share bits of himself. He had told her about himself, but he wasn't a man of words. He didn't know how to tell her that he...

Baring his teeth in an angry snarl, he shot up into the air above the moon pool. Too fast, really. Water sprayed from around him and he knew he wore a nasty glare which would make everyone in the dome nervous. Even Anya's eyes widened for a moment before her brows drew down in a frown.

"Daios?" she asked, her voice a little uncertain.

Now that he was up here, he didn't know what to do. All he knew was that he was so angry at the thought of Maketes gaining some of her attention. He didn't want anyone to know the little smiles she gave him, or the way her eyes wrinkled at the corners when she was happiest. He didn't want them to know her favorite food or what she sounded like when she hummed so off key.

He wanted her all to himself, and that was selfish. Daios knew that. But he wasn't willing to share any of her joy with others.

"I—" Struggling to find the words, he grunted instead. He placed his hand on her back underneath the water, hoping that the warmth of his palm would ease her fears.

Mira had changed a few things since the last time he'd stuck his head into her domain. There were more plants than ever, hanging from the ceiling and creating tendrils of vines that dripped above their head. The bed was hidden now in its own little room, a sheet hanging off of the ceiling that looked as though the sea had worn it down. Someone must have found that in the water for her, or stolen it from one of the city's trash heaps.

Metal bits and bobs were everywhere. Thrown about in every direction that he could see, along with the tools she used to mend them. He could see at least four welders from where he was, and he was sure there were more if he looked a little harder.

Mira stood just beyond reach. With her arms crossed over her chest and her bright red hair billowing around her head, she was an intimidating creature to look at. That scowl reached deep into his soul, letting him know she thought he was nothing more than a nuisance.

She had a few more freckles dusted across her nose, a sight he found intensely uncomfortable. Humans shouldn't be able to change their colors that easily. His kind couldn't.

"Daios," Mira said, her voice rusty even to his ears. "I see you actually brought her back. Do you have any idea how pissed I was when Arges told me your plan?"

"No more than you always are."

"Okay, asshole. Listen to me. Next time you want to fuck up the plan that we have, maybe consider that you're fucking up a lot more than just my personal life. Since you seem to enjoy doing that more than anyone else—"

At least Mira's rant stopped when a rusty squeak filled the room. Without thinking, he leaned over to nudge Anya's chin so she looked over at the sound she couldn't hear.

Byte rolled into the room. He'd gotten new wheels a while ago, some bigger ones that Arges had found on the bottom of the sea floor. But they were squeakier than the last ones, and that was saying something.

"Oh," Anya breathed, her voice a little too loud. "You don't say?"

Obviously, she wasn't talking to him or Mira. Bracing himself on the lip of the moon pool with his bad arm, he reached for her droid and gently pulled it off her head.

The words on the glass were a hundred rainbow marks, all dancing up and down with a single word. Byte's name. It danced around the lens, bumping off all the rainbows and sending them scattering in her excitement.

"She knows the droid?" he asked, before realizing that he was holding Bitsy, so Anya couldn't understand him.

Handing Bitsy back, he flashed a few of the signs she'd taught him. He still knew very little of her language, but he knew enough to gesture between the two droids and then signed half of the word "friend". He completed the word by miming what his other hand should have done afterward.

The pleased smile on Anya's face was worth every ounce of brain power it took to remember that word.

Affixing Bitsy back onto her head, she adjusted the lens before saying, "Yes, I think Bitsy knows him. Is your droid's name Byte?"

Mira looked between the two of them, clearly confused. "Yes, that's his name."

"They must have known each other from a long time ago." Anya smiled, then patted her hand onto Bitsy where her body rested on top of her head. "She's sweet on him, it seems, so we should let them have a chat when they can."

Byte rolled to a stop in the middle of the room, and his little binocular eyes rose to blink at the droid on top of her head. "All of her models were decommissioned years ago," the droid advised.

"Not all of them." Anya grinned. "Besides, Bitsy's had a few upgrades in the time since."

Daios leaned, peering through the lens from behind Anya's head to see bright pink hearts radiating around Byte's little body.

He wasn't sure how to feel about this. The droids were already abominations in his eyes. Metal creations with souls were somehow even harder to swallow.

"Well," Mira muttered. "That's unexpected. Regardless, my name is Mira and I'm happy to welcome you to our home. We haven't named it yet, but maybe you'll be helpful in that. Let's get you out of the water first, shall we?"

She took a step closer to Anya, but he didn't like that either. With a low growl rumbling in his chest, he planted his hand underneath Anya's thighs and lifted her out of the water himself. She was so light, he didn't need someone else helping her.

The little squeak that came out of her when he did so was decidedly satisfying, anyway. It was worth every ounce of pressure it put on his shoulder.

With an arched brow, he watched her sit at the edge of the moon pool and glare at him. "I could do it myself."

"I know."

She tilted her head to the side, eyes narrowing. "You're acting strange."

Mira snorted from behind her. "You're not kidding. I've never seen the big lug talk this much."

"He talks." Anya's tone was almost... defensive. She glared at the woman behind her before getting to her feet. Water rushed out of her wetsuit, splashing on the floor and rolling into the water around his rib gills.

He wasn't so prideful that he didn't suck that water into himself, coating his gills with her scent for later. For when he would no longer be permitted to see her.

"He talks?" Mira repeated, before another snort followed her words. "The man doesn't talk. He barely even breathes in my direction."

"That's because I don't like you," he growled before turning his attention to Anya. "Are you well?"

She was still looking at him with that shocked expression. Like she didn't know why he was asking, or that she hadn't expected him to come up with her. And it made him feel… awful. She shouldn't expect him to drop her off in a place she'd never been before, with people she hadn't ever met, and then just leave.

Of course, that is what he had planned to do. But he didn't want to do that anymore.

Maybe it was because he'd thought he had seen her curl into him a little. Like she hadn't wanted to release him from her grip, either. But right now, she seemed fine. She stood on her own two feet, looking down at him with surprise, but not with fear. She wasn't begging him to take her back into the water.

Maybe he had read this situation wrong.

Her little brows furrowed at his question. "I'm fine," she said, shrugging her shoulders. "It's not so different from Alpha, just a lot smaller."

"Is it?" Mira walked forward and held out her hand. "Sorry, again, I'm Mira."

"Anya." The two women shook hands, all while he narrowed his eyes and couldn't stop looking at where Mira was touching her.

Was she gripping Anya too hard? She wasn't so delicate that she couldn't handle a firm handshake, but he didn't want her to be uncomfortable here. He didn't want her to be afraid of anyone here.

The water stirred beside him and Arges lifted himself onto the mats beside the moon pool. The graceful movement didn't startle the other two women in the slightest, not like Daios had. Instead, Arges shook his hair back and grinned at Anya.

"Making friends, yet?"

"I don't know." Anya replied with a laugh. She adjusted Bitsy again, the only sign that she was slightly nervous. "I'm still not sure what you want me to do here."

"We're not either." Arges shrugged. "I think there's a lot you could do for us, but we want to talk with you about that first. We'll let you get settled before we fill your mind with all the possibilities. We don't want you to think you're stuck here."

Right. Because they were all still under the impression that he had kidnapped her. Stolen her away from her home like a creature who had snuck out of the depths to drag her into the undercurrents with him.

He awkwardly yanked himself out of the water as well, having to brace himself on his good arm as his gills flared a little wider. "She's not afraid of us," he growled.

Mira crossed her arms in front of her chest and he noticed how she moved just slightly in between him and Anya. "Daios. It's a lot for anyone to process, especially someone who grew up in Alpha. I know you think you're helping, but you're very large and intimidating."

"She's not afraid of me," he hissed.

All his fins flared even more. He wanted to puff himself up even larger. Intimidate the hell out of this achromo who thought she had the right to stand between him and Anya.

He knew this was ridiculous. Anya was somewhere safe. He should be happy and satisfied knowing that nothing would happen to her here. But he wanted... something. Something that he couldn't figure out and that was so frustrating.

Anya stepped around Mira, walking over to him until she was all that he could see. She blocked out everyone else in the room, with her sweet face and golden hair that always reminded him of sunlight. Her expression was soft, not like the others, who looked at him with distrust and sometimes disgust on their features.

He knew he was lacking in many things. Kindness, softness, the ability to see what other people were feeling and react accordingly. His outside now matched that monstrous interior, and some days he was ashamed of that.

But when she placed her hand on his wounded shoulder, so covered with scars that some of his scales had lifted over the worn skin, he didn't feel so ugly. Daios forgot what he looked like when she touched him like that.

"I'm going to be fine here," she said, a soft smile on her face. "But they are right. You are very large and you take up quite a bit of room."

He didn't mind it so much when she said that. In fact, it almost felt like a compliment. Especially when her fingers squeezed the broad muscles of his shoulders and danced up to the side of his neck.

The slightest brush against his gills had his eyes rolling back in his head. In mixed company, she shouldn't touch him like this. But she didn't know... couldn't know...

When he finally opened his eyes again, he saw a vixen smile on her lips. She knew what she did to him. And she liked having that control.

"I promise, I won't talk about too much while you aren't here," she said. "But I think that I want to settle in, and perhaps let Bitsy and

Byte catch up. I'd like to get warm, change out of this wetsuit into something more comfortable. Then we'll call you back so we can all talk together. How does that sound?"

Even though he didn't love it, he nodded all the same. "I'll find you something to eat."

"I think she has food here."

"Nothing like what I can get you." He brushed his shorter arm down hers, gently tracing the soft skin there. And he imagined that his phantom hand also slid down her back. "Be safe, kalon."

He saw his brother twitch at the word, but then Daios was already sinking into the water of the moon pool. He had to pretend he didn't overhear Mira's exclaimed, "Well, you're a beast tamer, aren't you?"

Chapter 24

As soon as Daios left, a whirlwind of movement swept her up. Mira meant the best, Anya could tell. The other woman was a veritable storm of a human being, though. She was loud and boisterous, or at least that's what Anya thought, from the way she used her hands when she talked and the constant exclamation points that Bitsy threw up. She could only imagine that Mira was nearly shouting whenever she opened her mouth.

The amount of swears that woman uttered, it was impressive to say the least. And they were usually directed at Arges, who stayed at the edge of the moon pool with an amused expression on his face. Mira wasn't scared of him at all.

Neither was Anya, when she looked inside herself. She should have had some amount of healthy apprehension about the new undines. After all, this was a group of people who had ordered her to be kidnapped and then brought to their doorstep. She had no idea what they wanted with her, or what their plans were.

But they didn't seem like they wanted to hurt her. And she also didn't think Daios would let them.

"Right?"

Anya blinked, and Bitsy threw up a mess of words that must have been an entire one-sided conversation that she'd just missed because she was thinking about Daios. Thankfully, she had the age-old story she could fall back on.

"I'm sorry." Anya tapped her ears. "I'm hard of hearing, so I missed what you said."

Of course, Bitsy had not. She didn't get to use that excuse if someone knew her. Daios would give her a look that said he was unimpressed before he just crossed his arms and waited for her to read what he'd said before. The man was one of few words, and he had no intention of repeating himself if he could help it.

Mira's expression turned to surprise, her eyebrows raising high and revealing wrinkles on her forehead before she nodded. "Right, sorry. I forget. I was saying, this is the bathing room. I'll leave some clothes out here for you to change into when you're ready. I'm sure it was a harrowing experience for you."

"It wasn't so bad, really. Cold. The life support in the facility wasn't able to run at full power because we didn't want anyone to realize we were there." Anya shrugged. "But the company wasn't terrible, and I was able to work on my own plan for a while until it all blew up. I hope you have a better idea than I did."

The redhead in front of her turned calculating. "Are you suggesting that you've been working against your father?"

"For years."

"You and I are going to get along just fine." Mira dumped an armful of clothing onto a bench outside the small curtain. "Take your time. I'm sure you want to wash the salt off. There's a tube of gunk in there that looks terrible, but it does wonders for your hair."

That was all she needed. Placing Bitsy on the floor, she patted her droid on the top of the head. "Go speak with Byte while I shower."

Anya didn't have any other words. Besides, everything was hard to hear in this dome. As she slipped into the room and closed herself away from sight, she sighed. There was the indistinct murmur of people, a sensation of sound that she couldn't quite hear. Not to mention the shower itself. She remembered metal making a noise when she turned the knobs, but she couldn't hear that at all.

Her time with Daios had given her a small reprieve from what her life was actually like. If she tilted her head back and let the water run over her face, she could almost assume it had all been a dream.

A really lovely, wonderful dream that she would hold close for the rest of her life. But a dream, nonetheless. Now she was here, and she felt like she owed them all something.

Sighing, she let her head fall forward against the small wall of the shower that was just a tiny room with a small shower curtain to prevent them from seeing her. Forehead against the cool metal, it almost felt like she was home.

But that didn't make her feel better. In fact, it made her feel worse. She had hated being in Alpha, but now that she was free, she still felt like she was in shackles. These people had gotten her out of a terrible situation and that meant she had to repay them. Somehow. Which meant she was still beholden to someone and something and a larger picture when she just wanted to be herself for a little while.

She couldn't stay in the shower forever, though, and she certainly couldn't go back home. The only way forward was... well, forward. That meant she had to meet with these people.

Sighing, she turned the water off and grabbed the towel that hung just out of reach. At least her hair felt better using that strange "gunk" as Mira called it.

A part of her whispered that she should pretend Bitsy needed work and she couldn't hear anything of what they were saying. Then she could have a few moments of rest.

But there was only the one dome that she'd seen. And considering Mira was already in this one, she assumed she'd be staying here with the other rather intimidating woman.

The clothes were nice. They fit her well enough. Just a plain white shirt and pants that had seen better days, but they were still vaguely denim in color. Stepping out of the shower, she headed toward the other two on the opposite side of the small pod.

Arges was still out of the water, although he was glistening like he'd just dunked his body back into the moon pool. He watched Mira's movements with obvious interest, and perhaps a bit of rapt attention that suggested he just liked watching her. No matter what she did.

What was she doing? Mira seemed to mostly like working with metal, but her arm was lifting like she was chopping something and then…

"Oh!" Anya's shocked gasp was maybe a little too loud, since the other two turned toward her.

Mira grinned. "I had a feeling you haven't seen vegetables in a bit."

Thankfully, Anya could read her lips well enough to know what she meant. Mira faced her directly, and that certainly made it easier.

Maybe her thoughts played across her face a little too loudly, because Mira's grin spread a little wider. "I was an engineer in Beta." She said each word slowly, giving Anya plenty of time to make out what each word was. "A lot of engineers had hearing damage. So I know it's important that I face you when I talk to you."

That made sense. Everything she'd heard of Beta was that it was a hard place to live. She knew that the people there had very little resources, in particular food and water. But they worked hard, and they fixed everything that Alpha needed fixed.

It took every ounce of her self control to walk calmly over to that table laden with green food. "I have heard that Beta just went through a rather difficult time."

Bitsy's sharp appendages climbed up her leg and all the way to her shoulder. With a dramatic flare, she dropped the lens over Anya's eye and wrapped one of her spindly legs around her neck.

Good enough, she supposed. Anya took a seat and tried not to let her hands shake as she grabbed whatever she could. Lettuce. Sliced peppers to go on top. Tomatoes, riper than she had ever seen in Alpha. Brightly colored banana peppers and even what looked like strawberries. She didn't know how that was possible, considering they were very much out of season right now.

Mira took a seat opposite from her, arms crossed over her chest with that ever present grin on her face. "It might not be Alpha, but we have food here. Good food."

She didn't even care if there wasn't salad dressing. She'd been missing vegetables so much that her stomach clenched and her mouth watered embarrassingly. Still, she put a good chunk on her fork and held it still while she said, "To be honest, I didn't know what I was getting myself into when I agreed to leave my home."

And then she shoved the fork full into her mouth so she couldn't say anything else. Maybe she'd learned a thing or two from Daios after all.

Mira's head tilted to the side. "Well, at first we thought we would sell you back to your father. Get him all riled up that the princess of Alpha had been taken right from underneath his nose, and force him into a deal that allowed the undines to live without the achromos involvement."

"Achromos?" she asked, mouth stuffed with food. "I've heard Daios say that."

"It's what they call humans."

"Right." She remembered that, she did. Maybe she was drunk on vegetables.

"So here's the thing. Your dad doesn't seem all that upset you're missing, which goes against everything I've heard about him and you. Every city knows that the General and his daughter are two peas in a pod, closer than a normal family should be." Mira leaned her elbows on the table, her eyes searching Anya's as though she could see right into her mind. "Why do I feel like that's not the case? From what I've heard, he's not panicking at all."

She just wanted to eat in peace. Why couldn't they let her at least do that? Around another mouth full of food, she replied, "Dad already knows where I am."

"Here?"

"Well, not exactly. He has cameras outside Alpha, so he saw Daios take me. They sent ships after us, but none of them could find us. We were in the..." She waved the fork in the air, jabbing at the air. "Spiky coral."

"Ah. So he knows you aren't in the city. That's why he's not sending messages out to the other cities for people to find you." Mira and Arges shared a look. "That makes things a little more complicated. But Byte should be able to send messages to Alpha if we still want to try that."

"It won't work, anyway." Anya set her fork down, putting temptation aside for this long conversation. "He doesn't care if I'm missing. He cares if I behave. The only way to get the city to work against him is to show them all the terrible things he's done. And the only way to do that is through a broadcast from the inside. I've already thought all of this over with the other people I work with. Trust me when I say I know exactly how to take my father down with the least amount of bloodshed."

Arges leaned forward, and she noticed he did so specifically so she could see his lips as he repeated, "The people you work with?"

She wanted to tell him it didn't matter if she could see his lips. He was speaking in a language she did not know. But instead of being snippy and tired, she said, "There are a group of us who have been working for ages together. This is the best plan."

"Then how do you expect us to get someone into Alpha? We barely got you out." Mira spread her hands wide, as though the issue was only getting bigger. "Unless you and your friends have a plan for that?"

They didn't. She didn't think, at least. "I can ask."

"Please do."

Anya stood, stepping a little distance away so she could talk with Ace, but then she rounded back to the table and grabbed the bowl to take with her.

Wandering toward a back wall, she started when the wall moved. The panel must be motion censored, and it slid open to reveal a massive garden on the other side. But even better, there was a glass ceiling on this one.

She could send messages much easier without all that metal getting in the way. This was perfect.

"Bitsy," she said, chewing another bite. "Send a message to Ace to see if we can connect."

"On it." The words floated along with little hearts bubbling up from the plants. Clearly, Bitsy was in a good mood. Soon enough, she'd ask about Byte and what that history was. Just not right now.

As she stood in the garden, looking up at the glass, she saw a shadow in the distance. And she'd know that body anywhere. The massive shadow glowed red the moment her eyes locked on it, like he knew she was looking at him.

With a wave of her hand, she waited for him to mimic the movement. Even from this distance, she felt better knowing he was out there. Waiting for her to come into the water and see him again.

Bubbles appeared as Ace jotted out a quick message. "I've been trying to get in touch with you."

"Been a little busy."

"We've got a problem."

"What do you mean, we have a problem? Did the new guy not get into the city?"

Bitsy even seemed to hesitate before the message appeared in front of her eyes. A long message that made her heart break. "He's dead, Queenie. We sent him in, just like we planned, but your dad has everything locked down. One moment he was there, and the next, all I saw was nothing. I saw the footage after hacking into it. Your father had one of his goons cut his head off and left him there at the port for other people to find. It was a message. Anyone who gets in your father's way? Dead."

"I'm sorry to hear that." A shiver went down her spine, and she couldn't pinpoint why. Her father had always been ruthless. But that? That was more than he'd ever been before.

"It's over."

The words played in front of her eyes and she had to read them six times before she blurted, "Over? What do you mean, over?"

"No one will work with us. I've been trying to get someone else, but no one wants to take the risk. Too many people have died, and everyone knows. We're dead in the water with your father's blade in our back."

"It can't be over. I'm so close, Ace. I found other people who are willing to help us. You can't give up on me now. Do you hear me?" She almost wanted to hit something. She wanted to throw the bowl in her hands and watch it shatter on the floor. "I need you to stay in this. With me."

Silence. So much silence from the other end that her tinnitus started acting up. Or maybe that was because no one else was in the room with her, and she was alone yet again.

Always alone. Now Ace was going to leave her too, and no one would ever do anything about her father. No one would ever do anything about... anything.

Hands shaking, she set the bowl down before she broke what was likely one of the few that Mira owned. "Ace?" she tried again. "Ace, talk to me."

Bitsy let raindrops play down the screen, and that's when she knew Ace had disconnected the call. She would not get any help from her friend. She was alone in this, as she had been from the start.

Swallowing hard, she tried not to cry even though she could feel the sound pressing against her throat.

Until Bitsy put an arrow in front of her face and she saw the shadow had moved much, much closer. Daios was on the other side of the glass, still slightly above her. But he had his webbed hand pressed against it. And she knew, she just knew, that he'd known she needed him with her.

Reaching up to the glass, she pressed her hand on the opposite side like she was holding onto him. Or perhaps, like he was holding her together.

Chapter 25

How did he show her how he felt? That seemed like an impossible ask from a woman who should have known just from his body language. Daios wasn't good at telling anyone anything. He'd never been a talker, even when he was just a boy. His mother used to say that he was as stoic as a stone wall, immovable, and sometimes a little cold.

He didn't see the value in chatting with people when he could show them what he wanted. Of course, that hadn't gotten him very far with women. And it would not get him very far with his little achromo.

After all, Anya had settled in rather nicely.

He hated how much that made him upset. Logically, Daios knew she did better with a task at hand. He looked at how she had worked in the facility, and he knew it made her feel more comfortable to be needed. He even understood it, because he was very similar.

Sighing, he fanned his fluke over the dust that had settled in this small, deep sea canyon. He was doing the same thing right now. Trying to appease his emotions and his thoughts by keeping himself busy.

This was not a task that kept his mind busy, though. All he had to do was uncover lost items on the sea floor, if there were any. And fanning the dust with his tail certainly didn't make him feel like he had something to do. Instead, all he could think about was her.

His distance from her had created unwanted side effects. The visions were back. The memories of all those dead bodies who had floated in the currents, all because of what he'd done. All because he had no self control when it came to his own hatred. Even now, he could feel those icy fingers grabbing onto his shoulders, pulling at the hand that should have still been there.

"Daios," they whispered. "Come, seek your retribution."

He didn't want to do that. He wanted to go back home, to a woman with a golden smile and a soul that eased his own. Only weeks ago he would have claimed it was a shame that the woman was an achromo. He would have told himself to sever this connection and break free from her siren call.

But now? Now he knew what it was to stand in the light of her smile and bask in the glow of her joy. He would trade the entire sea for a few moments with her.

"Why are we doing this again?" The words snapped Daios out of his fugue state. A yellow fin draped down on top of his head, only to be whisked away when he swiped at it with his claws.

"Mira thinks this was a dumping ground for the droids like Byte and Bitsy," he grumbled. "If we can find one of their... kin, then she will be pleased."

Maketes floated ahead of him, tail flicking to keep him lying down on the current. He had his arms behind his head, fully trusting the ocean to keep him cradled in her arms. If only the ocean were so contented with Daios.

"Ah right," Maketes lifted one of his hands in the air as if pulling a thought out of his head. "Fabricators. That's what she called them. Fascinating what the humans can make, isn't it? I never thought they would be such interesting people."

"They aren't," he grumbled.

"You seem to have found one in particular very fascinating. Or do you think no one has noticed how much you hang around the dome?" He spun in the water, putting a ridiculous frown on his face. "You're very mopey lately, Daios."

"I am not moping." Daios did his best to keep the emotion out of his words, but he knew that Maketes could see right through him.

His brother grinned, the expression one of utter triumph. "Not mopey at all? Not when you've been dragging yourself around the sea like you've got the weight of the world on your shoulders? I've never had such trouble getting you to leave our pod. Not since the achromos found our first home. Do you know what that makes me think?"

He didn't care. He didn't want to know what his brother thought, and he certainly did not care what Maketes had told himself. There was no story. There was nothing at all.

Grunting, he pushed past Maketes and off into an area of this graveyard they had not searched yet. But he knew that his brother wouldn't give up this teasing. Not when he was so certain that he had something to tear into.

"Daios," Maketes called, drawing out each sound of his name. "You like the woman! Far more than any other achromo we've met before."

"I do not."

"You think I haven't seen you watching her? Mira's home is glass. I can see your eyes are on her all the time. Not just when she's looking at you." Maketes floated by him again, his arms behind his head as though he didn't have a care in the world. "She doesn't watch you nearly as much. I wonder why that is?"

"She is an achromo. She is unaware of her surroundings and does not have our natural ability to see far in the water." At least, that's what he'd been telling himself.

Because he had noticed she didn't look at him as much as he wanted her to. Daios had been swimming by the glass dome multiple times a day in the hopes that he would catch a glimpse of her lovely eyes. But no, he was not so lucky. If she looked at him every other day, that was a surprise.

"Arges said she's settling in well, but seems a little off herself. I wonder if you're both mopey for the same reason."

"We are not," Daios snapped. "That is ridiculous."

"Are you so sure? You were alone together for an awfully long time." Maketes pressed both of his hands to either side of his face, squishing his cheeks forward. "I can only imagine all the things you got into! So much... conversation."

He knew what Maketes meant, and he did not mean that they were conversing. But still, there was a part of him that thrust forward to say, "I do not know how to speak with her."

"You..." Maketes frowned, twisting his body so he was upright in the water. "What do you mean?"

"I..." Exasperated, he gestured toward his face. "This."

"That ugly face of yours is why you can't talk?"

Snarling, he turned away to start searching again. "Forget I said it."

"No, no, I'm sorry. I didn't mean to make fun of the situation. I've just never seen you all tongue tied over a woman before." Maketes rushed forward, careful not to touch Daios and make him even angrier, but clearly wanting to show support. "You can't talk with her? You seemed fine when you brought her here. I'm certain I saw you speaking with her."

"That was different."

When it was just the two of them, it was easier. He didn't think about all the things her people had done to his. He barely even noticed their differences when she was laughing or locking his gaze on hers. She had a way about her that made him forget to be uncomfortable.

But here? All of that was different.

Everyone looked at him all the time. Like they were just waiting for him to explode and murder her. And he didn't like that. He didn't want people to think that he could ever hurt her, let alone that he'd thought about it.

Yes, he hated the achromos. Her people were a plague upon this sea and he would gladly see them all dead. Just not... her. And that was a strange emotion to even get through on his own, regardless of everyone judging him while he did it.

"Well," Maketes said, his voice low and slow. "Why don't we... practice?"

"What?"

"Pretend I'm the lovely Miss Anya." He fluttered his lashes, gills flapping flat against his neck as though he were trying to make himself look more like a female. "Oh, Daios, I haven't seen you in weeks!"

He blinked at Maketes once, twice, then just grunted, "No."

Again, his brother swam in front of him, flaring all his fins out to the side as though that might stop Daios from swimming away. "I'm taking this seriously. You need to practice how you're going to talk to her if that's what you want to do. I'm good at conversing."

"No."

"I'm better than you." Maketes even stretched his arms out, forcing

Daios to remain where he was. "You need me, Daios. Let me help."

He didn't want anyone to help him. He wanted to wallow for a bit and then figure this out on his own. But Maketes was right, he was a better conversationalist...

Sighing, he rolled his eyes above Maketes's head and tried to shove down his pride. "I do not know how to tell her that I prefer her company."

"Over?"

"Everyone else." Why was this so hard to say? All he had to do was let the words fall from his tongue. That was it. But instead, they pressed against the back of his throat like a warning that telling anyone how he really felt would only end in disaster.

"Oh, well, that's easy enough. You could just tell her that you miss her."

Daios looked at Maketes. His brother's expression had softened, his brows coming down to create wrinkles in between his eyes. It almost was an expression of pity, which he refused to look too much into.

"I do not..." He couldn't even finish the sentence.

Of course he missed her. The sensation had grown every day since he had last spoken with her, even though he could see her from afar. His gills felt like they couldn't suck in enough air, and no matter how much he did, he wasn't tired at night. His body was exhausted, but his mind wondered what she had done during the day. If she was comfortable here. If Mira and Arges were filling her head with stories about how dangerous he was when all he wanted was to talk to her.

He just wanted to hear her voice. And that was terrifying on its own.

Maketes tilted his head to the side. "You do miss her. Quite a bit, it seems."

The dust settled around them. Daios didn't even dare to breathe because suddenly it was all laid out right in front of him. He missed her, and he didn't know how to tell her that.

It was stupid to be so shocked by it all, and yet he was. He didn't know how to do... this.

Maketes flicked his waist fins, coming just slightly closer. "Missing her doesn't make you weak, brother. But you should tell her. Maybe she's missing you just as much as you're missing her."

"There's no way either of us can know that."

"I suppose I could ask her for you, but that seems rather childish, don't you think? You should just talk to her, Daios."

"I can't do that." It was too risky. What if she didn't miss him at all? He'd handed her back to someone who at least looked like her. It was warm in Mira's pod, and it was safe there as well.

Plenty of his people here were more fitting for her, regardless. They could provide for her easier than the one armed warrior who didn't know how to tell her how he felt, or even that there were words he wished he could say to her. She was better off without him, just as he was better off without her.

This was his place. He was meant to take the risky jobs and run from his home. It was how it had always been.

And how it should always be.

Shaking his head, he expelled dust from his gills hard and turned away from Maketes. "She's fine where she is."

Maketes groaned. "Oh, you stubborn finhead! Maybe she would be better off if she were with you!"

He couldn't believe that, not even for a moment. Because if he did, then he would rush back to that glass dome. He would take her away again, burying her so far under the sea that no one would ever find her again but him.

Daios knew those thoughts were wrong. Deviant. Horrible things to do to someone he cared about, and so he had to keep himself away from her. He couldn't do it to her.

"Keep searching," he grumbled. "I'm going deeper."

"You can't go deeper, and you know it. We're on the very edge of our territory as it is. We don't need the depthstriders to be involved in any of this." Maketes arched his brow. "Unless you're heading their way again?"

He hadn't thought about the depthstriders in a while, but... Well, maybe it wasn't a terrible idea.

"Perhaps I should seek out their treatments," he muttered. "It might clear my head."

"Daios..."

He knew his brother was worried. The last time he'd gotten this confused, he'd headed down into the darkness to find the depthstriders. They were the few who guarded the gaseous vents at the bottom of the sea floor. They claimed inhaling the fumes provided them with visions of the future and sights that no one else could see.

Daios hadn't found it to do that at all. Instead, it had let him float. In his mind, in his scales, all of it disappeared, so he didn't have to exist.

It was a heady sensation. And an addictive one at that.

He knew that he'd lost himself to it for a while, but he had never let it make decisions for him. Or at the very least, that's what he told himself.

Maketes watched him a little too closely, and he wondered how far gone he'd been in those days of drifting.

"I just..." Maketes swallowed. "I just want to make sure you don't wander off too far."

"I won't."

But he probably would. If he was being honest with himself, the depthstriders felt more like family than his own people did. Perhaps that was because they were creatures of few words. Or perhaps it was that he'd always thought they buried themselves in the darkness for reasons that were too close to his own problems.

With a quick nod to his brother, he flexed his tail and off he went. Sinking deeper and deeper until there was no light left. Only the faint red glow from his body as he searched the murk.

He lost himself in his thoughts. They rioted in his mind. The up and down of emotion as he thought about telling her how he felt, and what she meant to him. He wanted to let her know that he felt more free with her than he had in a very long time. She didn't judge him. There was no fear of rejection between the two of them because she didn't know how bloodthirsty he was, and all the mistakes he'd made.

But he didn't know how to say any of that.

Daios lifted a hunk of rusted metal out of the ground, then let it fall back to the sea floor with a puff of silt. He was wasting his time down here. He knew it. Mira knew it. And still, she had sent him on this mission to keep him out of trouble.

She'd almost succeeded in doing so, if he hadn't come down alone to the depths.

Daios only had a second to realize there was a current rushing toward him. He curled his tail tightly into his body as a solid wall of muscle and rage slammed into him and dragged him even deeper into the abyss.

Chapter 26

Anya laid her cheek down on the table and watched the two droids as they interacted with each other. Bitsy couldn't speak out loud, which she'd been informed Byte could do. So the two droids ended up talking in projections.

It appeared they were telling each other the story of what had happened since the last time they'd seen each other. Just the highlights. A lot of what Byte projected onto the wall were images from underneath the sea. Giant whales swam above their head, squid tangled around his little metal body, and how he'd been dragged even deeper into the water.

In contrast, Bitsy projected Alpha. She showed them all around the city, and Anya had tried to read the lips of both Mira and Arges for a while before she'd given up. Mira wasn't looking at her. She was walking through the projected city of gold with rapture in her eyes. Arges wasn't even speaking the same language she could read the lips of, so it didn't matter what she thought he was saying.

Instead, she laid her head down on the desk and tried her best to not feel... off.

She'd felt like it for a while now, and it didn't make any sense. She'd gotten out of the city. Now she was here, with these people, who wanted the same thing she wanted. They intended to bring her father down and rebuild Alpha in a new image.

Sure, it was dangerous. They wanted the undines to go completely unbothered, and Anya didn't know if she could convince anyone of that. But at least there was hope now that she was here.

Unfortunately, that meant... nothing at all. Ace wasn't talking to her. No one cared to hear what her thoughts were, because she had always been intended to be nothing more than a pawn. They knew what they wanted to do already.

Where did that leave her? Staring off into the distance while her only means of communication talked to a long lost... What did she even call Byte? Did droids have lovers?

Sighing, she tilted her head away from them a bit and looked up through the glass. At least she got a glimpse of Daios every day. He swam by the glass dome often. Whenever she caught his eye, he would nod at her and angle his body away from her sight. Just like he used to.

All that forward momentum was lost. She worried maybe he didn't even want to see her. He'd delivered her like a package he'd wanted to get rid of. Then he'd disappeared into the ocean.

How was she supposed to feel? After that kiss, the way he'd touched her, and how she'd come apart in his arms... He'd dumped her and left, like he hadn't wanted to be around her anymore. After everything they'd talked about and everything...

Well, maybe she'd just been entertainment while they laid low so her father's ships couldn't find them. Maybe she was the only weird one who saw a man who had needed someone to see him.

Just like she'd wanted someone to see her.

Blowing out a breath, she realized the barely there murmur of talking had stopped. She'd gotten so lost in her thoughts that she'd forgotten to stay aware of the rest of the room.

Sitting up and shoving her hair out of her face, she tried to look like she'd been involved. At the very least, she could assume what they were saying. Bitsy had been showing them Alpha, which meant that they were probably asking about the city of her home. No need to ask her, though. They could just ask the droid.

Anya was a little harder to understand than Bitsy or Byte, anyway. Her words were maybe said a little differently, just enough for people to get uncomfortable. They had to focus on facing her, at least while Bitsy wasn't on her head. And then, of course, there was the ever present knowledge that she couldn't hear them.

Maybe she was too tired. She normally didn't care this much.

"Oh, right," she read from Mira's lips. "Bitsy —" and then some words that didn't really make a ton of sense because Mira had tilted to look at the droids on the table and her mouth wasn't facing Anya any longer.

Considering Bitsy charged toward her and climbed up her arm, she could assume Mira had ordered the little droid up so they could talk.

The lens came down over her eye and Anya tried a smile that felt fake on her face. "Sorry, I didn't think it was necessary for me to be part of the conversation."

Mira winced. "That's not how we want you to feel at all, and I apologize if that was how it seemed. Bitsy was showing us the inside of your home. It's very different from where I grew up."

"Beta?"

Mira shrugged. "I just assumed we were all living in tin cans that were falling the fuck apart."

Right. Of course, that's what Alpha wanted everyone to think. The last thing they needed was for the other cities to realize there was one in particular that was green and full of life.

"My father didn't want people to know just how much we had." She twisted her hands in her lap, trying to keep them from shaking. "He wanted to keep Alpha a utopia where only the rich and the better off could go. That way, when he needed someone talented like a doctor or an artist, they were being given a gift that no one else was often given. It makes controlling people very easy."

A shadow of doubt crossed through Mira's expression. She flicked her gaze over to the undine half in the water and half on the landing area of the moon pool.

Perhaps they didn't think she understood their facial expressions, but Anya had spent the better part of her life observing others. She had to know how to read faces as much as she had to know how to read lips. What she'd just said worried them, as it should.

Coughing into her hand for attention, she adjusted Bitsy, so it was easier to read a lot of words very quickly. "Is there a problem?"

Mira bit her lip, that worrying movement already telling Anya what she was going to say. "We're not sure what to do at this point. You say your contact is incapable of doing any more than what they already have. There is no easy way into the city. We cannot use your propaganda idea without your friend. And if what you say is true, your father has very little interest in getting you back."

"I would suggest that me being missing is only helping him spread the idea that the undines are dangerous," she said with a slow nod. "Look at the reality of all this. He has footage of Daios kidnapping me. The people of the city have already been told that undines are dangerous monsters who would feast upon their children's flesh if they could. They have seen footage of attacks on other cities. And now I've gone missing."

"So our only other choice is to bring you back." Mira frowned, though. As if even she heard the flaw in that plan.

"We can't get me back in," Anya replied, even as Bitsy sent warning signals all over the lens. "I don't think he would let me return to the city, to be honest. It's easier for him now to say I'm dead."

There was the worst part of all this. It was easier to claim the death of his daughter. It was easier for him to play the martyr, the father who had lost a dear daughter and who couldn't possibly ever recover from it without the help of his loyal city.

They'd fallen right into his greatest dreams, and now they had to suffer through the consequences.

Arges's gills flared and then flattened. "I will seek my brothers. Perhaps they will have some idea."

Mira gave him a kiss before he left. It made Anya's cheeks flare bright red, and she wasn't sure why. But then again, yes, she did. Jealousy burned in her heart every time she looked at them. It was so easy for them, and far too painful to watch their interactions when she wished it was herself and another undine who had forgotten she existed.

Bitsy fidgeted on her head while Anya stood and wandered into the small garden area. This needed to be expanded greatly. Two humans went through a lot more food than one human did. If she was going to stay for a while, then they needed more plants. More space.

Unfortunately, it didn't seem like that was going to be very easy.

Bitsy put an arrow in front of her face, pointing behind her. Of course, Mira would follow her. Of course, she would also want to talk about… whatever it was Mira talked about.

Sighing, she turned and pasted that fake smile on her face. "Hi. I assume he's gone?"

She still hadn't figured out how to say 'Arges'. The undines used their lips in such a strange way, and it was hard to guess what that might sound like. She'd said it a few times, but considering the way his eyes had pinched in, she knew she'd said it wrong.

"He's headed out." Mira leaned against the wall, her arms looped over her chest and her ankles crossed as well. "So you're here. I can only imagine it's a relief to be with us instead of wherever Daios was keeping you."

She'd brought this up a few times, and it always made Anya strangely defensive. "It wasn't so bad."

"The facility you talked about? I looked it up. You barely had power enough for heat, let alone for whatever else you were doing. So I can't imagine it was easy. Especially with…"

That's when Mira always stopped talking, as though she were fishing for information about Daios. Anya knew people like this in Alpha. They were always interested in the gossip, although they never said anything themselves. They hoarded information, likely because they felt like it gave them power.

Unfortunately, it gave Mira power. And she didn't want to tell anyone about anything but also…

She wanted a friend.

Bitsy drew a large circle around Mira with the words, "You can trust her."

Taking a deep breath, she looked up at the glass dome and wished there was a familiar red scaled undine floating above her head. "He makes me feel safe."

Bitsy had to highlight a few exclamation points, and the animated figure of a person shaking with laughter. She could see the image of Mira laughing in the reflection of the glass above her head.

Let her laugh. She didn't need the other woman to understand how she felt.

But then Bitsy got more insistent, and she looked back to Mira.

The redhead was suddenly quiet, staring at her with an expression that said she was shocked, horrified, and maybe a little bit ill. "Wait, you're not kidding?"

Anya shook her head. "No, I'm not. He made me feel very safe the whole time I was there."

"He's huge, though. You must have been terrified of him when you first saw him."

Anya tried to remember whether or not she was. It was hard to think back on those moments when she'd first seen him and thought of him as a monster, now that she knew Daios a little better. But she didn't think she had ever been terrified.

"Not really." She shrugged. "He was my best option at escape. I grew up with the real monsters, Mira. I have seen what they do and how terrible they are. An undine never seemed so bad when I knew just how powerful they could be. I was looking for a protector, I suppose, and he fit into that role all too well."

The ghost of his lips against hers pressed to her skin. She could still feel the strength of that powerful arm as he'd dragged her closer. The press of his claws against her flesh. But it wasn't just those memories that made her feel so soft around him. It was also waking up to him brushing his claws through her hair so there weren't any tangles when she woke up. It was the low murmur of his voice that she could actually hear, and the way he softened when he looked at her.

"I've never felt so cherished," she said, not even certain that her voice was loud enough to be heard. "I know that's insanity. He's someone I don't know, not really. I haven't talked to him much about his life or where he came from. I don't know his struggles or his family or what it was like for him growing up. All I know is that the core of him..." She thumped her fist against her chest. "It's the same as what is in here."

Mira watched her with wide eyes, and she thought maybe the other woman wouldn't believe her. Maybe all those words would feel like a lie.

But then Mira nodded, slowly, but still a nod. "When Arges first kidnapped me, he took me to a facility underwater as well. He hid me away from the others to see if he could convince me to turn on our kind. But then, something happened. The more I saw his resilience, the stoic ferocity that made him who he was, it called out to me. I know what you mean when you say something in here feels the same as what lives in them."

Anya watched Mira press a hand to her heart as well, and she felt something inside herself unravel. "It should not exist."

"Perhaps not. Your father would call us abominations for feeling it." Mira shrugged. "But I have never followed the rules, and I'm not going to start now. I still can't believe you feel that way about Daios, though. He sucks."

A little giggle slipped out, and then another. Then, soon enough, Anya had lost all control over her mirth. Laughter bubbled up and out of her mouth, boiling over in hysterics. She'd almost gotten herself under control when she saw Mira was also laughing, and then that set her off all over again.

Finally, they stopped laughing after her stomach muscles screamed in protest. Mira had slid down the wall to sit on her butt, and Anya was braced against a box of growing basil. Her nose was filled with the scent of green things growing, of earth and loam and the calming smell of herbs.

Wiping tears from her eyes, Anya finally managed, "He doesn't suck."

"He does! He tried to kill me multiple times when I first came here. Even after he'd decided that he wouldn't do that, he's always been a gruff bastard."

"Not to me," she replied, laughter probably making her words almost impossible to understand. "He's always been so sweet to me."

"That's so hard to imagine."

She couldn't imagine why. He always seemed aware of his own strength around her. And he was kinder than any of the people in her city, because he was kind without an ulterior motive. He didn't want something from her. He just wanted her to smile.

Sighing, she slid down until she was sitting on the floor as well. Leaning her head back against the worn wood, she replied, "He brushed my hair."

"He what?" Mira even leaned forward with the force of the word. "When?"

"All the time." She shrugged. "He likes my hair."

"That's..." Mira shook her head. "Tell me everything. All I know is the grumbly asshole who tried to kill me. Clearly, I do not know this version of the man."

And for the first time since she'd been abducted, Anya just relaxed. She told her new friend everything, well, other than the more physical aspects they'd indulged in. She told her all the stories and all the kindness and all the strangeness she'd been feeling.

Mira never judged her, not even once. All she saw was another woman who had fallen in love with an undine, and Anya knew she would be accepted here.

It was a good feeling, even if it was a little terrifying.

Chapter 27

aios was cast down into the muck and mire of the depthstrider home. Long ago, when he was just a child, he remembered hearing so many stories about these creatures. They were pale from lack of sunlight. They were dangerous, with claws much larger than his own, and eyes that saw into the future.

There were rumors that the woman who ran their pod, Mitera, was descended from them. It was why she appeared more like a jellyfish than the other People of Water. She could see the future with her multicolored eyes swirling as she peered into a person's very soul.

Dangerous creatures, indeed. They could look inside someone they touched and know what and how and when they were going to swim throughout their lives. He'd been terrified of them. Or perhaps he'd been more terrified of what they would see.

His back ached as he struck the ground. Dust plumed around him, pressing against every part of his body and threatening to choke him through his gills. This was the same as the first time the depthstriders had brought him here. Years ago. He had been young and foolish, then.

A part of him had always thought he was better than the others. Pride had been his downfall. And when Arges was given the esteemed position of taking over their pod of warriors, he'd lost his mind. His ego had sent him careening into the depths as though he could change what had happened. Just like now, he'd been struck in the side and thrown into the dirt.

Daios was big. This creature was so much larger.

Breathing hard, he curled his fingers in the muck at the bottom of the sea. He knew what he would find when he looked up, and still he had to steel himself for what he would see.

Pale skin on the male's chest tapered into a deep purple that was only seen this far in the abyss. The depthstrider who loomed above him did not have fins that flared on his sides like the other undines, but tendrils. Tentacles that ended with bulbous tips that lit up with his anger. Though he still had the tell-tale fins on the sides of his face, his hair was much finer. Where Daios's locks were tangled into their own similar tentacles, this one had fine strands that billowed around his head like a plume of dark ink.

A severe face etched white as the moon, with lines of deep purple that streaked down from his eyes like tears, stared down at him. Powerful muscles flexed, his tail stretched so far behind him that it disappeared in the meager light both of their bodies let off.

"Fortis," he snarled.

"You have returned too soon," Fortis replied, his voice crackling with misuse. "Or perhaps far too late."

The tips of his tentacles glowed brighter, their ends reaching for him with what he knew would be an electric zap that would render him unconscious.

Rolling, he flicked his tail to get away from the much larger male.

It was rare to meet anything in this sea that was larger than him, and it always made him uncomfortable.

Fortis grabbed onto his fluke, claws digging mercilessly into the delicate membrane there. Daios arched his back, his teeth bared as white hot pain raced up his spine all the way into the small of his back.

He fought. Writhing and wriggling like he could get away from this much larger creature who had absolutely no intention of letting him go. He fought until blood filled his gills, flowing out of the deep wounds that Fortis continued to rip through him. And still, he was stuck. Like a fish on a hook.

Hissing out an angry breath, he stilled. "What do you want with me, Fortis?"

"I wish for you to see."

"I have seen enough from your kind," he spat. Twisting so he could see the other male, he bared his fangs and gnashed his jaw. "Or did you forget how long I was here last time? Because I did not. I know exactly how long I was here and how much you plied me with your sulfuric medicine. It took me months to get it out of my system."

"Because you had not yet seen," Fortis replied, those soulless black eyes meeting his and uncaring of the discomfort he caused. "Now you have seen some, but not enough. You have been summoned."

"By who?" Daios snarled.

"By all of those who have been before, all of those suffer now, and those you meant to save." Fortis's voice raised until the booming sound nearly made Daios's ears bleed.

The depthstrider reeled him in, clawed hand over clawed hand, digging into his scales and ripping through his tail until the much larger creature could hold him in front of his face and snarl, "You didn't listen the first time."

In those black orbs, he could see colors moving. He fought harder, wrapping his own claws around the wrist that held onto him. Daios dug his talons in, tasting the black blood of the depthstrider that was so tainted with sulfur and metallic poison that it filled his lungs as though he had ingested the drug himself.

Maybe if he had both arms, he would have been able to fight harder. He would have been able to grapple with the other creature better, rather than just use his body like a battering ram. He couldn't get out of this depthstrider's grip, and he couldn't stop the darkness that swept around them both.

The colors in Fortis's eyes slowed, then stopped. That blackness sucked him in and suddenly he wasn't Daios any more. He wasn't anyone at all.

There was the briefest moment when he could still feel hatred that depthstriders could do this. That they were so connected to the sea itself that they could take a person out of their body and show them something that the sea wished for them to know. He had always hated how powerless moments like this made him feel. And Daios was tired of feeling weak.

Fortis sent him careening not through the ocean, but through a memory that flashed through his mind as though he was there. One moment, he was Daios at the bottom of the sea with a creature who had his hand wrapped around his neck. The next, he was back in Alpha.

Or at least, he thought it was Alpha. The room was still filled with wealth and gleaming walls as he had seen before. The opulence was almost blinding. But this room was not like the one he had seen, or any of the others he had seen while searching out Anya.

He floated in the water like the room was filled with it, but surely that wasn't possible. Groggy, he could feel both of his shoulders lifting and falling with each breath. Flexing his fingers, he felt them twitch, but he couldn't lift them. No, he had lost an arm. This wasn't him, it was someone else.

Blinking his eyes open, he stared down the length of his pale, purple body only to look up and see two achromos standing right in front of him. His vision was blurry, but he could see they were standing, not swimming. Two of them. Both men, one with hair barely covering his shiny skull and the other, younger man looking up at him with a dark grin on his face.

They wore white clothing and held something rectangular in their hands. He could see they were talking, but in this memory, he did not have the chip attached to his head. He didn't know what they were saying, only that they were saying something.

He took a deep breath, steadying himself to reach for them, to fight. But something was in the water. Something bitter that tasted like bile after his body rebelled over something he ate. It filled his gills and suddenly he wanted to sleep again. He wanted to let his head loll to the side and not even think of what was or could be.

Belatedly, he knew he should reach out to someone. But Daios didn't know how to do that. His people did not have the abilities of the depthstriders to reach out through the distances. He knew that there was nothing and no one who could hear him.

The achromos spoke for a while longer, then reached out and hit their hands against twin red orbs on either side of his container. One moment he was surrounded by water, and the next, he was spilling out onto the floor. He couldn't stop himself. His body was strangely limp, as though there wasn't a fiber of his being that could fight any longer.

Gills flaring wide, he tried to breathe, but he couldn't. There was no water around him, just air. His body just reacted. Water expelled through his gills, soaking his body as he shivered. Lungs he hadn't used in years filled with air as he breathed through his mouth, an unnatural feeling that seemed to thrill the achromos now standing above him.

Others reached for him. But he couldn't do anything with this body. All he could do was lie there, limp and trying to fight. It was in his blood to fight. He could hardly even bare his teeth to let them know that he intended to rip their guts out and make them wear them like a necklace.

They weren't afraid of him. It took six of them to lift his body, and not even smaller achromos. The ones who surrounded him were the larger of their species, and they still were not afraid.

He was placed on a cold, hard object. Higher up. He could feel his tail hanging off of it, limp as the fluke slapped heavily against the floor. The achromos converged on him, touching his body as though they had a right to.

And then he felt it. The first flick of pain that radiated through his body. It was enough to send his neck curving, just to look down at the achromo who had ripped off one of his scales.

The creature held up the purple specimen. He could see the light glinting off it, and there were gestures made as though the achromo was surprised at how thick it was. They'd torn a piece off of him. Like sharks in the water.

But then he saw next to them a table of implements that had been wheeled over. Blades and knives and glinting metal that were all meant to rip and maim. What was he supposed to do?

He couldn't move. He couldn't tell them to stop. He couldn't even beg for mercy once they had done all they intended to do.

Daios endured. Every inch of that memory was forced to be replayed as though he lived it himself. He felt their blades as they sliced through his skin while he was wide awake. They watched him for any sense that he might be able to move, but he wasn't ever able to defend himself. One moment he had been swimming through the sea and the next he was here.

Sharp blades cut into his belly. And his earlier threat became his reality. He watched his entrails pulled from his body, then measured and weighed on some gleaming scale that quickly grew mottled with his black blood. Throughout all of it, they watched him as though they were waiting for him to die. But his people were a hardy race. It took a lot to kill him, and so he endured.

Long hours of torment. What felt like forever while he suffered and silently begged them to stop.

When the first and last tear slid down his temple, he felt the spasm of death take him. His powerful tail curled up toward his body, the muscles bunching despite the drugs they had filled him with. Then and only then did he feel the sea reach to take him back.

Slamming back into his body, he gasped and reeled away from the creature who had held him. Fortis let him go. He knew Daios needed a few minutes to piece his soul and body back together. He needed to shake the feeling of death's claws from his shoulder and gather the taste of the sea on his tongue.

"Who?" he wheezed, his gills flaring wide and the oxygen in the water not feeding his lungs nearly enough.

"A friend," Fortis replied. Even this stoic creature seemed moved by the memory. Yellow tendrils shook at his sides, sending a strange strobe-like effect through the sea as they blinked on and off in his anger. "I found his body at the bottom of the sea. Half rotten with crabs crawling through his ribcage."

The image sent Daios's mind into a tailspin. He saw Hamartia's rotting face. He heard her screams and saw the water turning black around them. His breath caught in his lungs as he felt the cold claws of the dead scraping down the back of his neck.

And he knew if he turned, he would see her again. Or perhaps it would be someone else. Yet another person who had trusted him because he had listened to the depthstriders the first time they'd given him memories.

"I did your bidding," he whispered. "I did what you asked, and I failed. What makes you think I can do better this time?"

"Because this time you have more information. This time, I am not telling you what to do with the information I am giving you. I am showing you what has happened and now it is up to you to fix it."

"Why can't you?" he snarled, all of his fins flaring wide as though he were preparing to fight. "You are the one who told me all of this. You discovered the truth of the future that would happen if we do not stop them. What are you doing, Fortis? Other than sewing the seeds of malcontent for a future you know will come to pass no matter what we do?"

For the first time, the expression on Fortis's face changed. It wasn't much, just a twitch of his cheek, but Daios had a feeling that said far more than he could guess. "I have my own battle to fight."

"What battle, Fortis?" he shouted. "I see all of us risking our lives for this future you have seen. I see all of us above having to deal with the achromos far more than your kind, and still you all do nothing but sit in your muck and prophesy futures that have yet to come!"

A blur of pale color and surging rage rushed forward. Fortis stopped right in front of his face, so close that Daios could see the lines down his cheeks pulsed with a darker light. "Do you really believe there are only three cities? There are more, my brother. Do not make me kill you and find another messenger. The depthstriders are doing what we can down here so that those up above do not have to be attacked in the same way."

"You've already made me lose my arm," he replied, his own colors flaring bright. "I am not willing to lose anything else for you."

"Oh, because of the woman? Is that it? You will lose her and everything else if you do not control this. I could show you your future without her, if you wish. I could show you one with her as well. The ancients already gave your brother that gift, but it is not one I so readily share with those who do not appreciate what I can give them."

"Don't you dare speak of her."

"Or what? You'll kill me?" Fortis shoved him hard, sending him floating back a few feet before he flared his fins to stop himself. "You are lacking in more than just your arm, Daios. But the sea has tentatively cast you in her favor once again. So do not squander this opportunity, or she will swallow you herself."

With a flick of his massive tail, the pale creature disappeared into the darkness. But Daios stayed where he was until the pinpricks of light disappeared entirely. Until it was just him and the sea, at the bottom of the icy depths where he swore he could still feel Anya's arms around him.

Then it all hit him. Harder than the depthstrider who had grabbed him.

His people were dying. Anya's people were not just killing them, but experimenting on them. There was nothing either of them could do to stop them, but they had to try.

They would fight again. Battle and wage war until nothing remained but blood in this ocean. He should gather his warriors, create a pod of his own and attack every city until there was nothing remaining but rubble.

Instead, all he wanted was to see her.

Chapter 28

"Anya." The word flashed in front of her eyes and she didn't know if it was said by Bitsy or Mira. She didn't really care.

It had been days since anyone had seen Daios. Maketes had come back, his head hanging low, and he'd spoken with Arges, who appeared troubled. Mira hadn't even told her until right now that Daios had been off in the depths with Maketes. For whatever reason, Maketes had come home alone, and no one had thought to tell her that Daios was missing.

"Anya." The word again flashed, and this time Bitsy added an arrow so she knew that it was Mira speaking.

"You're not stopping me," she said, yanking on the wetsuit. She did so a little roughly, and she was already out of breath.

He was out there, somewhere, alone. And no one had thought that was a problem? Not a single person in this entire place had thought they should maybe send someone out to look for him?

"Maketes will find him," Mira said, moving in front of her with her hands held up. She approached her like she was a wild animal, trying her best to keep her calm. "They already have an idea of where he's gone off to, so it's okay. They're going to get him back and there's nothing you or I can do."

"There's nothing you can do," she replied with a glare. "But I'm going out there. Give me your rebreather."

"And if I don't?"

Anya had to take a deep, steadying breath. "Then I will take it from you."

Mira tilted her head to the side in a shrug. "I'm a lot bigger than you are. I'm stronger, too. No offense, but you've been living in Alpha while everyone waited on you hand and foot. I grew up an engineer, and I've kept those muscles since living here. If you want to fight me, I promise it's not going to end the way you think."

Maybe not. But she had to try. She could be scrappy if she wanted to be, and Anya wasn't above playing dirty.

Her eyes flicked over to the rebreather on the opposite side of Mira. If she hit the other woman over the head with something, she could definitely slip out before Mira got her feet back under her.

Bitsy put exclamations around Mira, which suggested the other woman might be laughing.

Mira shook her head. "If you're really going to attack me, then take the rebreather. There's nothing you or I can do right now, though. All you're going to do is get lost."

Sure. She might. But maybe if she got lost, he would find her again.

Glaring, she took the rebreather the moment the hood of her wetsuit covered her face. "I might get lost," she said, the words probably garbled as she dragged the rebreather on. "But at least I'm not sitting here doing nothing."

"Yeah, yeah." Mira waved her hand at her. "Go on, then. I'll come out with you. Just give me a second."

She didn't care if Mira came out with her. There was only one person she intended to see in that water, and that was the only person who might have an idea of what happened to Daios. She dove into the moon pool without even noticing how cold it was. The icy shivers running through her body had nothing to do with temperature, and everything to do with the fear.

Maketes wasn't too far. She could see the yellow flash of his scales as though he were waiting for her. As though he knew that she would come for him.

Anya hadn't swum on her own in a while, though. Daios had always carried her because he was much faster. But she hadn't realized she would get used to that speed so quickly. It felt like something was holding her back as she tried to reach Maketes's side.

At least the man took pity on her. With a flick of his tail and a graceful twirling motion that spun him in a circle, he was at her side in seconds.

"Anya," he said, the words rushing past her lens as he spoke almost too fast for her to read. "I'm so sorry. He was there one second and then he was gone the next. I have no idea what happened."

"Why were you somewhere dangerous to begin with?" Anger spiked, and she shoved at him. But he didn't even move, and that made her all the more angry. Hitting him again on the chest, she felt marginally better when he did at least flinch. "You've all lived here your entire life and you lose someone?"

"It happens more than you would think—"

"I don't care if it happens to other people! Where is he?"

Maketes eyed her, his expression a little lost and obviously just as affected. "I don't know! All I saw was a flash of pale scales and then they were both plunging off the edge of a cliff. I have no idea where it took him."

Her breath caught in her lungs, and she knew it had nothing to do with the rebreather malfunctioning. "It?"

He hesitated, his eyes flicking above her head before he looked back at her. Of course, there was another undine behind her. They had an audience, because why wouldn't they? A little human like her shoving around an undine was sure to be a spectacle that everyone wanted to see.

Let them watch. She'd been watched her entire life by more people than she could count on all her fingers and toes. They could judge her, think ill of her, they could claim she'd lost her mind. None of it mattered.

"What do you mean, it took him?" she repeated.

"A..." Again he hesitated, his throat bobbing in a harsh swallow. "We call them depthstriders."

"What is a depthstrider?"

He looked like she asked him to pull his own teeth out. "They are still People of Water, but they are... different from us."

Bitsy threw up words in a different color. The blue that she used matched Arges's coloring so Anya turned to see the other undine swimming up to them as well. "They are a dangerous lot, who keep to the abyss where they belong. Daios has met with them before, but they are not like us. They see things that others do not. And they take those they believe can help them in their cause."

"So that's where he disappeared to? Into the hands of some fanatics?"

She wanted to rip the mask off her face just so they all could see how angry she was. She wanted to scream and yell and throw something at these people who were just floating here and doing absolutely nothing.

"All of you call him your brother," she said, feeling the ache in her throat as though the words were pinched. "And you're doing absolutely nothing to save him."

Bitsy threw up an image that was supposed to soothe her, a cup of hot tea with steam rising out of it, but she shook her head hard to clear the image. She wanted to look right at them while she scolded them. She wanted them to know just how much this angered her.

Arges didn't rise to her bait, though. "We do not know where they have taken him, and as I said, they are dangerous. Unpredictable. I could send a hundred of our people after him and none of them would be likely to find out where they've taken him. Daios has been there before, and he is the only one who knows where their homes are hidden. It's safest for all of us to wait until he returns."

"What if he doesn't?" No one seemed to know how to reply to that, and it made her even more enraged. "What if he doesn't make it back this time, Arges? What then? Do you go and try to find him when it's been a week? A month? How long until you decide it is time to search for the brother you have left on his own?"

Bitsy circled a little area behind Arges where Mira was swimming up to all of them. And she knew this was going to be even more of an argument. Because if she had seen someone yelling at Daios, and implying what Anya was implying, then she would have swum to his rescue as well.

The redhead hadn't even put on a wetsuit. She was in her regular brown trousers and a billowing white shirt that clung to her body while her hair created a cloud of red around her head. The rebreather on her face was the only thing that hid the anger radiating through her body.

"Careful what you say, Anya. We've taken you in and given you this much leeway, but don't think we cannot make you an unwilling captive."

"Where are you going to put me?" she practically shouted. "There's only one dome. What's next? Chain me to the wall? You can do that if you want, but we both know you were the one who sent a wounded soldier into a dangerous city to find someone who inevitably proved useless."

The words fell between them and plummeted like stones.

Therein lay the worst of her emotions. The worst of her heartache.

Anya had always wanted to be the solution for her people. Even if that was just a dream of a princess who had never faced what it might take to actually save them. But she still wanted to do it. She had still endured the looks, and the judgement. She'd gone into the middle of the sea with a creature who she should have thought was a monster because it might help someone someday.

She'd been the one on the outskirts for her entire life, the one who was different and maybe even a little wrong. Now she was here, and she was still the different one. She was one of two humans who were trying to justify their use. At any point, the undines could decide she wasn't worth the trouble.

And the only undine who had given a shit thus far was missing.

The rebreather wasn't getting enough oxygen into her lungs. She felt like she couldn't breathe. All she wanted was to reach up and rip the damn thing off because it was suffocating her, but she couldn't do that without drowning.

How did anyone live like this? How did Mira stay with them when this was how she had to feel all the time?

Fingers already scrabbling at the edges of the rebreather, she suddenly froze when Maketes grabbed onto her arms. "Anya, we're doing everything that we can. I hope you know that."

"No, you aren't," she replied, her voice breaking just slightly. "You're doing nothing."

Then, over Arges's shoulder and beyond Mira's billowing red hair, she swore she saw a red light. A glimmering beacon that might have made other people wary, but she knew that light.

She'd seen it in the darkness many times, and she'd always risen to the occasion of facing him without fear. Because how could she fear him? To her, he was not a monster. He never had been.

"There," she whispered, her eyes widening above the rebreather until the saltwater stung. "Isn't that..."

She couldn't even say the words, but she knew it was. The other two undines with her turned, and Arges wrapped one of his arms around Mira to anchor her at his side. They all waited there, frozen, as the red undine sluggishly approached them.

Even from here, she could see he was moving too slow. There was the faintest trail of black that followed him, like silk ribbons fluttering in a breeze. But he was alive, and that was all that mattered.

He was alive, and he'd come back to her.

Anya held her breath until she saw his face. Until she saw the missing arm that always made her so certain this red undine was hers, and she didn't have to struggle to look at his face or pretend that she knew his voice over all the others.

He looked up and their eyes locked. She could feel his exhaustion, the ache that spread through his body, but even more, she could feel the relief that coursed through him at the sight of her. Because it was the same emotion she felt.

With a sudden surge of his tail and a flash of fluke, he sped toward her at twice the speed. She barely had time to open her arms before he thudded into her. Hard enough that bubbles erupted from the seal around the rebreather, and her chest ached with the impact. She wrapped her arms and legs around him, holding on as he didn't slow down.

He just struck her with all the force of a hurricane and carried her away from the others without a word.

"Daios!" Arges shouted, and she knew that Maketes was trying to follow them. None of them could keep up with her undine, though. A burst of energy and power renewed his speed, and soon enough, the others were just specks in the distance.

He was shaking, she realized. Quaking against her chest until she felt as rattled as he was. Tears pricked her eyes, and she held onto him tightly, rubbing her palms up and down his back because she didn't know what else to do. What to say.

Instead, she just held him to her heart and let him hold her against his.

At one point in their mad dash, he reached up and ripped the rebreather off of her face. Before she could even protest, he'd connected that tentacle to her throat, and she felt him breathing for her. Perhaps a little too fast, and certainly ragged. But it was there.

"Just need to feel you," he growled against her ear, the tones so low that they practically vibrated through her.

She went limp in his arms. How could she do anything else? She'd been so worried, so frantic, that he might be harmed. Which he was. He'd arrived with banners of blood trailing after his body and yet still he carried her through the sea. Perhaps to somewhere he considered safe.

Anya didn't stop stroking his back for a second, not even when he dove into a tall kelp forest. Not even when the sticky tendrils brushed against her face and coiled around their arms. Not even when she felt like maybe she was a little trapped.

Because if she was trapped with him, she knew without a doubt that she was safe.

She felt his massive sigh radiate throughout both of their bodies. Daios tangled them in the kelp until they floated together without him needing to move a single muscle. He wrapped the kelp in an intricately woven pattern, almost like they were lying in a hammock, with her draped across his chest.

Only then did she hold his face in her hands and force him to look at her. Carefully signing her words, she spoke along with the movements so he could be certain what she was saying.

"What happened?"

He sighed again, and his warm hand cupped her thigh. He jerked her a little higher up his body and then slid his hand up her back. Slowly, almost reverently, he pressed his hand to the back of her head and drew her down to rest against his shoulder. "I am worn and ragged. My kalon, let me rest with you before I must face what I have seen."

Chapter 29

It was remarkable how the voices suddenly silenced the moment he wrapped his arms around her. And that was insanity. He'd kidnapped her from her home, stolen her away into the ocean where she was constantly in danger. He'd made her rely on him for everything—warmth, breath, and food. She should hate him. She should want to see him rotting at the bottom of the ocean and revel in the sight of his dying writhe.

But she didn't. Anya wrapped her arms around him and held onto him as though she'd missed him just as much as he'd missed her.

Perhaps they were both mad. Lost in the future the ocean had promised them when they both knew it wouldn't be so easy to catch that future. No matter what they did, there was a journey ahead of them that could not and would not be stopped.

He was one of the People of Water. He would always fight against her kind, just as Arges still fought. But Mira had no real ties to her people, whereas Anya did. Anya loved her city and every person in it.

Otherwise, she wouldn't have fought so hard to keep them all alive. She wouldn't have struggled and pulled herself up every time something had gone wrong. She wouldn't have fought tooth and nail to bring her father down and liberate them from the leader that was destroying their lives.

She wouldn't have fled that city with a monster.

Tightening his arm around her, he relaxed back into the kelp and told himself that this was a place out of time. He could lay with her wrapped around him. He could pretend that they didn't need to leave this place. All he had to do was feel her.

And oh, he did. The soft press of her belly against his. The sensation of her ribs moving with each breath that he gave her. Her tiny fingers toying with the ends of his hair, gently separating the knots and then draping the strands out across his mangled shoulder.

Daios told himself that she didn't even see the old wound. That she touched him without fear because his arm was still there. That he was a whole man who could do whatever it took to keep her safe and happy. Together, they would live out their lives without struggle or fear. It was just... them. Breathing in the ocean as he exhaled into her lungs.

He'd forgotten what true relaxation felt like. How long had it been since he didn't feel like he needed his guard up? But he knew this place like he knew his own heart. There were no dangers here that he had to keep his ears and senses awake for. He could open his gills wide and fill himself with the scent of her. For later. For when all this fell apart again.

"What happened?" she asked again some time later, her words muffled by the water that pressed against her lips.

He didn't want to talk about it. He didn't want to say anything at all. He just wanted to sit here and hold her and listen to her breathe. But he knew that wasn't possible, not when his little kalon had a curiosity that burned through her.

Sighing, he tightened his grip on her waist. "I trust my brothers told you about the depthstriders?"

"Barely," she grumbled. Then she reached up to adjust Bitsy, tapping the glass as though his words hadn't come through clearly. "They don't like to tell me much. I don't think they trust me yet."

"They probably won't for a while." Though he hated letting go of her, he also knew that it was important for him to speak her language.

Arges had never done that for Mira. And suddenly, he wanted to be better than his brother at something.

So he nudged her, rolling her over his broad chest until she lay in the crook of his shorter arm. He braced her there, grateful for the wetsuit that prevented her from being pressed skin to skin with his gnarled scars. Then he lifted his hand, and brokenly signed what words he knew as he spoke.

"Depthstriders are like us and not. The woman who controls our pods, we call her Mitera, she is of their kind as well. They see the future in a way that none of us can. They have... contacted me before." He knew so few of these words. Frustration sank into his voice before she reached up and cupped his hand in hers. Together, they signed the other words, as she taught him what was the right way to move his hand, and filled in the words when he needed a second. "I failed them before, and I fear I will fail them again."

"Why would you be afraid? What are they asking you to do?"

He untangled their fingers and ran his hand down his face in frustration. "They do not often tell us what to do, only what is to come. We are meant to discern for ourselves what is the correct next step, and from there, we do what we think is right."

"They don't sound like very good oracles," she grumbled.

With a soft chuckle, he shook his head at her blasphemy. "Perhaps not. But I have endured some kind of friendship with one for years, so they have their place."

"You're friends with one?" She sat up on his chest, her hair floating in front of her face before she shoved it back. "What do you mean, friends?"

"Not in the way you're thinking. They are not a species of creature who readily maintain relationships with anyone. They are solitary creatures." He couldn't help himself. Daios smoothed her hair back from her face as it started to float forward again, if only so he could feel his fingers dancing past her ear. "But Fortis and I have worked together before. I do not enjoy disappointing people, if you have not noticed that about me yet."

"Oh, I have seen it."

To his utter delight, she mimicked what he was doing. Her fingers moved through his hair, gently pressing against his skull before dragging her nails down the back of his neck. He arched into her touch, letting his eyes drift shut as she trailed her light touch down his face and the delicate frills that framed it.

"You all have such interesting names," she murmured, her voice light as rain. "They all seem to end in a hiss."

"Most do. They all have great meaning to them. My people believe that names have power."

"Of course they do. Humans don't believe that as much, but quite a few of us believe there is power in names."

He blinked one of his eyes open, keeping that narrow-eyed suspicion on her. "What does Anya mean?"

Her face split into a bright smile. "I don't really think it's as deep as your name meanings. Anya means 'grace', I have been told. I did not grow into that name very well."

He disagreed. For their people, grace was something that was given in someone else's hour of need. She certainly had done that for him.

Licking his lips, he nodded. "My brother's name, Arges, means brilliant and shining. I grew up with a clutch mate who shared the same name meaning as how we would describe a bolt of lightning, or the shimmering of a fish's scales. He was always born to be the better of the two of us."

Daios knew he was baiting her. He wanted her to ask what he did not want to tell her. It was a foolish thing to do, an endeavor that would only end in pain for him.

And then she asked, "What does Daios mean?"

He cupped her cheek in his hand, watching as she tilted her face into his palm. Her lips pressed against his skin. Not a single part of her flinched away from him, and perhaps that was why he let the words slip from his tongue.

"Enemy," he whispered, the words suddenly pouring out of him. "It is a word we use to describe hostile or destructive beings. Creatures who consume all that stand in their way. So it means enemy in the way you call evil beings demons."

The skin around her eyes pinched. "They named you the enemy of your people from the day you were born?"

"No, my kalon." Cupping the back of her neck, he drew her down until he could press their foreheads together. Here he could breathe her in. Here he could hope that this would not ruin all that they had built. "They named me the enemy of yours."

He felt the shudder run through her body as though it ran through his own. And he knew what it meant.

For the first time since meeting him, perhaps she understood that she should fear him. He was created to be a weapon, and he had been aimed at her people for his entire life. Daios had killed more achromos than any other undine. And he killed them with pleasure.

Even now, he did not think he would hesitate to kill one of her kind. The pleasure and enjoyment he drew out of their suffering was the same as it had always been. He longed to taste their metallic blood in the currents. He still enjoyed seeing the horror in their eyes as their life fled from them while his claws ripped and tore into their beings.

But this one? This was not one he wished to kill. He only wanted to see her safe and so far from his violence that she would never be touched by it.

He heard her swallow, the clicking of her throat a warning. "You have called me kalon more times than I can count. If all your names have meaning, what does that one mean?"

Telling her that would bare his soul. It would say so much more than he was willing to say in this moment, because he knew that word was special. He'd seen the faces of the other undines when they'd heard him say it. They knew what that word meant.

He almost didn't tell her. He almost kept the secret to himself for a little while longer, because to everyone and now to her, he was a beast. A weapon. The brute who attacked and killed whomever and whatever he was told to kill. He was a murderer and a monster through and through.

But when she pulled back and looked down at him, her hand holding his palm to her cheek, all of that faded away. All the screams. All the creatures he'd killed a hundred times over, and all the lives that had been lost because he'd made the wrong choice. All of it was gone.

Only she remained.

He stroked her jaw with his thumb, tracing the outline of her bottom lip with the pad of it. His black claw arched over her mouth and she didn't look afraid of him.

Perhaps that was why he could murmur, "It is a special word. We save it only for a rare pearl that we find only once in our life. It means a beauty that is more than skin deep. It refers to a soul that radiates inside a person, so much so that you can see it on the outside as well."

"Daios," she whispered, her eyes wide.

"I hate your kind." He needed her to know that. "I will kill them again. I will fight until there is no breath left in this body and I have lost every limb I can stand to lose. That will never change."

"I know."

"I find your people disgusting. From your ugly toes to the horrid white color that surrounds your eyes. Every bit of your people is revolting, and your bodies are a nightmare to look upon."

Her lips twisted with a soft smile. "So you have said."

He slid his hand into her hair, dragging her close to him again. "But I do not find you ugly."

"Do you not?"

"How could I? When your hair is the color of the sun on a cloudless day? When your smile warms the entire ocean around me? When I touch you, your soul is so familiar to me. It is like I have known you in a hundred lifetimes before this, and some part of me that I've forgotten wishes to bury itself inside you. It tells me to cling to the curve of your waist, to clutch at the feeling in my chest that lingers when you are near. My soul wishes to keep you and never let you go."

Somehow, they had drawn closer to each other. He could feel the warmth of her lips through the thin veil of water that separated them. Her words were tiny currents that rippled over his face.

"What are you so afraid of?" she asked. "You have been holding yourself back, and I want to know why."

He swallowed. "I am made of rage and pain. I do not want to give you any of that, my kalon."

"I want you, Daios. I don't know why or how, but I do. Every bit of you. Your anger, your rage, your pain. I want that just as much as I want your attention and your adoration." Her hand pressed flat against his chest, her palm so warm against his skin. "I am not afraid of you."

"I am."

The words seared through him. Sometimes, the truth burned. It was worse than when he'd lost his arm, knowing that he was so terrified to touch her even when she lay on top of him and begged.

"Of me?" she asked.

"No."

"Then what are you afraid of?"

He stared into those strange eyes and replied, "Of hurting you."

Anya looked back at him, and he knew she stared into his very soul. Those blue orbs saw too much of him. In that look, she saw he was terrified of hurting her with his claws, his spines, with every bit of what he was. He could so easily tear into her flesh and for a long time, he'd thought that wasn't fair.

Now he knew he wasn't the only one with claws. Because with one word, she could break him. Snap him into a thousand pieces and shatter his soul into shards that dusted the sands of his home.

He'd given her that power. He had handed her the leash to his heart and now he couldn't take it back.

"You won't hurt me," she whispered, using both of her hands to hold on to his face. "Do you know how I know this?"

"You cannot know that."

"I do, though. I know you won't hurt me because you don't want to.

And that is good enough for me."

He stared up at this brave woman, and he wondered just how far she was willing to take this. "Then what are you proposing, my kalon?"

She licked her lips, that pink tongue flickering in a way that he wanted to follow. "Let me ease your pain, Daios. In whatever way I desire."

Who was he to deny this siren? "Whatever you desire, Anya."

Daios breathed her in, that citrusy smell that coiled around his heart and flooded his tongue with her flavor, and he wondered if this was what it felt like to fall in love.

Chapter 30

Anya was done trying to deny this. Whatever was between them, she intended to see it through.

They didn't need any more words. She was so afraid if they said one more thing, she'd blurt out that she was in love with him. And that was insane.

She was a human. He was an undine. They were two very different creatures who shouldn't be together. It shouldn't even be possible that they were talking underwater, let alone what she was about to encourage him to do.

But she'd seen Mira and Arges together. She'd seen the way they looked at each other and it had made a part of her awaken and scream inside her chest. She wanted this.

She wanted him.

So it took so little effort to spread her legs wide around his thick waist and to kiss him. She didn't know if undines even did this, but the last time he'd been very good at it. All she wanted was to feel him against her like they had in that facility where he had lost control for a few moments.

She wanted to know if that had been a mistake or if it had been real. She hoped it was real.

His hand at the back of her neck tightened, and she could feel the moment he let go of all his hesitation. One moment, he kissed her so softly, and the next, he devoured her.

With lips and tongue, teeth and sharp bites, he consumed whatever she gave him. Like he was trying to swallow her whole. Like he wanted to crawl inside her and never leave and in this moment she couldn't think of a reason why he shouldn't.

"What do you wish of me?" he said between kisses, and she could feel how restrained the words were.

He was holding himself back. Desperately trying to keep some chains around himself so he didn't hurt her. But that wasn't what she wanted.

She wanted him unleashed. She wanted to be overwhelmed in every sense with him. Just him. So she kissed him back, her tongue tracing the deadly points of his fangs, before she whispered, "I want all of it, Daios. I want to think of nothing else but you."

The mood shifted. She could feel it in the current and in the way his hand clenched at the back of her neck. With a flick of his tail, he rolled on top of her. Kelp tangled at her back, keeping her exactly where he wanted her.

Daios loomed above her head. All flashing colors of red that turned her entire world into a deep crimson. He licked his lips, that black tongue catching her attention because she knew the ridges on it would feel incredible.

She watched his gills flare wide, all of them. His neck, his ribs, until she could see the delicate pink membranes deep inside his body. "You smell so good," he growled, his voice so low that it vibrated between her legs. "Whatever that scent is, I want to coat myself in it."

"You can smell me?" That didn't sound good. But considering the way he inhaled and arched back, she had a feeling it was a very good thing.

"Yes," he growled. "I can smell you."

Then he dove upon her and she knew what it felt like to be the prey. His claws skated down her body, his hand touching everything he could before she realized that he was surgically slicing the wetsuit away from her. She wanted to tell him to stop. She'd have to go back to the dome naked, but at the moment she didn't care.

Cool water flowed over her skin, pebbling the peaks of her breasts as he pulled the fabric away from her body. He watched every inch of skin revealed as though possessed. Even his eyes consumed every bit of her.

Anya almost said something, but then he pulled the wetsuit down to her waist. His hand spasmed against her hip where he held her still and then leaned down to press one long lick against her breast. She arched into him, her back bowing as the ridges of his tongue dragged against her nipple. The growl he let out made every part of her body heat. She felt like she could boil the ocean as he drew her into his mouth and sucked.

The tip of his tongue flicked at her while his hand dug into her skin so she couldn't think. She grabbed onto his head with both hands, holding him against her as she writhed.

Those ridges. They were so distracting. So different. So much a reminder that he was not a human man and all she wanted was to know what was so different about the rest of him.

Dragging her nails down the back of his neck, she grabbed onto whatever she could. Another low growl erupted from his chest, the vibrations making her want to dig into him harder. More.

Until he froze and pulled back. His eyes were wide as he stared down at where he touched her.

Why was he stopping? But then she looked down with him and saw little pinpricks where his claws had dug into her. Tiny tendrils of blood floated up from the holes. Little ripples, just like she'd seen in his tail.

"It's fine," she said, covering his hand with hers. "Daios, look at me."

"This is what I feared."

"Daios," she said again, her voice sharper this time. And when he looked at her, she said, "I like it."

His eyes were so clouded with emotion that she didn't think he heard her.

So she said it again, this time digging his claws into her with her hand. He fought her, but she persisted. "It doesn't hurt. I like what you do to me. This will not hurt me, you hear? I like knowing that you touched me. Just don't drag your claws through my skin, and it's fine."

It really was. She didn't mind the little salty pricks of pain. In fact, it was... thrilling. They were a reminder that she was taking an undine to her bed. He was no human man, he was something else entirely and he would take her how he wanted.

He was looking at her like he was trying to sense the lie, but then something in him gave. Those gills flared wide again, and she watched the tendrils of her blood suck into his lungs, and then he licked his lips like he could taste it.

"Good enough," he mumbled, before he drew her wetsuit down to her thighs, then her knees, where it caught and locked her feet together. "I lose myself when you touch me, kalon."

"That's fine with me."

"I want to savor you, not rush this." He reached above her head and grabbed something. Then he lifted her arms, one by one, squeezing her wrists gently when they were over her head so she knew not to move them. He rocked over her, giving her the sight of rippling muscles as he flexed and moved. Leaning up, she licked a line from his ribs to those delicate gills.

A shudder passed through him at the same time she felt a loop of kelp wrap around each of her wrists. He tightened them until she couldn't move her arms at all.

Then he slid down her body, a wicked glint in his eyes. "No more touching, kalon. Not this time."

She gave the kelp a tug, surprised at how something so slippery could be so effective. But then he slid down her body, and she stopped thinking about the kelp.

He rested between her legs, his gaze on hers as he pulled her wetsuit off completely. Spreading her thighs, he made sure she was looking as he gave her one long lick between her folds. Then his eyes rolled and his lids closed.

"Gods, kalon. You taste so fucking perfect. I've wanted to taste you since you rode my hand."

That ridged tongue traced every inch of her. He did not devour as she wanted him to. Instead, he took his time. He traced her. Learning every part that made her gasp or wiggle in his grasp. He hummed, that low sound vibrating his tongue as he pressed it against her clit and held it there. The vibration made a keening cry erupt from her mouth.

"Good," he murmured against her, another long lick driving her wild. "That's what I like to hear."

He'd learned her enough then, because the onslaught of his passion was unleashed with those words. She became incoherent as he plunged his tongue into her. That appendage belonged to a man possessed. Claws dug into her thigh and the one time she opened her eyes and looked down at the beast between her legs, she could see him breathing her blood into his gills.

He looked up at her, those flashing teeth glinting above her mound, and then he grinned.

Daios fucked her with his tongue, diving deep inside her. And it was big. Bigger than a tongue had any right to be, because it felt the same size as a human man's cock. Should she be worried? What if all of him was this large?

But oh, that thought was just as tempting. Just as tantalizing.

"Daios," she whined, twisting the kelp around her arms as she tried to reach for him. "I'm going to... to..."

"Yes," he growled. "More."

She ground against his face, searching for that pressure and the need and the desire and then splintered apart on his tongue as his teeth dug just a bit into her skin and she couldn't think beyond the pain and the pleasure of it all.

Thank the heavens he was breathing for her, because she might have forgotten to do that.

Breathing hard, she finally opened her eyes as water flowed over her body. It was replaced by scorching heat as he settled against her. His abs pressed against her, the hard muscles pressing against her clit so hard it was distracting. And yet, she noticed that he dragged her hair out of her face to make her look at him again.

"Beautiful," he said as he dragged a single claw down her temple.

She didn't know what to say. Other than, "I still need you."

"Then you shall have me. But we are not the same as achromo males."

"Good," she replied, her voice ragged and raw. "I don't want one of them."

How could she? Not when he released her wrists from the kelp so she could drag her hand down his chest and over those rippling abs. He was a massive creature, and she knew that this should terrify her, but it didn't matter. When she got somewhere around where his hips where, all she felt was scales. But then she went a little lower—because he was much larger than her—and palmed his cock.

Oh, he was huge. Significantly larger than even her imagination could conjure up, but the tapered tip made her think they could work this time. It might hurt, but clearly she enjoyed the pain when it came to him. This was doable. She could manage—

Then something bumped against the back of her fingers. He must have seen the slight widening of her gaze because he grinned down at her. "That's right, kalon. I have two."

"Two," she whispered, all the possibilities running wild in her head. "Well, that's an interesting development."

Anya stroked her hand up and down him, marveling at the width and length of the appendage that could easily tear her in two. But she wanted to try. With its slick texture, she felt like this might slide effortlessly and the thought made everything inside her clench.

He groaned, his hips bucking against her, and she wasn't sure what to do now. Did she guide him to her? Yes, that's what she was already doing. Like her body knew what she wanted.

She drew him closer, the wildness inside her screaming that she needed him.

Daios tilted, his chest arching away from hers because he was so big and he needed room. Through the haze of desire, she noticed he tied another kelp strand around his shorter arm, weaving it around another so he could pull on it as though he had a second hand. Then he slid his free hand underneath her neck, his teeth nipping at the long length as she moved with him between her legs.

Her fingers brushed against her clit, sending fire igniting through her entire form as the head of his cock brushed against her. It wasn't that large, compared to the thickness at the base. But she knew there was so much more that would stretch her beyond breath.

"Slow," she whispered against his mouth. "Slower than you ever have before."

"We fight to breed," he growled against her. His hips rocked, dragging his cock up and down her entrance, sliding along her clit. "We battle and whoever wins is the one who pins the other. It is unnatural to fuck with someone tied up like this."

"Is it? Because you seem to enjoy it."

"Oh, I do, kalon. I love nothing more than to see you helpless and writhing."

Then he reached between them. She leaned back on the kelp hammock, watching as he presented his cocks to her. That massive clawed hand grasped the bottom one, squeezing it hard enough that a drop of pearlescent liquid appeared at the end. Lining it up with her entrance, he stuttered out a breath that she felt through her entire body.

He pushed inside her, just the tip, just enough so that she arched her back and felt every muscle in her pussy spasm around him. She looked down, watching the dark flesh sinking inside her. His top cock slid over her clit, pressing down and moving slick over her skin.

He was a burning brand that she knew no one else would ever

compare to. He sank deeper until she gasped, her mouth opening as she had to remind herself she didn't have to breathe. He was doing it for her.

"Tell me how it feels," she whispered, the words ragged and raw in her throat. "Tell me."

She looked up to see him shaking his head. Instead, his shorter arm nudged her head to the side and she could just barely see his fingers moving as he spoke, her head rocking as he sank even deeper.

"Home. It feels like home."

He sank deeper, that ever present stretch making her see stars. It was more and more, but he kept going. Every time he paused, she thought that was it, but there was more every time. He consumed her. Every inch of him sliding deep into her body until she didn't know where he began and where she ended. It was so much and then she felt the heat of his scales pressing between her legs, spreading her thighs so wide they burned.

His deep exhale filled her lungs, and then they just stared at each other. They'd done it. She was certain every bit of herself was crammed full of him and...

"Please move," she whispered.

"We don't—"

"I don't care what undines do. I want to feel you moving inside me."

There was the faintest hint of confusion before his hips flexed and he started to pull out. When he got to the point where she was certain he was actually going to withdraw, she locked her legs around him. With one quick clench of her hips, she pushed him back inside her with a long, slow glide.

They both groaned at that, and she stopped being able to see. All she could do was feel him as he did it again. Then again. Each time grinding into her a little harder, a little more forcefully.

His head came down, catching one of her nipples between his teeth and biting down on it so hard bubbles blew out of her lips. Eyes flashing open, she felt that tight coil building again.

"Daios," she whimpered. "Please, I'm—"

"I know, kalon." He released her nipple to catch her mouth with his. Those sharp teeth nipped at her lips, sipping at her mouth as though he were drunk. "Gods, you take me so well."

"I can't... I'm—" She couldn't think straight as he slammed into her again.

His arm flexed, tilting her head so he could better reach to kiss her. And then she wasn't sure what happened, but one moment she was fine and the next she came so hard that she bit down on his lip. Hard.

The low growl that vibrated through him went straight into her heart. That sound was not one that she would ever forget. That sound lived inside her now.

Anya hadn't realized she could come again. Not this hard, not this soon. He came with her, flooding her with a heat as his cock kicked deep inside her. But her orgasm went on and on until it barely started to wane. Then he pulled out, and she could feel the whine in her throat until she was suddenly filled again. This time with a cock that was even larger, harder, how...

The second cock. Oh, fuck, he had a second cock and suddenly her orgasm burst again. Her thighs started to shake, her toes curling in on herself as suddenly the vibration of his growl grew even stronger and she felt him coming again inside her. A spurt of heat that turned her inside out. He arched, his lower back tightening so much she could feel it before that ragged breath slowed.

"That was..." She didn't have the words.

"Yes," he replied as he untied her wrists. "It was, my kalon."

She wanted to stay awake longer. She wanted to know what would happen if she asked about his second cock, or if she could take them at the same time. But her eyes were already drifting shut. The languid warmth of her muscles made it feel like she was floating on a cloud. And when he gathered her up and dragged her against his chest, she couldn't stay awake if she tried.

So she stayed limp on top of him, her head pressed to the sound of one heart beating and her hand pressed the other.

Chapter 31

He could have held her like this forever. Daios had never had such a peaceful morning when he woke to the light of the sun filtering through the water above them. The kelp turned everything emerald green. Spears of light illuminated the small school of silver fish that darted above their heads. Their hair tangled together, floating above them. Strands of darkness and beams of the sun as her gold hair snagged in his.

When he looked down, he was surprised at the beauty of her. She laid on top of him, all long limbs and lean body. Though there were small bumps dotting up and down her body, he knew he had warmed her enough through the night with his own heat.

One of his hip fins had naturally fallen over her waist. The red tinged fin looked like sheer fabric, draped over her body to hide her from any passing glances. Her leg was hiked up over his hip, her foot pressed flat against his tail. One of her arms reached around him and hugged him tightly while her face rested so close to his gills that all he could taste was her.

And oh, he would not forget her taste any time soon.

Sighing, he tailed his claws up her back and everything in him settled as she wiggled closer. Even in her sleep, she wanted to be close to him. That eased some animalistic part of his mind that was so afraid she would wake and scream. Or worse, regret what they had done. But after everything they'd been through together, now he knew for certain that she was his.

Why he'd ever questioned it, he had no idea. Because at every turn of their time together, she had proven that she wanted to be with him. No matter how mad that desire was.

They were together. And that was all that mattered.

A shadow passed over his head, and he looked up to see a yellow fin facing the opposite direction. Maketes even had his hand over his eyes as he blindly approached them, swimming by scent rather than sight. He held a yellow dress in his hand, the fabric trembling with the movement of the sea.

"Here," Maketes said, his voice pitched low and quiet. "I'm not looking. I wouldn't dare."

Rolling his eyes, he draped the other hip fin over Anya's legs, completely covering her from sight. "You can look."

"Ah, we used to play this game when we were children. You'd tell me to do something, I'd do it, and then you'd hit me. I'm not falling for that as an adult."

"I won't hit you, Maketes."

Anya stirred in his arms, propping herself up on his stomach and opening her mouth wide. He wasn't sure what that was, but she sucked an impressive amount of air out of his lungs. Her long blonde hair tangled against her chest, but those sleepy eyes and that soft smile only reminded him that he didn't actually want Maketes to see her.

This sleepy side of her, this soft version of the woman he adored, was for his eyes only.

"Nevermind," he grunted. "I don't want you to look."

"See? I knew it was a trap," Maketes grunted. "Just tell me when I'm above you so I can drop the dress."

Anya reached around him to grab Bitsy where he had taken the droid off her head and hung her on the kelp. He'd been afraid they would crush her in their sleep.

He was almost disgusted with himself, caring for a droid like it was a person. But the droid meant something to her, and that meant he had to take care of it as much as he had to take care of her.

Disgusting, yes. Weak? No.

Anya slipped Bitsy over her head, her eyes flicking over the words that Bitsy had been recording for her. Her lips twitched before she looked above them and noticed Maketes floating there, his back to them and the dress in his hands. "If you move back a bit, it'll be right on top of us."

"Good enough for me," Maketes grunted, holding the dress behind him and letting it drop. "Make it back in time for breakfast, yeah? Mira and Arges want to make a decision about Alpha soon. Apparently, your father has been causing lots of trouble."

And all of it rushed back. Everything that Fortis had told him, everything that the depthstrider had shown him. He needed to tell the others. He needed to tell her.

But he didn't rush them out of this warm, comforting morning. So he said nothing as he reached up to snag the dress that floated down toward them. He helped her into it as much as he could with one arm, but he braced her where she sat on top of him, holding her still so she could wiggle it over her form.

Fingers fanned wide around her ribcage, he couldn't help himself from taking her in. Every inch of her was so lovely, and he'd touched and licked every part of it last night. Yet still, he felt as though there was so much of her he had yet to explore.

"Don't look at me like that," she said, her voice a low murmur as she finished buttoning the small pearls up her torso and between her breasts.

"Like what?"

"Like that." Anya leaned down and kissed him hard. "We're never going to leave this place if you keep looking at me like you want to take me again."

His cocks kicked against his scales, and in an instant he was ready to go again. He wanted to take her in the kelp, maybe this time tie her up in a way that left her more at his mercy. He'd liked that.

The women of his people fought so hard while mating, and few of them had been tempted to try him out. Daios was too big for them to overpower, and that's what they wanted. To overpower, to control, and to leave scars that would last a lifetime. He had no such scars of his own. Some of his people would claim that was a sign of disgrace.

But his little kalon was all too happy to be pinned. She had writhed underneath him, those little moans coming out of her mouth like a symphony of hallowed songs.

His claws clutched the borrowed dress, dragging her close to him again so he could nip at her lips. "If you wish to stay, then we certainly can."

"I love how much this has felt like a bubble where only you and I exist." Anya carded her hands through his hair, gently separating the tangled locks. "But the world does exist. And we should probably get back to them before something worse happens."

He groaned, kicking his hips up into hers before stilling. "I hate that I agree with you."

"Come on, big guy."

She moved as though she were going to kick off him and start swimming, which was absolutely ridiculous. The mere thought that she could keep up with him was laughable, but also...

A low rumble vibrated through his chest before he caught her against him. "I'm not ready for you to be so far from me, kalon."

Anya bit her lip, looking up at him through those thick lashes. "Is that so?"

"Don't tempt me," he grumbled.

"What if I want to tempt you?"

He burst out of the kelp and started toward their home, shaking his head as she tangled herself around him as strong as the kelp. "Gods of the sea, cast pity on me. I have found myself a woman who dares to test me at every turn."

Her laughter filled his ears and heart with a sensation of peace. Just like he'd felt when they woke up together. And though he did not laugh or smile with her, he felt the warmth of her happiness blooming in his chest. It was hard not to feel warm around her, and someday he would tell her that.

If he took his time getting back to the pod and the dome, he tried to tell himself that it was because he wanted more time with her alone. Not that he was afraid of what he had seen.

But eventually they made it back. A few of his people who had relocated from their original pod gave him surprised looks. Perhaps the first time he'd arrived with her, they had assumed it was merely part of his assignment that he'd been sent out on. But this time, it was hard to ignore the fact that they both smelled like each other. They were intertwined, as only lovers could be.

He tried not to wince. He did his best not to look at those shocked features and feel as though they judged him for it. One part of him wondered if they thought he was above falling under the spell of an achromo. Another part wondered if they had thought he was truly unloveable, and thus even an achromo should not have found him acceptable.

But then her hand spread over one of his hearts and he looked down at her soft smile. "They don't matter," she said, a little too loud. "All that matters is you and me. Right?"

He nodded. "Just you and me."

Perhaps it was a little funny how easy it was to swim with her to the dome. He didn't even mind coming out of the water with her. Daios flicked his tail, propelling them high enough that he could slide up onto the platform of the moon pool with her still in his arm. It was not graceful, and perhaps jolted her around a bit, but at least he didn't have to let go of her.

The other two people in the room looked at him with wide eyes. Mira because he had rarely shown up without some attempt to kill her. And Arges because he was looking at Anya, still trapped in his arm, and likely considering how he could get her away from Daios without injuring her in the fight.

Another burble of water suggested that Maketes had joined them. His brother hooked his arms on the metal edge of the moon pool, leaning there comfortably as he said, "Found them."

"Found them?" Arges repeated.

"Yeah. In the kelp." Maketes shrugged. "We all knew it was going to happen at some point. Is it really all that surprising?"

Arges looked at him, then back to Anya, then back to Maketes.

He could see where his brother's thoughts were going and there was something in him that wanted to deny what was laid out so obviously. He wanted to keep their moment, their passion, to himself. He didn't want anyone else to judge them for it.

Then his blue brother blurted out, "That's not possible."

He leaned down and signed in front of Anya, "This is going to take him a moment."

She rolled her eyes and said aloud, "Do you think it's because they know how much you hate my people?"

Arges pointed at her with a long claw. "That. That is exactly the issue here. You hate achromos. I have seen you kill more of them than I have seen you kill fish!"

With a nod, Daios gently set Anya on her own so she could stand. "I still hate them, yes."

Another jab at Anya was the only response from his brother.

Daios puffed up with pride when he noticed she didn't move far from his side. Instead, she stood beside him with her hands planted firmly on her hips.

She looked his brother in the eye with zero fear and stated, "I can choose to be with who I wish. I'm an adult."

"You aren't the problem here," Arges growled. "I know my brother, and I know he always has some plan. Do you think this will make her work with us? We already have that figured out. She's been more than helpful since she's come here, Daios."

"Right," he said. "I'm going to ignore that you said that because I still respect you as a brother. But say one more thing and I will remove your jaw from your skull."

All the lights on Arges's body flickered to life, and he knew they were about two more sentences from launching at each other. They'd always argued like this, even when they were boys. The two of them went for the throat, and that was just how they were. But right now, he didn't want to risk the two achromo in the room who were clearly far more delicate than his kind were.

"Just stop talking." Daios took a deep breath and readied himself. "I met with the depthstriders."

That sobered everyone up in the room. Anya still looked at him with questions in her eyes. She didn't understand why the word made everyone so uncomfortable. He'd explain it all to her soon enough.

The other two males in the room watched him with rapt attention, though. Quickly and efficiently, with as few words as possible, he told them everything that Fortis had revealed.

And while he did so, he could see Anya tensing with every word. Her eyes flew over the lens, so he knew that Bitsy was adding her own commentary to every word he said.

He didn't want to hurt her. He didn't want her to know what her people were doing, because he knew how much this would impact her. He could see her heart bleeding through her eyes, but there was nothing he could do to prevent her from feeling this wound.

Perhaps it was better to stab hard and quick than it was to slide this knife in slowly.

Tears welled in her eyes and dripped down her cheeks by the end of his story. Arges and Maketes were both flared up. Their colors lit the room as much as his did, turning their blues, reds and yellows into oranges and violets that played along the walls. Mira had her hand over her mouth, and he had a feeling nausea pressed against the back of her throat.

"They're experimenting on your people?" Anya finally said, those tears still dripping down her face.

"That is what Fortis has seen." He reached for her. Daios couldn't stand seeing that expression any longer, not without touching her. Soothing her.

She came to him without hesitation, tucking herself into his side as the others began to all speak over each other.

"Anya," Mira said. "Did you have any idea this was happening?"

A bright blue flash illuminated that corner of the room while Arges said, "We cannot waste any more time. We have to move now if they've already been capturing people this long."

But it was Maketes's voice that made his heart shatter. "I wonder how many people we thought were lost on raids who were actually just waiting for us to save them."

The quiet words ended with a silence that burned. That anger and hatred that had always flowed in him had merged together with the others. He knew his people would stop at nothing to get their own back. He knew without a doubt that the battle was soon to flood this sea.

Yet his heart also thundered with warning. Because tiny hands were pressed against his chest, feeling the rage that coursed through his skin and he knew she was right here with him. She could hear every word. She suffered every injustice that her people had done to his.

Anya's feelings were different from Mira's. The city she had come from was the one who had done the worst to his kind, but even more, it was her own family that held the blade.

Everyone remained silent. All he could hear was the staggered breath from Anya's lips that ghosted over his wet neck and cooled his skin. The fire that burned inside him was one that she could easily stoke or extinguish.

He'd always thought his rage and hatred would come before anything else. But this woman could make him pause if she wished. A single order from her, and he would take her away from all of this.

Instead, Anya lifted her head from his neck. Her eyes were ringed with red and her cheeks slick with tears.

Her voice, when she spoke, was ragged and raw. "This does not surprise me. As much as I wish it did. I have always known my father to be bloodthirsty in both battle and in knowledge. I'm sorry. If I had known I would have done... more."

"There is nothing you could have done." He lifted his hand and smoothed the tears away from her face, propping her up with his shorter arm. "Your father would have killed you. We've proven already that the lack of you has only made him stronger. He would have discovered that with or without us."

Mira's voice interrupted him with a hissed, "That's the most words I've ever heard him say in one sitting."

He silenced her with a glare before returning his attention to the woman in his arms. "This is not your fault, kalon."

"No, it's not my fault, but it's still my people." Something shifted in her eyes. Something hard and familiar at the same time. She looked at the others in the room before, with a flat tone, she announced, "Blow it up."

Silence was her answer before Mira scoffed. "What? What do you mean, blow it up?"

"I can get inside. I know where everything is. You want Alpha out of the picture? You want to save your people? Attacking Beta with a handful of undine gets you nowhere. You have to make drastic decisions that will echo through the entire ocean."

Mira shook her head. "You're calling for a war."

In his arms, she shook. He could feel her trembling with emotion, and some part of him whispered it might be fear.

"No," Anya replied. "I'm calling for a massacre. I know where to hit so some people will still be able to leave if they are quick. You want them to take you seriously? To know that they cannot and should not ever fuck with the undines again?" She made eye contact with each and every one of them in the room, saving him for last. Her gaze met his, and he knew that hardness was the same rage he felt burning in his own chest. "Then you need to tear the golden city to the ground."

Chapter 32

It all became a bit of a whirlwind after that. Anya was ashamed to admit she mostly stood there in shock.

She'd always known her father to be ruthless. But experiments? On live specimens? It was wrong on so many levels, and it was painful to hear. She didn't want to think of all those people who had suffered, all because her father couldn't see their people as alive. Or at least, people worth respecting.

And then it had all hit her.

No matter what she did, she couldn't save the city.

She couldn't save her people. They would forever be in the clutches of the man who had made her life so terrible. And then she realized, they didn't want to be saved.

Her father was no scientist. He wasn't capable of finding the undines, cutting them up, or researching about them on his own. There were countless people who helped him.

Her own people. Good people she had always thought were worth saving. They had helped him, and then they had walked through those gilded streets with blood on their hands and smiled like nothing had happened.

It tore her up inside to realize that maybe her people weren't worth saving after all.

She told the undines everything they wanted to know. Mira was quick to jump into learning about the city, and Anya had no intention of hiding anything. She hooked Bitsy up to Byte and let the two droids work. They downloaded every schematic and map that Bitsy had access to. Then Anya had her call up Ace to get her friend involved. It took a while before Ace even answered, but she had known her friend wouldn't remain silent for too long.

"I know it sounds insane, but I need to know this is a secure channel," she said as Bitsy projected the words up on the screen.

"Always."

"Good. I'm working with the undines, and I think I know how to break Alpha."

There was a long pause after she said the words, three bubbles bouncing on the screen, which meant Ace was typing. Considering how long it took, she assumed Ace was typing out an entire monologue.

Then all that came through was, "The fuck did you just say?"

Mira's lips quirked with a wry grin. "Your friend seems nice."

"Yeah, they're pretty great." Anya shrugged before replying. "I know it sounds crazy, but the undines are our ticket in. We're going to destroy the city, and I need you to figure out refugee arrangements."

Again, more bubbles. More time that her friend needed to figure out what to say. In the end, Anya decided to tell Ace everything.

It made the undines behind her bristle. Clearly, they didn't want to trust yet another human with more information about their whereabouts or who they were. But Ace was someone she would trust with her life, and so it was pretty easy to hand that connection over to Mira and Byte.

Almost two days passed before she realized how tired she was. Before she stared down at the map of her city and realized there was only one way this was going to happen. She looked up at Mira once all the men had left, all of them agreeing that the two women needed to eat and rest.

"They'll hunt the biggest thing that they can find," Mira said, sighing as she cracked her neck. "They need to blow off steam and we both need rest."

Anya didn't need rest. She needed a miracle. "You see the same thing here that I see, don't you?"

She didn't have to ask twice. It was clear in the way Mira's shoulders tensed and lifted to her ears. "Yeah. I think I do. But I'm doing my damnedest to find another option, because I don't like what you're planning."

Neither did she. Anya knew there were such limited chances for them to attack Alpha. They would get one more time to make an impact before they'd be locked out of the city for good.

She couldn't take that risk. Not with so many lives at stake.

Mira watched her, her eyes seeing too much. "You know he's not going to let you fucking do this without a fight."

"I know."

"I don't like the guy. He made my life a living hell when Arges first kidnapped me, and he's tried to kill me multiple times." Then she softened a bit, the wrinkles between her eyes easing a little and her shoulders dropping back down. "But even I can see how much you mean to him, and I'm not that heartless. You soften him, and I worry that if he loses you..."

"I will not accept that pressure," she interrupted. "We're both adults and we both have always had the same goal. I don't like Alpha any more than you do, and I intend to save my people and yours by doing this. I know destruction seems insane, but I believe that this is the only path we can take."

"So you really think you're the only one who can set off a bomb?"

God, it was so much worse when someone else said it. Anya shifted Bitsy up so she could rub her eyes before nodding. "Yeah, I do. I know where my father keeps all the weapons in the city. That's where I lost my hearing. I can get in. I can detonate the bombs before anyone has a chance to stop me."

"And you think you can walk right in without your father finding you?"

No. She didn't. She had a feeling her father would know that she was arriving the moment the cameras picked up on them. And there wasn't a way into the city without someone seeing her.

But that was what she was hoping for. She wanted her father to see her. She wanted him to know that she was coming and that he needed to save face because he'd already told everyone that she was dead.

Maybe he knew, in some deep, horrible way, that she'd been trying to get rid of him. Perhaps he had hoped that eventually they would need to fight it out like they were going to in the end. It fit everything she knew about the man.

"And you think Daios is going to let you do that?" Mira asked, her voice echoing through the room.

A shadow passed over the glass. She looked up to see that Daios was the first to return. He carried with him a reasonably sized tuna, and one that she absolutely would not eat. She couldn't stomach anything right now.

Sighing, she shook her head. "No, I don't think he's going to like this one bit."

Both women waited until he poked his head through the moon pool, much slower than when he'd arrived with Anya. Slapping the fish down onto the metal floor, he looked them both over before growling, "Why do you both look guilty?"

Flicking her gaze to Mira, she tried to convey that she needed the other woman to step in. She couldn't do this on her own. She couldn't tell him right now when she was so vulnerable and everything felt so raw.

Mira nodded, her hand hitting the table in what was likely a very loud clap before standing. Bitsy ran words over her eyes that startled even Anya.

"I have something for you, Daios. I've been working on it for a while, but it wasn't working the way I want it to. It's good enough for what we're about to do, though."

She disappeared into a side room, one that had always smelled like metal and oil.

Daios arched a brow. "What's this about?"

"I don't know." But it didn't matter. She had to tell him. She couldn't stand here and look at him like she wasn't lying, just by not telling him what the plan had to be. "Daios…"

Getting up, she sat down beside him on the metal. He reached for her without thinking. That massive arm of his scooped underneath her legs and dragged her closer.

He smelled like the sea. A briny scent mixed with salt that burned her nose, or maybe that was the tears that she refused to let fall. Because he was holding onto her without hesitation. Like she was right where she belonged.

Her forehead came down on his shoulder, and she let him prop her up as though he could take away the weight that was so heavy on her shoulders. Without Mira in the room, he was so quick to run his hand over the back of her head. He smoothed her hair back from her face, hooking the strands behind her ears.

"My kalon," he whispered, and she could feel his lips press to the top of her head. "Did you miss me?"

"Yes," she said with a breathy laugh. "Isn't that crazy?"

"Not so crazy."

"You were only gone for a couple hours, if that. And already I feel like..." She didn't know how to say the words. Only that she didn't like it when they weren't together.

And maybe that was partly because she was afraid all of this was going to shatter around them. What she knew she had to do was only going to make everything else difficult. Or she'd lose her life in this insane battle that wasn't necessarily hers to fight and yet, here she was. Fighting.

He hummed long and low, his chest vibrating with the sound that she could still hear. If she failed in doing this, she'd never hear someone speak so clearly again. Her father wouldn't ever let her leave their home and she would be stuck back in her cage. How could she lose the sound of him when she knew how dear it was now?

Swallowing hard, she forced herself to draw back. "Daios, I think the only way to—"

Bitsy flashed red all throughout the lens, startling her so much with the bright light that she stopped talking mid sentence, only to realize the droid had thrown up an arrow. And Daios was looking over her shoulder with a frown on his face that almost terrified her.

"What?" Anya asked, turning around to see Mira was standing in the doorway of that room with an... arm.

Or at least, a metal arm.

It was massive, and her arms shook as she held it up for them both to see. Strangely, it sort of looked like a undine arm. The wrist flopped, and the fingers were clearly jointed with fine webbing between them.

"I wasn't going to show you for a bit, because it's still very much a prototype." Mira frowned down at the arm. "There's a lot it can't do. Please don't use this arm on anything that can be bruised, broken, or killed. The tension on it is really touchy."

"What is that?" Daios hissed.

"It's an arm," Mira grumbled, walking toward them while tilting her head down. Bitsy put a little warning that said "murmuring" before she read, "Pretty fucking obvious, I thought."

Neither Anya nor Daios said anything as Mira stepped up next to him. They watched as she lifted the hole in the fake arm up to his half arm, and something felt... wrong inside of her.

Anya didn't know how to feel about him getting "fixed" when she'd never thought of him as broken. He lacked an arm, yes, but that didn't make him less of a person. He had figured out how to live without one and now it felt a little cruel to hand him something like this. Even if he had wanted it, she wasn't sure how to feel.

If someone had offered her a tool to get her hearing back after all these years, she wasn't even sure that she would take it. There were risks to using any new tool. And she was fine the way she was. Sure, she had Bitsy to translate for her, but that wasn't the same thing as something to "fix" what had made her... better.

Years and years of practice had turned her into a different person. Her lack of hearing was part of her, just as much as her eye color or what food she liked. She wouldn't want someone to come in and save her.

But the way his eyes lit up as he slid his arm into the arm hole and how he held so still for Mira to affix a sling around his neck to hold the metal a little tighter against his skin? It made something in her chest squeeze really hard. Because that wasn't the expression of a man who agreed with her. That was the expression of a man who was remembering what it felt like to be whole.

And suddenly, she was alone again. Years and years of practice at not feeling like she was the only person on the planet who had suffered, and now she watched someone else get fixed.

The feelings were so complicated, and she didn't like them.

"This has to connect to your nerves," Mira said, her head tilting to look underneath his arm. "I'd like to affix it more permanently for you, but this will have to do for now. Quick jab."

Daios winced, and then he lifted the arm. The elbow bent at his will, and when he held the metal fingers up to the air, he could open and close them. The fingers clinked together, and they were definitely clumsy. He could only move all of them at the same time, but that was all. Maybe with practice, he'd get better.

He met her gaze, those eyes filled with hope, and she felt like an awful person for not wanting him to wear it.

Daios saw right through her, though. He always had from the very first day. "Mira?" he asked. "Can you give us some time alone?"

"Of course."

They both stared at each other while Mira retreated to her workshop. And then they were alone. Two souls who were different from other people, and now one who was closer to normal than the other.

Why were her eyes watering?

Dashing away the tears, she smiled at him. "How does it feel?"

"You are upset."

"No, I'm just... happy for you." She scooted away from him, taking in the sight of him. "It looks good. With a little practice, I bet you'll be able to use it like a normal arm."

"Why are you upset?"

"I'm not."

Daios sighed, his shoulders lifting and falling with the gust of breath she couldn't hear. "Anya."

"I'm really happy for you." She smiled, but she could feel how watery the expression was. "Really."

He reached for the strap over his shoulder, shaking his head. "This can't work."

"Daios, don't take it off." She lunged forward, her fingers catching onto his and stopping him. "It will be helpful. I have to go back to the city, anyway, and who knows what's waiting for us there? You might need it."

He stared into her eyes, frozen as they were locked together. "You're going back?"

"I'm going to be the one to blow up the city."

His lips parted, and for a moment she thought he was going to tell her no. He would argue that it wasn't safe. She would tell him that nothing they did was safe. They would go to bed angry at each other and maybe ruin all of this before it had a chance to really start.

Instead, his warm hand came up to cup her jaw. "You are brave, kalon. Far more than you have any right to be."

Relief, unlike anything she'd ever felt, flooded through her. With a sharp nod, she stopped looking into his eyes and instead locked her gaze on the arm. "I am glad for you. It's a complicated feeling, that's all. Seeing you like this... whole now..."

He moved so quickly she didn't even see him twitch. The strap went up and over his head. He wrenched the arm off, and she could see there were tiny wires that had wriggled their way into his skin. He pulled those out without a single flinch. Blood dripped from the little holes that were left behind as he dropped the arm onto the floor.

"Whole?" he growled, wrapping his hand around her waist and tugging her against him. Water splashed up to her knees with the force of his movement as he dragged her against his chest. "My lack of arm has nothing to do with feeling whole. A metal device or not, I was never whole before you. You were the first person to look at me and see a man after my injury. Not a mistake, not a failure. You were the one to see me. My kalon, if you wished me to shed my skin, I would. If the arm makes you uncomfortable, then I will drop it into the deepest pits of the sea."

"That's not what I want," she said with a watery laugh. "I don't want you to not be whole again because of me."

"I am only whole because of you." He pressed his lips to hers, the long kiss tasting of salty tears and seawater. When he drew back, he pressed their foreheads together and took a deep breath with her. In and out. "Anya. It's just an arm. A tool to be used, but never something that is part of me. I will use it to bring you to victory, but it does not change who I am."

Nodding frantically, she licked her lips before replying, "I know. I know that."

"Do you?"

She hoped that she did. Because she was going to need him, and she was so afraid that she loved him far more than was acceptable.

Chapter 33

Anya was terrified. It was a risk to go back into Alpha. A risk to even think her father would let her walk around the city without immediately throwing her into a prison. Daios hadn't argued with her too much. And yet, he swam with her crushed so tightly to his chest that it wasn't hard to guess what his innermost thoughts were.

He didn't want her to do this any more than she wanted to. They both knew this might be the last time they ever see each other. And they'd just found each other.

Some part of her wanted to turn right around. She wanted to tell him to bring her back to his home and then they could leave all this behind. There were other abandoned facilities out there. Maybe they could even investigate to see if the land above was more habitable now that there had been centuries between when humans lived above and not. She didn't know.

All of these thoughts were fantasies, though. Because she knew they couldn't live with themselves if they left their people behind.

His arms tightened around her, his feelings likely turning in the same direction as her own as they neared Alpha.

She still wasn't used to the sensation of the metal arm around her back. It wasn't quite an unnatural feeling. She couldn't tell that it was any different from his other arm with her borrowed wetsuit on. But she was so used to knowing that he only had half an arm on that side. It felt... different.

On top of the arm, Mira had given them both more than enough gear to complete their mission. Byte and Bitsy had gone through the systems that once would have stumped Anya's droid. But Byte had been upgraded too, and because he was a research drone, he had a lot more access than Bitsy did. Together, and with some help from Ace, they'd given enough information for Mira to create something she called a jammer.

It was big and bulky, a square box that was unwieldy at best. She currently carried it so Daios could carry her. The giant block had turned to ice the moment they'd hit the water, and it had been burning her hands since.

"Are you ready?" he asked, his voice deep and guttural. The words flickered in front of her face as Bitsy reacted to the cold as well.

She'd noticed the droid slowing down. It took longer for her to translate the words, and she wasn't sure if she should be worried about that or not. Considering there was a lot more for her to worry about, she had to focus on the moment and not on what might happen afterward.

Still, she found it hard to lie to him. "No," she replied with a soft laugh. "I'm not ready at all. But we're here and I have to do this."

"We can leave."

She looked up at him and that strong jaw that had already

sharpened with frustration. "You know we can't. I have to do this for everyone in that city and for your people. There is no other choice, Daios."

The muscles of his jaw jumped even more until he looked down at her. Then everything in him seemed to freeze. Pausing as his eyes danced over her features.

"If we do not see each other again, my kalon, I wish for you to know that I have never been more honored than to have a woman like you at my side." He swallowed hard again, his eyes still flicking over hers. "I do not know how your people say this."

Oh, this sweet, wonderful man who had no idea how much he had wriggled his way into her heart. She reached up and framed his face with both of her hands, staring into those black eyes that showed so much more than he knew how to say. "We say I love you."

"I have heard this from Mira before."

"From Mira?" she repeated with a laugh.

He shook his head. "She has said it to Arges. Tell me what this word means."

"It's not about the word itself. It's about the feeling in here." She moved one of her hands to his chest. "It means that living without you feels wrong. That to be parted from your side makes me miss you more than I miss breathing fresh air. And that I will always think of you, no matter how far I am from you."

"This feels right," he said. His hand scooped underneath her hair and drew her close to him, breathing in the scent of her. "Know as you dive into danger that I love you, my kalon. I will hold you in my heart until you return to my side."

She kissed him fiercely, because there were no words she could say to tell him how much she loved him. How much she admired his strength and his valor. And how, even now, he was letting her do what was right, even though it could take everything away from them both.

Daios was a warrior himself. He was the one who fixed things when they went wrong and he was the one who went into danger for others. He allowed her to do this with no argument, no fighting, just a tension radiating in his body and his claws clutching at her sides as though he would have to force himself to let her go.

"I will find my way back to you," she whispered against his lips, almost desperately. "I will come home, Daios."

"Home," he replied, that deep voice radiating through her entire body. "That is what you have given me, kalon. Wherever you are, I am home."

They stared at each other for a few more moments before she felt his arm reach in between them. He clicked the small button that would turn on the device that Mira had built, and she knew it was time.

Time to let him go. To move forward with this plan. To put her life on the line to save his people and her own. Would it be easy? Absolutely not. Would she do everything possible to get back to him? She sure would.

Together, they raced through the towers that had shot at him the first time he'd done this. But Mira's jammer seemed to work. The towers didn't activate close to them, and the ones in the distance didn't react either. Perhaps whatever signal the box in his arms was giving off had worked. Or maybe her father just didn't want to show that he knew they were coming.

Either way, they made it to the original tunnel they had escaped from. And there she could see someone had capped it. A massive metal door stood in the way of their plan.

Daios put her down on the ground with the box beside her. He slid her rebreather over her face and detached the cord from her neck, leaving her feeling bereft without his breath.

The current here was unusually strong, so she had to hold on to the side of the building and sink her legs into the muck as she watched him move above her. His tail flicked, and then he was grabbing both sides of that metal cap.

It was welded into the building. She could see how much metal they had poured onto it. The bolts dug deep into the concrete that made up Alpha's exterior. Muscles bulging, teeth bared, Daios heaved.

His entire body lit up with his efforts. All of his form was bared, those muscles straining with effort, and she could see the cords as his pectorals strained. The metal arm of his was reacting better than his natural one. But even those wires sparked in the water. And then the cap gave. She watched in shock and a bit of horror as he peeled it back enough that air rushed out of it.

The bubbles erupted and they would give up their position easier with that white flag of bubbles. He held out his hand for her to take, and she kicked off the bottom, reaching for him.

The current threatened to whip her away from the building and out into the middle of nowhere. But he grabbed onto her wrist and hauled her right up against him. He held onto Alpha with that metal arm that didn't seem to budge, even though they were both flung against the side of the building until he yanked them both closer to the opening.

"Come back to me," he growled, before shoving the rebreather aside with his nose and kissing her once again. It felt like a brand. Like he knew this could be the last time either of them saw each other, and he refused to let this end without her knowing how much he wanted her.

Heart thundering in her chest, she kissed him back with every ounce of hope in her chest. She would get back to him, no matter how hard that was.

Daios shoved her closer to the pressure coming out of the vent. She knew there were only a few moments for her to get through this gap before he had to close it. Anya yanked the rebreather back over her face, focusing on her new obstacle. She could see in his eyes that he was going to seal her inside the city she'd come from, and then it was up to her.

Her. A girl who had been pampered her entire life and liked to pretend hero. They were all hoping that nothing went wrong and that she could figure all this out, with no one else helping her.

Swallowing hard, she grabbed onto the edge of the vent and yanked with him. The two of them shoved her right through the wall of air and into the vent. On her hands and knees in the now empty tunnel, she ripped the rebreather off before whirling around.

The suction from the tunnel threatened to throw her back into the sea. But she wanted to see him. Needed to see the heat in his eyes, the passion that burned there even now. And the hope that flared in his chest as all his muscles bunched again.

She crab walked away from him, watching until the last second. But then the vent closed, and all the lights went out.

She was alone. Cold and freezing in the tunnels underneath Alpha, where she knew so many terrible things had happened.

With a shuddering breath, she reached up to tap Bitsy. "Do you have any lights?"

Her lens flickered to life again, this time with a little more force. "So cold."

The words floated in pitch black and lanced through her heart. She hated that this was hurting her oldest friend as well, but there were only so many things she could do to help the little droid.

She should hurry. Someone might be wondering what had happened.

But she took the time to remove her droid from her head and to press the little one to her chest. Carefully breathing onto Bitsy, she warmed up the droid until she felt her fidgeting in her grip. Only then did she put her back on her head and read the messages on the lens.

"Ok," Bitsy put on the lens. "I am ok."

"Good," she whispered. "Light?"

A small light appeared out of one of Bitsy's arms. They'd only had to use it once when the power had gone out in Alpha, and she'd never thought to use it again. The beam of light illuminated the tunnels that clearly no one had been taking care of. They'd just sealed it off and filled it with air. She couldn't imagine the strain on the filtration systems.

The tunnels were bone dry now. And as she started walking up them, the bodies of dead crabs crunched underneath her feet. So much death, all because her father had been mad at her.

Anya glanced down and saw the little wave pattern carved into their shells. These were the ones who had helped her find Daios, all those weeks ago. And they had died because of her.

Determination settled on her shoulders like a heavy weight. She would not let anyone else die because of her. Not if she could get her hands around the throat of this situation.

"Contact Ace," she said, bracing herself against the concrete walls.

Bitsy made quick work of it, and Ace had been waiting for her.

"You in?"

"I'm in. Show me the map to get back to my old rooms."

A map projected right in front of her. The blue lines showed her which tunnels to trace her way back to her old room, although there would likely be an issue as soon as she got there. After all, there was no entrance into the pool systems anymore.

"Have you gotten anywhere in draining the pool?" she asked, turning left and almost slipping on some left over algae.

"No. Looks like they sealed off the entrance to your pool. I don't know if there's even water in it. But there seem to be service tunnels that might be of use."

"Just let me know which ones to break into."

"You have the tools Mira gave you?"

Yes, but she wasn't very good at using them. Mira had given her the run down on how to use all the tools themselves, but now that she was freezing with shaking hands and absolute terror dogging her steps, she wasn't sure if she could do it.

"Yes," she replied, turning again. "I have the tools."

"Good."

"I'm not sure I can..." she trailed off, not sure what to say.

There were a few blinking lights before Ace replied, "You have to."

Of course she did. Because no one else could do this as easily as she could. No more lives deserved to be risked because she was afraid to face her father.

Anya steeled herself and kept moving. There was a service entrance, just like Ace had suggested. The short ladder took her right up to the small hatch that had apparently been hidden behind a wall near her pool her entire life. How many times had someone come in here? Had her father ever had someone spy on her?

It took her four times to get the screwdriver into the marks that Mira had told her to put them in. Her hands were shaking so badly she almost dropped the automatic tool.

With a deep breath, she let the hatch drop and then released Bitsy into the room. Even though her droid was a little worse for wear, and moving slower than she should, she made quick work of her job. Climbing up the wall, she scrambled the camera long enough for Anya to get out of the hatch and step into her old bathing room.

As she shucked her wetsuit off, she marveled at how nothing had changed. If she stood still, she could almost pretend that nothing had happened. She had been here her entire life. Maybe she'd fallen and clocked her head on the side of the pool and dreamt all of this up. But then she felt the aching bruise on her neck where Daios's tentacle sank underneath her skin, and she knew it had been real.

And she had a job to do.

Mira had offered her one of her few dresses that was still in good shape. The bright blue fabric was pretty and almost looked like it fit Anya. It was still dry enough to convince her father that she had been here for a while.

"Come on," she said, reaching her arm out so Bitsy could jump onto it. "It's show time."

Smoothing her hair back, she made one more check to make sure she didn't have a drop of water on her, and then strode into her bedroom. Nothing had changed here, either. All of it was exactly where she had left it. Like she'd just walked out yesterday.

That would only make it easier for her argument. Sitting down at her dresser, she started pulling out small pieces of makeup. Lipstick. Eyeliner. Pieces she hadn't had at her disposal for a while.

It took exactly three minutes and forty-two seconds before the door to her bedroom slammed open and her father strode through with rage turning his face ugly. "Where have you been?"

She pretended to look startled, not even struggling when two of her father's men stomped in after him and grabbed her by the arms.

"Dad? What is going on? You said you knew where I was going! I told you I was spending a few days with my friend."

"Days? You've been gone for over four months!"

Of course she had. She knew that. But she blinked up at him, making her eyes a little wider and even more innocent. "I lost track of time, Daddy! I'm so sorry to have worried you. I've been back for a while, though. Surely you noticed?"

Let the games begin.

Chapter 34

Leaving her was the hardest thing he'd ever done in his life. All the voices in him raged to the front, screaming a myriad of grievances. He would get her killed, just like he had killed them. He was leaving her to her doom like a coward. If he wasn't there with her, then she would die. She would wallow in the pits of the sea with the rest of them. Her soul would never rest.

Their hands plucked at his shoulders, trying to turn him toward them. They wanted to scratch out his eyes, to rip out his throat, to make him feel their pain.

Of all the things that he had done, this was the one that he knew he would regret the most. Because if he lost her, if he lost the only grip on reality he still had... he wasn't sure what he would do.

Breathing hard, he darted through the sea, back toward his brothers. He was not supposed to linger near the city, and he knew it was for the best. He was supposed to go back to where Mira had rigged Byte up to have a direct connection to Bitsy.

The two droids could now speak over long distances, and that would allow them to see what Anya saw. They could know for certain that she was safe and nothing was happening to her.

But his fins stopped working, freezing in place at the thought that he would be so far away from her that if anything did go wrong, there was nothing he could do to stop it. He would be stuck far away, forced to watch as she was murdered or tortured like depthstrider from the memory Fortis had shown him.

His body wouldn't work. He simply could not leave this place, no matter how hard he tried to make himself. Daios wanted to stay here in a silent vigil, not eating, not sleeping, just waiting until he knew she was safe in his arms.

Swallowing hard, he turned to see the small speck of Alpha in the distance. He wanted... Fuck. He didn't know what he wanted.

He wanted her to save their people. Every ounce of that glory would be hers. Pride swelled in him just at the mere thought. His people would be far more accepting of an achromo who had helped them, and far more understanding of his love for her as well.

But those thoughts were chased by the knowledge that she was alone and could so easily be hurt. He remembered how she felt as they finally joined with each other. The softness of her skin, the way her body had dimpled underneath his touch.

How easily she bled.

He could still taste her blood in his gills and now feared he would taste it outside of pleasure. The phantom scent played over his gills, filling his mouth with blood, and he feared something was wrong. She could already have failed. Her father had seen them coming. Who knew what that evil man had planned for her? Daios had to get back to her.

Now.

He turned, but there was a darkness blocking his way. At first, he thought it was another one of the ghosts that followed him. A part of his guilt that had manifested in the size of a large male who had likely died in the first battle with Beta.

But then a blue glow erupted, and he knew exactly who was stopping him.

"Arges," he growled. "Move."

"No," his clutch brother replied. "I will not. You cannot go back to her, Daios. You have to come back to the dome."

"My place is with her."

"As the sea commands," Arges said in agreement. But he did not move. "You cannot ruin all that we have worked for. There are more people at stake than just Anya."

"If you do not move, I will make you move."

His claws were already flexing at his side. Perhaps a fight would make him feel better. If he tore into his brother, expressing all his frustration, maybe he could hold himself back from swimming to her side.

"You can't make me move, Daios."

Baring his teeth in anger, he snarled, "Have you forgotten the last time we fought? I have not. Even fresh out of battle and missing an arm, I tossed you into the air like you were nothing more than a child."

It had felt like the right thing to do at the moment. He had been certain Mira was an omen of the end. The depthstriders had warned him that the achromos would only bring destruction. Fortis had told him time and time again while he inhaled the steam from the heart of the sea. The achromos were a threat to all of their lives.

Perhaps Fortis had not meant Mira specifically, but what else was Daios meant to think? She had shown up at the worst possible moment. And in a way, she had changed everything. In his mind, that had been enough.

But if his brother wished to fight again, then that was what they would do. He would rip and tear into Arges's scales and throw him in to the abyss if that was what it took.

"Daios," Arges said, his voice little more than a sigh. "I know how you are feeling. I understand your need, but you cannot go back."

Already his chest rose and fell with anger. He could feel his gills flaring wider as he drew air into his lungs for a battle. He didn't care if Arges knew how he felt.

"Mira is safe!" he almost shouted. "Your mate is within reach. She stays in her dome. If she goes out, she leaves with you. You have never sent her straight into danger without you."

"What do you think happened when she returned to her city? You've forgotten that we had to raid Beta to get her back. That I crawled through that place without water, squeezing my body through doorways so that I could get her back!" Arges thundered. "I have almost lost her and I know what goes through your heart. But no one can help you if you do not let us."

He didn't need their help, though. Nor did he want Arges's help. He just wanted Anya home.

His hearts hurt in his chest. Rubbing at them, he shook his head and charged Arges. Pain was what he needed right now, and he knew an easy way to get it.

They came together in two massive forces that struck so hard he saw stars. Arges grappled with him as he had expected him to. His brother always fought in the same way, no matter how many times they battled. With a flick of his tail, he tossed Arges over his shoulder and surged toward the city.

But Arges was smaller, and that made him just a little more agile. A blue fin came down over his shoulder, Arges's tail wrapping around his own and pinning his hip fins to his sides. With a slithering movement, Arges anchored them together and tightened the grip of his tail as he coiled around Daios.

Hissing out an angry breath, Daios reached back with his metal arm and caught one of Arges's hip fins.

"Remember when I almost ripped this off?" he snarled, bloodlust rushing through him. "This time I'm keeping it so you can't sew it back on."

He would have yanked on the fin if Arges hadn't leaned forward and hit a button on the arm. It went dead. Limp and useless other than as a weight that suddenly dragged him in the opposite direction.

His brother released him with a feral flash of fangs. "Do you think Mira would build you anything that I couldn't turn off?"

Those two were going to be the death of him. An angry snarl rippled through his body while he yanked the arm off. He let it drop onto the sands below them and blew out an angry breath that cleared his gills of debris.

He stared his brother down across the water. Arges was now once again between him and the city that kept his mate from him.

His mate.

Fuck, that was the first time he'd ever thought of her like that. But it was true. She was so much a part of him that he didn't know how to be without her. Anya had taken his pain and rage and turned it into something he could use. He was someone else when he had her and now he could... he could lose her.

His lights flickered. Once, twice, then burned again as he forced himself to fight again. He needed to get to her.

But this time, Arges caught onto his arm as he darted forward and held Daios close. His brother looped his tail around him as many times as he could, squeezing hard enough to freeze the breath in his lungs. Daios's arm was pinned down at his side, and though he could have likely broken this hold, he found something in him was breaking.

All he wanted was to know that she was alive.

Breathing hard, Arges hissed in his ear, "We are doing everything we can to keep her safe. You have to come back with me so you can see for yourself."

"We are so far," he wheezed. "If she is in danger, what would you have me do? Stay there and watch her die?"

A ripple spread from his body into Arges's. He knew the moment his brother understood where Daios's fear came from. "We will have more warning than that."

"We won't, and you know it. Her father is an eel in the depths, waiting to bite. She will not know what is happening until the very last moment, and we will all lose her." His voice fractured on the last word. And then he stopped talking.

Because talking had never gotten him anywhere. Daios never said the right thing, no matter how hard he tried to do that. The only person who ever understood what he was trying to say was locked away where he could not get her.

Even though Arges knew the fear, Arges could not understand the depth of Daios's emotions. At least in Beta, there was a chance. Arges had climbed into the city and he had gotten his woman.

Alpha was a city built of air and wide spaces. One of their people would only greet death if they even managed to get within those walls.

Arges slowly released him, his tail dropping until only his arms around Daios's shoulders remained. That tight squeeze eased, just enough to feel like the embrace it was.

"She is a brave woman," Arges said, his voice a low murmur that the sea caught and echoed. "She honors you, brother, by going into that city with no fear. Her memory is one that all our people will talk about for years to come. Honor, brother. That is important."

"Life is important." Something in him shattered as he added, "Her life is important."

Arges's arms squeezed a little tighter. And for a moment, they just floated there together. Watching the city that would soon be nothing more than a ruin. He rolled the plan over in his mind for the hundredth time. Maketes and Anya's friend were ready to get the survivors somewhere safe. There was a small pod they had given to Maketes to save any of the people who might end up drowning. They wanted the other cities to hear that the People of Water had made an effort to save the achromos.

Anya would be the first one in an escape pod. She knew where they all were. He would be waiting for her when the time came, but they had to make sure that everything was in line first. But none of them knew how long that would take.

It was better if he stayed here. He had to wait for her to give him some kind of signal to prepare himself and he would be ready.

"We have put so much trust in a single person," he whispered. "Everything rests on her shoulders."

"And she is strong enough to do it," Arges replied.

"But she is so small. Her shoulders barely fit in my grip if I wished to hold her. She gets cold in the warmest of waters. She doesn't like raw fish or oysters, and she doesn't know how to gather her own food. If someone tries to attack her, she does not know how to fight. My woman is soft."

He loved that about her. He loved how she was a soft place for his tormented heart to rest, but he did not know what it would mean for her while she was not safe in his arms.

"Just because she is soft does not mean she is easily broken," Arges said as his arms dropped away. "The most you can do right now is trust her. Come back with me, Daios. Together, we will watch over your little kalon."

He nodded, slowly. But it took a long time for him to pull his gaze away from the city of light that glowed on the horizon. If only he could capture it in his palms, perhaps he could hold her against his heart a little longer.

Eventually, he turned. He joined his brother on the many hour journey back to their own home. The dome was still lit up, and even from the outside, he could see the projection that Byte had cast up on the wall. It was a familiar room. A familiar place.

Perhaps he had taken a bit of Anya into himself. Because he could feel her softness in his chest as he looked at the same vision where he had seen her for the second time. Where he had taken her into his arms and he had never let her go. Until now.

Maketes saw him first, slipping into the water through the moon pool and darting toward them. All of his fins and gills were flared wide, and his eyes were a little mad with glee. "It works. Daios, Arges, it works."

"What does?" he asked.

"The connection between the droids. As long as Bitsy is on her head, we can see everything she can see. We can guide her too, because Byte can connect with Bitsy." Maketes stopped in front of them, his fluke still twitching with excitement and jerking him left and right.

"We can see everything."

"She's alive?" he asked, even though it made his stomach rebel to ask.

"Of course she's alive," Maketes said. "And she's already convinced her father to let her keep Bitsy. They're all very confused because she's lied through her teeth so well. It almost seemed like maybe her father believed her and that she was just visiting a friend."

He didn't think that was possible. The old man was more wily than that, but for now, it seemed like his mate would see another sunrise.

Arges wrapped an arm around his shoulders again, this time keeping him from sagging with relief in front of the others. Leaning down, he murmured in Daios's ear, "Breathe, my brother. I believe you can do this. Yes?"

"Yes," he replied, dazed and a little shocked.

She was alive. And he had to make sure she stayed that way.

Chapter 35

Two weeks.

That's how long it took for her father to make a mistake.

Two weeks of constant surveillance and someone even standing in her room while she slept. Two weeks of distrust and everyone looking at her like she had somehow turned into a witch in the short amount of time since they had last seen her.

In the first week, she had gone to her father's office multiple times a day. Just to check in on him. To pretend to beg for his forgiveness while she fake cried and told him how much she had missed him and that she really had just been having a wonderful time.

Anya spun a story about where she was. She'd stayed with a friend named Jessica who had invited her to go to Beta because she'd never seen it. She swore up and down that she'd talked to him about it, even made mention of the story to her maids, who apparently had forgotten as well. Her father did not believe her in the slightest. Not a single detail, even though she was meticulous about remembering everything she'd told him.

Because he asked. Every day he asked different questions, each one meant to trip her up. But Anya had lived with this man her entire life. She knew exactly what he was going to ask and why he was going to ask it. He had his own opinions about where she was.

And he had the footage.

But he didn't want anyone to know that he had the footage of her leaving with an undine. So she continued to mock him. To tell him this story that she knew he would never believe, but maybe those who had seen the footage would start to question their own sanity.

A woman dragged into the depths of the sea by an undine? How could she possibly survive? She even dropped in a few conversations about how Beta was so cold compared to here, and she couldn't stand the cold.

Little details that she had thought would win people in her favor. That was always the game with her father.

Who was more popular? He was the old man who ruled them all. The General who kept them safe.

But she was the golden daughter who sat on the pillar he had built her.

At the end of the first week, she stole a keycard from her father's desk. She'd purposefully made him so angry that he grabbed the back of her neck and slammed her face down on the table. Even though she knew the sight of this treatment would make Daios fly into a rage, she needed it to happen. He always kept the keycards in the same hidden place underneath his desk, where his legs fit into the slots of the massive amount of wood that should have been used for anything other than a desk.

She'd palmed it, and then taken the enraged yelling and the bruises down her back and shoulders. He wouldn't ever injure her in a way anyone else could see, though.

When she left the room, she'd looked down into her hand and showed them. A keycard. One of her father's personal cards, which meant it should open every door in Alpha.

All of that, and it still took another week before she could slip out of her room. This was her chance, if she didn't take it now, then she might have to wait another two weeks to do this.

But she was done waiting. And she was done being here. Now that she'd had a taste of freedom, this life felt even more controlled. Anya was done with the cage. Now she wanted to go home.

Bitsy affixed to her head, she made sure that all of her black clothing covered her almost completely. She'd even torn a piece of black fabric off one of her dresses to wrap around her face. The only thing anyone would be able to see was her eyes, and the faint glow of the lens as Bitsy guided her through the city.

"Ready?" she whispered, knowing it was the last thing she would say until she was certain no one could overhear her.

Bitsy put a little thumbs up on the lens, and then they were off. The guard outside her door had fallen asleep. The poor man had been here three nights in a row, and she assumed that someone else had traded their shift so that he would be here yet again. There had been a second man, but he'd gone off to pee, which meant this one had fallen right into a deep sleep without the distraction.

All she had to do was open her door and creep past him. Not exactly easy when she couldn't hear what she was doing, but it was simple enough. Sliding through the smallest crack, she relied on Bitsy to show her a small bar with the level of the sound she was making.

Down the street from her small home, she still had to keep being quiet. There were people here that her father had likely planted. So she yanked her black hood up over her face and made her way down the street like she was hurrying home.

"Quickly," Bitsy said. "Go right, there's another person coming your way."

She didn't hesitate. She turned every time her droid said to.

Anya made her way through Alpha in the dead of night, guided by Bitsy and all the schematics that she'd downloaded before they left. Every step, every sound, all of it was up to her droid.

Artificial starlight lit her way. All the twinkling lights on the top of her largest cage reminded her of why she was doing this. Everyone here was in a cage; they just didn't know it yet. Soon, she would set them free.

They would join other cities. They would learn what it meant to work for what they had, and soon they would realize that life was so much more than indulgence and petty parties where everyone hated each other.

She was giving them a gift. They might not know it now, but soon enough, they would.

"Right again," Bitsy said. "There's a service entrance on the wall. Press the fourth flower on the mural."

They'd discussed how this would go. If they wanted everything to run smoothly, she had to move like she wasn't taking orders. Fluid and natural was the plan. Bitsy would tell her something just moments before she had to do it. If anyone was watching, they would think she was a service engineer if she didn't hesitate. So she planted her palm on the fourth flower and a small door opened up to the right of it.

She had to plunge into the darkness while holding her breath, not knowing what waited for her on the other side.

And then she was in the depths of the city. She remembered these worn down corridors from the day she'd lost her hearing. They weren't like the rest of Alpha. Bare metal bars overlapped over her head, faintly tinted orange with the bare bulbed lights that hung along the ceiling of the metal hall. Steam filled the room, making the fabric of her clothing cling to her skin. Already sweat dripped down her temples, but that could be nerves.

"Keycard," Bitsy said.

She reached into her pocket for it, quickly pulling it out as though she knew there was a door coming up soon that would require her credentials.

"Head down, person coming."

Ducking her face into the shadow of her hoodie, she nodded at the man who walked by her. He had a bandana around his neck as well, likely because he used it to wipe the sweat from his face. The man's exhausted expression didn't change as he returned her nod.

Some of the tension eased in her back as he walked away from her.

"Two doors down, pretend to be resting. Take the door on the left when the group of people walk by you. Be quick."

Quick wasn't easy the deeper they went into this place. Her footsteps likely echoed as she walked, boots clacking against the metal. But here she was supposed to make noise. After all, she was just another worker. Just another person who had come to Alpha hoping for utopia and instead had been thrown into the bowels of Hell itself.

Anya leaned against the wall, one foot pressed flat against it and her arms crossed over her chest. A group of people walked past her, all men heading home likely. Although their homes were nowhere near where she had come from.

One of them paused as he looked her up and down. The others continued moving, but he didn't. No words appeared on her lens, so she had to read his lips. Thankfully, he was staring right at her. "You all right?"

She nodded, not sure if she should trust her voice.

"If you're hurt, you're supposed to go to the infirmary." He hooked a finger in the direction the group had come from. "You need help getting there?"

Bitsy flashed a little red light over her eye, likely trying to pretend to be one of the devices that people used to see through the walls to find broken pipes. But she couldn't put any words there or the man would see them too.

"I'm fine," she replied, trying to deepen her voice but having no idea if she succeeded. "Just needed a breather."

"You're telling me. Been a long day." He palmed the back of his neck and dropped his head. That's when she lost sight of his lips. All of a sudden, she couldn't tell what he was saying. Then he looked at her, and she knew he had said something she was supposed to respond to.

Fuck.

What did he say? What was she supposed to say in response? He was going to know that something was off and she didn't belong here. She was so fucked. So...

He tilted his head to the side. "You can't hear me, can you?"

She shook her head. Why would she lie? She couldn't hear him, and could only make out a bit of what he was saying right now. It wasn't like she could say just anything, and he'd believe she was realistically continuing the conversation.

"That's all right." He enunciated the words better this time. "My brother lost his hearing down here, too. All of us take something home from Alpha. You sure you are good?"

Nodding, Anya wondered if it would really be this easy to convince him to leave her alone.

"Night, then."

And then he walked away.

He just walked away, and she waited a few breaths until Bitsy flared up again. "Left door."

"Right," she whispered before using her father's key card to spill into the lab.

None of the technicians or scientists were here at this time of night. But she still made Bitsy do a sweep for any heat signatures before she felt safe enough to yank the stifling fabric off her face. Only then did she breathe a little easier.

They'd made it into the room where she had lost her hearing and where everything in her life had changed. She didn't even look at the area where the explosion had gone off. All she did was walk right to the back, where she had never been. It was one of the few unlisted rooms in the schematics they had found.

Another set of words flashed in front of her eyes as she approached it, these in the reddish pink color that was usually Daios. "What are you doing, kalon?"

"This is the only time, big guy." She flashed her father's card and watched as the door opened. "I know it's the middle of the night, but I'm getting tired of waiting."

"Wait until I get the others."

"Can't do that."

"Wait." Bitsy even underlined the word, as though he had said it with more command than normal. "You will wait, Anya. It's too risky. What if something happens while you are in there? What if your father comes in? I cannot help you from here."

"I know," she whispered, the words breaking in her throat. "But this is what I came here to do. Bitsy, end contact with the dome. Only provide visuals."

"Anya wait—"

And then the contact was severed. She felt a bit like she'd cut off one of her own limbs, but this had to be done. She couldn't be distracted, not even by him.

Stepping into the room, she covered her mouth with her hand. They weren't even hiding what they were doing. An undine laid out on a table, dissected. Their tail was limp on the ground, the lovely pale lavender color dulled into a shade of sickly grey in death. It was a female, she thought, considering the breasts that caused the gaping open chest to droop.

Anya couldn't look at her for very long, so she turned the lens in that direction and closed her eyes. She counted to twenty, slowly turning her head up and down so that they could see the entirety of the woman who had been killed. And then, when her head was turned away again, she opened her eyes.

There were four cylindrical tanks on the wall opposite her. They looked like tubes, except three of them had undines in them. One already looked dead. She wasn't sure how she could tell, but there wasn't a spark of life in the floating body. The other two were alive, though.

One was still asleep. She walked up to the tank, tears already burning in her eyes because she knew the sleeping one was probably the next one to be experimented on. If she didn't do this in time, then this undine's life was on her hands.

The male was so pretty. Delicate green fins fanned out around his young face, not a single mark of a scar on his features. Not like Daios.

"The dome is trying to contact you," Bitsy said. "They are saying you should be focusing on getting the explosives. I agree. You are risking yourself every moment you are here."

"I know," she replied. Then she turned her attention to the last tank.

This undine was awake. It bared its sharp teeth at her, those black eyes flashing with hatred. A deep purple color went up from its tail and onto its belly. It was significantly paler than the other undines she had seen thus far, and didn't have the same kind of fins.

She could only guess this was a depthstrider. This was one of the creatures that everyone was so afraid of and yet it was trapped just like the other.

Anya lifted her hand and pressed it flat to the glass of the tube. She knew Daios was likely growling and raging wherever he was because she was taking a risk. But the depthstrider calmed. Its eyes swirled with a hundred colors as it pressed its hand opposite to hers, and she knew, somehow, it understood she wanted to help them.

In a blink, she saw where it came from. The deep dark sea with all the flashing lights of rainbow creatures that lived with them. She saw a small child, held in the arms of a female undine, who looked at her with a soft smile on her face. And she knew... she knew she couldn't leave them here.

Swallowing hard, she shook her head to clear it of the vision the depthstrider had given her and sighed out a ragged breath.

"Bitsy?"

A flash of light illuminated her droid's lens.

Her throat was thick with emotion, and she wasn't sure her words were anything other than a garbled mess. "Tell the others there's been a change of plan. We're moving now. Get Maketes and Ace ready. The moment they can get here, get them here. There's about to be a lot of alarms going off."

"What are you doing?" Bitsy asked, but she could see the messages were sent off into the ether where the others would get them.

"Daios? I know you can hear me." Anya walked over to the shoot near the dead body. Her father was always efficient. She knew there was a tunnel for them to dump these bodies out into the sea. Hitting the button for release, she grabbed the tray of tools beside it and jammed it into the shoot to keep it open. "I love you. Try not to be mad at me for too long."

She knew where the explosives were. She knew where everything was because they hadn't moved them since her accident. Everyone here was so arrogant. They didn't believe for a second that their little golden princess would be the one to destroy everything from the inside out.

Bubbles appeared on the lens, and she knew Bitsy had let him through the channel to send one last message to her.

"Kalon, what are you going to do?"

Stalking out of the room, she reached for the axe that hung in a glass box in case of emergencies. It was so much heavier than she thought, and she had to drag it across the floor after her into the room of ammunitions.

The explosives were small silver balls, just like the ones that had damaged her hearing. But she knew these were meant to be lobbed into the sea where they would set off an explosive that was powerful enough to clear a field of at least one hundred undine.

That was the plan, at least. Her father had never had to use them, but he liked having weapons just in case. She ran her finger over the top of one and it lit up with numbers along the top. Bitsy helped, showing her exactly where to press to give her enough time to save the undines and get out.

Setting a timer for thirty minutes, she assumed that would be plenty of time. Besides, she only had to set one off. There were at least fifteen of them sitting next to each other. A single explosive would set off all the others until it became a massive bomb.

Heaving the axe up onto her shoulder, she stalked back into the room where the two living undines remained. "I'm getting them out. No matter what."

Chapter 36

Daios watched the life-sized projection with horror turning his blood ice cold.

Fortis hadn't lied. The achromos had their hands on undines, and they were ripping them apart. Why? He had no idea. They likely would get no answers out of these monsters who thought nothing of killing just to discover answers about his people.

If anyone else was in that room, he would have told them to search more. He would have wanted an answer for why the bodies were just lying there like garbage. But it was Anya who stood looking at them. It was his woman who risked her life just being in that room with the others.

He shifted where he leaned against the moon pool, doing his best to not bump into Maketes, who was holding onto another ear piece that Mira had rigged up so he could contact Ace. His low murmur was distracting, but not enough for him to change what his real worry was.

"Byte," he ground out. "Make a connection with Bitsy. I need to talk with Anya."

Byte chirped out a disgruntled sound. "I cannot just do that. It is a great breach of privacy and considered to be highly rude amongst droids."

"I do not care. Connect with her and force her to let me talk to Anya, or I will smash you into a hundred pieces that even Mira cannot fix."

Mira gave him a dirty look at the threat, but it worked. Byte allowed a connection to go through.

"Kalon," he said, his voice low and sharp. "What are you going to do?"

Arges shifted where he had braced himself inside the room. Already Arges's scales were drying out, but he didn't move from his place, staring at the projection alongside Daios. Anya was dragging something behind her, and her breathing was labored. What was she doing? She was going to hurt herself if she didn't stop.

Daios should be there with her. He could have figured out a way to get into that room so he could join her. Then, whatever she wanted to do, he could do with her.

"I'm getting them out," she said, her voice ringing true and strong through the connection. "No matter what."

"What do you mean you're getting them out?" he growled. "You just set the explosives. We could see that you put a timer on them, Anya!"

But she didn't reply. She just heaved that axe over her shoulders, turned to the tank with the awake undine, and brought it down on the glass. The depthstrider inside flinched, but then it looked at the small indent on the glass and it seemed to know what was happening.

Arges stirred, his blue tail looping closer to him as he pushed himself closer to the screen. "She's going to break it out of the glass."

"It's going to kill her," Daios growled.

"I don't think so. It looks like he understands what is happening." Arges pointed to the other of their people trapped inside the other tube. "That one is still asleep, though."

"Anya," he said, hoping that Bitsy would throw his words at her again. "Stop what you are doing. There are only two of them and an entire city for you to save. Maketes is speaking with Ace, but they need more time."

"Tell them they have thirty minutes," she grunted as she slammed the axe into the glass again. The spiderweb of cracks fractured around the edges. Not quite a break, but enough for the depthstrider to hit it from the other side as well.

"Thirty minutes?" He looked over his shoulder, hearing Maketes repeat the words into the translator and then shaking his head as he read it from the device himself.

His yellow finned brother's eyes were wide with panic before he said, "We can't be ready in thirty minutes."

"Did you hear that, Anya?" Daios shouted, as though she was right in front of him and he could rage at her. "There isn't enough time for them to get there."

"There is." She let out a little yell this time as she slammed the axe down. The spiderwebs grew larger, this time with water leaking out of the small holes between them. "I already calculated it with Bitsy. Tell Ace to use Alpha's safety ships. They can be activated remotely. The explosion will be far away from the housing of pretty much everyone, so only people close to the blast will be affected. They'll get out just fine, and anyone around here deserves to be stuck."

Something about that struck him as odd. The way she said the words, it all felt wrong. Thirty minutes was shorter than how long it had taken her to get to the safety pods herself.

All he could hear was a high-pitched shriek in his head, and time seemed to slow. He looked at Maketes. His brother was completely lit up, repeating the words to Ace and then waiting for the translation of what they said to come through. Apparently that was fine. They could make this work even if Ace had to hack into Alpha's system again.

Mira and Arges were saying something to his mate, but he wasn't listening to their words. All he knew was that he felt like he needed to lie down. Because he knew what she was saying. She'd told him before going in there and he'd been too stuck in his ways to hear what she was saying.

Bracing himself on the edge of the moon pool, he croaked, "You're not getting out, are you?"

Everyone froze. Even Byte tilted his head just slightly before relaying the words to Anya, who had lifted the axe one more time over her head. She seemed to hesitate, that heavy weapon held over her head.

Then she said, "I don't know if I'm getting out of this one, Daios. My family was the one to do this. There's an old human saying, Mira can explain it to you. A captain goes down with his ship. I have to make sure that happens."

The axe flew through the air and struck the glass hard. The projection suddenly whirled as the water caught Anya up and she was tossed back against the table where the dead female was. Sharp objects rained down on her head from the table and she hissed as one of them sliced through her pant leg. The bright bloom of blood was all he could see until a webbed hand came down on the wound.

Again she made a pained noise, and he could see the depthstrider had grabbed her too hard.

"Anya," he said, his voice cracking. "You have to listen to me. Get out, now. The depthstrider will do what he must."

When the depthstrider did nothing other than keep his hand on her leg, she reached up and took Bitsy off her head. Anya turned the projection toward herself and he could see the sweat dripping down her face. There was a grease smudge on her nose and black blood dripping through her hair from the dead body above her. Her eyes were a little wild, perhaps with fear.

"I love you," she said into the camera, with a smile that he knew was fake. "Ace can find me. I'll keep Bitsy on. There's still a chance, Daios. Just a small one, but... Find me? Even if I'm not alive."

"Anya!" he shouted, but then the connection went black.

Byte struggled to reconnect. He could see the blue and green text flying where he tried to make Bitsy listen, but then... nothing. There was no connection. No projection of what Anya was doing.

Nothing at all.

He let out a sound of rage that burst from his chest as anger unlike anything he'd ever felt thrust through his entire body. He slammed his fists down on the floor, denting the metal as he bared his teeth at the others.

"I'm going to get her," he snarled before turning to the water.

"You don't even know where she is!" Mira shouted.

He didn't care. He had to do something. The depthstrider in there was just as dangerous as the people that surrounded her. He had sent her into a pool of sharks to swim while she bled freely. What had he expected?

Maketes moved in front of him, his tail wrapping around Daios's to stop him from moving. "Listen to us, Daios. Give me a moment to talk with Ace, and I will tell you where she is. We can find a way to get to her."

He didn't want to wait a single second more. The words ground out of him before he could stop them. "Every moment I am here lengthens my journey to her side. If she dies, I will blame all of you. I will boil the very sea that you live in. I will hunt every one of you down until your lineage is nothing more than chum in this sea."

The heavy weight of their stares and silence pressed down upon him, but he would not bend. He would not bow to their expectations when his woman's life was on the line.

Maketes nodded. "Noted. Let me talk with Ace first, and then we'll figure out a faster way to get you there."

"I can do that," Mira said with a sudden snap of her fingers. "I've been working on a device to help me swim faster. It has a motor on it. With you swimming and the motor pulling you, you should move faster than without it. It's not teleportation, but it might cut it down by an hour or so."

An hour was half the time. He could do that fast enough. But it was still thirty minutes after the bomb went off, and time was ticking.

His muscles and tail twitched with the need for action. He did not move, though, when Arges approached him. His brother held the metal arm, retrieved from the bottom of the sea. "You will need this."

He did not want to wear it. Anya hadn't liked it, and in the end, neither did he. But he still threw it over his head as Mira came out of her back room, affixing the terrible sensation of needles digging into his skin and flexing the fingers of the metal arm.

Arges took the strange device out of Mira's hands and approached him. "We are here for you, brother." He handed it over and then pointed out the switch to turn it on. "We'll be right behind you. But I need you to hear me when I say you are not alone."

"I hear you, brother," he replied. What he did not say was that he didn't think they could help him now.

"Go get her."

Maketes made a tsking noise and handed the strange rectangle over. "This is the city map. She's somewhere in here. Ace thinks there's a way to get into it through these tubes. Apparently, that's what her father has been using to dump those bodies. As long as the blast doesn't damage those, you should be able to get through."

"Are you sure?"

"As sure as we can be in a few moments." Maketes shrugged. "It's the best chance you've got right now."

"Then I'll take it."

He didn't look at the others. He couldn't. There wasn't any time for reassurance or for any more words. He knew exactly where to go, and that was where he had to continue.

The device that Mira had built would help him swim faster. Already it was pulling him, and he could only hope that would jolt him through the water with all the speed of a sailfish. If he could manage that and maintain that speed, he could get to her. Hopefully. Sooner rather than later.

He darted through the water, feeling the currents running over his sides. The goddess was with him. As he darted away from their home, arcing up in a big circle and then plunging into the fastest current he could find, he knew this to be true. It had been a long time since he'd been so certain that the sea was on his side.

He could feel their goddess in the way the ocean moved with him. He could feel it the moment that the sea knew he was going to save the only woman who had ever meant anything to him. His mate. His heart. His soul.

The goddess was there with him as the first sparkle of Alpha appeared on the horizon. A tiny golden gemstone in the distance and it was still in one piece. He would make it. He could go a little faster now, because the adrenaline running through his body had yet to wear out. The currents pushed with him, sending him careening through the water. Soon he would be at her side. Soon.

The city was the size of his fist now. Not far at all. If only his fins worked a little faster. He could get there, he could...

The explosion rocked throughout the entire ocean. He saw it first. A bubble appeared around a large section of Alpha and then it popped. Debris and dust billowed around the gold. And for a moment, he couldn't see anything at all there. It was the gray texture of muck that had been stirred up, then fell slowly to reveal the golden city of Alpha. Than it all compressed. Sucking back into the city like the hand of a goddess had pressed it back together. Forming a gemstone on the horizon that turned red as the city burst into flame.

Then he felt it. The explosion blasted through the entire sea, shoving him back a countless distance as debris and dust surrounded him. It filled his gills, shoving him into the dirt even as he struggled against it. Fighting for her.

And then it all stilled. Eerily calm again as the sound finally hit him. The strange sound of popping and the echoing thunder of ruin.

"No!" he screamed, the word raw and ragged.

His hearts exploded with that city. Because she was there. His woman had saved them all, but there had not been enough time for her to run.

A fissure opened up in his chest. All that madness that she'd locked away streamed out of it, choking him with the finality that everything he loved, everything he touched, died. And it was his fault.

All the ghosts trailed their hands along his face, but this time, it didn't feel like they were trying to dig into his skin. Instead, they were wiping away tears he couldn't feel.

"Go get her," they whispered in his ears. These voices were no longer full of rage, but of sadness and heartbreak along with him. "Go bring her home, Daios. Lay her down to rest with us. We will care for her."

The choked sound that came out of him was unlike any he'd ever made before. His hearts shattered. He could barely see through the ache in his body. All of it was gone now. Every hope. Every dream. All of it decimated in the wake of that beautiful light that had been snuffed out.

The device in his hands kicked, and he let it fall. Perhaps they would find it later, but right now, he swam with his own body. He used every muscle, every fiber, every twitching pain to get him to her side.

"My love," he called out, his voice echoing through the ocean and pushing through the currents. "I am coming."

He hoped her soul knew. That perhaps some part of her could find peace in knowing that she might have died alone, but she would not stay that way. He would find every piece of her and bring her back. Every bone, even the smallest one, he would carry it to her final resting place. With him, as she deserved.

When he reached Alpha, all the city's defenses were down. None of the other undines had made it before him, but that was all right. Right now, he needed to find a way into the underbelly of this city. Even it meant he had to dig through the mire to get to her.

Chapter 37

30 MINUTES EARLIER

The undine loomed over her. No, not undine. Depthstrider. He was breathing hard, all of his gills flared wide as though he had forgotten he had a second set of lungs that could help him breathe easier here. Regardless, it mattered very little. He was going to kill her, and maybe she deserved it.

Her people had been the ones to hurt him. Her people had been the ones to capture him, bring him to this place, and then force him to watch them experimenting on all of his friends. Perhaps family. The woman on the table behind her was someone who had a life before this.

A life Anya's people had stolen.

He lifted a hand to her neck, those deadly claws dragging down her skin in fine pinpricks of pain. She'd already disconnected all communications with Daios and the others. She didn't want them to see her die. Not like this.

But then the depthstrider touched Bitsy gently and turned. He leaned down to pick up the axe she had broken him out of his case with and dragged himself toward the other undine.

She thought to ask if he needed help, but she recognized the posture of his body. He had to do this, just like she had to let them out. An alarm suddenly blared over their head. Delayed, of course. But someone had figured out that the undine's cage had been broken and soon enough, there would be swarms of people in this room with them.

"Hurry," she said, her throat aching with the sound.

She didn't have to say anything. The depthstrider coiled his tail underneath himself, pushing up to a great height but still able to use his body like a weapon. Unlike her, it only took him one strike to break through the glass.

The other undine fell to the floor with a wet slap. Water rushed out of this one too, but she was prepared for it this time. Grabbing onto the legs of the table weighted down with the massive dead body above her, she held on until the water had stopped flowing.

Blowing out a long breath, she dragged herself upright. Her leg was on fire where she'd been sliced with that stupid tool. Who knew what had gotten into the wound, but did it really matter? Her father wouldn't let her live after this.

The depthstrider picked up the other undine in his arms. Somehow, the sleeping male looked so small in the arms of the other.

She pointed to the disposal shoot she'd wedged open. "I already opened it for you. I don't know if you can understand me, but you have to go now. I can distract them long enough for you to get out."

But not enough time for her to get out. Her father would send countless people to this room. There was only one way these undines would get out, and that way was her. Her cover was blown. Now, she could only hope that she'd set enough bombs off to do some real damage.

The depthstrider nodded, almost as though he understood her, and then slipped into the shoot. She could already hear boots outside the room in the metal halls, so she waited until the last possible moment before yanking out the metal she'd jammed it with. The shoot closed with a finalistic thud, and she knew this was it.

She was going to have to distract a group of men and women who had been told to stop her at all costs. Lives depended on it.

The doors slammed open. Metal struck metal, the room shaking with the force of it as she turned to look at the last person she had expected to walk through the room with a wall of people behind him.

"Hi Dad," she breathed.

The General stood in the central area of his research lab, face beet red, so angry that he didn't know what to do with himself. His eyes scanned over what she had done. The broken tubes. The way she leaned against the table with the dead body, obviously injured. His eyes saw everything but back to the room with all the weapons.

Because why would she go linger in the room that had caused her permanent damage? Why would she ever risk herself like that again? To him, she was still a foolish little girl who had too much pity for creatures he hated.

"Anya," he said, clearly trying his best to not yell at her. "What have you done, child?"

"I'm not a child. And I set them free."

"Why?"

"Because they are people. They have intricate cultures and lives that we do not understand. And because you were cutting them open while they were awake for your own sick and twisted games. I don't know why you want to rip something living open while it can feel every single cut, but I refuse to let you do it any longer."

His face got more and more red with every word she said. But then he played right into her hand. "Everyone out."

The soldier beside him turned in surprise. "Sir?"

He must have been her father's newest brainwashed recruit. The man not only thought he was right where he needed to be, but he was also openly questioning her father in front of other people.

Some soldiers never learned.

"Get out," her father snapped. "Do not make me tell you twice. This is a family matter."

In the days when she was afraid of him, she would have flinched at the words. As a child, he would have taken these moments to add to the bruises that no one could see. But she was a grown woman, and she knew what freedom tasted like.

The memory of that was enough to fight for. Even if she would never taste it again.

Anya curled her hand around a scalpel still on the table. If this required her to get her hands dirty, then she would do that. Her father had it coming to him.

It took a while for everyone to filter back out through the doors, but then they were sealed into the room together. Her father's expression changed from one of chiding annoyance to downright rage.

"First, you're back from the dead," he started, his voice deep and rough. "Then you're freeing experiments? I have to ask, daughter, how did you find out what was happening down here?"

"The undines talk."

"No undine makes it out of this room alive, so you'll have to do better than that." He took a few steps toward her, only to raise his hands and pause as she brandished the scalpel at him. "That little pigsticker won't do anything, Anya. Put it down."

"No," she hissed, adjusting Bitsy so she could see both the lens and her father easier.

"Did you think I wasn't aware of your contact outside the city? I've had you watched since you were just a little girl. I know everything you do."

She would not rise to that challenge. Bitsy was bugged often, of course, but she'd fixed her every time. "You have no idea what I do in my spare time."

"Ace?" He lifted his eyebrow. "Your little friend in Gamma? She's already been taken care of, I hope you know. I sent men to remove the problem the day you got back."

The first inklings of panic rose in her throat. She could feel it squeezing like he'd wrapped his hands around her neck. "You don't know who Ace even is."

"No, Anya. You don't know who Ace is. I know exactly who she is, where she lives, and how long she's been helping you. Just like I knew where you were when that monster stole you away from me. But it worked, you see? I had a daughter who gave me every reason I needed to keep fighting against the monsters in this sea. You could have stayed with them and I would have left you alone. As much as a man can leave his daughter alone when she's fighting on the wrong side of a war." He shrugged. "But you had to come back."

How much longer was there on the bombs? She knew it had to be under twenty minutes. It had taken her a while to get the undines out of the tanks. But how long had it actually taken? It felt like only a moment, but she had to have wasted more time than she thought.

"Of course I came back," she said. "After they told me what you were doing, I knew I was the only one who could stop it."

"Stop what? The death of two undines?" The smile twisting his lips was downright cruel. "They're going to swim off and maybe live a couple more years, certainly. I'll just catch more."

"I am going to do everything in my power to make sure you can't do that."

"I'm sure you will. You always were an obstinate fool."

That's when she noticed his hand was at his waist. His fingers toyed with the handle of a gun. And what was she supposed to do? She had to keep him talking.

"Are you going to shoot me, Dad?" She threw the words at him, because they were her only weapons. "Really? Your daughter?"

"It's a shame that you got it into your head that the undines were actual people. When you returned, I saw the footage of your kidnapping and it was obvious they had brainwashed you. The alarms went off and what a horrible feeling I got in my stomach. A sickness like I knew I was about to lose my daughter. I found you down here dead after you tried to release them, and they killed you on the way out." He shook his head, taking the gun out of his waistband and pointing it at her head. "But the city will always remember you."

"Why?" she asked. Some desperation in her knew she was about to die, but she had to understand the reasoning behind it. "Why kill me? Why go to all this trouble?"

"Because I have always needed a figurehead!" Spit flew out of his mouth. "Your mother never understood that, either. I pursued her for years. Years of me telling her that I would become the next general and she would stand by my side. Only the greatest generals in the history of Alpha had wives as beautiful as her. I would become a god in their eyes with her at my side!"

"Mom didn't want to marry you?" She didn't really care all that much, but this would keep him talking.

"No, she didn't want to marry me." His face warped, as though he was trying to pretend to be sad. "But when your father tragically died in a horrible diving accident, she had nowhere to go but to crawl her way back to me. And she would have been the perfect bride if she hadn't taken the coward's way out and slit her wrists in that fucking bathtub! If she wanted to die, I could have made her a martyr, but no. She had to take that from me as well. Thankfully, I had a replacement ready to go."

Bitsy circled the gun in her father's hand and put up the word "click". He'd taken the safety off the gun. He was going to shoot her. He was going to put a bullet in her head and there was nothing she could do to stop him.

"Mom killed herself?" she whispered, taking one step back as though the words hurt her. But really, her head was reeling with all this new information. "You're not even my father?"

"No. It was easier to tell you that I was, though. Kept you real quiet over all these years." He gestured up and down her body with the gun. "You look just like her. The golden dream of Alpha. Proof that our city was born in nothing but beauty. Years ago, they would have worshipped you as a paragon. Perhaps they would have said you were sent to us by god himself. Do you know that? You've always wielded that beauty so well. Just like her."

No. She hadn't. She hadn't wanted any ounce of her looks, nor had she ever wanted the attention.

"But then I went and touched something I wasn't supposed to," she whispered. "And I wasn't perfect anymore."

Bitsy threw up an image of someone giving another person a hug, and she'd strangely forgotten that the droid was even on her head. She was so used to reading the words from her father's lips that she hadn't noticed she was reading the words transcribed in front of her. She'd just… existed.

Her shoulders rounded forward in defeat. And the General's head tilted back with a laugh that she knew must be cruel and cutting.

"Yes, you ruined that a bit. But surprisingly, people seemed to love you even more after your little mistake. Strange, I had thought it would prove that you were just as broken as we all thought you were. But no. They loved you because you were a little broken bird who needed them to put you back together."

"I was never broken." She curled her fingers even more tightly around the scalpel blade, as though to remind herself that she wasn't defenseless. "I became so much stronger. It's a shame that you haven't recognized that, General. But allow me to tell you that I am far more than you could ever dream."

"That's good to know. I'll tell them all those were your last words. They'll love that."

He pointed the gun at her head again, and she had the feeling that now was the time. That everything was about to happen and if she was right, she had saved them all.

The soft smile on her face gave him pause. "What are you grinning about?" he snarled.

"You don't know everything, General. Even though you like to think that you do."

"I have my eyes everywhere. Even in your little pod. I know they're coming for you, and we will be ready to mow them down with all the gunfire that exists in this city. I will destroy them and become the General that no one ever forgets."

"Right," she replied. "If only I hadn't set off the bombs."

"What bombs?" His face twisted in a snarl and he turned, giving her the smallest window of time.

Anya spun and ran. She darted behind another table before turning it onto its side. She could feel it shaking, and could only assume that her father was shooting at her. But she was behind enough metal to keep her safe for a few moments, pressed against the wall as she was. It was the best chance for her to survive the coming explosion.

As she whispered a countdown to herself, she let memories of her few moments with Daios play through her eyes. She'd tried so hard not to think of him through all of this, because if she got lost in those memories she wasn't certain that she would ever do it.

But now she could remember the soft surprise in his eyes at her touch. The soft way he'd brushed his fingers through her hair. The wide-eyed expression he got when she touched him. All of those wonderful memories as she counted down with Bitsy.

Love you, appeared on her screen.

Touching her fingers to the small droid on her head, she whispered, "I love you too, you know."

The words hovered above her eyes as the countdown hit one. And then everything exploded.

Chapter 38

He'd nearly made it to the city when he noticed there were others. People of Water who he did not recognize, all of them swimming toward Alpha with him. He had made it so quickly. How were others able to join him?

They must have been lying in wait, he realized. Maketes must have done something, but he couldn't focus on what his brother had done at all.

There was a hole in one of his hearts that bled. One of them beat for the other, because half of him had died the moment that bomb went off. She was gone. He was so certain of it that even the lights on his body wouldn't work. She was dead, and he had to find her body to bring her home.

He watched the other undines join him with a numbness that spread throughout all of his fins. He could hardly swim at all. Everything felt rather mechanical, as though the sea goddess herself pulled the strings of his body to move him forward. Not that he wanted to.

Would she be limp in the water when he found her? Already he could see the blood surrounding her like a graceful dress of crimson. She would float down within the glass of the city, a creature trapped beyond measure. Golden hair would coil around her head, stained red with more blood as her graceful spine would curl in on itself.

Even in death, he knew she would be the prettiest thing he'd ever seen. An otherworldly creature who had come from the sky to give him a moment of bright light.

How was he supposed to go back into the darkness without her to guide him?

"Brother." The word sliced through him, because he knew that voice. These weren't People of Water, not like he knew at least.

Turning his head as he sped through the currents toward the city, he realized it was Fortis beside him. The dark purple coloring lit up the moment he glanced over at the man who had once been a friend.

"Fortis?" he asked, feeling as though perhaps he slurred the word. "What are you doing here?"

"We knew it would happen. We are here to help."

"Since when do the depthstriders help anyone but themselves?" He shook his head, trying to clear himself out of the fog of rage and heartbreak. "What could you possibly help with?"

"You won't make it in time." Fortis pointed toward the city, and that was when Daios's mind cleared enough to see what was happening in front of him.

She'd blasted a hole in the side of the city. Not a huge hole, but enough that water was rushing in through that area. It was so small that only three of his kind could have moved through it, a surprisingly small amount of damage for the destruction it had caused.

But then his eyes moved up the glass casing that protected the city. Fractures were creaking through it, fissures moving all the way up the glass dome until he could see there were thousands of them.

Cracks in not just the first layer, but the second as well. Cracks that were getting worse and worse with the pressure of the ocean.

"She did it," he said, his voice little more than a croak. "She brought the city down."

"That she did." Fortis cleared his throat before placing a hand on his back and shoving him forward even faster. "We perhaps saw the future wrong when it came to her. I feared she would fold under the weight of her father's disappointment. But she is an impressive woman, brother. Impressive enough to win the favor of the depthstriders."

That numbness crept back into his soul. Because how was he supposed to say yes she was, when he knew that was in past tense? She had to be dead. That hole was big enough to drown her, even if she had survived the blast.

She was gone.

Two figures appeared in the murky darkness surrounding the city and, for a moment, his heart leapt once more. Perhaps she had made it out. The People of Water she had saved. Surely they had taken her with them. They had to have...

But it was a depthstrider with one of his own people in his arms. The two males were worse for wear, too thin to be healthy and barely making it through the water.

Fortis moved faster than he did toward them. He grabbed the limp one from the other's arms, passing the body off to another of their kind before he gathered the depthstrider up in a hug. They coiled around each other for a moment, their tails looping and twisting before they broke apart.

"You are well?" Fortis asked, his voice croaking.

"I am alive," the younger depthstrider said.

And Daios realized they were the spitting image of each other. The younger one looked almost identical to Fortis, even down to the spots on his tail and the yellow tips of his tentacles.

"You have a son?" he asked.

"I have a son. And her people took him from me."

"Why didn't you just say that?" he spat. Anger rose again, and some of his lights flickered back to life with the force of it. "Instead, you spun this story of a dead creature you ripped the memories from, when you could have just told me that your son was in danger!"

"I didn't know if we could trust you." Fortis never let go of his son's shoulder. "You were so entangled with her, I did not know if you would tell her and she would get a message to her father to kill him. I could not take the risk."

"And yet she took the risk for you and your people." Again that burning in his chest, that ache that he could not rub away. He turned his face from his friend, not able to look at either of them. "I have to go inside and get her."

"Daios, it is too risky. We need to return to the others and help the achromos with their escape pods. We will guide them to Gamma, where it is safe. That is the plan, is it not?"

He didn't want to know how Fortis knew even that much. It was all pressing down on him until he felt like he couldn't breathe again.

Fortis's son cleared his gills of dust before saying, "She saved our lives. I could see the danger she was in, and I could smell how terrified she was. But she still did it. If a woman exists who could survive that blast, it is her."

The words should have made him feel better, but they didn't. Instead, all they reminded him of was that no one could have survived the blast. No one. And he had tried so hard to do everything possible to keep her safe.

Until she had chosen to put herself in danger. Until she had chosen to take her own life to save so many others. And who was he to stop her from seeking that honor?

Feeling like a broken man, he nodded at the younger one before locking his eyes with the elder. "Fortis, make sure everyone gets out who needs to get out. Gather our people and make it known they are not to kill those who remain alive."

"I will. Until your brother gets here, they will all be safe."

He turned back toward the city and felt that ache jagged like a dagger in his chest. He hadn't realized that it would hurt this much to lose her. If he had known, would he have taken the risk?

Daios went into the murky dust blind, feeling with his hand for the ragged edges of the metal. They scraped at the delicate webs between his fingers, ripping at his nail beds. And through all the pain, he knew that he would do it a thousand times over to have the memories of her living in his chest. He would give anything to touch the golden strands of her hair.

Flames illuminated everything around him. All he could see, however, was the way her eyes crinkled at the edges when she smiled at him. How she had seen straight through all of his anger and instead trusted that he wasn't a monster. No matter how surly he'd been, no matter how much he'd tried to make her hate him.

Anya had looked at him with affection and love from the beginning. Not as a pet or some strange creature from the sea. But as a man who had seen too much in life, and she knew what that felt like.

There was air above him. Flames that flickered to life as well, but there was still a pocket of air.

His gills felt frozen as he poked his head into the room. The blast had ripped open the metal floor and flooded a majority of the area. The floor had cracked in two, and it seemed somehow the entire room had tilted. Part of it was still out of the water, quite a bit, actually. The flooding seemed to be sucking into tubes that funneled the water deeper into the city. From the faint sound of screams, he had a feeling it was flooding the lower levels, and that there were quite a few people who could not get out.

He should feel some sort of pity for them. After all, he was in love with one of their kind and yet... he felt nothing.

Emerging from the water, he cast his eyes throughout the room that he remembered having walls. At least, that's what it looked like from Anya's perspective. There were no walls in this room any more. Just shattered rubble and a ceiling that looked like it was going to cave in at any point.

The floor had cracked open so far that there was a small water pathway he could use to get deeper into the room, so he did. Slowly swimming through the current and avoiding the areas where wires had fallen into the sea and sparked bright hot shards into the air that burned when they first touched his skin.

Hissing, he turned toward a sound as something moved in the distance. Metal crunched and there was the faintest sound of a groan.

If someone had survived, he would rip them limb from limb. Violence would ease the loss of his love. He would coat himself in the blood of their enemies, dripping with it in honor of her sacrifice.

Yanking himself out of the water, he forcefully expelled everything from his gills. Instantly, all he could smell was smoke and burning wires. This place was going to cave in at any second, so he had to find her body and get out.

But first, he would slake his bloodlust.

Grabbing onto the warped and dented metal sheet, he yanked it free from the person hiding beneath it. Teeth bared and lights glowing blood red, he knew he was a looming creature of the depths that would terrify even the bravest of souls.

But it was not an enemy hidden beneath the dark, warped metal. It was a little blonde woman, curled in on herself like she'd just been tucked inside an egg. A gift from the gods, it seemed.

All of that rage seeped out of him in one swell and he couldn't even hold himself up anymore. The muscles of his tail spasmed. Suddenly, he was right there in front of her. Cupping her face with his hands, one cold and metal and the other warm and alive.

"Anya?" he whispered, his voice shaking because he would swear he heard a moan from this corner. He thought he saw her chest rise with a breath. "Kalon? Please tell me you live."

Another moan, this time as she rolled her head. There was blood on her face where the lens had shattered against her cheekbone and forehead. More lines of blood dotted through her scalp where Bitsy had been crushed against her head. The little droid wasn't moving, and he wasn't sure it ever would again.

Dragging her into him, he leaned against the wall and pulled her into his lap. Looping his tail around her, he created a shield out of his body so not even a spark of heat would touch her skin.

He was shaking. Trembling with her in his arms so hard, he was afraid the movement would hurt her. But then he dragged her closer, pressing her head underneath his chin and squeezed his eyes shut as hot tears trailed down his cheeks.

Rocking her back and forth, he tried to get control over what he was feeling. But these emotions refused to be tamed or named in any way. They were a typhoon of madness and hope and relief and love.

So much love.

All of it shuddered through him as he pressed his lips to her head while she slowly woke in his arms. He'd found her. He had found her before she was lost and he didn't know what god to thank for sparing her, even if she was covered in blood and even if she was not the same. He didn't care. If the head injuries changed her, he would keep her safe for the rest of her life.

Just knowing that she breathed was enough for him. Nothing would ever risk that again.

His breath came in short gasps as he curled himself tighter around her. That metal arm didn't feel right, so he made sure it was farther from her skin so he didn't accidentally crush her.

Again, he pressed his lips to her hair, tasting her blood in his mouth.

"Wake up, my kalon," he whispered, though he did not recognize the sound of his own voice. "You have to wake up now, my love. We have to go before this city takes us with it."

Another moan, and then he felt something shift in her body. A tension that came to life as she woke.

"Daios?" she said, even though her eyes were barely open.

He leaned back, trying to give her enough space to breathe but also not wanting to stop touching her. "My kalon," he said again, breathless with relief. "That's it. There you are."

"Daios?" she repeated, that tension coiling ever tighter. "I can't hear… Where is Bitsy?"

He didn't feel right pulling any of the shards of glass out of her cheek. He was no healer, nor had he ever been talented at helping others through pain. The mere thought of her in more pain, caused by his own hand, made his stomach roll.

So instead, he lifted both of his hands so she could see what he said. "Broken."

"Broken?" she whispered, and then her fingers fluttered up to touch the wounds on her face. She made a terrible sound as her fingers skittered over the shards of what remained. "What happened?"

Cupping her neck, he turned her attention toward the rubble and then signed, "You did it."

"I did it." She repeated the words one more time before nodding. She seemed a little... shell shocked. "I destroyed Alpha."

He would have held her in his arms for hours longer, but another part of the wreckage shifted and moved. A large portion of the ceiling had fallen in the back corner, and he had assumed that was immovable. But something did move underneath it. Something that groaned and started swearing.

Wrapping his arms a little tighter around her, he moved toward the water before whatever else was in the room saw them. He needed to get her to safety. The water was safe. It was...

"Wait," she said, her voice a little too loud. "Wait, Daios."

That moment of hesitation, where he would have done anything she asked, was the moment the rubble finally cleared. A man stood, covered in dust and black soot and blood of his own.

A man that looked surprisingly familiar.

Every fin flared on his body, and he bared his teeth as that familiar rage swelled yet again. For the first time in his life, he stared at the living version of the General.

And oh, he had never wanted to kill someone more.

Chapter 39

She couldn't touch her face. Anya wasn't sure what had happened, but she had a feeling her mind wasn't entirely with her yet. There had felt like shards of glass in her cheek, and she wasn't sure how they'd gotten there.

All she knew was that she had woken up a little too warm with arms around her that were sturdy and safe. She'd known who was holding her. How could she not?

Daios was always the dream. She wanted to feel his arms around her, so of course she had dreamt of them. Snuggled into the muscles of his body and the steady thuds of his hearts, nothing could hurt her.

In some part of her mind, she had known she was hurting. She had felt it. And when she'd woken enough to realize maybe this wasn't a dream, she'd felt the glass in her face. She could also feel the strange feeling of pressure in her skull. No, on her skull.

That panicky feeling started rising in her chest again. She didn't want to think that the feeling was Bitsy, but... What would she do if her droid was destroyed? She couldn't hear anything at all. Not

Daios. Not the groan of the building around her. The explosion right beside her had only made everything all that much harder. It was just a pressing silence that weighed down on her.

She couldn't breathe. She couldn't stay in his arms either because there was something else she was supposed to remember, but her mind was so scattered.

Anya couldn't sit still like this. She couldn't stay in his arms when she needed some air. Some space to process that everything she had relied on was just stripped away from her. Struggling, she ignored his frustrated sounds until she could stand up beside him and just... breathe.

But the damn air was full of smoke because she'd just destroyed her entire home and she was bleeding.

Drips of warm blood trailed down her arms. She couldn't stop staring at them as they raced down her skin. For the first time since she'd woken, she wondered if there was something seriously wrong with her. Anya couldn't put any weight on her leg, but she remembered getting stabbed there when she'd been trying to set the undines free and then...

A cold sensation traveled down her spine as she remembered the other important part of all this. The most important part, she realized, considering he was now standing on the opposite side of the room.

Somehow, impossibly so, the General was still alive. He stood on shaky legs, just like her. Two pillars on either side of the room that was crumbling, but somehow they were holding all of this up with their mutual hatred of the other.

She could see the gun on the floor right in front of him. He saw it the same time she did and cocked his head to the side as he looked at her and the undine beside her.

Clearly he was thinking the same thing she was. He had time to get it. If he was quick. But he had just as much blood and dirt covering him, and it wouldn't be all that easy for him to do so.

He said something, but he was too far away for her to read his lips. Daios's hand wrapped around her ankle, and when she looked down at him, he signed something close to, "He wants you dead."

She knew. As much as it hurt, she knew.

The General stood there, his lips still moving, but she had no idea what he was saying. Part of her didn't want to know. He was spewing out words of hatred and absolute honesty that he didn't want her. He never had.

He'd already told her everything that he needed to say. The General believed she was less because of her mother. He had always thought of her as nothing but a replacement. A figurehead that should have been just like her mother, but she'd not been easily controlled either.

He had taken her from her mother in the hopes that he would create a tool that he could do whatever he wanted with. All the memories of her childhood were suddenly tainted.

They'd never gotten along. He wasn't a good father, but she had always thought, at the very least, he had some pride in her. Now she knew it was all brainwashing. All of it was just a way for him to control her. To manipulate her into the little doll so he could move her limbs at will and puppet her to say the words he wanted her to say.

She'd been a fool to ever trust him, but she couldn't change her past. All she could do was continue moving forward in a way she was proud of.

"Shut up," she shouted, squeezing her belly so the words came out as loud as she knew how to make them. "I don't want to hear anything you have to say anymore. I'm leaving. You can stay in your crumbling city to save what little there is left. I broke my cage. And now I'm going to fly free."

As if everything moved in slow motion, she watched the General grab the gun so close to his feet. He lifted it and pointed it directly at her, and she knew there was a part of him that wanted to see her in pain. He didn't aim at her head. He aimed at her chest, as though he knew that was where it would hurt the worst. Right through her broken and bleeding heart.

She hadn't heard loud sounds for a very long time. Especially not a gun shot. She'd heard them when she still had her hearing, and when she was just a child.

But she knew what this one sounded like. Anya could imagine the sound of it leaving his gun, and the ricochet of noise that came after. Squeezing her eyes shut, she waited for the pain to join the rest that had already burned through her entire body.

But that pain never came. Not in the slightest.

Peeling her eyes open, she was astounded to find Daios in front of her again. His teeth were bared, those black eyes seeing right into her soul as he became a living shield. He jerked again, leaning into her with a puff of breath that feathered over her face.

He said nothing. Perhaps because he wasn't sure if she could hear him. All he did was lift his hand and touch his middle and ring finger to his palm.

"I love you," he said, and she hadn't taught him how to sign that. Where he'd learned it from, she couldn't even guess.

"Are you okay?" she whispered.

At his quick nod, she said, "Get rid of him, and then take me home."

He stared down into her eyes with a softer expression than she'd ever seen on his face. Like he knew how horrible that was for her to ask, and how much she had to fight against herself to say the words. Anya never thought she would be the person to order another life to end. But she also knew the repercussions of letting the General live.

It was the one thing none of them had talked about. And as Daios tucked her behind one of the mangled metal tables and then slipped into the water, she repeated all the reasons why this was the right choice.

If they let the General go, then he would find his supporters amongst those who made it to the life boats. He would be given a grand entrance to any of the other cities where he would just continue what he had been doing, and nothing would change.

The General started shouting. She could see his lips moving and his chest heaving with the words as he pointed the gun at the water. It kicked back, jerking with a violence that mirrored his rage. A small part of her was afraid that Daios would get hit, but she also knew her undine had done this many times. Fighting her people was what he did.

If the General got to the other cities, then they would have even less of a chance to work with them. She knew Beta was already quiet considering the undine attack, and her father hadn't sent them any help afterward. They wanted nothing to do with Alpha or the people in it. Which only left Gamma, and that was a problem. For all that she'd been friends with Ace for a long time, Gamma was still dangerous. The people in that city were convicts, the ones that were thrown to the wolves and to a city that ran entirely on its own.

No government, no one to police them. It was a lawless place.

The water rippled behind the man she used to call father. He stood there, legs braced as though he was prepared for anything that attacked him. But he was just a human.

And Daios was so much more than that.

A metal arm appeared out of the water. She watched each finger settle on the remains of the floor before it flexed and suddenly all the bulk of her undine moved like a snake striking its prey. His tail lashed, muscles bunching, every bit of his strength on stark display. One moment, all she could see was the barest hint of his head and then he was on her father.

The large, metal hand had her father's wrist in his grasp. Then the bones were... wrong. The gun dropped from the General's grip, but he still fought with the other unbroken hand. The General struggled even as he fell onto the ground with the heavy weight of a massive undine on top of him.

Daios bared his teeth and all his fins rose. They shook, vibrating with his anger as he glared down at the man who had caused so much pain and hatred for his people.

She knew he wanted to make this slow. He wanted to take his time peeling off the skin of the man who was responsible for so much heartache and pain. But as Daios looked up at her, catching her gaze through the haze of smoke and fire, he jerked his chin as though telling her not to look.

But Anya thought she should. She should watch and know what he unleashed because she was the one who had asked for this. She told him to take care of her father. No, not her father. Her thoughts were so jumbled and her heart was racing in her chest.

Then she saw Daios lift his hand and palm the General's face. The muscles of his chest and back flexed, his tail coiling as though to give him significantly more power and she knew...

She knew what he was going to do.

She turned her face away from the sight, squeezing her eyes shut even though she knew she wouldn't hear what happened. Her mind, though, it played through it for her. The massive undine who had always protected her had just crushed her father's skull in his hand.

That shouldn't make her breath race or her heart thud in her chest. Or maybe it should. She told herself that this was the first time she'd seen him actually act like a monster, and shouldn't she hate him for it? Shouldn't she be terrified that he had the capability of doing this? He could do it to her whenever he wanted, and there was nothing she could do to stop him.

Anya didn't know how long she stayed where she was, frozen behind that dented table as though it was the only shield protecting her from the world. Everything had changed. Yet again. Her face and head were on fire, and she didn't think there was a part of her body that wasn't bruised. Every time she inhaled, there was a distinct pinching feeling that she was a little terrified might be a broken rib.

All of that was so overwhelming. She couldn't think about all of it at once or she might break. Or maybe that was the head injury. How was she supposed to know?

Cool hands slid up her legs, and she opened her eyes to see him in the water. Waiting for her to look at him. Those black eyes were filled with so much patience and kindness that it made tears prick in her own.

He looked at her like she had hung the moon. Like he knew what he had just done would scare her and he would patiently wait for her on the other side.

And now they could barely even communicate. She couldn't ask him for reassurance because that had been so terrifying. Because she'd almost died and maybe they never would have come back together again if she hadn't just gotten lucky. She wanted to hear him tell her that he was all right too, and that she was going to be all right. That together, they were going to get through this.

Instead, all she heard was the faintest ringing in her ears and all she saw was that his lips were moving. But she couldn't quite read them on those cracked lips. Maybe because they weren't actual words to her. She couldn't see where the syllables started or ended. She couldn't read his lips and she couldn't tell what he wanted her to hear or say or...

He lifted her hands from her knees, cradling them as he pressed a kiss to her knuckles. So gently. Like he knew she was fragile right now, and that she felt as though she could shatter into a thousand pieces of what used to be herself.

She broke. Anya reached for him, tears sliding down her cheeks as his hands slid around her back. There wasn't a hint of blood on him because he'd swum to her side and soon, there would be no blood or ash on her either.

He connected them through the breathing tentacle, and even that was more gentle than she had realized it could be. She barely felt it slide into her neck and when he breathed for her, it was like he took so much of the weight off her shoulders.

With him, she didn't have to do anything but stay in his arms and let him take the burden of it all for her.

Daios sank into the water with her, his hands never stopping as they smoothed up and down her spine. The warm one counted the vertebrae down her back, holding onto her ribs as he felt her breathing while clutching her to his hearts. The cold metal one cupped the back of her head and held her face against the side of his neck.

She wasn't warm enough to swim with him. There were no wetsuits. Nothing for her to keep herself safe in.

But then she felt his fins fold over her hips. He curled himself around her, tucking her fingers into his gills that were warm with every breath he took for the both of them. He wrapped himself around her so tightly she didn't even feel the cold chill of the ocean.

And then she felt his lips press to her head, and she knew nothing bad was going to happen. He was taking her home.

It was done. All of it was done.

Chapter 40

Daios brought them back to the dome faster than he thought possible. With her wrapped in his arms, he had known it would be a slower journey just to make sure she didn't freeze off any of her limbs. But it felt like a blink of an eye for the two of them to be sitting in the dome that was filled with more people than it ever had before.

Mira walked between the two of them, a tube in her hand that dispensed an ooze that healed whatever it touched. She tsked at Anya's broken ribs and had to peel the remains of the droid out of her head. At least Byte had a medkit for that pain as well.

Arges and Maketes had yanked themselves onto the floor of the dome to give the depthstriders a space to argue. The others were beyond angry at what had happened.

So many words flowed past him, and he knew he should pay attention more than he was, but he didn't care to.

"Were all the pods delivered safely to Gamma?" Maketes asked, that tablet in his hands beeping with words that Daios could only assume was Anya's friend still getting in touch with him.

"Yes, of course. They were all delivered with the inhabitants alive," Fortis said, his son floating next to him with a hard expression on his features. "My people did not take our blood price, if that's what you're asking, Maketes. I would be honest if we had murdered any who deserved it."

Then he could only hear Mira scolding Anya, who couldn't hear a word anyone was saying. "What were you thinking, doing all that by yourself? You should have set the bombs and run. That's some stupid shit I would have pulled and I don't appreciate anyone else doing it."

Arges looked over the both of their heads, his neck gills wiggling with amusement. "Oh? It's not as fun when someone else does it?"

"Hush, you. I'm trying to get her healed. None of the med packs will do anything about the worsened hearing problems, though. I'm not a healer. I have no idea what I'm doing."

If she didn't know what she was doing, then she should let Daios do it. Then at least he could be certain someone wasn't hurting her as Mira poured more of that goo down the still bleeding lines that marred Anya's head.

She looked… wrong. Dissociated, he might have said. Her features were so much paler than he'd ever seen them, and her eyes were a little too glassy. She looked very much like she wasn't even in the room.

He wanted her here with him. He wanted to know that she was alive and well and that no matter what had happened, she didn't look at him like he was still a monster.

After all, he'd killed her father. Or at least, the man she thought was her father. He'd listened while she told Mira and Arges everything that had happened the moment he swam up with her into the moon pool. Before the entire place was swarmed with people and she stopped looking like she was seeing what was going on right in front of her.

"We're going," he announced. "Or everyone else is leaving."

"Excuse me?" Mira said, whipping around with a glare on her face and that strange tool suddenly wielded like a weapon. "You're going nowhere with her. She needs to rest."

"Then everyone else get in the water and we will continue our conversation outside."

Arges blinked at him. "Do you have some disagreement about how we're doing things now?"

"I do." He tightened his arms around Anya. "She needs rest. You are not letting her rest."

Everyone whipped around to look at her and they must have seen the same thing he did. A woman who was now a little bit fractured and frayed around the edges. They all needed to give her space.

The depthstriders were the first to sink out of the room. Then Maketes, who gave Anya one last worried look before he disappeared. Arges was the last, his eyes on both of the humans before he looked at Daios.

"Be nice," he said, his voice low and soothing.

Daios bared his teeth in a snarl and ignored his brother's laughter. He shifted even closer to Anya, gently tugging her trembling hands from her lap and bringing them to his mouth. "I wish I could tell you how much I love you. How your light has brought more wonder and joy to my life than I have ever felt in it. I have been a warrior my entire life, and before you, that was all I was. You make me want to put my weapons down and find out what it really means to live."

He ignored that Mira pressed her hands to her mouth, and slipped into the water as well. He had to work to do. Business to finish that would mean he could let all this go. But he had to do this first.

It took about a week for him to get everything done. His people had decided to go back to Alpha and rip the entire city apart. The one fracture was too easy to fix. Maketes was still in contact with Anya's friend, so Ace sent them a little help as well. Ace claimed there were cameras ready to broadcast everything they did to all the other cities. So he and all the other large People of Water pulled the city apart, glass panel by glass panel.

They shattered everything on the stones, leaving nothing but rubble. He took what he wanted out of it, because there were quite a few things to salvage. None of what remained would be given to the humans.

Jewelry, dresses, whatever looked useful, he took. He even brought back a droid that looked a lot like Bitsy for Mira to fix up. Hopefully, there was a way to bring the little droid back to life.

And a week later, when all of it was done, he felt like he could return to her side as a good man. As the man who had changed everything for her.

No longer did he need to struggle or fight. He had set that life aside. And Daios found that he was quite looking forward to what he would find in the future.

Poking his head into the moon pool, he peered through the dark room. It was still early. Mira was probably asleep, but he knew they had set up another small bed for Anya in the garden room.

"Anya," he called out, before tossing a pebble into that room, but he didn't need to wake her. She was waiting for him. Like her soul had known he was coming for her today and he wasn't leaving without her.

She appeared like a ghost, wearing a soft pale gown that he had gotten her. She said it was for sleeping, but he had wanted to see her like this. With the moonlight streaming through the water and turning her skin and the fabric to ivory. She slipped into the sea with him without a sound, but he noticed there was a new droid wrapped around her head.

"My gift worked?" he asked, his claw tapping the metal as he drew them both into the water.

She nodded, then grabbed onto the tentacle at the base of his skull and affixed it to her throat. Now that he was breathing for her, he didn't have to worry as much. She was safe in his arms, right where she should be.

He took his time gliding through the currents, drawing her off into a hidden area of the ocean where no one would bother them.

"Where are you taking me?" she asked, her voice light as air.

"I thought we could enjoy each other for a while." He had hopes for more, but if it was just holding her, then he would be happy. "There's something I want to show you."

They said nothing else, but he knew she had understood him. He could see the words reflected on her lens.

Daios thought maybe he should be a little worried that she was saying nothing. She had been through a lot, and he didn't want to be the one to push her. After all, it had been... hard for both of them. The distance. The knowledge that they had succeeded in doing what they had set out to do.

Arcing over a plateau, he paused on the outskirts of a vented area. It was warmer here, the water almost too hot for him. But she would be able to float comfortably. And then there were the bubbles. Every time a vent released, it scattered a thousand bubbles that at this time of the day... Ah. There it was. They all turned into a thousand rainbows the moment the sun hit them.

"Beautiful, isn't it?" he asked, his mouth against her neck. "Just like you."

She let out a little sound, a moan that filled him with hope. Then suddenly she was twisting in his arm, grabbing at him. Gripping his hand and dragging it to her waist, to her breasts, to anything she could get him to touch.

"I'm better now," she whispered, her lips finding his and pressing the words against him. "I've been waiting for a week and you've been gone and I... I'm okay. I just need you."

He groaned, the sound part need and part relief. He had been feeling the same way, but he wasn't certain that she wanted to be pushed. After all the things he'd done, all the things they had both been through, he wanted to give her time. He wanted to let her breathe. He wanted...

Her.

Fuck, he just wanted her.

Arm banding around her, he dragged her against his chest so her breasts were crushed against him. He kissed her like he was a starving man. Trying his best to press into her very soul all the things that he'd been afraid to say in the past week. He wanted her. He needed her. She was everything to him, and he would give up the entire world if that made her happy. He would give up the sea itself to see her smile.

Breathing hard, he bit at her bottom lip. "I need to see you, kalon. I've been dying to see you for too long now."

She didn't need to be told twice. Anya twisted in his arms, dragging the fabric of her nightgown up over her head. He had seen nothing like her before. The ivory beauty of her skin reflected the colors of the thousand bubbles behind her. The sunlight beaming through the water heated her flesh and warmed it even more to his touch.

But even better, beyond the soft curve of her waist and the pretty softness that gave underneath his fingers, were the scars that marked her head. Like braids, they twisted along one side of her skull and just barely kissed where her face began. They were the marks of the woman he loved, and of the strength she possessed to survive.

He touched his fingers to the patch of circular scars underneath her eye. Lingering where the new lens just barely covered before he heaved her up in his arms.

She gasped, but then her head fell back as his claws parted her lovely folds.

"Look at you," he praised, his mouth already watering. "Already so wet for me, kalon. Gods, I have waited to taste you for too long."

He allowed the water to buoy her upward until her legs were tangled around his shoulders. With one long lick, he finally had his mate's taste back on his tongue. His eyes rolled back in his head as he did it again and she let out that little moan that always made his heart race and his blood thunder in his body. This was what he had needed. This was what he had been missing his entire life.

A groan vibrated through him, his gills flaring wide as he licked and sucked at her skin. If he could crawl inside her, he would. He planned to. Fuck, he needed years to explore the woman writhing in his arms.

He glanced up the long line of her body. She'd lifted her arms above her head, all those soft curves his to claim if he wished. Her hands were sunk into her hair, the coiled tangles of gold catching in the light and fuck, she was beautiful. Every inch of her. Her eyes squeezed shut, her cheeks just slightly blushed. She was everything he had always wanted and more.

"You taste so fucking good," he growled, sinking his tongue deep inside her. This was what he had discovered she enjoyed. Her legs locked around the back of his neck, squeezing tight as he slowly rolled the entire length of this tongue inside her body.

When he had her writhing so hard he feared for her heart, he pulled back just long enough to growl, "I'm going to fill you up, Anya. And then I'm going to watch my cum seep out of that pretty little slit of yours. And you're going to take me, aren't you? All of me."

She whimpered, looking down at him with those heated eyes. She nodded, but that wasn't enough for him. Not at all.

"Say it," he growled.

"Yes," she croaked.

And so he feasted. He licked and sucked and tasted until she came apart in his arms. Until her tiny claws dug into his arms and she dragged him even closer at the same time as she tried to push him away.

Pleasure pounded in his chest. His cocks were so hard he thought a single touch would send him off the edge, but he'd never been happier in his life. He'd never known that a woman like her could exist.

He thought he'd pleasured her speechless until those warm blue eyes looked him over and she suddenly twisted. Locking herself around him, she moved down his body until he was poised right where he wanted to enter her.

"I won't be able to stop like last time," he said, his voice still low and guttural. "There's two for a reason, my kalon. Last time was just the beginning."

"Last time was learning," she replied. Her gaze was just as heated as his as she reached between them to cup him. "This time is for me."

He didn't have the faintest idea what she meant until she guided him inside her.

Clenching his teeth, now he was the one who had to close his eyes as she slid him up and down her wet slit. By the gods, she was hot. So hot that it warmed him all the way into his depths. He wanted, no, needed, more than this. He wanted to thrust into her as she'd taught him. He wanted to feel her surrounding him and clenching as he moved.

And then she was. She sank her hips over him and drew him down until she bumped against his scales.

They both gasped at the intrusion. She was so fucking tight. Every time.

"Anya," he hissed, as she moved herself up and down with her arms braced on his shoulders.

She moved against him, rolling her hips before she blew out a long breath. Her bubbles joined all the others that surrounded them. She was surrounded by a kaleidoscope of colors and then she said something that made him even more shocked.

"I want them both." Her words were breathless, and he swore he heard her wrong.

"Both?" That wasn't something his people did. They enjoyed long sexual encounters, that was for certain. Two were better than one to ensure that a female was properly fertilized, at least that's what the stories said. He just liked that he could linger with her longer than a human male ever could.

"Both," she repeated, the sound so certain that he wasn't able to argue.

How was she going to do that? He had no idea what she meant.

Until she suddenly pulled herself off him and held both of his cocks in one hand. The tips brushed against each other, one much warmer after the heat of her body. He couldn't speak. He couldn't breathe. All he could do was hold himself still as she squeezed him tightly in her little grip and then lined him up.

"Anya, maybe we should…"

She sank down. Just the tips inside of her, their tapered ends much easier until she got to the thicker part.

He hissed out a long breath, and she looked at him, pupils blasted wide as though drugged. "Fuck."

He should tell her to stop. He should tell her that this was dangerous, and she was still healing, but she had just introduced him to heaven itself and who was he to deny that gift? So Daios cupped her thighs with each hand, holding her spread with that metal hand, and his webs pressed against her overheated skin.

"Look how well you take me," he murmured, the heated words barely understandable. "Spread wide for me."

"Daios," she whimpered, sliding lower on him, more of him pushing inside of her body.

"I know," he whispered, his hips moving to help her. "I know. You're so needy for me, aren't you? You need this?"

She nodded, her bottom lip caught between her teeth as she stared down at where they were joined. Together, they worked him inside of her. Inch by inch. Until he could barely breathe because it was so tight and she was whimpering to a point of concern.

"Kalon?" he asked, his voice little more than a rasp.

"You fill me so much," she whispered.

"Watch us." He cupped the back of her head, bringing her face down to look at them again. "Now beg for me."

That whimper again nearly sent him racing to the end. But he wouldn't, not when she needed him right here. He knew it. She knew it.

Then she bit that little lip that he wanted to capture between his and she moaned, "Please."

It was all he could take.

Daios slammed home. They both bowed into each other, foreheads pressed together with ragged breaths as they touched. Flesh to scale. Heart to heart. He was inside her, both of his cocks were inside her and he couldn't fucking think.

"Move," she said, that voice aching and rough. "Move now, Daios."

And so he did. He plunged inside of her again and again, watching as she writhed in his arms. He pressed his thumb to that bead above where they joined and watched her shatter in his arms. She clenched so hard around him that he saw stars, and it still wasn't enough. It was never enough. So he slammed into her harder, every inch of him wanting her, needing her, knowing that this was the only woman that would ever be for him.

And when he came, he swore it plunged him into another existence. One where nothing had ever existed but them.

As they spiraled down, he pulled out to watch the glistening evidence of their love shimmering in the water. Pressing a kiss to her head, he snuggled her tightly in his arms.

He didn't know what to say, because he wasn't very good with words. So instead, he held up the sign for "I love you" as Mira had taught him when he'd asked if she knew any sign language that Anya hadn't taught him.

And all the ugly bits of his soul knit back together as she mimicked the sign and pressed their hands together. Whole. Because she loved him as he hadn't realized he wanted to be loved.

Epilogue

D o you think this is going to work?" Anya asked, looking over the monstrosity in front of them.

"I'm positive." Mira floated beside her, held aloft by Arges's tail as he talked to the other undines behind them. "I stand by my work. I know what will happen when we turn the air on. I think this is going to be the best thing I've built yet."

Maybe it would be.

Anya and Mira got along well enough, but the dome was small. So tiny that they were often running into each other and sometimes that got a little frustrating. They had realized quickly that they couldn't live together forever.

Anya had spent a lot of time with Daios in the ocean after they realized how difficult it was going to be. He didn't mind. But sleeping under the water and being entirely reliant on him to breathe for her... it was a little hard. She knew when she woke up that she was fine, but the panic attacks of feeling like she couldn't breathe were really getting to her.

Not to mention the amount of times she'd gulped in a giant mouthful of salt water and ended up having to swallow it. Her stomach couldn't take much more.

That was when Mira had decided they would expand. There were plenty of materials left over from Alpha. Huge chunks of glass and metal and big panels they could use to make more living space here.

Mira wanted to keep the original dome for herself, so a large portion of their efforts had gone into building a new section. Anya had been asking Ace for schematics that would work, and Mira took them and welded the whole thing together. Once the inside was finished and there was air flowing inside it—something she still wasn't sure was going to be possible—then Anya could get in and do whatever else needed to be done.

There would even be a moon pool in her section. Daios could visit her whenever they wanted, and she was very much looking forward to enjoying her mate without being under the water.

Even now, the thought heated her cheeks. He grunted behind her, the sound shaking against her back as his arm tightened around her waist. The metal one he mostly left off these days, unless he was helping with building the extension of the dome.

Otherwise, it was just him and her.

His short arm joined the other, and she hugged the stump tight to her belly.

"Ready?" Mira called out.

They all shouted and she felt the elation expelling from her body with all the others. She knew they were pleased, even if it didn't work. Even if they hadn't built this entire building to spec, at the very least, they had tried their best.

She held her breath and then watched as the windows drained

of water. They'd have to test if that air was breathable, of course but... there was no water in those rooms.

She could walk in there and decorate it how she wanted, live the way she deserved, and do… anything. There was air, which meant that at least four more rooms of space were theirs. Another garden so they didn't have to ration vegetables. A bedroom, a big shower for both of them to share?

Something rumbled through her chest and then she had to press her hands against her mouth because she wasn't sure what sound she had just made.

Daios chuckled behind her, and some of the tension eased. He pressed his mouth to her shoulder as he signed in front of her, "You sound happy."

She was. She really, really was.

Signing back, she replied, "I don't think I've ever been happier."

And it was the truth. She had fled from her cage. Freedom was something she never dreamt would feel like this. She was so happy, all the time. Exploring the ocean with him. Kissing him. Loving him. Working on making friends and doing everything in her power to find adventure every single day.

Daios tapped the droid on her head and signed, "How is she?"

Bitsy was... "Complicated," she replied.

The droid wasn't back to herself yet. Sure, the functions worked. There was a small hard drive that had survived the blast and the subsequent smashing against Anya's skull. But she missed the little quips and jokes that Bitsy had put on her lens at all hours of the day. She was starting to get some of that, and Byte claimed that Bitsy was still in there. A droid just needed time to heal.

She wasn't sure how a droid healed, but... Well, she wasn't one to question it. If she could get Bitsy back someday, then she would keep holding onto hope that one day her friend would return.

"Droids are all complicated," Daios grunted, snuggling her a little tighter against his chest.

"I suppose they can be."

Anya glanced over to see everyone so happy. Mira and Arges were twisted up in each other now, and he tossed her up into the water with a laugh as they disengaged from their air tentacle. Mira rolled her eyes but floated down into his arms gently and without any issues.

A few of the depthstriders had stuck around, although she wasn't entirely sure why. Fortis and his son were a remarkable duo, but the two of them were terrifying as they stalked around camp.

And then Maketes. She had a soft spot for that yellow finned brother. He laughed all the time, but she noticed that laugh wasn't reaching his eyes as much as she thought it should. When she'd asked, he just shrugged and gestured around him as though that was an explanation.

If she had to guess, it was starting to sting that he was the only one without someone here. So many mated pairs. Well, two of them. And here he was, still the odd one out.

At least he had Fortis. As much as anyone had Fortis.

"Anya!" Mira called out. "Let's go inside!"

She nodded, wanting nothing more than to do that. But then a message flashed on her lens and she froze.

She read it over three times, barely noticing that Mira and all the others were giving her an odd look. Then she shook her head, took Bitsy off, and handed her to Daios.

He frowned at the words as well, and then she watched him read over it again.

"Anya?" Mira asked, her tone a little more serious now. "What's going on?"

"I..." She didn't know what to say.

"Spit it out. We've already had more go wrong in our lives than most people do in a century. How bad is it?"

"It's not bad." She took Bitsy back when Daios offered it, looking up at him as though he might be able to answer for her. "It's just... Ace."

Maketes reacted like he'd been struck by lightning. He stiffened, his entire body lighting up with a sharp glow before he quickly asked, "What's wrong with Ace?"

"Nothing, brother." Daios expelled water from his throat gills, hard enough that it stirred Anya's hair. "Ace has been speaking with the leaders of Gamma and they would like an audience."

"Here?" Arges gestured around them. "Where would we host achromos?"

"No, they wish for us to send an ambassador to their city. To Gamma."

Mira was already shaking her head. "No, that's a trap. None of us are going until we know more about that. I know Ace is your friend, Anya, but we can't trust anyone who claims that they can fix everything by—"

"I'll go."

The words interrupted all of them. Anya turned with the others to see Maketes floating by himself, his hands twisting at his waist. He sighed before repeating, "I'll go."

"Go where?" Mira blurted.

"I'll go to Gamma." He grinned, that smile never quite reaching his eyes. "I'm the only one with nothing to lose now, don't you think?

Besides. I'd like to meet Ace in person, if possible."

Anya focused on her lens to see Bitsy had already sent that message to Ace. All that remained was one more message from her friend, hovering in the air like everyone could see it.

I can't wait to meet him.

Follow me on socials or Amazon to keep your eye out for the next book!

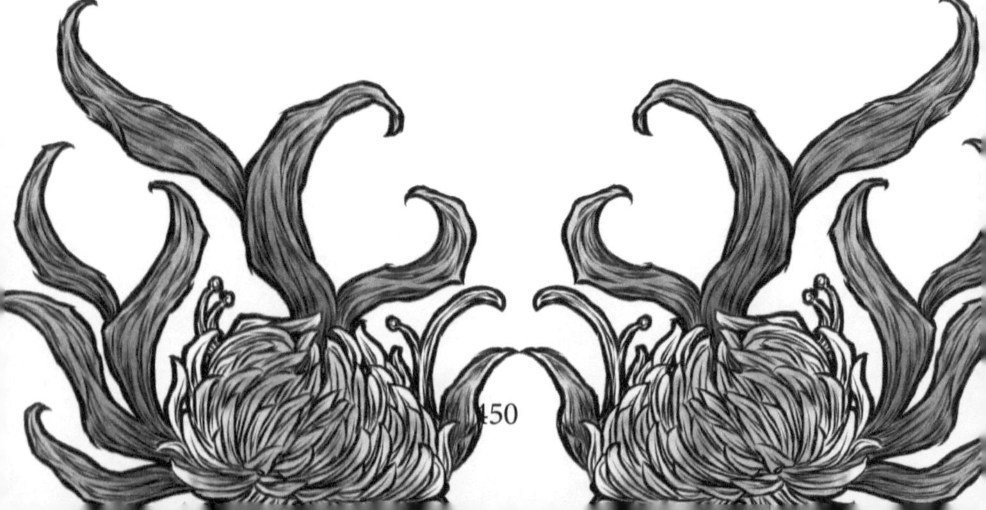

Acknowledgements

As always with each book I write, I thank a couple people in the acknowledgements who mean a lot to me. Usually it's my fiance (hi babe!), then sometimes it's something silly like my pets (Arrow, get the cats), and other times, it's a serious acknowledgement thanking my beta readers (Look at all those hotties!).

But today I just want to thank you.

My readers.

The people who picked up this book, gave this monster fucker weirdness a chance, and then loved it.

You're... the best. You're incredible. You are my world, my moon, and my stars.

I love you all so much.

I really, really do.

About the Author

Emma Hamm is a small town girl on a blueberry field in Maine. She writes stories that remind her of home, of fairytales, and of myths and legends that make her mind wander.

She can be found by the fireplace with a cup of tea and her two Maine Coon cats dipping their paws into the water without her knowing.

For more updates, join my newsletter!

www.emmahamm.com

Song of the Abyss

455

Song of the Abyss

Song of the Abyss

www.ingramcontent.com/pod-product-compliance
Lightning Source LLC
Chambersburg PA
CBHW030013010826
48973CB00009B/2794